ZOMBIE APOCALYPSE!

WASHINGTON DECEASED

Public audience Chamber

entirely unfinished, the cieling has given way.

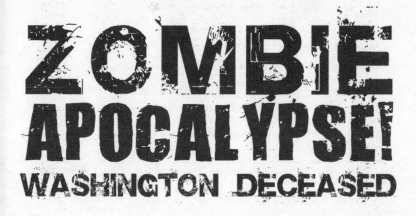

ZOMBIE APOCALYPSE!
WASHINGTON DECEASED

Lisa Morton

Created by Stephen Jones

ROBINSON

RUNNING PRESS
PHILADELPHIA • LONDON

Constable & Robinson Ltd
55–56 Russell Square
London WC1B 4HP
www.constablerobinson.com

First published in the UK by Robinson,
An imprint of Constable & Robinson Ltd., 2014

Zombie Apocalypse! Washington Deceased
Copyright © Stephen Jones and Lisa Morton 2014

Frontispiece: Plan of the White House in 1803 by Benjamin Henry Latrobe
Endpiece: "Old Gory" copyright © Smith & Jones 2014

"Zombie Apocalypse!" and "ZA!" copyright © Stephen Jones

The right of Stephen Jones and Lisa Morton to be identified as the
authors of this work has been asserted by them in accordance
with the Copyright, Designs and Patents Act 1988

A copy of the British Library Cataloguing in
Publication data is available from the British Library

UK ISBN 978-1-47211-067-1 (paperback)
UK ISBN 978-1-47211-080-0 (ebook)

1 3 5 7 9 10 8 6 4 2

First published in the United States in 2014 by Running Press Book Publishers,
A Member of the Perseus Books Group

Books published by Running Press are available at special discounts for bulk purchases in
the United States by corporations, institutions, and other organizations. For more
information, please contact the Special Markets Department at the Perseus Books Group,
2300 Chestnut Street, Suite 200, Philadelphia, PA 19103, or call (800) 810-4145, ext. 5000,
or email special.markets@perseusbooks.com.

US ISBN: 978-0-7624-5462-4
US Library of Congress Control Number: 2014932205

9 8 7 6 5 4 3 2 1
Digit on the right indicates the number of this printing

Running Press Book Publishers
2300 Chestnut Street
Philadelphia, PA 19103-4371

Visit us on the web!
www.runningpress.com

Printed and bound by CPI Group (UK) Ltd, Croydon, CR0 4YY

October 3rd, 1803
London

My Dear Benjamin,

I am most pleased with your last communication.
You have completed the work asked of you in a
timely and precise fashion, and the new American
capitol of Washington has been suitably prepared
for the future.

Did you know that one hill of your Washington
was once called Rome? There is no question that the
stars foretell a great destiny for this city. You, the
Frenchman designer L'Enfant, your colleague
Hoban and the surveyor Ellicott have done a fine
job of creating a truly occult metropolis, with
L'Enfant's streets forming a pentagram and the

cornerstones all washed in the rituals of the Masons.

The crypts you have just finished building, as per my designs, will prove especially vital, as you well know. And in previous letters I have given you a taste of what the future holds for this city and the new nation it governs.

We have, however, spoken little of the past, and the time has now come to remedy that. We shall begin with my birth — or, more properly, my re-birth — which occurred in 1672, when certain occult researches on my part led me to the city of Chorazin, on the edge of the Sea of Galilee. There, in a metropolis which was cursed more than a millennium ago for rejecting the works of that abhorrent Shepherd, I encountered He whom I sought: Anarchon, the demon sometimes known as "the One Who Watches in Darkness". I brought Anarchon out of Chorazin, and in return He blessed me with the secrets of life eternal.

But Anarchon promised me more than mere immortality; for, after all, what good is it to live forever as a servant, when one could ascend to master? Anarchon taught me magicks and rituals through which I could raise myself while consigning the majority of humanity to my servitude. These practices depended on many particulars, some of which comprise the arcane mysteries of architecture.

You, Benjamin, have laid the groundwork — or, dare I say, the under-groundwork — for these plans to blossom in the New World. During our time together here in London, you were a most worthy student, and so I know that you understand that the complex which you have constructed beneath America's Capitol is more than simply an elaborate design for the Masons.

Yes, geography and structure are vitally important in realising the Master's plans, but timing is even more crucial. And so it is that I eagerly await the seventh of October — a mere four days hence — the third day of the new moon when Saturn is in conjunction with Venus. On that day, I shall offer a sacrifice of that ridiculous creature I call my wife to our Lord, Anarchon.

(And yes, as with most of these sorts of things, the ritual does require that the object of sacrifice be in a virginal state; let me assure you that, although I admit she is not without some fleshly charms, I have laid not so much as a hand on the girl, who will come to the altar in a pure and satisfactory condition.) This most sacred of rituals will take place in that chamber especially prepared beneath an acolyte's residence in Hob's Lane (yes, the same chamber that you and I once toured, in order for you to more clearly re-create it in the New World), and the sacrifice will be attended by seven of England's most pre-eminent men and women, all of whom have prepared for this very event for decades. I have chosen these faithful as the most qualified to govern with me; they will serve as my cabinet in the brave new world which is to come.

There is another name which Anarchon is also known by, a title which might sound ridiculous at first: He is "Master of Fleas". Yes, those seemingly insignificant nuisances which have caused irritation to millions throughout history. But more than irritation as well: Fleas, carried from house to house, from ship to shore, from wagon to town,

spread the Great Plagues which have ravaged
Europe for centuries.

Now those same fleas will carry a different kind of
plague — a _divine_ plague, if you will.

Because, after our ritual is successful, Anarchon
will release fleas whose bite will prove both lethal
. . . and restorative. These fleas will spread a
sickness which will first kill its host, then
resurrect them, but as lowly, witless beings who
will exist only to spread the sickness further . . .
and to serve my will. This new plague — this
plague of un-death — will rage with a speed that
will make all prior plagues seem slow and
constrained by comparison. It will swiftly
overwhelm not just these isles and the Continent,
but _all_ continents, including your New World.

Now, Benjamin, let me ask you: When you

opened this letter, perhaps using a knife blade, or more simply a finger, did you not notice a tiny red speck leap forth? Did you not feel a pinprick on an exposed patch of skin — the back of your wrist perhaps, or even your neck, or ear? Have you already, unthinkingly, scratched a small itch?

Yes, words can be powerful, but do not actions sometimes scream? In pursuit of those actions, one of my agents will have placed several of Anarchon's fleas in with this epistle. These fleas have been blessed by the Master Himself, and if our ritual on October 7th has been successful, then my little bloodsucking friends presently carry the Black Un-death.

By now, I am quite certain that you have been bitten. Soon, you will feel more than an itch. I am afraid the first part will prove unpleasant — you will suffer an illness similar to the Plague, with attendant agonies and fevers. These, however, will pass, as will you. And then you will awaken again, as the first of Anarchon's followers in America. You will be our messenger, our Angel of Death, to those former colonists who will realise how little they have gained in turning against their Mother England. You will be — what is it you have there, that absurd title? — President of a country of the dead. I will arrive soon enough to claim the land, but until then it will be yours . . . if you only have enough consciousness remaining to realise it.

Farewell, Benjamin. I wish you all success in bringing Anarchon's dark gift to America.

Yours in Service to the Great Master of Fleas,

Thomas Moreby, Esq.

Chapter One

"HEY, STEELE . . ."

The woman in the lightweight body armour looked up from her place on the Black Hawk's bench. It took her a moment to figure out which of the eight other similarly outfitted passengers had spoken, then she saw D'Agostino peering at her curiously.

Of course it would be Aggy. Although she liked the former cop, D'Agostino was always the one with questions.

"What, Aggy?"

"You met her before, right?"

Steele weighed her words for a few seconds; she knew that Aggy might have been the one to ask the question, but she saw the gazes of the rest turned on her. "You mean the package? Not really."

"But you're Secret Service . . ."

She almost sighed. Steele had hoped that maybe a cop knew more about the Secret Service than the average civilian. Before she could answer, the man to her immediate left answered. "I believe *Director* Steele has served briefly in presidential protection, but the Secret Service does a lot more than that, you know."

Steele couldn't suppress a smile at how Agent Anderson had emphasized the word "Director". The others assigned to this job came from a mix of backgrounds – two cops, three Army soldiers, a Navy SEAL and three Secret Service agents, including her, Anderson and tough little Chavez – but there was no question that she was in command. In the past, the mission would have been crewed only with Secret Service agents, but today they'd had to scrounge whoever they could get.

There weren't many of them left. Not since the dead had overrun everything.

"Holy crap, look at 'em . . ." That was Petrosyan, an Army private who Steele had concerns about, but he'd been vetted as capable; he was, after all, still alive.

Right now Petrosyan was looking out the open door of the Black Hawk, down at the rural New York countryside passing beneath them. Steele didn't need to join him to know what he was seeing – pastoral farmland, green and tan hillside, and lazy winding road, all dotted with staggering, shambling figures.

They were everywhere. Not just in the cities – like Manhattan, nuked in a fruitless effort to quell their rising numbers, or Washington, that'd been taken over by the living dead – but in the suburbs and small towns as well. No matter how many of them the survivors put down, with a shot to the head or a massive explosion that tore the brain apart, they continued to increase their numbers. A single nip, a light scratch and a survivor became one of *them*. Of course most of the survivors didn't sustain only a few toothmarks or a lone red scrape; most were partially consumed, and when they died and returned the cycle continued. The dead were ever hungry.

"Petrosyan . . ." Steele called out to the young soldier, who reluctantly yanked his gaze from the passing panorama and looked up at her. "Remember your assignment today."

Petrosyan gulped, nodded, and leaned back against the wall of the 'copter. Steele saw some of the other faces all reflect renewed intent. The other ex-cop, a thirty-ish woman named Schechter, turned away from Petrosyan, trying to distance herself, to stay focused.

If they succeeded today, the human survivors might have another chance. If this worked, what was left of the U.S. would no longer be under martial law. General Parker had done well holding them together until now, but he didn't want the job permanently. If they were to move forward, they needed someone strong to lead them.

If . . .

The pilot's voice barked over the receiver in Steele's ear, "Two minutes."

Beside her, Steele saw Chavez fidget with her body armour. "What's the matter, Angie? You haven't finally decided to join the rest of us and get nervous, have you?"

Chavez gave her a lopsided *fuck you* grin and tugged at her suit again. "Hell with that. Just never worn this stuff before. I think I'd prefer a nice padded jumpsuit and a football helmet."

Steele smiled. "I hear that, but this is gel armour. They would've started outfitting our troops overseas with these suits if—"

"They hadn't been eaten first".

Steele laughed. Chavez could always be counted on for the mordant jibe. When she'd received news of the death of her beloved brother Manny, she'd turned her head for a moment before muttering something about hoping that the "*pendejo* that ate him got heartburn."

Adjusting her own suit, Steele noted, "If this stuff can stop bullets, it should be able to withstand a bite."

From the other side of the helicopter, the S.E.A.L. – Byrne – overheard them and said, "I've already done three missions in this suit. It's the shit. We could've conquered the fuckin' world if we'd had these earlier."

Chavez and Steele exchanged a look, and Steele had to work to hold back a laugh.

From her other side, Anderson fixed Byrne with a glare and said, "And weren't half the guys in your last squad killed even with the suits?" Before Byrne could answer, Anderson flipped his helmet visor down, concealing his face.

Steele hoped they'd survive long enough to share a beer and make jokes about this.

"One minute."

As the pilot's voice in her headset cut out, a beep announced an incoming call. "Go."

It was Marissa Cheung back at HQ. "Director Steele? Just letting you know that we've still been unable to establish communication."

"Copy that. We're one minute from set-down, Cheung. I'll get back to you after we pick up the package."

The call ended, Steele took in a deep breath and held it, calming herself. *If there's still anything to pick up.*

They'd had communication with their target until last week. Then, yesterday, Ames Parker had made the decision, and Steele had been told to assemble a team. It wasn't required or even approved that she lead the team, but this mission was too important.

Besides . . . it was history in the making. Steele couldn't lie and say that didn't appeal to her. It was one of the reasons a fourteen-year-old high schooler named Sandra Steele had first thought of joining the Secret Service – her Aunt Jen had taken her to a presidential rally, and she'd felt the intensity of the crowd, all focused on one person on the stage, and it had energized her into an instant career choice.

She didn't want to be the person at the centre of the attention, but the idea of being in the immediate circle of that little piece of history fascinated her. She'd joined the Secret Service, worked hard, made connections, and when her male peers had nearly brought the agency down with a series of tawdry scandals, Sandra Steele had been the obvious choice to restore the Secret Service's tarnished lustre.

It was too bad the rest of the world had fallen apart not long after her appointment. But if they succeeded today . . .

"Where the fuck are we gonna land?" Petrosyan was peering out of the open side of the Black Hawk again, and this time Steele joined him.

For a change, Petrosyan was right: the land below them was crawling with the dead. They were converging on a large country mansion, one that had been surrounded by a solid stone wall, but a stone wall that was now rubble in several places. Steele guessed that wall had probably stood for over a century, but had given way in the past twenty-four hours.

"Oh man . . ." Petrosyan looked out, his head jerking back and forth. "Anybody who was in that house has gotta be dead . . ."

"No." As the 'copter circled the mansion, Steele nodded down. "Look at the doors and windows – all boarded up. And the dead wouldn't all be hammering on the walls like that if they'd already found a way in."

Behind her, Steele heard Chavez say, "Those boards aren't gonna hold much longer, though. If they could push down the stone wall . . ."

Steele exchanged a look with her agent and realized the younger woman thought this mission was pointless. That she'd stayed committed was why she'd always been one of Steele's favourites.

Anderson joined them, peeking out. "In all seriousness . . . where *are* we going to land?"

The 'copter had circled around to the back of the mansion, revealing an unbroken ring of zombies. They were packed in around the house at least six deep, with more spread out farther away. As the Black Hawk passed overhead, they looked up, some even raising partial, half-eaten limbs.

Steele leaned farther out of the bird and spotted something a short distance to her left. Squinting, she made out a wooden outbuilding, a simple post fence . . .

"The corral." She adjusted her mike, addressing the pilot. "What do you think about that corral to the north?"

A short distance behind the main house was a barn, a stable and a fenced-in corral. The corral was empty; obviously the zombies had been uninterested in an empty corral and had trudged around it, leaving the wooden fence miraculously in place.

The pilot's voice came back. "That'll work, although it'll put you a good two hundred yards from the house. And they'll come for us as soon as we set down."

"Well, unless you see anything better—"

"I don't. Okay, Director, get ready."

As the Black Hawk headed for the corral, Steele felt the adrenaline begin to pump. She turned to address her team, starting with Myers and Allmon, the two Army sharpshooters she'd recruited.

"Okay, we're about to do this. Myers, Allmon, you're with the 'copter keeping the way clear for us." The two snipers nodded; they were experienced and cool, and Steele knew she wouldn't have to worry about them. "The rest of us are the main team. We make for the house, we find the package, we get out – *all* of us. Any questions?"

Steele shot Aggy a look, and he didn't disappoint her. "Yeah, I got one: What if we don't find her?"

"Then we pack up and get out fast in one piece."

D'Agostino gulped and pulled his helmet visor down. Next to him, Schechter gave Steele a quick look before sliding her visor closed. Petrosyan, Byrne and Chavez did the same. Steele didn't like the way Petrosyan nervously hugged his assault rifle, but she kept quiet.

As the Black Hawk touched down, Steele pulled her own visor into place, grabbed a backpack at her feet and shrugged into the straps. She leapt out, crouched and ran twenty feet, then stopped to look for the best way to the house.

There was no best way. The space between the house and the corral was packed with the dead. And now they were turning towards Steele and her team. She felt their glassy eyes on her and shivered beneath her gel suit.

Chavez and Anderson moved up beside her, their presence reassuring, and she heard somebody behind her mutter, "Jesus Christ . . ."

She forced her mind to work, to focus on her job. "Chavez, Anderson – we need a distraction . . ."

Chavez grinned. "I can do that." The small Latina broke to the left, running and waving her arms while shouting, "Hey, douchebags, c'mon, got some nice meat on these bones for ya, this way . . ."

Anderson picked up on the routine and ran with her. "This way, you fuckers, come and get some prime USDA choice . . ."

It was working: The dead on the other side of the corral fence were turning, staggering after the two loud targets . . . but not all of the dead. A few remained behind – they'd reached the fence now, their hands were scrabbling at the wood.

Small red holes blossomed on their foreheads and they fell. Steele glanced back at the 'copter and saw Myers and Allmon crouched in the Black Hawk's belly, picking off zombies with M40 sniper rifles. She threw them a thumbs-up, drew her Glock 21, and waved her team forward.

She raised the Glock – and froze. It was impossible; despite how many of the zombies had been drawn away by Chavez and Anderson and how many more were falling to sniper rounds, she was still faced with a wall of un-humanity. They had reached the corral fence now, mouths open and moaning, tattered fingers reaching . . .

We can't do this.

Steele had only faced a horde like this once before, when DC had first been overrun. She'd tried to storm the White House in the hope of saving the President; she knew her agents were already dead, and she'd hoped against hope that she might still find the Commander-in-Chief.

But as she'd seen the Oval Office at the end of the corridor, a familiar figure had come lurching out; his suit might have been shredded, his eyes limned in blood, but it had been *him*, the President, and she'd been too late. With only a few rounds left in her last magazine, she'd turned and fled.

But this, today, was different. There were more zombies – but also more firepower. And she wasn't alone.

We have to do this.

The wooden crossbeams of the fence were creaking, and Steele knew they'd give way any second. She raised the Glock with both hands, sighted and fired. She told herself these things weren't human: the handsome young man with chiselled biceps was a monster, the elderly woman with a kind face was no longer kind, the little boy in cartoon-print pyjamas was nobody's son.

Her action spurred her team, and shots sounded from either side of her. Then came the rapid-fire *rat-a-tat* of an automatic weapon, spraying wildly. "No!" Steele whirled, even though she knew what she'd find.

Petrosyan was firing his M16 into the zombie mass, not even aiming. Steele had to shout his name twice to get him to stop. "What the hell are you doing, Petrosyan? Semi-automatic only, remember?"

Petrosyan's eyes were wide, his face sweat-sheened. "That isn't gonna work. Look at 'em—"

"We can't risk hitting the house. And you're not even stopping them. *Look.*"

The ex-cop followed her gesture and saw the dead he'd just shot at still coming, the bullet holes in their chests and limbs having done nothing to halt their progress. "Shit . . ."

As Petrosyan stared, Steele reached down to his M16 and flipped it to semi-automatic. "Now *aim* before you fire." She waited until Petrosyan gulped and nodded before turning away.

They'd made a good hole in the zombie mass, though, and she strode forward. The fence was splintering under the weight of dead flesh, so Steele kicked at the beams until they split. She waved the Glock towards the immobile corpses. "Petrosyan, D'Agostino, Schechter – pull those bodies away so we'll have a clear path. We'll need it coming back. Byrne and I will cover until you're done."

Petrosyan made a face, but when D'Agostino and Schechter got to work, he reluctantly slung his rifle back and joined them. Steele glanced at Byrne, and saw him grinning. "You look like you're enjoying this."

Byrne chuckled and said, "Not *yet*. But just wait . . ."

Steele heard shots off to her left, and saw Anderson and Chavez backing away – the zombies at the far end of the corral had breached the fence and were spilling in. Steele shouted and waved. "Back here!"

Anderson and Chavez didn't hear. They were popping off shots, dancing back. In the Black Hawk, Myers and Allmon were concentrating on the dead around Steele's group.

Steele felt her gut clench. She reached under her visor and grabbed her mike. "Chavez, Anderson, do you read?"

Angie's voice came through, although it sounded as if she spoke through gritted teeth. "We got it here, ma'am. Just keep working on your part."

"We're through." That was Schechter, motioning at the path they'd created through the fence. For an instant, she was split: help her agents, or head for the house while they had the chance?

There was no choice. Anderson and Chavez were on their own. She turned to the house.

She emptied the Glock's magazine on two zombies – teenagers, both of them, one still wearing the remnants of a Marilyn Manson T-shirt – and popped it out. She was just slamming a full magazine back into the gun when she felt something tug at the backpack she bore.

Byrne moved up beside her. "Allow me." She saw that Byrne was carrying a three-foot-long length of metal pipe. With both hands wrapped around it, he swung at something behind Steele and she felt the pull on the backpack ease. Excited by the first kill, Byrne waded in.

As Steele and the others watched in disbelief, Byrne transformed into a human fury, whirling the length of pipe in every direction, battering skulls and kicking corpses out of the way. Steele had to appreciate the pipe as a weapon: it worked better in close quarters than a gun, didn't need to be reloaded and rarely required multiple hits. Byrne did have to pause once to wipe his visor free of gore, but then he laid into the zombies again.

Somehow, the writhing mass of walking dead didn't seem to thin out, and they were still ten yards from the house when Byrne's stamina started to flag. He panted and had to lower the pipe after every swing, and the zombies were closing in.

"Fuck!" That was D'Agostino, just behind Steele. She whirled and saw that a fat middle-aged man in crimson-splattered overalls had grabbed Aggy from behind and was trying to sink his teeth into the cop's upper arm. The gel suit held, and the zombie's teeth shattered on the tough material; but Aggy couldn't pull his arm free from the zombie's grip. Steele raised the Glock, fired on two other zombies that were about to reach Aggy, but couldn't get a clear sight on the one holding his arm.

"Aggy, duck!"

D'Agostino dropped – and came face to face with a legless woman clawing at his feet. He screamed and fell back just as Steele shot the zombie that held him. The zombie fell – but so did Aggy, pinned beneath the bulk of the flabby corpse. "Get it off me, get it off me!"

More zombies circled in. Steele and Schechter shot them while Petrosyan covered Byrne. When Steele could finally get back to Aggy, she looked down just in time to see the crawling woman yanking Aggy's left boot off and sinking her teeth through his sock into the foot.

D'Agostino screamed again. Steele shouted.

But she couldn't get to him. The dead were between her and the downed man. As three of them descended on him, she knew his agonized scream was his last and she forced her focus away from him.

Aggy was done.

Schechter kept firing as Steele finished off another magazine and slammed a new one in. "Byrne, get us to that house!"

"Working on it!"

Something fell against Steele and she tensed, but saw that it was a real corpse, its head barely recognizable as a result of having met Byrne's pipe. She side-stepped the falling body, watched as Byrne brought the bar around in a side swing and sent another zombie to its final rest, and she could see the house now, just a few feet away.

She heard Byrne grunting with the effort of the last few blows, but then they'd reached the house, with Petrosyan, Schechter and Steele covering the sides and rear of their trail. Steele shot a zombie to her right as she edged that way to a back door, its inset window boarded over. She pounded on it with a fist as she called out, "Hello! Anyone alive in there? *Hello!*"

There was no answer.

"What now?" Petrosyan asked, as he sighted along his rifle barrel and took out another zombie shambling towards them.

"We go in. Everybody stand back." Steele pointed her pistol at the doorknob and fired. When she aimed at the deadbolt lock, one of the bullets ricocheted off and struck a zombie in the chest, staggering it.

"Good shot, Director," Schechter said, as she pumped a round into the thing's head to finish it off.

Steele pulled the door back only to see the backboard of a large cabinet blocking the way. She waved Byrne and Petrosyan up. "Can you push that out of the way?"

They put their shoulders against the heavy furniture and grunted with effort as Steele and Schechter guarded the rear. Steele heard wood scrape on tile and knew they'd managed to slide the cabinet aside. She didn't wait, but stepped into the house. She was in the kitchen, which was large and modern, with a centre island and chrome fixtures. "Hello?" Again, there was no answer.

"We blew it. Nobody home," Petrosyan muttered.

The power was out, so Steele pulled a small maglite from a pocket of the gel suit and swung it around the dim interior. "No, look – this place is sealed tight from the inside. And everything's clean . . . no sign of struggle."

A cry sounded from outside, and Steele turned to see a grey hand pulling Schechter away by the left shoulder. The ex-cop struggled to raise her gun, but another zombie yanked her right arm and from Schechter's scream Steele knew the arm had been broken.

"Petrosyan, Byrne—!"

Steele lifted the Glock, trying to get a shot, but Schechter was in the way. She could only watch helplessly as a zombie tore at Schechter's helmet visor, flipped it up and bit into her face.

Byrne rained blows on Schechter's attackers, but it was too late – Schechter's face was a bloodied ruin, her eyes closed, body sagging.

"Byrne, let her go." It was one of the hardest commands Steele had ever given, but she couldn't afford to lose Byrne as well, not when they were so close . . .

She heard Byrne utter a curse as he stepped back into the house. "You better make this quick, because we can't hold them much longer."

Steele called, "Copy that. Just give me a minute."

She slid out of the backpack, dropped it and ran from the kitchen. It took her less than a minute to check out the rest of the two-storey house, and she was panting by the time she returned to the kitchen. Petrosyan and Byrne were sweating it at the door. "We gotta go," Petrosyan shouted back, "they're bunching up again outside."

"Not yet," Steele said. Her gut told her their quarry was still here, somewhere . . .

"C'mon, ma'am, the place is empty," Byrne said. Even his resolve was fraying into panic.

Steele whirled. "The basement."

Byrne glanced back at her. "What?"

"The basement. It's where I'd hole up if the house I was in was surrounded."

There – a door at the other side of the kitchen that could only go down. Steele ran to it, turned the knob and pulled. The door didn't move; it was somehow secured from the inside.

"Hello? Anybody down there?" Steele called through the heavy wood.

She was rewarded with a response from the other side: "Who are you?"

Relief washed through Steele, so intense she had to put a hand on the door for a second to steady herself. "We're from Washington, ma'am. We're here to get you to safety. We've got transport just outside."

Steele waited anxiously, listening. It seemed like hours passed before she made out the sound of stairs creaking on the other side, and then something metallic being moved. Finally the door opened and a woman stood on the steps just inside, a heavy chain still held in one hand.

As she stepped up into the kitchen, they all stared for a moment. Petrosyan and Byrne forgot the murderous hordes outside. The blonde woman in her sixties smiled at them in gratitude. "Am I glad to see you. It was getting boring down there."

Steele held out a supporting hand. "Are you okay to move?"

The other woman nodded. Steele reached down to her backpack; she unzipped it and drew out a gel armour jacket and pants and a helmet, which she handed to her charge. "Put these on."

The woman eyed the armour; then, as she drew on the jacket she said, "Gel armour. I knew it was in the development stage, but I had no idea it was a done deal. How many suits were completed?"

Steele gestured briefly around the kitchen. "Pretty much what you see here." Then, speaking into her headset, Steele said, "We've got the package ready for delivery."

On the other end, Cheung answered, "Holy shit. I can't believe you actually found her."

"Well, we've still got to get back to the bird. I'll call again once we're airborne."

"Copy. Good luck."

Steele gestured the woman to the door. "Let's get you back where you belong . . . Madame President."

The woman arched her eyebrows. "When did *that* happen?"

Petrosyan popped off three shots, a grim reminder of the difficulties that still lay before them. "We'll have to save the explanations. Let's go."

Petrosyan shot twice, and then Byrne leapt out, the pipe already swinging. Steele ushered the other woman out. "Petrosyan, behind us."

The zombies were still thinned out slightly, but closing in on their path back to the Black Hawk. "Keep up the speed, Byrne!"

"Right."

Behind them, Steele heard Petrosyan scream; his rifle threw out a series of shots, and something slammed into Steele's back with enough force to throw her forward. She caught herself before she went down; pain exploded in her back, and she knew she'd taken one of Petrosyan's bullets at close range, but the gel suit had kept it from doing more than just slamming into her.

"You okay?"

Steele didn't take the time to nod or to look back at Petrosyan. "Just keep moving," she called.

She fired off six more shots from the Glock, taking down three zombies; she was getting tired and sloppy. An obese middle-aged man with one black eye socket and a missing ear lunged at her from the right. She raised the Glock, pulled the trigger – and the hammer clicked on an empty chamber. She dug a hand into a pouch on the gel suit, looking for a replacement magazine, and realized: there were no more magazines. She was out.

Byrne jumped back, putting himself between her and the huge dead thing. "Go!" he called.

Steele had just enough time to see Byrne raise the pipe, only to have it stopped in mid-swing by the zombie's upraised arm. Then it raised its other hand and grabbed Byrne by the throat. Steele didn't stay to see the rest; doing her best to protect her charge, she pushed through the zombies, ducking and dodging, dread curdling within her . . .

A dead boy reaching for her fell back as a bullet exploded into his forehead. Steele looked up and saw they'd almost reached the 'copter, where Myers was aiming his sniper rifle. He paused long enough to help the two women into the bird.

"Where's Allmon?" Steele asked, panting.

Between gritted teeth as he sighted and fired, Myers answered, "Gone. He tried to move up to the house and they got him."

"Chavez and Anderson?"

"I don't know, but I think they're gone, too."

Steele looked out, saw zombies starting to converge on the Black Hawk and decided. Speaking into the headset, she said, "Get us out of here."

"Happy to," answered the pilot.

Steele made sure her charge was secured on the bench, then glanced out – and saw Chavez staggering out of the encroaching mass.

"Wait!"

The bird hovered a few feet off the ground. Steele leaned out, grabbed Chavez's hands, and helped her in. The zombies were only a few feet behind. "Go, *Go!*"

The Black Hawk lifted up, engines roaring. Steele saw the hungry mob falling away beneath them, and she turned to Chavez. The agent's armour was covered in blood, the visor was missing from her helmet and she'd lost her gun somewhere along the way. But what alarmed Steele most was the look in Chavez's eyes.

It was defeat.

"Chavez . . .?"

A tear leaked out of one of the agent's eyes. "They got me, Steele. The fuckers."

Steele was confused – she didn't see a bite mark, the armour was still in place. "No, you're—"

Chavez cut her off, angling her jaw so Steele could see the thin red line there. It wasn't deep, not even really bleeding, but it was . . .

"A scratch."

"Yeah." Chavez lowered her head.

"Are you sure you got it from one of *them*? Maybe . . . maybe your helmet, or . . ."

Chavez shook her head. "No, it was this fuckin' girl. Just a girl. Half my age, but . . . dead."

Steele saw Myers looking at her, his expression unreadable. She turned her attention back to Chavez. "We'll get you back to HQ, maybe—"

Chavez shook her head. "No. I don't want to risk infecting anyone else. Especially—" she directed her look at the blonde woman who sat across from her, "—especially not now." Chavez pulled off the rest of the helmet, hurled it away and moved to the open hatchway in the side of the Black Hawk. Facing them, she gripped the edges tightly and nodded at Steele's holstered Glock. "Do it. Now."

Steele drew the Glock, remembered. "I can't. I'm out."

Myers was surprisingly gentle as he held the sniper rifle out to Steele. "Here."

Steele took it. Her fingers felt numb, the rifle too heavy as she tried to raise it.

Chavez closed her eyes and leaned back, letting the downdraft from the helicopter's rotor whip her dark hair. Steele tried to sight on Chavez's forehead, tried to force herself to imagine Chavez as a hungry dead thing tearing at her, eyes glassy, teeth champing . . .

It didn't work. She lowered the rifle. "Chavez, I—"

Before she could continue, the blonde woman had unstrapped herself and knelt beside Steele. She looked into Steele's eyes, and Steele saw reserves of strength and courage there that left her stunned. Steele let the rifle be taken from her, but she turned away until after she heard the shot. Chavez made no sound as she fell, and there was only a heavy *thunk* as the rifle hit the deck of the Black Hawk before Steele felt a hand grip hers.

She turned to look at the new President and said only, "Thank you."

The other woman nodded, gently.

In that moment, Steele knew she would gladly die to defend this woman.

From: Bobby Van Arndt <virginboybva@vi.rr.com>
To: Kevin Moon <moonykev@laex.com>
Sent: FRI, Jun 28, 2:14 PM
Subject: Okay?

Hey, Kev, we keep hearing a lot of bad shit is going down out there in L.A. Hope you're hanging in and it's just the media over-hyping everything as usual. Out here in Virginia we aren't seeing a lot of the dead yet, but of course we're out here in the sticks. We did finally put up an honest-to-God fence around the farm, so I think we're safe. Grandpa has dug out the old shotgun and bought a bunch of cartridges for it. Wow, this could be the first time I've ever been pro-gun.

Let me know how you are. I worry, you know. ☺

Love,
Bobby

——Original Message——
From: Kevin Moon <moonykev@laex.com>
To: Bobby Van Arndt <virginboybva@vi.rr.com>
Sent: FRI, Jun 28, 2:16 PM
Subject: RE: Okay?

Thanks for the note, bro. And yeah, it's bad out here and getting worse. Fucking zombies are everywhere. I had to leave West Hollywood because it got so bad. I'm staying now with friends at a house up in the hills (remember cute Scotty? He knows this guy who's a rich music producer who's letting us all crash here because it's hard to reach and a little safer). But we're running out of food, the power keeps going in and out, and frankly I don't know how much longer anyone will be able to stay in L.A.

I miss you.

Kevin

—Original Message—

From: Bobby Van Arndt <virginboybva@vi.rr.com>

To: Kevin Moon <moonykev@laex.com>

Sent: FRI, Jun 28, 2:18 PM

Subject: RE: RE: Okay?

Kevin, srsly – get your ass out of there. Can you get to a truck or a car or something? I was hoping the news reports were all lies, but it sounds like they may have actually understated how bad it was.

Come out here, Kevin. You can stay with Grandpa and me at the farm. We've got plenty of food, we've got candles if the power gives out, we've got a well for fresh water, and . . . well, we've got ME. ☺

Please be safe, and please please PLEASE get out of there, whether you decide to come to ol' Virginia or not.

Love,

Bobby

Chapter Two

THE SILVER LEXUS GX SUV circled the parking lot of the huge warehouse store in Burbank, moving slowly from the south entrance to the far north parking lot and around the building. The three men and one woman inside peered through the tinted windows, nervously squeezing tools and homemade weapons.

In the rear seat, Kevin said, "Damn. The parking lot was never this empty when I shopped here in the past."

The woman in the front passenger seat, Nancy, nodded as they rounded a corner. "It's not completely empty, Moony."

Kevin gritted his teeth – he hated that nickname. Yes, his last name was Moon, but it was a fine Korean surname and he'd heard "Moony" and "Moon the Loon" since his days as a first-grader in Oregon. Nancy – probably the smartest person in the car – must have known how irritating that jibe was, so Kevin figured she wanted to annoy him. Maybe she just found the rest of the apocalypse boring and was trying to entertain herself.

Kevin tried to move past the obnoxious name to see what she was looking at. There, maybe fifty feet away – a single figure walking purposelessly near the store's entrance.

The blonde man next to Kevin saw the walker, threw back another gulp from the bottle of Jack Daniel's he cradled in his lap and muttered, "Fuck . . ."

Kevin peered at his friend Scotty in concern. Scotty had once possessed the sharpest wit and the biggest strut of anyone he'd ever met, and he was so boyishly handsome that he'd been propositioned by both male and female porn stars. But ever since the Human Reanimation Virus had turned much of LA into a graveyard, Scotty's confidence had vanished. He'd become a sweating, trembling drunk, and Kevin wished again that they hadn't brought him with them today.

But they were all hungry.

Two weeks ago, it had seemed like a good idea. "I've got this friend, Howard. He's a rich music producer, has a big house just off Laurel Canyon, says we can come up and crash there until all this blows over," Scotty had said one night, as they'd been drinking vodka in Kevin's tiny studio apartment off Gardner in West Hollywood. Kevin hadn't liked the bars over the windows when he'd moved in, but since the shit had gone down, he'd been damn glad they were there.

Even so, he knew he couldn't stay in the apartment much longer; the streets of WeHo were thronged now with the infected. Kevin and Scotty had left the restaurant where they both waited tables three days ago, when one of *them* had crashed right through the front glass window to dine on a patron, and they hadn't left Kevin's apartment since.

Now there were more of the dead outside every hour, and Kevin knew that, despite the bars, it wouldn't be long before they'd find a way in. He'd already heard one of his neighbours shrieking as his door had been torn off its hinges.

So they'd peeked out, and waited until none of the things were around, and then sprinted to Kevin's old Toyota Camry. They'd barely made it inside and locked the doors before a once-attractive burly man in leather had beat on the front windshield. Kevin had gunned the motor, and they'd endured a frantic drive into the Hollywood hills, swerving to avoid car wrecks and the dead, taking the canyon roads' sharp turns too fast when a group of five or six zombies had run after the car.

Howard Karan's house had at first proved a functional sanctuary. It was isolated, on a steep hillside, and could only be entered by a narrow walkway between heavy cement-block walls that led to a solid front door. Kevin, Scotty, Howard and Howard's sister, Nancy, had formed a kind of family, taking turns on lookout, cooking and cleaning, and partying. Lots of partying. Howard had a plentiful stash of coke and weed and booze, and he didn't mind sharing. Scotty and Howard occasionally adjourned to Howard's bedroom, leaving Kevin and the forty-ish, acerbic Nancy to fend for themselves.

But then the food had run low, and soon they were down to stale crackers and the last jar of pickle slices. They'd discussed their options and had decided to try the Food Club warehouse in the east end of the Valley. Even if Burbank was as full of the dead as West Hollywood was, the massive Food Club was the likeliest place to still have supplies.

First they'd decided they needed weapons; Howard didn't believe in guns, which left a fireplace poker for Nancy, a length of metal chain for Scotty, a piece of 2 x 4 studded with nails for Kevin (who was proud of his homemade mace), and a crowbar for Howard. Then they'd clambered into the SUV, Scotty making sure he was already drunk when they left and had a bottle with him.

The drive had taken two hours, as they'd frequently backtracked and swerved and reversed, but they'd finally made it. Now they pulled up forty feet from the front entrance to the gigantic, dark building.

"Doors are open," said Nancy.

"Good, 'cause I left my lock picks at home," Kevin answered.

Scotty gestured at the lone zombie, now shambling towards them. "What about him?"

"Well . . ." Howard gunned the engine.

Nancy looked over at her brother. "You can't be serious."

Howard gave her a grin – more of a grimace – and hit the accelerator.

The Lexus shot forward, tyres squealing on the asphalt, and was doing probably forty miles an hour when it hit the zombie, a gangly fifty-something man missing his left arm. The impact threw him clean over the car, and Howard braked to a halt, shoved the gearshift into reverse and rolled back over the body. The car thumped twice, and then Howard let it roll back far enough to where they could see the corpse in front of them.

"Nope, still moving," Nancy said.

"Not for long." Howard slammed the car into DRIVE, and steered over the zombie's head. The passengers all heard a mushy *crunck*, then Howard stopped and looked back. "*Violà* – no more zombie."

"But how you gonna fit the Lexus in the store, Howie?" said Kevin.

"I can't believe you didn't make it as a screenwriter."

Kevin allowed himself the luxury of a bitter smile. "I can't either. Well, hell – maybe soon there'll be a market for human-zombie bromances. Or I could invent a whole new genre: zomances."

Scotty didn't seem to have heard. He looked out of the Lexus at the wide-open doors into the warehouse, gaping like a hungry maw, and twisted his hands around the sweat-slick bottle. "This isn't gonna work. It's too dark in there – the place could be crawling with them . . ."

Kevin put his hand on Scotty's arm, trying to reassure his friend. "This *has* to work, Scotty. We'll starve to death otherwise."

For an instant, Kevin was glad he and Scotty had never become lovers; at first he'd been attracted to Scotty (who wasn't?), but now that he'd seen how Scotty reacted to stress, he knew they would never have worked.

One of the car doors opened, startling them all, and Nancy stepped out. Holding the poker in one hand, she leaned back inside just long enough to say, "Am I the only one here with balls?"

Howard howled in protest, grabbed the crowbar and got out. Kevin followed suit, wrestling his 2 x 4 club out of the rear compartment as well as a large flashlight.

Scotty wasn't moving. He just kept staring at the black opening into the store.

"There should've been more of 'em around here. They're probably all in there, in the dark, just waiting for us."

Kevin glanced at Howard and Nancy, already moving towards the entrance, before turning back to Scotty. "I think you should stay in the car, man . . ."

With that, Scotty undid his seatbelt and threw his door open. "No fucking way am I sitting out here alone."

He got out, chugged the last of the whiskey, pulled his arm back, and threw the empty bottle as hard as he could. He whooped when it shattered on the pavement, then he followed after Howard and Nancy, the metal chain looped between his fists.

Kevin wasn't sure he liked this any better than motionless anxiety. Scotty was abruptly reckless, and reckless (combined with drunk) could get them all killed. Or worse.

"Kevin, bring the flashlight up here." That was Howard, waving from the doors. Kevin swallowed back his reluctance and joined his friends.

Scotty and Nancy had grabbed shopping carts, and they waited at the entrance like racers at a starting line. Howard was straining to listen. "You hear that?"

"What?" Kevin heard small noises from somewhere in the store, but not much more.

"They're in here. I heard one moan."

Kevin thumbed the flashlight's power button and swung the beam around the dark interior. The light fell on mostly empty shelves, smashed cardboard cartons, paper wrappers . . . but no zombies.

And no food.

Nancy frowned. "Looks picked clean."

Kevin shook his head. "Nah – they always put non-food specials up front, shit like plants and towels and crap. The food's back in that corner." Kevin pointed with the flashlight. The warehouse fell away into shadow; it was impossible to tell how big it was, or what lay just beyond the light beam.

"C'mon, let's get this over with." That was Scotty, already shoving his cart around piles of refuse and boxes.

"Scotty, wait—!" Kevin ran after his friend, trying to light the way. Nancy and Howard followed.

They passed ceiling-high metal racks; the ones that held appliances and glassware still had a few products left, but for the most part they held little more than dust.

"This isn't looking good," Howard murmured.

"Yeah, but—" Kevin broke off as a zombie staggered from around the end of an aisle.

It was a chunky middle-aged woman with blonde hair, although half of her scalp had been torn away, leaving shreds of hair on that side of her head. She was coming towards them silently, and they all froze. After a few seconds, Scotty whispered, "Why isn't this one moaning?"

"And more importantly," Nancy added, "who's going to do something?"

Kevin decided now was as good a time as any to try out his weapon. He tossed the flashlight to Scotty, leapt forward, swung the length of wood, buried the nails in the zombie's skull, and it collapsed almost instantly . . . taking Kevin's 2 x 4 down with it as it fell, nails embedded firmly. "Shit."

Planting a foot on the corpse's jaw, Kevin struggled to pull the nails free – and was still struggling when he heard Scotty say, "Uh . . . more company, Kev."

Another one was coming around the end of the aisle. And another after that. These two did moan; one was a former executive whose pale crown sported a bad comb-over, and the other was a young Asian woman who wore the store's T-shirt and apron. The white apron was stained red, and the fact that much of her neck had been torn away caused her head to tilt a full forty-five degrees to the left.

"Uh . . . Kev . . ."

Kevin finally gave up on removing the board from the dead zombie's skull and started back-pedalling. Behind him, he heard somebody – Howard, he guessed – cry out, followed by the sound of the crowbar smashing into tissue and bone. "Fuck you, too!"

Behind Scotty, Howard was still standing over a zombie he'd just brained with the crowbar; his shirt had been torn away from one shoulder. Nancy turned to help him, but he held up his hands. "I got it, no problem."

Nancy looked back at Scotty and Kevin. "This was a bad idea. We're going. *Now*."

Just then Kevin glanced past her and saw the flashlight's beam bounce off something wrapped in plastic. "Wait a minute . . ." He took the flashlight back from Scotty and ran to what he'd glimpsed.

"Kevin, in case you've got blood in your ears – we are leaving."

Kevin held up what he'd just grabbed – a carton of two-dozen cans, all still in shrink-wrap. "Canned peaches." He threw the carton into Scotty's shopping cart.

Nancy started pushing Howard towards the exit. "Fine. You stay and get killed for peaches."

Kevin looked into Scotty's eyes. "You hungry?"

Eyes jittering back and forth between Kevin and the two approaching zombies, Scotty answered, "Yeah . . ."

"Watch this." Kevin turned and ran right past the shuffling pair. They were slow, impaired, and although they reached out for him and turned, he dodged by them easily. Freed from their attention, Scotty ran with the shopping cart, rushing past them.

From several aisles farther into the store, Kevin uttered a victory whoop. "Scotty, get that cart back here – we struck gold, bro!"

As Scotty joined him with the cart, Kevin was hefting more wrapped cartons of food. "What is it?"

"Tuna fish, I think. And hot damn, mushrooms!" Kevin began piling boxes into the cart.

Scotty glanced back nervously and saw the two zombies rounding the end of the aisle behind them. "Kevin, man, they're coming . . ."

Kevin cast a quick eye at the dead and then ran in the other direction. "Let 'em come. We'll just outrun 'em."

They sped down the next aisle, where they scored coffee, peanut butter and creamed corn. Kevin started to reach for pickles, but stopped when Scotty said, "I'm really fucking sick of pickles, okay?"

They avoided the produce area – most of the fruit and vegetables had gone bad and the stench was nauseating – but grabbed several cases of bottled water. The cart was piled high, and Scotty was struggling to push it.

"We got enough. Want me to push it from here on?" Kevin joined Scotty behind the cart – and felt something brush his back. He whirled to see a dead man reaching for him, but the man was missing three of his fingers. "Go!" Kevin kicked out and the man stumbled back.

He joined Scotty to push the cart and they ran, heading for the block of light that marked the exit. When a zombie lurched into their path they had to stop abruptly, sending a case of soft drinks flying. Scotty started to bend to retrieve it, but Kevin shouted, "Forget it – let's go around him!"

They curved past the zombie, and a few seconds later they were outside. They ran the cart to the Lexus, where Nancy was examining Howard as he cradled one arm. "Look what we got!"

Scotty was already tossing cases into the back of the SUV, but Kevin went to see what was going on with Nancy and Howard. "Fuck . . ." Howard moaned softly.

"What?"

Nancy pulled away the edge of Howard's torn sleeve to reveal a long, bloody line. "He got scratched."

"By one of them?"

She nodded.

Kevin's elation vanished instantly. "Oh fuck . . . I'm . . . really sorry, Howard."

"Don't be – this was my idea."

What they all knew, what they'd heard repeated endlessly on the news during the early stages of the outbreak, was that a single bite or scratch from one of the living dead caused the virus to be passed on. Kevin had never actually seen anyone turn, and he had no idea how long it would take . . . but he didn't doubt that it would eventually happen to Howard.

"So what do we do?"

Nancy answered, "We take him home and care for him, of course."

Kevin stared at her, dumbfounded. "Nancy, we can't take him home. He's been infected—"

"We don't know that. We don't really know much about how this works, except what we've heard on the news, and who knows how accurate any of that was?"

"He'll turn—"

"Maybe not. Besides, even if he does . . . we have to take care of him. He's my brother."

Kevin looked into Howard's eyes. "Howard . . . you know what'll happen . . ."

"I just want to go home, Kevin. Okay?"

Kevin spun, angry, irritated with himself for hating Nancy's compassion, wishing he was far away from here, and his gaze fell on the store's automotive wing, where tyres were changed and new batteries installed.

A black Hummer sat in one of the repair bays; it was an older model, big and boxy. They'd had a drunken discussion one night when they'd talked about the best car to have in a bad situation, and they'd all agreed on the solid, militaristic Hummer H2s.

Kevin started walking towards the repair bays. Behind him, Scotty called out, "Where you goin'?"

"To get that Hummer."

"What are you doing, Kevin?" That was Nancy, but he didn't stop to look back. "We don't need another car."

"You don't, but I do."

"Why?"

Kevin didn't answer. Instead he looked into the bay, cautiously. It seemed empty. There was a small sedan to the left of the Hummer; to the right of it sat an empty slot.

He heard footsteps behind him, then Scotty's voice. "They probably didn't even fix the tyres yet . . ."

Kevin bent down and examined the Hummer's tyres – they were obviously new, even still had stickers. "No, it's done." He moved up the side of the car, looking in the windows. It was empty. And the keys were in the ignition.

"Kevin . . ."

"Give me a minute." He walked around to the driver's side, reached for the door handle – and jumped at the sound of flesh slapping on glass. The sound, though, came from behind him, and when he turned he saw a dead child's face pressed up against the window inside the sedan. The child's mouth worked on instinct, gnawing, and its eyes seemed desperate. Kevin felt for it, even as he was repulsed by it. He knew without hesitation then that he had to leave this place.

The Hummer started up when he turned the ignition. He backed it out of the bay and was pleased with the way it handled. Pulling it around in a circle, he drove up and parked next to Howard's SUV. Nancy had just finished securing Howard in the front passenger seat and was moving around to the driver's side; she stopped halfway when Kevin got out of the Hummer, its engine idling.

"I'm going," he said.

"Where?"

"To Virginia. I've got a friend there."

Nancy eyed him with pity. "You won't make it, you know."

"Yeah, well . . ." Kevin nodded towards Howard, " . . . you're not gonna make it here, either. I'm going to take a couple of the cases of food and water with me."

Nancy just nodded.

Kevin loaded the Hummer. When he finished, he saw Scotty watching him, torn. "You can come with me."

Scotty considered for a moment, and then shook his head. "You go on. Sorry, but I'll take my chances here."

Kevin nodded. He realized that in one of his screenplays, his protagonist would have hugged his friend goodbye here, but he just wanted to be gone. Without another word he climbed behind the wheel, put the gear into DRIVE, and headed off.

The Hummer had nearly a full tank. He had no idea how far it would get him, but at least it would get him away from here.

He found the on-ramp to the 5 freeway, drove up, and headed out of town. For the first time in weeks, the heaviness that had settled on him lifted.

He felt free.

Rhonebach Dispatch

May 30, 2013

LOCAL WAR HERO TY WARD DEFENDS TOWN

By Missy Welbeck

TY WARD, 30, walks with a limp as a result of firefights with Iraqi insurgents, but former Army Private First Class Ward says he won't let it slow him down.

"Rhonebach welcomed me back after my tour," Ward explains, during an interview that took place in the family home he still lives in, "and I'll do what I have to do to defend my town now."

Ward, of course, is talking about those infected by HRV, who have already brought down a number of major American cities, although here in Rhonebach cases are still scarce. Ty Ward intends on keeping it that way.

"I've studied this HRV, and I don't see any reason why we can't keep Rhonebach free of infection." Ward, who possesses first-hand combat experience and a Purple Heart thanks to his 2007 tour of duty in Iraq, told the *Dispatch*. "As long as we guard the entrances to the town and remain vigilant, we should be safe."

Ward, who makes his living with his own computer repair service, has been instrumental in assisting local law enforcement officials in setting up barricades on either end of Main Street, and in instructing citizens on the proper uses of firearms.

A wiry man with prematurely gray hair, Ward projects experience and confidence.

"We can lick this thing," he says. ●

Chapter Three

THE DESERT AT night . . . a mission to investigate an abandoned village . . . gunfire, and the man on the right goes down . . . more men shout, it's hard to hear over the deafening sound of assault weapons, something thuds into my back, I go down, there's blood on my hands, my blood *. . . but there – fifty feet away, the pops of light where the gunman is firing, and my rifle comes up, aims, the trigger is pulled, a body falls, the gunfire stops. I crawl forward to check the dead man, but something's wrong – the body's too small. I reach it, nudge it with the barrel of my M16A2, flip it over and see it's a kid, can't be more than eight or nine, his weapon – the one he shot me with – is almost bigger than he is, and* Oh dear God, I killed a little boy—

Ty jerked upright to the feel of his heart slamming in his chest and an overwhelming sense of panic. He felt around for his gun, didn't find it, looked at the light coming into the room . . .

. . . and realized he was home, in Rhonebach. He wasn't in a barracks somewhere in Iraq, or a military hospital. That'd been six years ago.

Six years, and he still awoke almost every morning with nightmares. The doctors had called it post-traumatic stress disorder, and had assured him it would pass. It hadn't.

He jumped as a knock sounded, followed by a muffled voice saying, "Ty? You awake?"

Ty collected himself from the bed of his small guest house, the one his brother had magnanimously allowed him to live in after his return from the veteran's hospital, and limped to the front door. His back was in agony this morning and the pain reminded him of the metal he still carried there, the bits of shrapnel they'd been unable to remove because of their proximity to the spinal cord.

He ignored the knocking to massage the sore spot for a few seconds, then opened the door a crack and stared out.

Mike Symonds, the diner owner, was there looking like a kid on the first day of school. "We got one. Gerald spotted it coming out of the forest around his back field."

Ty rubbed his eyes and glanced around. The day was warm and clear, closing in fast on afternoon. "So Gerald shot it?"

Mike's enthusiasm was undimmed. "No – he just hid in his house and watched it walk right on by. I guess they really are pretty stupid."

Ty literally bit his tongue, and then asked, "So where's the fucker now?"

"C'mon, Ty, do you have to use that language?"

Restraining the urge to reach out and slap the other man, Ty smiled tightly and said through gritted teeth, "I'm sorry. Where is the lovely shambling rotten corpse now?"

"Coming towards the barricade at the west end of Main."

"Those folks at the barricade know to aim for the head, right?"

"They were kind of hoping you'd do it, Ty. Being the war hero and all."

Ty grabbed the door frame, looked away for a moment, and said, "Fine. Give me two minutes."

"But—"

Ty slammed the door in the man's face.

He tore off the stained Red Sox shirt he'd slept in, went into the bathroom, splashed water on his face, then looked into the mirror.

The only thing that newspaper article had gotten right was his grey hair; they'd missed the rest of his face, though. He didn't look thirty. With his red-rimmed eyes surrounded by black circles and his unshaven silver stubble, he looked fifteen years older.

And he was sure as shit no hero. The article hadn't mentioned that his Purple Heart had come courtesy of a kid . . . a kid Ty had shot. Now he was supposed to pick up a gun again and protect this town.

He briefly considered not going. The town fools could let the zombie blunder through, nipping at everyone it passed, taking a few with it, none of them smart or steady or brave enough to stop it. He could hide out here, in the guest house his brother let him stay in for free. He could just lock the doors and wait until it was all over, then maybe just sit in the corner and rot away slowly with the rest of the world.

But they'd find him. Not the zombies, but the townies, all the ones out there like Mike who were looking to Ty as their leader now.

That's a laugh. 'Bout the only thing I can lead is a pill to my mouth.

But there was his nephew Ben to think about, too. Ben was one of the only things that kept him going; Ty and Ben had always been close, but at sixteen Ben had finally grasped exactly why Ty limped, and he admired him now as well as loved him. Ty might have been an antisocial, disabled ex-vet saddled with uncurable PTSD and a computer repair business that didn't pay enough for a real place to live, but Ben almost made him believe in a future.

Ty sighed, left the bathroom, threw on the closest thing to a clean shirt he had (it featured the logo of a rock band Ty knew only through Ben – most of his clothes were cast-offs from his nephew) and headed out.

Mike was still waiting for him outside, practically dancing with eagerness as he walked beside Ty. "Why aren't you bringin' a gun? I thought you'd have your Army pistol or something . . ."

"They don't let you keep that stuff."

"Well, a shotgun, or a rifle—"

Ty stopped walking and turned to face Mike. "I don't own a fucking gun, okay?"

"So," Mike swallowed, and then asked, "what are you going to do?"

Yeah, war hero, what are *you going to do? Because you're sure as hell not going to shoot it.*

Ty hadn't been able to lift a gun since that night in Iraq. He'd had to pick up a hunting rifle two days ago to show someone how to use it, and he'd promptly staggered off and vomited into a bush. He had told his "students" – three middle-aged women, one young man and an ancient farmer – that he had food poisoning.

Just the idea of raising a gun – pistol, rifle, shotgun, *any* gun – made Ty queasy. After a moment, Ty turned away from Mike and kept walking towards the centre of town. "The point, Mike, is to make sure you all know what to do. I won't always be around when you need to have a zombie shot."

They walked past Rhonebach's quaint white clapboard church, a row of antique stores and gift shops, and turned the corner on to Main. Ty walked into the middle of the wide street, momentarily disoriented, not sure which way was west.

He heard a scream.

It came from the right, and Ty's head jerked towards the source. He jogged a block down the street, heading for a group surrounding a single lurching shape. As Ty drew closer, he saw people he recognized in the circle – Mike's waitress Selma, Jake from the hardware store, the Mason's oldest boy Roger, the local paper's reporter Missy – all battling a zombie that staggered because a large part of its right thigh was gone.

Ty stopped, gaping, as he saw the townspeople were wielding bats, shovels and rakes, which they used to keep the zombie at bay.

"There it is," Mike burst out.

Ty muttered to himself, "Are they fucking *crazy*?"

As he watched, Dean Fetter, who owned Rhonebach's sporting goods store, came running up with a hunting rifle that still had the price tag dangling from it. "I got it!"

As Fetter raised the barrel, still running, Ty shouted, "*No!*"

Fetter stopped and stared at Ty. "But—!"

Ty limped up, motioning at the circle. "Wait until you've got a clear shot – right now there are people all around that thing."

Fetter stopped and stared, almost as if he didn't understand. He considered for a moment before thrusting the rifle at Ty. "You do it."

Ty's vision seemed to contract until he could see nothing but the rifle. He was frozen, rooted . . . but then shouts and cries broke his paralysis and he snatched the gun from Fetter. He swallowed against a lump in his throat as he raised the weapon (why was it so heavy?), but he knew his hands were shaking too badly to get a steady shot.

And everyone was watching him. Or at least it seemed that way to Ty.

The sound of approaching tyres interrupted the scene, turning attention away from Ty. An expensive hybrid car appeared and braked to a stop until the barricade – two wooden sawhorses – was pushed aside. A young woman was behind the wheel; as she came abreast of the crowd, she rolled down her window and shouted, "There are a lot of them coming this way – you should all take shelter."

As she sped on past them, Ty got a glimpse of her face and there was something familiar about her. Had they met somewhere? Or . . .

His attempt at recollection was shattered when Fetter grabbed the rifle away from him and ran. Everyone was fleeing now, both the single zombie and Ty forgotten. They raced back to their stores and homes.

Ty heard moaning. He turned and saw the zombie now trying to make its tortuous way towards him. It had once been a young man, although Ty didn't recognize him; there was nothing unusual or distinguishing about him. He'd looked like millions of other young men – he'd been a son, a brother, a friend.

He could have been Ben.

Now, as one of the hungry dead, the need in his eyes filled Ty with sadness. Ty couldn't have shot him.

But when the stench of the dead thing hit Ty, he turned and ran with all the rest of them – back to his guest house, where he locked the door, crouched shaking in a corner, and tried to wash the image of a murdered eight-year-old from his mind.

CENTRAL INTELLIGENCE AGENCY

CLASSIFIED – EYES ONLY
DATE: 06/28/13
SUBJECT: RENDITION OF PATIENT ZERO

On June 19, HRV Patient Zero was acquired by special U.S. forces who captured him from a renegade British intelligence agent in the countryside not far from Oxford, England. He was then flown to The Bunker, a special research facility run by NWP, where he underwent testing and observation in an attempt to isolate and study the Human Reanimation Virus. So far NWP is cooperating with us and providing information on Patient Zero (PZ), although we remain as always suspicious of their motives and the quality of the data they give us.

The history provided with PZ is frankly confusing and possibly suspect. According to the report, PZ claims to be a British national named Thomas James Moreby, who was released from a subterranean chamber beneath All Hallows Church, south London, when construction crews working on that country's New Festival of Britain (see separate report #1803-01/13/12 for security assessment and threat evaluation) accidentally broke into said crypt. Initial reports stated that Moreby was surrounded by a swarm of fleas that attacked those who came near; victims of the flea bites were apparently among the first to contract HRV, and soon spread it to others via the methods we are now familiar with (bites, scratches, or any contact which involves an exchange of bodily fluids or the breaking of the skin).

The report also indicates that a Thomas James Moreby was born in the early 18th century and was involved with various forms of occultism and black magic, including human sacrifice. After being caught in a particularly heinous act (with seven of his cult followers), Moreby was hauled through the streets of London and thrown into the crypt beneath All Hallows Church, where he remained in an unknown state of suspended animation until released. Yes, we are being asked to accept that Moreby survived imprisonment in this crypt for more than two centuries. While on the surface it seems unreasonable to accept this history, at this time we cannot provide any other verification concerning Moreby's background.

After disappearing for a short period, Moreby was subsequently captured by British intelligence forces, who were able to run a few preliminary tests and conduct interviews with Moreby. We have obtained copies of some (not all) of these interrogations and examinations, which suggest that:

1) Moreby is arrogant and believes himself to be some sort of "King of the Dead".
2) There are actually two strains of HRV present in Moreby's body – one of which may produce reanimated dead who are capable of limited thought and reasoning.
3) Moreby may have an unspecified sort of mental connection to some of the infected.

After Moreby's transfer to The Bunker, a team led by Dr Jason Willson began research, all overseen by NWP. Initially, Moreby was surprisingly cooperative (although as vain as the British reports had indicated); he also claimed to have been born even earlier than the 18th century.

Unfortunately, the project was terminated prematurely, and we are unsure as to the current disposition of Moreby, Dr Willson, or any of the other physicians involved. We have contacted Landen Jones, but he claims ignorance and has been of no use.

We are awaiting an update from W. Leonard Paryder, Senior Controller (East), and will continue to monitor and report on the Moreby situation.

PRELIMINARY REPORT PREPARED BY:
Marissa Cheung, C.I.A. Analyst

Chapter Four

STEELE WAITED, WATCHING, as the President read the report, then exhaled and leaned back in her chair. For a second Steele thought she saw doubt cross the woman's features, only to be replaced by a bitter smile.

"You've read this?"

Steele nodded. "I have."

"Did you believe it?"

"I . . ." Steele didn't know how to answer. A few months ago it would have been the stuff of pure fantasy – an immortal man trapped in a crypt beneath London, commanding hordes of virus-carrying fleas – but that was a few months before most of humanity had died and then come back as monsters. ". . . I'm truthfully not sure, ma'am."

"Who's in charge of the CIA now?"

"Director Gillespie survived. He'll be part of the meeting today at three."

"Good. He can explain this nonsense then." The President tossed the report to the side with a disdain that made Steele smile.

When they'd arrived at the OC yesterday, everything had still been in chaos. After General Parker had declared martial law, military bases – like Bolling in Washington – had become both fortresses and refugee camps. As the Black Hawk flew over the camp, and started to descend, Steele saw how the other woman took in the large, newly erected tent camp.

"What's that fenced-in area?"

Steele followed her gaze. "Quarantine. When civilians arrive, they're kept there for seventy-two hours to make sure they're not carrying HRV. Then, if they're virus-free, they're released into the tent city."

The new President looked down at the outdoor, fenced-in space, teeming with bodies, and asked, "Is it really necessary to keep them out in the open like that? It's like some kind of cattle pen."

"There's just nowhere else to put them."

As soon as the 'copter touched down, the President insisted on touring the tent city first. Even though she was exhausted, she moved with grace among the survivors, offering handshakes and waves. When an African-American woman with a five-year-old boy clutching at her legs saw the President, she burst into tears and ran forward. "You gotta keep us safe," she said between sobs. "I lost everything but my little boy, and he's all that matters now. I know you can save him." The President hugged the woman while the child stood back, shy and uncertain.

Two hours later, they left the refugee camp and entered an office building marked DEFENSE INTELLIGENCE ANALYSIS CENTER. The guard at the front desk nodded to Steele and then gaped when he saw who she accompanied.

They walked behind the guard, passing offices (mostly empty) until they reached the end of a long corridor and stepped through a plain, unmarked door. On the other side was a single large elevator with no call buttons, only a security card reader beside it. Steele handed the President a plastic card on a lanyard. "Keep this with you – it operates the elevator. Yours is also keyed to operate all secure areas of the complex."

"How many elevators are there?"

"Just this one that we know of, but we don't have the original plans and we haven't had time to assemble a complete map yet."

"It's that big?"

Steele smiled and slid her key through the slot. "It's that big."

During her years on Capitol Hill, prior to becoming President, she had heard rumours of the series of underground bunkers built beneath the city, but when they reached the bottom after a long descent and stepped out, she was still nonetheless surprised by the size and scope of the complex. As they walked past storage rooms, control rooms, offices and quarters, the President asked about the history of the complex.

"Amazingly," Steele said, "it was laid out along with most of the rest of the city in the early 19th century, and was the last part of the construction to be completed. The original White House architect was James Hoban, but the work was continued by an Englishman named Benjamin Henry Latrobe, who we think completed the underground area in 1803 and then vanished. After the Greenbrier Bunker in West Virginia was decommissioned in the '90s, a secret project was started to renovate this facility and bring it up to date. Here, look at this, for example . . ." Steele slid her card through a slot next to a door marked FOOD STORAGE 4, and opened the door to show the President a cavernous space filled with metal racks extending off into the distance, the racks filled with cardboard boxes.

"This place was stocked to house most of Washington in the event of nuclear war. We've theoretically got everything we need down here, from food stocks to apartments, offices, mess halls, even a brig. It's almost like a small city, one that could accommodate hundreds comfortably."

What Steele didn't add was that no one was comfortable. Those now living in the underground complex had been used to excesses of wealth and glamour; many had lived in staffed mansions with large families. Now they were crammed together in small, metal-and-concrete-lined rooms in a fluorescent-lit facility that had come to be known as the OC – short for "Occupied Caves". Tensions that had already been high before HRV – political foes and rivals jockeying for power and prestige – had escalated when set to simmer in the OC. Steele wondered how many of them would fare in the tent city above their heads.

Steele led the President to a suite of rooms reserved for her, and wasn't surprised when the woman told her she wanted to get started right away. She asked first for a roster of survivors; next, she wanted all the information they had on the zombies.

When Steele finally bid her good night, so weary she could barely stagger off to her own small quarters, the President was engrossed in studying and acknowledged Steele's departure with only a small wave.

That had been yesterday. Today had begun with the President asking about her daughter.

"I'm sorry, ma'am," Steele told her, "we know she got out of Manhattan before it was nuked, but we lost her after that. Hopefully she's safe somewhere. We'll keep looking."

The President's composure continued to astonish Steele. She knew the woman had already lost her husband during the battle for Washington, most of her friends and family were gone, the country she'd spent so much of her life working to serve was in a shambles, yet she remained calm and determined. Steele's own husband had been killed just last year – an agent for the ATF, he'd been temporarily unemployed during the government shutdown and had been shot in a coffee shop when he'd tried to stop a robbery.

Steele had taken a month off work and spent that time considering the "what ifs": What if he'd gone to another place for coffee that morning? What if there'd been no shutdown? What if he'd died regretting that they'd never had children? What if . . .

When she'd finally returned to work, she'd been grateful for her job and had thrown herself into it with renewed dedication – a dedication to keeping herself sane, mainly.

Maybe that's what the President was doing now. Since she had possibly the hardest job in the world, it shouldn't be a problem to lose herself in it.

Steele had kept the other survivors – the senators and representatives, cabinet officials and lobbyists and civil servants – from the President for the first twenty-four hours; even given the woman's remarkable self-possession, it would be counter-productive to overwhelm her. Today at 3:00 pm would be the first major meeting; that would surely be enough to test anyone's resolve, especially given the classified report they'd reviewed that suggested they were also dealing with impossible, maybe even magical forces.

But before that were two other meetings. The first one was with Steele, just the two women. The President told Steele to take a seat, and asked her to serve as an advisor.

"Me?" Steele was both flattered by and uncomfortable with the idea – she liked operating quietly, in the background. "I'm not sure that I'm right for that . . ."

"You're the best one for the job who's left, frankly. And I trust your judgement."

No more persuasion was required. "Then I accept."

The second meeting was with Bob Delancy. When the President asked Steele to arrange the meeting at noon, she didn't know why. She didn't like Delancy – he was a fifth-term senator who was an old school political hack and a hard-line hawk. He still chaired the Senate's Defense Committee, and was always the first to vote in favour of military action. During the shutdown, he'd voted with his party to refuse negotiation.

That was just his public face. Steele knew some of the private details as well: Delancy was a notorious womanizer who'd had affairs with everyone from high-priced Washington hookers to naive young interns. He'd even once suggested to Steele that he could "perform secret service" on her, and smirked when she'd declined. Steele had often wondered why his wife stayed with him; she guessed that a major alcohol and prescription pill habit helped. Last she'd heard, Delancy's wife had fled the country and was staying with relatives in Canada. Steele guessed that hadn't been a hard decision to make.

Trying not to imagine him ogling her ass, Steele had led Delancy to the President's hastily decorated office – a cubicle with nothing but a metallic desk, three chairs and mounds of cardboard boxes containing folders – and tried to tell herself that Delancy shouldn't make her skin crawl more than the zombies did.

In other words, she couldn't have been less prepared for the President's offer to Delancy.

"Bob, I want you to serve as my Vice President."

Delancy, who was at least sixty pounds overweight, with silver hair still perfectly cut, puffed up like a gigantic bird. "Well, ma'am, that's very flattering, if a little surprising, considering that you and I haven't exactly seen eye to eye on most issues in the past."

Steele had to agree. She remembered when the President had been a senator, with views as diametrically opposed to Delancy's as blue is to red. And she suspected that virtually *no* women, except for maybe a few starstruck young interns, could stand Delancy's undisguised leering.

"I've been over the list of survivors, and you're the most qualified. Plus, I'd like to think that us working together will send a loud and clear message that we're putting old party politics behind us and uniting against our common enemy."

The new Vice President chuckled. "Well, I don't know about putting *all* of the party politics behind us . . . but I'm sure we can come to terms."

They shook hands, and Delancy left. He hadn't even thanked her.

After he was gone, the President bent over papers on her desk, but spoke to Steele without looking up. "You don't approve, do you?"

"He'll still have to be ratified by Congress."

The President smiled. "C'mon, you know he'll be ratified. What's the real problem?"

"I . . ." Steele weighed her words, and then said, "Why *him*?"

"What I said about the united front was true. There aren't many of us left out there, all across the country . . . across the *world*. It's more important now that they believe we can still come together and triumph than that I pick an easy partner. And for whatever it's worth . . . I don't like him, either. But I need him."

"Just don't tell him that – he's liable to offer to lower your personal deficit right now."

As 3:00 pm neared, Steele led the way to a conference room, where the President took a seat at the head of the table, Steele immediately to her left. Those invited began to arrive, Steele mentally cataloguing them:

Ames Parker was a four-star general who was the highest-ranking military officer left, and had been something of a hero to many other African Americans. At sixty, Parker had been preparing for retirement, but had easily stepped back into the ranks after the initial zombie attacks had decimated all branches of the military. When they'd realized no one higher was left, Parker had assumed command under the dictates of martial law, but had almost immediately made it clear that he had no intention of keeping it that way. Three days ago he'd called Steele into his office, told her who he believed their only real choice was, and asked her if she'd oversee the mission.

"Everything's riding on this, which is why you're the only one I can ask," he'd said, in his clear, soft voice. Steele had agreed, of course, and started assembling her team. She liked Parker a great deal, and had been relieved when she'd heard earlier today that he'd already accepted the position of Secretary of Defense.

She was less sure of Aaron Gillespie, the CIA Director. When the Secret Service had been involved in a scandal two years ago, Gillespie had been open in his crude, taunting remarks about being caught with their pants down. After Steele had been named to replace the then-current Secret Service Director, she'd tried to make peace with the man, but had found him dismissive and close to insulting. He was also a friend of Bob Delancy, and Steele couldn't help but wonder how many times Gillespie might have used his agency to cover up Delancy's indiscretions.

But Gillespie was still a cut above Landen Jones, a Capitol Hill lobbyist whose medical degree unfortunately put him in line for the role of Surgeon General. Jones prided himself on always being the best-dressed man in any gathering; with his perfect hair and expensive suits, he reminded Steele of a strutting rooster. Before moving to Washington, Jones had headed Research and Development at New World Pharmaceuticals Group, the biggest drug company on the planet, and Steele had heard uncomfortable rumours ("some of his projects are even offensive to the rest of the New World eggheads") about why Landen Jones had traded his R&D job for lobbyist. Steele thought the man would probably happily lie for a sandwich or stab a friend in the back for a promotion, and she trusted him even less than Delancy.

Delancy himself was also present, but the remaining chairs around the table were left empty; they'd talk to other survivors later about agriculture and commerce and education. Right now they had more important things to discuss.

Once they'd all been seated, the President gestured at her tablet computer. "I've been over everything—"

Gillespie cut her off. "*Everything?* My office alone sent you at least a hundred reports—"

The President returned his interruption. "Aaron, I've been over *everything*. I'm a fast reader."

Gillespie settled back with an arched eyebrow, but kept his mouth shut. Delancy chuckled.

"I want to make retaking the White House a priority."

The four men shifted in their seats, and Steele knew they hadn't expected this. After a few seconds, Gillespie and Jones fixed on Parker, who ignored them, addressing the President. "Madame President, you know that will present considerable difficulties . . ."

"I do, General, but I have full confidence in you and I know you can pull it off. We need first and foremost to send a message; we need to let all of our citizens who are left out there – no, we need to let *the world* know – that we are in charge, and order is being re-established. The White House is a traditional seat of power, and we must be the ones to occupy it.

"I've heard a few of you jokingly refer to this place—" the President waved a hand around, indicating the entire underground complex, "—as the 'OC', which I understand stands for 'Occupied Caves'. Well, I have no intention of overseeing a government that operates in fear from *caves*, no matter how high-tech and secure those caves are. It makes us sound like terrorists. That is *not* the image I want the world to have of us."

Steele admired Parker's calm, even as she knew he was weighing the possibilities and seeing the word "defeat" at the end of every equation. "Madame President, just getting you out of a rural farmhouse was almost too much for us. I'm not sure we've got the troops necessary to take back the White House. Have you looked at the security cameras still functioning up there lately? There must be ten thousand infected just on the South Lawn."

The President looked Parker in the eye, not with challenge but determination. "I know how many troops we've got, but what I don't have in all these reports is an inventory of what arms we have left. How many of those special protective suits do we have, for instance?"

Parker shrugged. "Not enough to protect a force of the size we'd need to take the White House."

"Then we'll look at other options."

There was a second of silence before Delancy barked out, "Drones."

Steele looked at the President, who she suspected was struggling to keep from showing contempt. When the President had been a senator, she'd been part of a sub-committee that had investigated the use of drones in overseas operations; although the sub-committee's findings had done little to change the use of the unmanned weapons, rumours around Washington had suggested that at least one member of the sub-committee had been unhappy with the number of civilian deaths and still believed the use of drones in warfare needed more oversight. However, the President didn't override Delancy's suggestion, and instead asked, "What about drones?"

Parker nodded slowly, his mind working. "That's one option. Hancock Field in New York's got drones – MQ-9 Reapers with Hellfire missiles. If we could fly a few in first around the White House, cut ourselves a path—"

Chapter Five

THE HUMMER'S GAS gauge still showed a quarter-tank remaining, but Kevin didn't want to wait until he entered Oklahoma City proper to fill up. And the sun was going down.

No it would have to be here, in a village called Erick.

The Hummer idled at the top of the ramp leading down from Interstate 40. Kevin used the binoculars he'd acquired at a sporting goods store in Kingman, Arizona, to survey the town below. It looked like an average Midwestern settlement: he saw a motel and a truck stop near the freeway, with houses and flat farmland beyond. Overhead, the sky was slate-coloured and striped with clouds.

The zombies were here, too, just as they'd been in every other town Kevin had stopped at along the way, whether for gas or food or other supplies. The dead had been bad in metropolitan Southern California, but the small towns were often even worse. Zombies in stained jeans and baseball caps stumbled past white clapboard houses and churches, jaws gaping, hands reaching out as if for the American Dream they'd never found.

Erick was no different. The dead staggered along past the houses in the distance, but they were spread out and less concentrated near the interstate.

The truck stop offered the obvious first choice, but Kevin had stopped at two along the way and found out that both had been drained dry, as had virtually all the gas stations. Instead, he'd learned to refill his tank from other cars. The ones with their doors still hanging open made the best sources, because they usually hadn't gotten far and still had mostly full tanks.

Kevin was careful when opening the driver's side door to reach in for the lever that popped the gas tank cover; once, a zombie had sprung at him from the rear seat, and he'd banged his head badly as he'd leaped back.

He assessed his needs before leaving the comparative safety of the freeway: in Kingman he'd collected sodas and candy bars from the same convenience store where he'd found an ancient Cadillac with a full tank, and he'd taken a moth-eaten car blanket from the Caddy's rear seat that he'd used to bed down last night in the rear of the Hummer, parked right on the 40. He'd woken up shivering and sore, and realized he'd neglected to pick up water.

He could certainly get sheets and blankets at the motel, and there were at least half-a-dozen cars in the parking lot.

And the sun was touching the horizon.

He couldn't wait any longer. He made his decision and pulled off the 40, heading for the motel.

It was a two-storey L-shaped building with a parking lot facing the freeway. Kevin pulled in and scanned it, waiting, letting his engine idle. He knew the noise would draw any zombies who were nearby. After thirty seconds or so, he was satisfied that the area was unoccupied.

But he knew it might not stay that way, so he moved quickly.

He took a crowbar he'd found in the Cadillac and ran to the first car. The door was locked. He could just smash the window, but the car was a newer model and might have a still-functioning alarm; no point in drawing extra attention to himself.

The third car he approached was occupied – someone sat behind the wheel.

In the dimming light, it took Kevin a few seconds to realize what he was seeing: it was a dead man, unmoving. As Kevin neared, taking small cautious steps, he saw a dried splatter on the glass and a crumpled skull. He reached the car, and followed the corpse's right arm down to a hand still clutching a revolver.

He checked the rest of the car, verified it was empty, and then reached for the door handle. It opened.

Holding his breath, he leaned in past the corpse to the keys that still dangled from the ignition, and turned them to ACC. The dashboard lit up, and the gas gauge moved to almost the top of the F. A full tank.

Pay dirt.

Feeling a surge of relief, Kevin returned to the Hummer and moved it up near to the dead man's car. He popped the gas tank covers, unscrewed both gas caps, stuck one end of the plastic tubing into the dead man's tank and sucked on the other end until he saw brown liquid swirling up, then shoved it into the Hummer.

By the time he was done transferring the fuel, the sun had set but the sky was still light. He knew that he should probably have left already, but he didn't relish the idea of another cold Midwestern night on the rough floor of the Hummer's rear area. The motel rooms beckoned a short distance away, their simple treasures irresistible.

After capping his tank and storing his siphon tube away, Kevin did one other thing before heading to the motel – he walked around to the passenger door of the dead man's car, opened it and reached down to take the revolver.

The corpse's hand was still tight around the pistol, and Kevin felt his stomach clench as he broke a dead finger with a loud snap, being careful to keep the gun pointed away from him in case it went off. It didn't, and he finally pried it away from the cadaver's withered grasp. He wasn't sure he knew how to use it, but its heft was reassuring, and he held it at his side as he jogged to the Registration Office.

It was getting dark inside by now, but there was enough light to see that the motel was old-fashioned enough to have still been using metal keys, which hung from a numbered pegboard behind the desk. Kevin quickly scanned the office, saw nothing but dust and some old magazines, and he took the keys for Rooms #5 and #6. The keys for the first four rooms were missing.

He left the office and ran down the longer leg of the "L", past #2, #3 and #4, until he came to #5. He opened the door and stepped in.

The room was dark. He flipped the light switch, and was surprised to find the motel still had power. He smiled to himself at the thought of the ice machine outside still functioning, making perfect square cubes that no one would ever use. Maybe he'd take some just to give the machine a last sense of usefulness before its electricity failed forever.

He moved quickly, stripping the bed of sheets and blankets. Glancing at the bathroom he decided to add towels as well. He also grabbed soap, shampoo and toilet paper. Carrying his loot to the Hummer, he dumped it in the back, and decided to ransack Room #6 as well. When it came to blankets, better too many than not enough.

After stripping #6, he knew he'd stayed too long. The parking lot was growing darker, even though a few sodium lights popped on, their timers still working.

Kevin threw the last armfuls into the back of the Hummer, closed the door, turned – and stared at a zombie staggering towards him.

It had been a middle-aged woman, with a stout build and styled hair, but her lower jaw had been torn away when she'd been attacked and dried gore stained her floral-print blouse. She made no sound as she staggered towards Kevin, which was why he hadn't heard her. She was no more than ten feet away.

Kevin remembered he still held the pistol. He raised it and pulled the trigger.

The gun clicked on an empty chamber.

Adrenaline raced through Kevin as he tried to remember all the movies he'd seen in which gunslingers or cops had used revolvers. They did something with the hammer, didn't they? Had to pull it back . . . was that how the cartridge turned and brought a chambered round into place? Or did this gun even hold any bullets? Had the dead driver used the last one on himself?

While Kevin's mind raced through the possibilities, the zombie grabbed his arm.

He cried out and staggered back, but she held his hand in an iron grip. His finger pressed the trigger spasmodically, but the only result was an empty *click – click – click*—

She brought the teeth of her upper jaw down on his fingers.

Using all of his strength and fuelled by pure panic, Kevin jerked his hand away, dropping the gun. He stumbled back to the open door of the Hummer and fell into the seat, pulling the door shut behind him and locking it. The zombie pounded on the window, but Kevin ignored her, reaching for the keys he'd left in the ignition.

The engine roared to life and Kevin backed away, tyres squealing. He was shaking badly as he jammed the gear into DRIVE, and punched the accelerator, running the zombie down. He felt the wheels crush something, and he shouted victoriously. Then he turned and headed for the relative safety of the interstate.

He drove a few miles, then pulled over. He was miles from a town and didn't even see any houses clustered near the freeway. He'd be okay here. Only then did he realize he was crying, from fear and anger at himself.

Kevin forced himself to calm down, turned on the Hummer's overhead light . . . and froze in shock at what he saw:

There was blood on the back of his hand.

It wasn't a lot of blood, but it was *his* blood, flowing from two small incisions the zombie woman's teeth had made in his skin.

"Fuck," Kevin said, to no one. Then, screaming, "*Fuck! Fuck! Fuck!*"

He pounded the roof with his clean hand, and then forced himself to think:

Maybe I can still catch it. The first-aid kit . . . clean the wound out, it couldn't have spread far yet . . .

He scrabbled in the rear seat for the first-aid kit he'd found in Kingman. He managed to dump the contents as he lifted it into the front seat, but he found the anti-bacterial ointment, unscrewed the cap and squirted most of the tube's contents on to his hand. He then used a cotton swab to wipe at the wound. He looked at it again.

The bleeding had stopped.

But he knew, in his gut, that he was too late. He thought back to everything he'd heard or read about the progress of HRV. Was it days? Hours? When would he start to feel it, working inside him, changing him? Killing him?

Kevin did the only thing he could do then: he cried. He cried at the unfairness of it all, at the absurdity of losing his life to a tiny wound inflicted by a dead woman with no lower jaw, at never seeing his friends on either side of the country again, while he died alone in a stolen Hummer.

No, fuck that.

After a few minutes Kevin rubbed his sleeve across his face and forced himself to stop.

How far am I from Virginia? I am *going to see Bobby. And then I'll ask him to be the one to put me down. When I come back.*

Kevin almost started the Hummer up, to keep going, even though the sun had set and the freeway was already being eclipsed by darkness. But if he hit a wrecked car or a staggering figure that he couldn't see because it was night and he was doing 70 miles per hour, he'd never make it to Virginia.

So he took a deep breath, locked the doors, taped cardboard up over the windows, and crawled into the back. He looked at a bag of candy bars, chips and plastic-wrapped convenience store pastries, but he couldn't bring himself to eat.

He already feared the hunger that was to come.

POST FROM NYDSL FORUM

AUTHOR: Ty Ward

SUBJECT: Anybody alive around Rhonebach?

MESSAGE: If anybody else in or near Rhonebach reads this, please post a response. A bad joke, a cute cat photo, a political rant, ANYTHING. I think I'm alone here. ☹

Chapter Six

TY DIDN'T SO much awake as roll out of bed. He didn't really sleep any more. The following few nights after that first zombie had entered Rhonebach had been filled with the roar of distant gun blasts and an occasional shriek or shout.

Ty had stayed in the main house with his brother Rich and with Ben. Ben had spent a lot of the time on the phone with his mother, who had lived in Chicago since the divorce; but at the end of the second night the calls had stopped going through, and Ben had fled to his room to cry.

Rich and Ty had nailed boards up over the windows, but when things seemed to quieten down on the third day, Ben had taken his father's car, intending to head to Chicago. Rich had pedalled a bicycle into town, planning to borrow or just steal a vehicle to follow Ben.

Ty hadn't heard from either of them since.

He'd tried both of their cell phones, just in case. Ben had answered the first call, but said only that he couldn't talk. Those were the last words Ty had heard him say; after that, the calls hadn't gone through. Unable to bear the emptiness of the big main house any longer, Ty had returned to his guest house.

By the fifth day, Ty had barricaded the three windows and single doorway, but the moans of the dead outside kept him awake. He'd taken the additional precaution of taping plastic sheeting up over the windows to make them light-proof, he'd pushed his only heavy piece of furniture in front of his door, and he stayed as silent as possible, but somehow the dead still seemed to know he was here.

They'd ringed the house for two days, occasionally banging on a wall or board, their grunts and wails testimony to their desperation; but they'd finally given up, and it'd been three nights now since he'd heard them.

But he still couldn't sleep. When he tried to close his eyes, he saw nothing but his own failures, written large on his mental viewscreen.

He'd abandoned Rhonebach. Its people had looked to him, depended on him ("war hero!"), and he'd deserted them. When push had come to shove, he'd done neither; he'd run and hid. He hadn't been able to comfort Ben, or keep him from leaving.

Ty was a useless coward, broken beyond fixing. Even if he couldn't fire a gun, he could've used a bat, a broom; he could've made himself a weapon, a spear perhaps. He could have talked to Ben. He could have gone with him.

And he would've been dead with all the rest. Or dead and *undead*.

The local channel on his television had been taken over by the Emergency Broadcast System; announcers kept reading lists of emergency shelters and telling survivors to make their way to the nearest one. The shelters were set up in high schools, churches, underground storage bunkers. The announcers were running interviews with people camped out in the shelters who were calm, even jovial. They made jokes about lines for the bathrooms and how many tins of canned beans they'd eaten.

Ty stopped watching when he realized they'd been running the same interviews for two days. He wondered if the families in those clips were even still alive.

The nearest shelter was the public high school in Red Hook, twelve miles distant. Getting there on foot was out of the question. Even without zombies, his war injuries made walking that far nearly impossible.

And even if Ty could find a car – there were probably plenty without owners now in Rhonebach – he knew he wouldn't go there. If he did, he'd either find the remains of a bloodsoaked massacre, or resolute mothers and fathers, protecting their children, doing their best to convince the little ones that this was just like a big camping trip or summer camp, except Mom and Dad were there, too.

He couldn't handle it. Even before he'd been packed up and shipped off to the war, he hadn't done well with large groups. His family had made him attend a few town functions – a Christmas party, a town meeting – and he'd drawn into himself like a hermit crab, refusing to speak to anyone else and hugely relieved when they'd brought him home again. His computer repair service had eked by on word of mouth; Ty was better with motherboards and hard drives than he was with human beings.

No, pretending to be a decent, hardworking member of a survivors' camp was out.

But how long could he last on his own? He had enough food for another three days, maybe six if he rationed it. He thought there might still be food in the main house – Rich had always kept a well-stocked pantry – but he dreaded venturing back there. If Rich, or even worse, Ben, had turned . . .

Suicide seemed like his best option at this point.

But he couldn't imagine how he'd do it. He didn't have a gun, or even a length of rope. He supposed he could cut his wrists and bleed out; that seemed the easiest and fastest way. Last night, as he'd finished off the last of his bourbon, Ty had picked up a steak knife and pressed the point against the skin of his inner arm; the blade was dull, and it would take some doing to saw through the veins. Fortunately he'd never been opposed to a little hard work.

He wasn't ready for that yet, though.

Ty couldn't even understand why he hung on. He had nothing to live for – no wife, no children, no real career, no passions. He would probably have been better off if he'd done it six years ago, after he'd returned from Iraq; hell, if he'd done it *before* he'd shipped out, there might still be a kid alive there.

But he hadn't done it any of those times, and he wouldn't do it now, at least not yet. He refused to believe he was finished; he supposed everyone felt this way – as if their life had a mission they still had to complete – but that recognition didn't diminish his own determination to stay alive.

The knife's meeting with his wrists would have to wait for now.

After checking his computer again (there was still no response to his post on the forum, and he knew that the electricity would fail long before any appeared) and trying a call to Ben (just in case), Ty made an attempt to scrub himself clean, then looked over his cans. He finally opted for tuna instead of pork and beans or tomato soup; he had no mayonnaise or bread to make a sandwich, but he didn't mind eating it right out of the can.

He opened the container and was just raising the first forkful to his mouth when he heard something outside.

He froze mid-bite, ears straining. There: a shout. Ty set the can and fork back down and moved to the front door of the guest house, leaning forward over the bureau pushed up against it.

A woman's voice, shouting for help. It was coming closer.

It was the first human sound he'd heard in days, and it paralyzed him for a few seconds. He knew he should just stay put, let her go by outside. Her calls sounded hoarse, and Ty wondered if something was chasing her. Maybe even something still alive. A dog. A man.

Bam! A gunshot sounded not very far from where he stood, safe inside his barricaded house.

The woman's voice came again. She was close, possibly in his backyard.

"Help! Help me . . . is anybody here?"

He ground his jaws together and considered. He could stay hidden, and keep going as he was . . . to a lonely, probably self-inflicted death. Or he could push aside the bureau, open the door and let her in, which meant he'd probably have to share his food and it would cut his time in half.

He leaned against the bureau, but didn't push yet.

She shouted again. Now she'd gone past his door.

"Hello? Help!"

He was safe right now. He was warm and had food.

And he was lonely. He'd been lonely for a long time, but god*damn*, not like this.

Before he knew what he was doing, his shoulder was against the bureau, and he shouted, "Hold on!" as he pushed it across the wooden floor.

He heard a response outside. "Hello?"

With trembling fingers, he undid the locks on the door and flung it open.

A woman with unkempt hair and soiled clothing staggered to a halt near the corner of the guest house. She looked back at him, wary. Ty saw immediately that she was favouring one leg, but he didn't see any blood on her; he hoped it meant that she'd just sprained an ankle.

He waved her frantically in. "Come on!"

She hesitated, and he saw she held a pistol in one hand. He glanced in the direction she'd come from and made out the shape of a body face down in the dirt fifty yards away, near where the backyard gave way to a rolling meadow.

Ty turned back to the woman . . .

An arm reached from around the corner of the guest house and grabbed her. She screamed and pulled back, but her attacker held her wrist firmly. As she struggled she pulled the zombie around the corner into view.

It was Ben.

The golden-haired, handsome sixteen-year-old boy who'd kept him going for the past seven years, who he'd hoped was in Chicago with his Mom. Instead, Ben had never even made it out of Rhonebach.

The sight of Ben – now ash-grey, part of his face missing, his eyes glassy – stunned Ty. He watched in shock as his nephew's head ducked down to the woman's neck. His teeth clamped on to the soft meat just above her shoulder, he jerked back, and came away with a bloody hunk.

The action gave the woman the leverage she needed to jerk away, and she raised the pistol. The word "No" died on Ty's lips as she pulled the trigger, at point-blank range.

Ben collapsed, the large piece of the woman's shoulder still clamped in his jaws.

Ty stared through a haze, frozen in disbelief.

Not Ben.

He barely noticed as the woman staggered towards him, one hand holding the gun and the other clamped to her wound. Blood spouted through her fingers, and Ty forced his attention to her. She was already white, and he knew she'd be dead in minutes, maybe seconds.

"Damn . . ." she fell back against the side of the guest house, already dying. She slid down the wall, leaving a crimson swath, and Ty knelt beside her, the movement clumsy because of his back. Her blood spattered him and pooled around his knees in the dirt. He meant to ask her if he could help, but what came out was, "Ben."

She'd removed her hand from the wound and dug into a pocket of her down vest; using two fingers, she removed a smartphone, its screen glowing. "They're coming for me," she said.

"Who is?"

Ty looked at her face closely, and he realized two things: First, she'd been the woman in the car who had warned the town a few days ago.

"There are a lot of them coming this way – you should all take shelter."

He'd thought there'd been something familiar about her then, and now he saw her clearly, and could only gape in astonishment as the second realization dawned on him.

She was famous. In fact, she was probably the most famous daughter in the world. And now she was dying right in front of Ty.

"God, I'm so cold . . ." She tried to raise the gun, but her arm was too weak and it fell back to the ground. She looked up at Ty, her eyes pleading, her voice fading more with each syllable. "Please . . . you have to . . . take the gun . . ."

Ty looked from her to the gun and back – and understood.

She wanted him to kill her.

"I don't want . . . to come . . . back . . ."

Fingers numb, Ty pried the pistol from her grip. He saw, with some bitter irony, that it was a Beretta M9A1, the same pistol he'd had in the Army. Its heft in his hand felt familiar, if not entirely welcome.

The woman below him whispered something he couldn't make out; she uttered a garbled sound and coughed up blood. She only had seconds left, and then she'd be coming back, rising to attack, to spread the infection. Like Ben.

He put the barrel to her forehead. She closed her eyes, and he saw the slightest smile form on her lips.

Ty thought she probably died just before he pulled the trigger.

Her blood was warm on his hand and face, and he fell back in the dirt, still clutching the gun. He stared at her, overwhelmed by his feelings of grief and self-loathing. And he was tired, so *goddamn tired*. He thought he might just curl up right there in the dirt and wait until they found him, the ones who would feast on him and turn him. He'd finally belong to something bigger than him. It would almost be like the homecoming he hadn't had seven years ago.

He wasn't sure how much time passed until he heard voices, human but muffled. He opened his eyes and looked up to see strange figures moving through his yard; at first he thought they must be aliens, clad in spacesuits and helmets. Then he saw their all-too-human guns and one of them detached from the others and moved forward.

She squatted first by the dead woman, pushing hair out of her ruined face and examining the smartphone she'd dropped. She lifted the visor on her helmet, and Ty saw a middle-aged woman, her attractive features creased in disappointment.

"It's her. We're too late."

The others – who Ty now realized were soldiers of some sort – sagged, weapons lowering. Ty struggled to a sitting position as the woman turned to him.

"My name is Sandra Steele, and I'm with the United States Secret Service. Are you injured?"

Ty shook his head. He was too dazed and exhausted to speak.

"No bites? Scratches?"

Again – *no*.

"Do you know what happened to her?"

Ty opened his mouth, but only a whisper came out. "I shot her."

Steele's mouth tightened slightly, then she reached out towards him. "You'll need to come with us, sir. Can you walk?"

By way of answer, Ty rose uncertainly to his feet. Steele nodded at two of the soldiers, who ran forward and positioned themselves on either side of him. "We'll be taking you back to Washington. You're sure you haven't been at any risk of infection? We'll have to examine you thoroughly, so it'd be easier if you told us now."

"No. I've been . . ." Ty uttered a small, unhappy laugh, ". . . very safe."

"Okay. Let's go."

Two more soldiers moved in with a body bag to collect the dead woman. Steele led Ty and his escorts through the backyard, and he was surprised to see a big military 'copter in the meadow, blades revving up in readiness.

"What's your name?" Steele asked him.

"Ty Ward."

"Well, Mr Ward, I hope you're ready to meet the President."

Ty just shook his head in disbelief.

The world was still full of surprises. Perhaps eventually one of them might even be pleasant.

CENTRAL INTELLIGENCE AGENCY

CLASSIFIED – EYES ONLY
DATE: 06/30/13
SUBJECT: REPORT ON T. MOREBY AND NEW ZOMBIE STRAIN

Pursuant to earlier report, on June 28, NWP terminated its projects investigating "Patient Zero" (aka Thomas Moreby) at secret laboratory code-named "The Bunker". Although their cooperation with us faded and our intelligence is sorely lacking, as a result of the report by Senior Controller (East) W. Leonard Paryder we do know that NWP sealed the entire facility in which Moreby had been kept, that they are reporting the loss of Dr. Jason Willson, his wife Marianne, Professor M.T. Déesharné and all other team members, and that they are also reporting the termination of Moreby.

We have reason to believe they are lying about the latter, and that Moreby in fact escaped from the laboratory, accompanied by a woman who matches the physical description of Marianne Willson.

This is where reports become at best problematic, and at worst completely fictitious.

First off, if Moreby is accompanied by Marianne Willson, HRV is out of the picture because Mrs Willson died on June 7 nearly a month before the first sighting of her with Moreby. Although we cannot rule out that Mrs Willson was resurrected by her late husband under purely scientific means, we should also consider the possibility that Moreby may have somehow been involved with her rebirth.

We have received reports of sightings of a zombie that matches the description of Mrs Willson, although she was described as acting alone; we have no reports thus far on Moreby. What is significant is that in areas where Mrs Willson was seen (originally near Baltimore, more recently in Annapolis), we've also received reports of a new kind of zombie – an intelligent one.

Zombies have been reported speaking, driving vehicles and wielding weapons. In one particularly disturbing account from an eyewitness near Annapolis, a group of approximately twenty zombies were marching in unison as an obvious military unit, led by a commander who matches the description of former Major General Harland Dawson.

Dawson served our own forces with distinction, but died during the initial wave of zombie attacks on Washington D.C.. We originally believed that Dawson had succumbed to shrapnel wounds, but if our source was correct in identifying Dawson, then he may have been merely wounded in an explosion but was actually killed by HRV (it is significant that his remains were never recovered).

The larger question, of course, is not only why Dawson is lucid, but why there are enough intelligent zombies serving under him to form the beginnings of an army. It seems unlikely to be sheer coincidence that Mrs. Willson has been seen in these areas as well, and it is possible that she is responsible for the appearance of these intelligent zombies. If so, she is undoubtedly acting per Moreby's plan . . . wherever he is.

We will continue to track down Moreby, and to monitor the actions and movements of these new intelligent zombies, who I think we all agree could pose a serious threat to our security.

I also recommend increased surveillance of Landen Jones. We have reason to believe that Jones possesses far more knowledge of the inner workings of NWP than he has yet revealed. He has also been observed twice to disappear into lesser-used areas of the O.C. – areas that he has perhaps rightly guessed are wired for neither cameras nor microphones.

We should not rule out the possibility that he is contacting NWP during those times; unfortunately, we can no longer access phone records, so we can't be sure. I strongly urge you to consider interrogating Jones, employing whatever techniques are necessary to obtain information about NWP and Moreby.

I know you are personally opposed to interrogation of Jones and I agree that he has value for his medical knowledge (when we are admittedly short on trained medical personnel), but the threat posed by Moreby and Dawson surely outweighs the benefits of having Jones around.

REPORT PREPARED BY:
Marissa Cheung, C.I.A. Analyst

Chapter seven

"LANDEN," THE PRESIDENT said, and Steele heard distaste just in the way she spat the name out, "what the hell's going on? Intelligent zombies now?"

Jones shrugged. "I can only guess that this is the second strain the British doctors thought Moreby was carrying."

"So you're telling me that New World Pharmaceuticals is in the business of guesswork?"

Irritation flickered across Jones' features, but his smile never faltered. "No, ma'am. I'm telling you I'm not in communication with NWP enough to know . . . provided they know anything more."

Steele asked, "So you haven't been calling NWP lately, Mr Jones?"

Landen laughed. "Wow, this feels like the good ol' days, when we stuck our noses into everyone's phone records."

"Landen," the President added, her voice cool and firm, "answer the question."

"Look, I've got a phone. In fact, here it is." He removed a phone from his pocket and handed it to Steele. "Have it. The Seattle number is my sister, if that's any help."

Steele glanced at the phone, but handed it back. "I'm not interested in this one. You own a satellite phone as well, don't you?"

Jones' eyes narrowed as he answered, "Yes, but it doesn't work with our Wi-Fi, so it's useless down here."

"It wouldn't be," Steele said, picking up a sheet of paper, "if you went topside. In fact, I've got a list here of times you've done just that. Seems you do it about three times a day."

As Jones gaped, the President added, "Landen, for God's sakes – we're not accusing you of anything. I'm sure you can understand that we would be concerned if, for example, we thought that NWP was withholding information on Thomas Moreby."

"Well, you can rest easier, then, because we're not. In fact, we think we're close to having a vaccine for HRV."

Now it was the President's turn to stare silently for a few beats, before responding, "A vaccine? One that could be made widely available?"

"Absolutely."

The look the President shot at Steele was clear as ice: *I'd love to believe that, but I don't.*

"How close?"

"Weeks. Maybe days. All the tests are very promising."

"Have you shared any of this information with our CDC teams at Johns Hopkins?"

Jones spread his hands *mea culpa*-style. "Look, we're still a business and allowed to make a profit, right? Obviously the interests of the American people come first, and we'll share when we're in a better position to do so."

"Thank you, Landen."

The interview was over. Jones left, and Steele resisted the urge to slam the door behind him. Instead she closed it quietly and turned back to the President. "Do you really believe that they have a vaccine?"

"I'd like to, and I have no doubt they've been working on it, but . . . well, who knows. Right now I'm more concerned with the threat of intelligent zombies. Look at this." She tossed a report to Steele.

Curious, Steele picked it up and scanned it. As she did so, the President muttered, "There was a time when I might have used the phrase 'intelligent zombies' to refer to most of Congress."

Steele put the report back down. "'Intelligent' might be giving them a little more credit than they deserved."

The President returned her wry expression, and asked, "What do you know about this analyst, Marissa Cheung? Why haven't I met her yet?"

"I can certainly arrange that, if you think it's—"

The President interrupted, "I'm just wondering . . . she's reliable, right? Not someone who's basically all that's left?"

"I checked her out. She's been a targeting analyst in the Directorate of Intelligence for six years. From what I can tell, she was considered to be among the best. She was one of the first to identify and warn us about HRV when it appeared in Britain. Since she arrived here, she's basically become Aaron Gillespie's right hand."

"Have you spent any time with her?"

"No. Do you want me to?"

The President considered for a few beats. "Just be aware. I saw her yesterday with Delancy, and the idea of him being chummy with the CIA's second-in-command just made me a little . . . curious."

"You got it." Steele shared that curiosity; she knew that Delancy had ties into the intelligence community, but the idea of reforging those links here, in an underground bunker while the world above fell further into ruin, left her uneasy.

Abruptly remembering why she was here, Steele added, "Do you want to see Ty Ward now? He's waiting."

The other woman tensed. Steele dreaded this meeting, and couldn't imagine why the President had insisted on it. "Are you sure you want to go through with this?"

"I think I have to. Bring him in."

Steele started to turn away, but was called back. "Oh, and Steele – thank you. I know you took a big risk going out there, and I deeply appreciate what you did."

"It's just . . ." Steele almost added . . . *too bad I failed*, but instead she turned and walked out of the office.

A few yards down the hall, she entered a briefing room. Ty Ward was seated there, with guards on either side of him. Steele nodded at them. "I'll take it from here." Steele knew that the broken veteran before her posed no threat.

She waited until the soldiers had left before she leaned over towards Ty. "She wants to see you now."

Ty's eyes were haunted as he looked up at Steele. "Why? I mean, what the fuck am I going to say to her? 'Gee, sorry I killed your kid?'"

"Don't say anything unless she asks you a question."

Ty offered her a mocking salute. "Yes, ma'am."

The man rose to his feet, and Steele saw how difficult the movement was for him; she'd already scanned his file, and knew he carried shrapnel from a tour of duty in Iraq. Softening her tone, she said, "If it helps . . . I don't think she's angry."

"Well, that makes one of us."

Steele led the way to the office, knocked again and took Ty in. Even though she felt the man presented no danger, she stationed herself behind him, where she could easily restrain him if necessary.

The President gestured at a chair. "Have a seat, Mr Ward." She nodded at Steele, indicating that she should stay.

Ty lowered himself painfully into the metal chair. He stared at his hands, folded in his lap.

"Tell me what happened. Please."

Ty's Adam's apple bobbed twice before he spoke. "I was holed up in my place. I heard shouting outside – a woman. I opened my door and looked out. She was running, or trying to – looked like she'd already twisted an ankle. I tried to call her in, but when she turned, my—" Ty's voice choked, and he had to correct himself, "—*one of them* grabbed her and bit into her. She had a gun and shot the zombie, but it didn't matter – it'd taken a pretty big piece of her. She just kind of . . . slid down the wall, and then she asked me to shoot her."

"And you did?"

Steele forced herself not to look away. She couldn't imagine a more difficult conversation than this one, and she saw how the other woman's jaw was clenched rock-hard to hold all the emotion in . . . but she betrayed no more than that.

"Yes, ma'am." Ty rubbed at one eye, looking towards a far corner of the room.

There was a long silence before the President said, "Thank you, Mr Ward."

Ty looked up in surprise, his eyes still wet. "For what?"

"First, you risked your own safety to save my daughter. Then you did what she asked of you. I know she'd be very grateful."

The President studied Ty for a silent few seconds, and Steele knew something was coming, but she had no idea what. They'd already privately discussed Ty's history as a decorated war vet and Landen Jones' autopsy confirmation that the President's daughter had indeed carried HRV before she'd been shot, but Steele had no idea what the measuring look in the President's eyes meant. And so she was possibly even more shocked than Ty when the President finally said, "Mr Ward, would you like a job here?"

"As what?"

"My Chief of Staff."

Ty gaped before blurting out, "You're kidding."

"I'm not. I've gone over your file. I know that you enlisted because you wanted financial aid to obtain a degree in computer science. I know that you were being considered for promotion before your injury ended your Army career. I know that your former commanders all spoke highly of you. And I know that we're seriously understaffed here, and I really don't have anyone else I can ask."

"What . . . " Ty sputtered and finally got out, ". . . what would I be doing?"

"You'd help me stay organized. You might take meetings when I can't. Basically, Mr Ward, you'd help me put this country back together."

Ty's bitter laugh surprised Steele; she hadn't expected him to easily accept, but the vehemence in his voice took her aback even more. "'Put this country back together'? I'm sorry, ma'am, but you must have been down here too long, because this country is *dead*. And I'm not talking about HRV and all that shit going on right now – that's just the final nail in the coffin."

The President never took her eyes off Ty as she asked, "And what *are* you talking about?"

"As far as I'm concerned, this country died the day I found myself in the middle of a desert where nobody spoke my language, fighting some rich man's war I didn't understand and killing a boy who'd just shot me. It was dead by the time I got home, was given ninety days of treatment and then told to get the fuck out. It's been dead for the last seven years, while I've rotted in the only home I could find, with a small business that couldn't get any smaller and a couple of meaningless medals I couldn't even fucking sell on eBay. If anything, I think the zombies are doing us a favour."

Steele tensed, ready to escort Ty from the office, but the President made no gesture towards her. Instead, she addressed Ty. "I understand your feelings, Mr Ward, and I'm not without sympathy. I know you've suffered. So have a lot of people over the past decade. But you didn't give up, did you? Why is that?"

Ty's head dropped in guilt. "I . . . because there was still one person I cared about. My nephew, Ben. He's the one who took a chunk from your daughter, before she shot him."

A small shock spiked in Steele's mind. There'd been no reason to check the identity of the dead zombie they'd found near the President's daughter . . . or had there? Had she missed that, in her haste to exit the scene? She should've at least interviewed Ty Ward more thoroughly. She'd messed up . . .

The President's voice interrupted her thoughts. "Oh, dear God. I'm truly sorry, Ty."

"Ben was a great kid. He—" Ty broke off, unable to continue.

"So, even though you'd just seen your nephew shot, you still managed to comply with my daughter's final request?"

"Yeah, I guess I did," Ty muttered.

"Mr Ward, I think you're a man of more character and decency than you realize. I'd like to have you on my staff, because you're honest about what's going on; you've had first-hand combat experience both abroad and here, at home; and I'd like to help you find a second chance, because I think you deserve one.

"But I understand your reasons for not accepting the offer. I hope you can find some other work in the facility here that will suit you better."

Now the President did look at Steele, and she stepped forward, ready to lead Ty out . . . but he didn't move. Instead, he said, "I'm not good being on my feet for long periods of time. Because of the injury, I mean."

Steele saw the President's hand twitch, so she waited.

"When would I have to start?"

"As soon as possible. I'm sure Steele will assist you with whatever you need."

Ty considered briefly, then said, "A second chance, huh?"

"And not just for you, Ty. For . . . a lot of us."

"Okay. God help me, I'll try."

The President stood and thrust a hand out. "Welcome aboard."

Ty rose, grimacing at the pain, and accepted the hand, but stayed silent.

Steele led Ty back to the small cubicle that would serve as his quarters. She knew that later today she'd meet with the President and they'd discuss this, and Steele would voice concern. It was her job, after all.

But they had a new Chief of Staff, and Steele could only hope the President's instincts were right.

Chapter Eight

TY HAD BEEN surprised to receive the lunch request from General Parker on his first day on the new job, and he was even more surprised to realize, after spending five minutes with Parker, that he liked the man a great deal.

He'd had a love-hate relationship with military commanders ever since his experience in Iraq. On the one hand, his own sergeant had carried him back to base after he'd been shot; on the other hand, Ty felt as if the subsequent commanders had handed him a medal and then abandoned him. He'd been shoved out on to the street and forgotten by the system.

Added to Ty's uncertainty was the fact that Ames Parker was justifiably famous. He'd commanded battles, written books, lectured around the world, been a hero to many Americans. Parker had worked his way up from an impoverished Detroit childhood, had joined the ROTC in college and had eventually found himself in the position of Chairman of the Joint Chiefs of Staff.

They met in Parker's small office, where he offered Ty a chicken breast sandwich. After they shook hands and sat, Parker said, "We got lucky and had a baker survive and join the staff down here, so the bread's worth the whole meal. Go on, try it."

Ty took a bite, and had to agree – the chicken breast was simply prepared, but the bread was fluffy, slightly sweet and very fresh.

Parker started on his own sandwich, and after a bite he asked, "So, may I call you Ty? How are you settling in here?"

"Yes, sir," Ty said around swallows. "It takes some getting used to. I mean, you're all people I've read about for years, and now . . ." He finished with a helpless shrug.

Ames took another bite and set his sandwich aside. "I understand. I also know something of your history. I read your file."

Ty's appetite abruptly vanished and he returned his sandwich to the simple tin plate. "Yes, sir?"

"You don't have to stand on military address here, Ty. Please call me Ames."

Ty opened his mouth, but nothing came out.

Parker saw his discomfort and smiled warmly. "It's okay, you'll get used to it. We'll be seeing a lot of each other down here, with you serving as Chief of Staff now, and I . . . well, I wanted to talk to you about a possible second job."

"What would that be, si . . . I mean, Ames?"

Parker gazed for a few seconds at a photograph and then turned it around to show Ty a family portrait, taken perhaps ten years ago. In it, Parker sat next to a striking middle-aged woman while two twenty-something children, one son and one daughter, stood behind them. "My wife and children are still alive in our home in Michigan. They've got a military encampment in the backyard and the infected are pretty spread out up there, so they're safe. They've even got a little vegetable garden going; my wife's the one with the green thumb."

Ty was surprised and moved to hear the man choke up once; Parker had always been the calm, rational, smoothly modulated voice of whatever administration he'd worked with. It was startling to realize that the man missed his family and was as human as anyone else.

"Why don't you bring them here? To be with you?"

"Because they're better off where they are. This place is a dead end."

Ty found himself looking down at the sandwich – made with bread baked from stored flour and meat that had undoubtedly been frozen – and he knew it was the truth.

Parker continued, "It works as a temporary sanctuary, but the President understands that we can't retake the country from here. In a few days, I'll be leading an assault against the forces above us. It'll be the most dangerous military operation of my life. I think we can win, but can we hold it afterwards?"

"I don't know," said Ty.

Leaning forward, Parker spoke with the same soft intensity he'd once used when presenting plans in the most crucial briefings. "I'll level with you. You and I aren't the only vets down here – a few of the Congressmen served, but none of them saw any real action. You understand what that's like, and I think you're a decent, thoughtful man who won't risk any lives unnecessarily. I'll be taking every capable soldier with me when we make our attempt on the White House, and if we aren't successful, I want you to take over the military operations down here."

"Me?" Ty pushed his chair back and waved his hands. "I really appreciate your confidence in me, General Parker, but I don't share it. There have to be other choices – what about the man who runs Bolling topside . . .?"

"Colonel Marcus," Parker answered, "is a capable soldier, but he's got his hands full up there. I want someone who knows what's going on *here*."

"I understand, sir, but . . . that someone just isn't me."

Parker leaned back in his chair. "Well, please keep it in the back of your mind, Ty. Oh, and one other thing – I'll want you to be the one to notify my wife." Parker pushed an older model phone across the desk. "I use this to talk to them. Just punch 1 and it'll automatically dial."

"Got it, but . . . I'm awful on the phone."

Parker smiled at him, then picked up his half-eaten food. "Now finish up your sandwich – it's probably the best thing we've got left down here."

Ty took another bite, but even the bread had lost its appeal.

From: Kevin Moon <moonykev@laex.com>
To: Bobby Van Arndt <virginboybva@vi.rr.com>
Sent: SUN, Jun 30, 8:12 AM
Subject: Coming

Back on the 40 now. Had some trouble just outside of Oklahoma City, but . . . well, I'll tell you about it when I see you. Hopefully it won't be long now. Love, Kevin

——Original Message——
From: Bobby Van Arndt <virginboybva@vi.rr.com>
To: Kevin Moon <moonykev@laex.com>
Sent: SUN, Jun 30, 9:27 AM
Subject: I can relate

Trouble, huh? Yeah, we've had some of our own around here. Be careful, bro – they're every-fucking-where now. Proceed with caution . . . but please proceed. You're what I'm living for now.

XOXO, Bobby

——Original Message——
From: Kevin Moon <moonykev@laex.com>
To: Bobby Van Arndt <virginboybva@vi.rr.com>
Sent: WED, Jul 3, 10:27 AM
Subject: Got stuck

Sorry, man, had more problems just outside of Memphis. Ran out of gas, went to look for some, and got separated from the Hummer. Had to hide out in an office building for the last two days. But I finally got out, found some juice, and got back to the Hummer. I don't think I'm that far now. I'm thinking tomorrow.

Love, Kev

——Original Message——
From: Kevin Moon <moonykev@laex.com>
To: Bobby Van Arndt <virginboybva@vi.rr.com>
Sent: THU, Jul 4, 7:17 PM
Subject: You okay?

Didn't hear back from you yesterday. I guess emails are probably not getting through by now . . . but let me know if you get this, okay? Please? Okay? Love,

Kev

Chapter Nine

IT WAS FULL night as Kevin approached the Van Arndt farm. He'd been within thirty miles as the sun had set. He'd tried contacting Bobby one last time to let him know he was an hour away and finally had continued on.

He'd left Interstate 40 ten miles back, and had driven cautiously along narrow two-lane country roads since. The land was hilly and densely wooded, and even at twenty miles an hour he'd had to swerve dangerously on three occasions to miss a shambling figure. He knew the Hummer was safe, but he still found himself nervously re-checking the door locks.

And of course the gas gauge. What had happened just outside Memphis had almost ended the trip. He'd smashed in the window of a car parked in a convenience store lot, setting off the car's alarm. The zombies had converged from *everywhere*, and even though the Hummer was parked less than fifty feet away, they'd cut him off from reaching it. He'd considered fighting his way through with the crowbar, but there were too many. So he'd fled on foot, towards a large office block down the street, dodging more attackers as he went. He'd run into the parking garage first, giving cars as wide a berth as possible. Finally he'd spotted a door marked STAIRWAY.

Of course it'd been locked.

He'd managed to break the lock with the crowbar, and had yanked the door open just as the first of the zombies had staggered around the corner of the garage entrance. He knew they'd come soon.

He also knew he'd be trapped. If the floors above him were full of them . . .

But they weren't. He'd run up the stairs until he came to the fifth floor. Out of breath, he'd paused in the dim stairwell, then ventured to the landing and peered through the window inset into the exit door.

It was dark, but from what little he could see, it looked empty.

He heard moans from the stairwell below him, so he decided to risk it. The door was thankfully unlocked, and he pulled it open, stepping into the corridor beyond.

Kevin jogged down the hallway, trying doors as he went. Finally he came to one that was unlocked. He quickly stepped inside.

The office beyond was small – just a reception area and an inner office. Both were empty. He opened the blinds on the outer window to give himself working light, pushed the heavy metal reception desk up against the outer doorway, and waited.

The sun had gone down two hours later. He helped himself to room-temperature water from a cooler and hunkered down to wait. He managed to grab some sleep on a battered leather couch, but when dawn came, he heard the moans again from outside.

So he waited still longer. Through another day and another night. Relieving himself in the office trash can. Eating some wrapped crackers he found in a desk drawer. And waiting.

At some point he glanced at his hand and remembered a hotel parking lot in Erick, Oklahoma, where a woman with no lower jaw had sunk her upper teeth into his flesh. The woman had been a zombie, carrying HRV. All bite wounds were infectious. Shouldn't he be sick by now? Feverish? Aching? Vomiting?

Turning?

He wasn't, though. In fact, except for feeling anxious and bored and hungry, he was fine.

So he waited. And when the second day dawned to silence, he ventured out.

Only to find a zombie in the hallway, between him and the stairwell.

He almost ran back into his office sanctuary, but anger and desperation prevailed, and – virtually without being aware of it – he charged the dead woman, crowbar raised. She moved forward, reaching for him, but at the last second he dodged to the left and smacked her midsection. She went down and Kevin pounced, driving the end of the crowbar into her forehead.

He hadn't realized he was screaming until then.

Kevin continued on, even as he knew his voice had probably acted like a dinner bell for every zombie in the building. He rushed down the stairwell recklessly. When he reached the bottom, he burst into the parking garage like a force of nature. There was a dead man near the door. He went down in one bone-crunching blow.

After running back to the Hummer, Kevin had found the parking lot empty. The car he'd originally meant to check for gas turned out to have a full tank. The irony of the past two days was not lost on him.

He finally refilled the Hummer and got back on the road.

And now, thanks to GPS tracking and satellites that continued to orbit, beaming information down in disregard for the chaos below, his headlights picked out a mailbox with VAN ARNDT stencilled on the side in faded block letters.

He hadn't seen a zombie in the past mile, so he dared to hope that Bobby's farm had stayed untouched, pristine. Just past the mailbox was a gravel drive that led a short distance to a two-storey farmhouse and barn. A chain-link fence had recently been added around the structures, and Kevin had to stop the Hummer at a gate across the drive.

Kevin looked around, surveying the situation. He saw none of the dead, and there were lights on in the house. It would have all looked perfectly normal – cozy, even – had it not been for the fence.

Setting the Hummer's parking brake, he shifted into neutral, leaving the engine running as he climbed from the car. He examined the fence, but saw no sort of buzzer or bell. As much as he hated to use the car's horn (dinner bell!), he saw little choice.

He leaned into the car, gave the horn one tap and stood by the vehicle. He wanted to make sure he could be seen and identified.

A figure started forward from the house. Kevin wasn't sure who it was or where they'd come from; the front door hadn't opened, but they might have come from the rear of the house. They weren't in the path of the headlights and he couldn't make out a face.

"Bobby?" He'd shouted to be heard above the engine rumble, but there was no response.

His stomach clenched. The figure was walking evenly, but too slowly, mechanically. Finally it stepped into the light, just a few feet on the other side of the gate.

It was Bobby. And he was dead.

"Oh, God, no," Kevin cried out, as he saw his friend's eggshell-white eyes and cracked lips. Bobby had no obvious wounds, but as he reached the gate and thrust a hand through a gap in the chain link, he snarled.

"Damn it. I should've gotten here sooner. I'm so sorry, Bobby, I tried, I really tried—"

A gun blast split the night air. Kevin jumped back, and saw now that a man had come out on to the porch of the house, a smoking .22 rifle still clutched in his hands.

"You got no business here and we got nothin' you'd want, so just turn your vehicle around and get back on the road," he shouted at Kevin.

He was an elderly man, sparse white hair crowning a wrinkled face, and Kevin knew that this must be Bobby's grandfather. Bobby had spoken often about the old man, who'd raised him after his parents had been killed in a car accident; he practised what Bobby had jokingly referred to as "tough love", but Bobby had loved "the old bastard" anyway.

"Mr Van Arndt, my name is Kevin Moon. I'm a friend of Bobby's. I just drove here all the way from California to see him."

"Well, you're too late. He's gone."

Kevin glanced at Bobby again, who was now turning away from him and shuffling back towards the old man, who showed little concern.

"What happened? He was fine when I talked to him on email just a couple of days ago. He really wanted to see me—"

The old man cut him off, his voice strained. "*You* are what killed him! He heard somebody in the driveway three nights ago and thought it was you. Run out all excited like, came back with a scratch. Said it weren't nothin', but it killed him. He'd still be alive if it weren't for you."

Kevin shook his head. "No. I didn't . . . I wouldn't . . . he was . . ."

Bobby had almost reached the porch now, and his grandfather hit him in the chest with the butt of the rifle, knocking him on his ass. "You and your kind poisoned this boy. He should never have left. Now look what's happened to him."

His eyes streaming, Kevin clutched the fence. "Why don't you just shoot him?"

The look that the old man turned on Bobby revealed that he had lost his mind. "Shoot him? I'm not going to shoot my grandson. My Bobby. I just don't let him into the house, is all. We're fine. Or we will be, once you get the hell out of here."

Kevin wasn't happy about having to drive further through these country roads at night, but anything was better than watching his dead friend try to claw his way up to where his grandfather stood, waving a rifle as if it was a lecture pointer.

"Goodbye, Bobby," Kevin said under his breath. Before he returned to the Hummer, he called out to the old man, "Bobby was killed because his luck ran out, Mr Van Arndt – not because he was gay."

He turned his back, ignoring the protestations and curses that were hurled in his direction. He was still thankful to climb into the Hummer and slam the door, sealing himself away with nothing but the engine's reassuring roar. Throwing the car into sudden reverse, he backed down the drive, hit the road and sped away.

After a few miles, he stopped the car, pulling on to the shoulder from force of habit. He waited for his breathing to slow down and felt a sting on one cheek. He turned on the overhead light and looked into the rearview mirror.

Three long, fresh bloody furrows raked down the side of his face. He hadn't even realized that when Bobby had reached out through the fence he'd been that close, and he hadn't felt the physical pain until now.

It didn't much matter, though; he'd already been infected. That'd been three days ago. He didn't have much time left. Kevin had no idea where to go, but he didn't want to die in a stolen Hummer, by the side of a forgotten road. He'd find some place quiet, maybe even nice; he'd wait out the end there.

He decided he didn't want to go far, because after he turned, he hoped there'd be just enough left of him to go back for Bobby's grandfather.

CENTRAL INTELLIGENCE AGENCY

CLASSIFIED – EYES ONLY
DATE: 07/05/13
SUBJECT: ANALYSIS OF JULY 4 LETTER FROM "JAMES MOREBY"

Background: On July 4, remaining worldwide digital networks and broadcasting systems were flooded with a document (see attached) purporting to be a letter from "James Moreby, President of the United States of America". This letter – which served as a sort of victory proclamation – claims that intelligent zombies have taken over all parts of the United States except for isolated rural areas. The letter's author calls himself a former White House janitor who, by virtue of having consumed the brains of the Capitol's strategists and analysts (whom he refers to as "the greatest minds of our generation") has gained enough knowledge to declare himself President over a United States in which zombies have faced humans in "the great civil war" and emerged triumphant.

ANALYSIS: White House employment records do indeed confirm that a James Moreby was employed on the janitorial staff and was likely present in the building during the initial, most devastating waves of zombie attacks.

We do, of course, note the similarity of names between this self-proclaimed "President" James Moreby and "Zombie King" Thomas Moreby, aka "Patient Zero", who was supposedly terminated when New World Pharmaceuticals shut down its research facility known as "The Bunker". Tracing James Moreby's lineage back suggests that he may indeed be distantly related to Thomas Moreby.

When Moreby "died" in 1803, obituaries noted that he passed on with "no issue". However, we can follow James Moreby's heritage back to 1654, and an ancestor named "Amos Motherby". Motherby is a figure of much speculation within occult scholarship; he claimed, in 1672, to have discovered the secret of preserving a man's "Essential Saltes" – physical immortality, in other words.

More than a few scholars have noted that "Amos Motherby" is an anagram of "Thomas Moreby", and have suggested that they are one and the same. In the case of our subject James Moreby, the spelling of Motherby seems to have been altered to Moreby by Ellis Island officials when his distant kin emigrated from Britain to America in 1803. Perhaps coincidentally, this is the same year that Thomas Moreby reportedly "died" or, more accurately, disappeared.

Given that James Moreby may be a direct descendent of Thomas Moreby, and that James Moreby would have been one of the first of the intelligent zombies, we believe it is safe to assume that there is a direct tie between the two Morebys. James Moreby is probably a puppet ruler whose strings are being controlled by Thomas Moreby.

If this is the case, it suggests three things:

1) Landen Jones was lying when he claimed that New World Pharmaceuticals had terminated Moreby
2) Thomas Moreby is also currently in the White House and
3) Gaining the White House may indeed have been Moreby's goal all along.

Although Moreby was brought to America (or, more specifically, to New World Pharmaceuticals) supposedly for research purposes, there were rumors at the time of Moreby's transfer that indicated that Moreby had *arranged the transfer himself*. If Moreby's plan has always been world domination (as we must assume), then it would follow that placing himself in power in Washington would have been of paramount importance.

New information has recently come to light that supports this theory in other ways. Before he disappeared, Thomas Moreby formed a secret cabal called "The Well of Seven". This group was composed of high-ranking members of British society (including politicians, physicians, scholars and architects), and their purpose seems to have been the practice of occult rituals under Moreby's direction.

According to records on file with the British Museum, these activities came to a head on October 7, 1803, when a mob broke into a cellar of a brothel and found Moreby and the Well of Seven sacrificing Moreby's nineteen-year-old wife. The girl did not survive, and most of the members of The Well of Seven escaped. Moreby was carried by the mob to a vault beneath All Hallows Church,

Blackheath, where he was reportedly interred alive. Later, the members of The Well of Seven were either interred – *or interred themselves!* – together nearby, beneath a large stone circle.

If we accept that supernatural forces are in effect and Moreby wields some control over these forces, then it's not ridiculous to assume that Moreby plans to somehow resurrect this Well of Seven and install them as his government, operating under President James Moreby.

REPORT PREPARED BY:
Marissa Cheung, Deputy Director and C.I.A. Analyst

Chapter Ten

AFTER JUST FIVE days of working with Ty Ward, Steele had to admit that the President had been right about him.

He was surprisingly adept at organization and detail. At one point, when Steele had complimented the ease with which he set up a complex spreadsheet, he told her that he was planning on upgrading their network down here. He was at first shy with some of the Congressmen, but he loosened up as he got to know them, and by the end of the second day he'd sent a representative from Tennessee packing after he'd demanded to see the President immediately. Steele saw him grin as the man strode off, and she knew he'd do just fine.

She was less confident, though, about other aspects of what she saw happening in the OC.

Search-and-rescue teams had managed to locate a few more survivors hiding out in parts of Washington, and they now had 36 senators and 162 representatives. The largest assembly room in the complex, the auditorium, held ninety-nine seats, and the senators had claimed that for themselves, noting that it wasn't big enough to hold all the representatives. Left with little choice, the representatives had decided to go digital, and Ty had set them up with a discussion forum. Steele had logged into the forum and saw that a variety of bills were already being bandied about, everything from aid packages for virtually every state with a surviving Congressman to legislation that would make it illegal *not* to carry guns. When Steele saw a discussion about whether women should have any right to choose when "the survival of the very human race depended on their wombs", she had to shut the computer down and walk away.

The world was ending and it felt like business as usual. And of course the parties still fought.

The President's party was ahead by exactly one senator and three representatives (one member of the opposition party had already broached the subject of conspiracy), but she wanted a wider majority for key pieces of legislation. She'd even had one meeting with her Vice President in which she'd tried to persuade him to do away with the two-party system altogether. "Bob, there are so few of us left now," she'd argued, "doesn't it make the most sense for us to band together, at least until we've recaptured some of what we've lost?"

Delancy had chuckled and said (his drawl thicker than usual), "It probably does, but that doesn't mean it's goin' to happen."

Steele had other concerns about Delancy than just his old-boy morals. He had missed two meetings recently, and one senator who'd complained to Steele told her that his alibi – a long lunch with Ames Parker – hadn't checked out. Yesterday, she'd secretly followed him after he'd left the President's office; he'd met up with Marissa Cheung and together they'd disappeared into a large food storage area. Steele had waited nearly an hour, tucked into a dark tool storage alcove across the hallway, but they hadn't re-emerged and she'd given up. She couldn't imagine that Cheung – who'd been rumoured to be a lesbian – would have any sexual interest in Delancy, but she couldn't imagine anything other than an affair that would take so much time in a food locker.

Today's schedule was centred on a meeting with the intelligence and military heads to discuss the Moreby situation. Steele knew the President would try to force Ames Parker into taking action, whether he thought his troops were ready or not. Contact with the west coast was getting sketchier, Canada had sealed its borders and was refusing any communication with the US, and Moreby's puppet President was continuing to flood the Internet with victory messages.

Steele agreed: They either acted quickly, or they might as well settle into a life spent forever with powdered eggs, concrete walls and artificial lighting.

She entered the conference room where the meeting would take place; she was fifteen minutes early, but wanted to check on the set-up. Ty Ward was already there, going over arrangements on a tablet computer.

"How's it going?" Steele walked to the table but didn't sit; she knew Ty had a seating chart, and she intended to comply with it.

"Okay," he said, swiping at the screen. "Just making sure everyone got the documents."

Remembering, Steele pulled her phone from a pocket and brought up the files; she'd downloaded them an hour ago, but only glanced at the contents. Now she saw Marissa Cheung's earlier profile of Moreby, some military analyses from Parker and some recent updates on the situation overhead.

"What do you think of Marissa Cheung?" Steele asked, trying to sound casual.

Ty shrugged. "Efficient. Smart. Dedicated. But . . ."

"But?"

"She's got something going on with Delancy."

Steele nodded. "The President's noticed that, too. But I don't think it's an affair."

Ty grunted and said, "Well, considering that Delancy's old enough to be her thoroughly non-Asian father . . . and have you taken a good look at her face lately?"

"Yesterday, I noticed she looked a little under the weather."

"I saw her this morning, and she looks a *lot* under the weather."

Steele remembered the security protocol she'd helped Gillespie set up when they'd first come down to the OC: new arrivals were stripped and thoroughly examined for any open wounds. If any were found – no matter how solid the story behind the wound's origin – that individual was held in quarantine for seventy-two hours before being released into the underground population (or terminated and taken topside for cremation). Congressmen and cabinet secretaries had groused and complained as they'd been forced to shed clothing and ordered to lift their arms, but when the former Secretary of Homeland Security turned after twenty-four hours in quarantine and had to be shot, attitudes changed.

Steele knew that Marissa Cheung had undergone this ordeal with the rest of them. "There's no way she could have HRV. You were the last person to come down here, and we know you're not infected."

"Hey, let's hope it's just a cold. Hell, if we're really lucky it's morning sickness."

The door opened and Bob Delancy blustered his way into the room, effectively putting an end to the conversation. Steele suffered a moment of mingled amusement and disgust as she imagined Delancy being a contributing factor to Cheung's morning sickness.

Fifteen minutes later, a dozen people were seated around the table, discussing the latest reports on Thomas Moreby. Steele had been shocked by Marissa Cheung's appearance today: she was pale, sweating, hoarse. Whatever she had, it was obviously not a cold or a pregnancy. Steele decided that as soon as the meeting was over, she would confront Aaron Gillespie with her concerns.

Ames Parker had led off with good news. "Our first experiment with an unmanned drone strike proved extremely effective. An MQ-8B Fire Scout armed with Viper Strike glide bombs successfully opened a path through the insurgents surrounding the White House. The path closed again within seconds, but we now believe it would be possible to combine drone strikes with armoured vehicles and ground troops to create a victory for us."

"So," Delancy asked, "we can retake the White House?"

Parker took a beat before answering, "Yes."

Steele understood the meaning of Parker's hesitation, and asked, "But can we hold it?"

The General raised his hands. "Depending on what kind of casualty numbers we sustain in the initial assault, we're probably looking at being able to station around fifty troops in the area."

"Against thousands of zombies," Steele added. "That doesn't sound good."

Delancy butted in, turning to Aaron Gillespie. "What about this Moreby? Do we think a bullet through the head will kill him, like it does all the rest?"

Gillespie glanced at Cheung, but she seemed focused on just staying upright. Her breathing was shallow, face sheathed in sweat. Instead, Gillespie looked to Landen Jones. "Landen would be the likeliest person here to know the answer to that."

Landen spread his hands and smiled, feigning innocence. "Aaron, really . . . we've been over this – well, pardon the bad pun, but we've been over this *to death*. Your information on Moreby is quite clearly better than mine. If I knew something special about how to kill Moreby, I'd tell you. Believe me, I don't relish the thought of spending the rest of my life in a cave any more than the rest of you do."

Gillespie shot Jones a hard look, which Jones returned. Steele thought that if either one had touched alcohol, they'd have been in a fistfight by now.

Ty Ward jumped in, tapping his tablet. "I believe we were also going to discuss the possibility of setting up defensive perimeters that could be slowly expanded. General Parker, perhaps you'd like to take that . . .?"

Steele liked Ty more all the time.

"Of course," Parker said, with his usual disciplined poise. "We've got approximately two thousand linear feet of portable chain-link fence panels. It's not designed for permanent use, but should buy us enough time to dig defensive trenches and to . . ."

Parker continued talking about permanent fencing and lookout platforms and electrified enclosures, but Steele was no longer listening. She was looking at Marissa Cheung.

Cheung's eyes had rolled up into her head.

Before Steele could react, Cheung's head fell forward, hitting the conference table with a heavy *thud*. Parker broke off in mid-sentence, staring. Silence fell around the table for a moment, before someone asked, "Miss Cheung . . .?"

The President and Steele both stood. So did Gillespie, seated immediately to Cheung's right. However, while Steele and the President both moved towards the unconscious woman, Gillespie backed away.

The President started to reach out to help Cheung, but Steele grabbed her arm, holding her back. "Steele, what are you—?"

Steele cut her off as she stepped in between the President and Cheung. "I'm sorry, Madame President, but I can't let you do that." Turning to the rest, she shouted, "Everyone, please clear the room immediately."

As chairs scraped and feet pounded for the exit, Steele drew her gun.

The President was still behind her. "What the hell are you doing, Steele? She needs help . . ."

Steele wasn't listening. She stepped up to the unconscious woman and placed the Glock's barrel against the back of Marissa Cheung's skull.

One second . . . two . . .

Marissa Cheung's head jerked up. Her eyes were milky, and blood-tinged foam flew from her snarling lips.

Steele fired. The bullet went through Cheung's head and lodged in the thick wooden table. Cheung dropped again, truly dead this time.

"Oh my God," Steele heard someone breathe out behind her.

She saw Cheung's blood on her own hand and sprayed across her neat jacket, and she turned to check the President. "Did any of her blood hit you?"

"No, I don't think so."

Steele confirmed that, and then ran her eyes quickly over the paralyzed onlookers packed into the exit. "How about anyone else? Any contact?"

She heard murmurs of "No."

"I'll need to get to decontamination as soon as possible." Steele turned to go, but had a last thought. She scanned the witnesses for Gillespie.

He was already gone.

Steele turned to the President, speaking in low tones. "We've got a problem."

"Understood."

Before she left, Steele saw Delancy. He hadn't even risen from his seat throughout the scene; he'd stayed rooted, the only sign of anxiety the way his fingers were gripping the arms of his chair.

He didn't look stricken, and Steele knew there'd been no affair between Cheung and Delancy. Instead, he looked almost angry.

As Steele headed out to the decontamination showers, she vowed to herself to find out what Delancy had really been up to with the late Marissa Cheung. And if that something had led to the death of a capable woman . . .

Delancy would pay.

From: Kevin Moon <moonykev@laex.com>

To: "HottyScotty" <hottyscotty@laex.com>

Sent: SUN, Jul 07, 10:42 PM

Subject: Goodbye

I hope you get this, Scotty. There's no electricity where I am, but I've been using the Hummer to keep my phone charged. Kinda crazy, I know . . . like somebody's going to call me. But it's been useful for navigation, I guess.

Not that I'm going anywhere. Ever again. They got me. First some old bitch in Oklahoma, then Bobby. Fuckin Bobby was turned, can you believe it? I came all this way, and they got to him first, the dead fucks.

I'm gonna die now. Double dose, after all. I'm out in the country, not far from Richmond. I found a pretty little abandoned farmhouse. Even had a cellar full of homemade jams and pickles. They're pretty good.

It's a nice place. The weather's been good. I'll just wait it out here.

Stay alive, Scotty. Please.

Love,
Kevin

Chapter Eleven

KEVIN WOKE UP, squinting from the sunlight in his eyes. He reached for his phone, thumbed at the screen, saw it was after 3:00 pm. He felt the empty bottle of whiskey he still clutched, and groaned at the pain in his head.

After a few seconds, he staggered to his feet and made his way to the bathroom. He relieved his aching bladder and then swung the mirrored front of the medicine cabinet back, finding a half-full bottle of aspirin. He poured four into his hand, tossed them into his mouth, and endured the bitter taste as he chewed and dry-swallowed.

He returned to the bedroom and collapsed on to the narrow twin bed. The aspirin started to work, and he allowed himself to drift with the diminishing pain, just taking in the details of the room: floral print wallpaper. A dresser painted bright yellow, framed photos of grinning young girls on top of it. Lacy curtains, waving in a light breeze. A desk with a dead laptop, a few textbooks, some pencils.

It'd been a girl's bedroom. An undergraduate college student probably majoring in English, by the look of the textbooks (a Norton anthology, a few classic novels). Probably not even out of her teens yet.

Probably dead now.

Kevin fought against a tsunami of sadness that threatened to drag him under. He forced himself to sit up, wander out to the kitchen and retrieve a bottle of water from the refrigerator. There was no electricity and the water was room temperature, but it washed away the last of the acrid tang of the aspirins.

He was feeling better now, the hangover working its way out of his system. He was halfway through another long gulp of water when it hit him: he *was* feeling better. In fact, except for the fading throb of the headache and fatigue, he felt fine.

That shouldn't be possible. He'd been bitten by the woman . . . what, more than a week ago? Wouldn't infection have set in by now? Hell, shouldn't he have been long *dead* by now?

Startled, he set the water down and rushed back to retrieve his phone. He should be able to still reach the Center for Disease Control's web page on HRV. Maybe the virus had mutated, maybe they'd updated the page—

He glanced at his phone and stopped, staring. He'd been wrong about the date: it was later than he'd thought. He'd been infected *almost two weeks* ago. And again six days ago by Bobby.

He brought up the page on the CDC's website and read over the information: the first signs of infection (fever) usually set in within the first twenty-four to forty-eight hours and, depending on the wound inflicted, it could take anything between one and five days for the virus to cause you to completely turn.

But he had never had a fever. He ran a hand over his forehead, just in case, but his skin still felt cool and dry.

This shouldn't be possible. *He had been bitten nearly two weeks ago.*

He checked the date on the CDC's site. The page had not been updated for several days.

Kevin's mind raced through possibilities: the woman in Oklahoma hadn't bitten him deeply enough. He'd got the amount of time passed wrong. He had a fever but just couldn't feel it.

Bobby hadn't really been dead.

But he rejected them all; he knew they weren't true. The truth was that he'd been subjected to the usual means of spreading the infection – not once, but *twice* – and had survived. The only explanation that made sense was some sort of natural immunity.

He decided he'd spend another few days in the farmhouse, just to be certain. This was a good place to rest; it had food, water, sunlight, and he hadn't seen a zombie since Bobby. It was, in fact, tempting to stay here.

Kevin dismissed that quickly. He needed to find other survivors now; he had to know if there were more like him. If not, then maybe he could help.

It crossed his mind that he might even be important. It seemed unlikely; he'd never been more than a statistic: a gay man. A Korean. A Californian.

Surely that wouldn't have changed at the end of the world.

MORNING SCHEDULE for Saturday, 13 July

Prepared by Ty Ward

08:00 a.m.	Meeting with President and Aaron Gillespie
09:00 a.m.	Inspection of decontamination equipment
09:30 a.m.	Meeting with Landen Jones (re: revised decon. procedures)
10:30 a.m.	Strategy planning session with Ames Parker
11:00 a.m.	Work through files with President
01:00 p.m.	Break for lunch

Chapter Twelve

TY FINISHED WITH the morning schedule and examined it, and then emailed it to all involved. He'd prepare the afternoon schedule during the lunch break. They were planning little in advance right now, while they still struggled with issues of basic security and survival.

It was almost 7:30 am, and Ty pushed his tablet aside. He was already showered and dressed, with just enough time for a quick breakfast of powdered eggs and coffee. He stretched, moving carefully; his little apartment was barely big enough to be a closet, with nothing but a single army bed, a chair and table, and an adjoining bathroom.

At least he had his own bathroom. He was fielding daily complaints from Congressmen who had to share a facility.

Ty downed his rations and stopped to examine himself in the bathroom mirror a last time.

He froze at the unknown face that stared back at him. This man looked groomed and healthy, confident even. He was working harder than he ever had in his life – even when he'd been enduring basic training after his Army enlistment – but he looked well-rested.

Of course; he hadn't had a nightmare in three nights.

He thought about the dreams (*muzzle flash, blood explodes, child falls*) and felt a tremor start in his right hand, but he willed it away. No, no more.

As he left his cubicle and stepped out into the steel-lined hall, he felt the image of the murdered boy trailing after him like a ghost chained to his guilt. He knew that he would never truly escape that terrible night, but he thought he might finally have learned how to live with it. He was working again. He had purpose and goals. He was *alive*.

Those things mattered.

He made his way down several lengths of corridor, exchanging greetings and nods with those he passed. It occasionally surprised Ty to think that he'd once seen some of these people on television or in the newspaper, as distant from him as the moon. Now he saw them every day, and he was learning their personalities and foibles. He already knew that the senator from Alaska had a temper, the Democrat representative from Washington state possessed a delightful sense of humour and a craving for chocolate, and the young soldier with the boyish face from a little town in Iowa was about to be promoted to Major.

"Oh, Ty, I was looking for you."

Ty turned and saw Sandra Steele approaching. Steele had become his closest friend in this strange new world; the President may have been the one who had given him life again, but it was Steele who had saved it in the first place. And she'd taken a great deal of time with him over the past couple of weeks, giving him tips, insider information and even the gossip he'd need to blend in with Capitol Hill's political zoo.

"Good morning, Director Steele. What can I do for you?"

Steele waited until two Congressmen passed them, then she spoke in low tones. "We finally finished going over Marissa Cheung's body—"

"'We'? Is there anything around here you *don't* do?"

"Well, I don't trust Landen Jones. But I do trust you."

Ty was warmed by Steele's confidence, but he also shared her wariness about Jones. The man's slick exterior seemed like it was covering up something primordial and oozing. "Mr Jones seems . . . very knowledgeable."

"Unfortunately, he's the closest thing we've got to a medical examiner right now and he's hard to pin down. We found a wound on Marissa Cheung's right ankle. Nothing serious, but clearly infected."

"So she's been outside within the last few weeks . . ."

"Either that, or someone from topside has been down here."

Ty rolled it over in his mind. "But that someone would have to be infected, too . . ."

"Right. No, I think you nailed it: she found some way out of the OC, some exit we don't know about. And who did she keep disappearing with?"

Ty ran it through his head. "You don't think Delancy's infected, do you?"

Steele grimaced. "HRV might be a step up for Delancy, frankly. But no; I think Marissa Cheung's job was to keep him from getting infected." She hesitated, and then gave Ty a hard, direct stare. "Ty, I need a favour. It could be dangerous, so don't feel obligated—"

Interrupting, Ty said, "You want me to follow Delancy."

She nodded. "We need to know where he's been going, and what he's doing topside. If he's bringing potential threats to our safety back with him, I need to know *now*."

"Do you think he's in something with the CIA?"

"Yes, but . . ." Steele's jaw knotted for a moment before she shook her head. "I think they're protecting him. He used to chair the Senate Select Committee on Intelligence; hell, he used to *golf* with Gillespie's predecessor. Whatever's going on now, I don't think it's anything directly related to the CIA."

Ty resisted an urge to look around nervously; they were alone in the hallway, but they were also planning to spy on the Vice President of the United States. "Okay. Can you get me a webcam?"

"Probably."

"I'll set it up across from that food storage room you saw him go into, and make sure only I can access the live feed. I may need you to cover for me when he leaves."

"You got it."

Ty started to walk away, but Steele called after him, "Thank you, Ty."

"C'mon, Steele – I think I owe you pretty big."

Steele nodded and walked away, and Ty wondered just how expensive his debt to her would be.

REPORT ON THE ACTIVITIES OF R. DELANCY
FOR S. STEELE
FILED BY T. WARD

On the afternoon of Tuesday, 17 July, at approximately 12:30 pm, I observed, via a webcam live feed, Vice President Robert Delancy step through the door of Food Storage Room 7. I immediately excused myself from a meeting with Senator R. Kowalski and hurried to the indicated room.

I entered, and found a large storage warehouse. Steel racks holding rations and other supplies formed long aisles. At first I saw nothing else in the room – no other furnishings or side rooms.

The room, however, was empty, so unless Delancy had left while I'd been en route to the room, I knew he had left via some other means.

A more thorough search revealed one other exit in the form of a freight elevator at the rear of the room. I pressed the call button and stepped inside. The elevator only went to two floors: "G" and "U" (where I was). I pressed "G" and the elevator began to ascend.

After several seconds, the doors opened again, and I peered out cautiously. I saw daylight a short distance away, but I was still inside a large building. I quickly realized this was some sort of loading dock, with an opening perhaps fifty yards away. This was the edge of the dock, where incoming trucks would back up to unload. I made out parts of Bolling Air Field a short distance outside.

To the side the building continued, lit by overhead fixtures. I saw a hallway of offices. Voices were coming from within one of these; I clearly heard Delancy's laugh, and several men I could not identify.

I let the elevator doors close behind me, and heard the men approaching. I found a large stack of cardboard boxes to one side of the dock and hid behind them. Fortunately, I was able to observe around the edge of the boxes with little chance of being seen myself.

Delancy walked on to the loading dock, accompanied by two men in military fatigues. The Vice President had put on what looked to be a hunting jacket and hat. He carried a rifle, and I thought he might be inebriated. He took up position near the open front of the loading dock, which I now saw was lined with barbed wire.

A cell phone rang, and one of the uniformed men answered. He said a few words, then ended the call and turned to Delancy. "Get ready, sir. I think you're going to like what we've got for you today."

Delancy grinned. "I always do, Sergeant." Delancy threw the rifle's bolt, preparing to fire.

After a short time, I heard the distinctive sound of zombies moaning. The two uniformed men stood at the edge of the loading dock, just behind the barbed wire, and shouted, "This way, you fuckers! Come and get it, assholes."

A group of four zombies appeared around the edge of the building. They were perhaps forty feet away and staggering forward.

Delancy whooped, sighted through the scope mounted on his rifle and popped off a shot. It was a direct kill and one of the zombies fell.

A soldier shouted. "Good one, sir!" Delancy grinned and chambered his next round.

(Since all three men were preoccupied at this time, I was able to capture some of what happened next on video. I apologize for the shaky quality – I was still concerned with the possibility of discovery – but the audio is clear and will confirm my account.)

As the next zombie staggered up, Delancy peered through the sight and said, "By God, I know this one – this dipshit tried to filibuster a bill I sponsored once."

"We knew you'd like that one, sir."

Delancy fired, and the shot hit a middle-aged zombie in a tattered business suit. The zombie staggered back from the impact, but it was only a chest wound, not a kill shot. "Oh, yeah, you bastard," Delancy said, finger poised on the trigger, "you're going to suffer a little. Let's see: you wanted health care, is that right?" He fired again, hitting the zombie in the right foot so it stumbled and continued on with a shuffle. Delancy continued, "And you weren't too happy when I blocked your gun control bill, were you?" His next shot took the zombie in the stomach, and as it continued forward some of its organs began to ooze out through the wound. "Aw, hell," Delancy said, sighting again, "this might be the first time you ever showed any guts." He finally pumped a bullet into the zombie's brain, and it dropped, splattering blood and intestines on the pavement. The soldiers applauded.

Two of the zombies reached the loading dock and attempted to grab at the barbed wire. One of the soldiers pointed and laughed. "Look at this dumb fuck – he'll probably cut his fingers right off and not even notice."

The other uniformed man stepped forward and drew a pistol. "Hey, be careful, man – that's how Cheung got it. They may look stupid, but they can also reach through that barbed wire." He started to aim at the zombie's head, when a shot sounded and the zombie dropped. Delancy laughed like crazy, but the soldiers glared.

"Hey, you think maybe you could wait until we're out of the way?"

Delancy chuckled. "Oh, come on, boys, that shot was perfect."

He shot the remaining zombie and turned to the soldiers. "Any more coming?"

"Not today. It's not so easy to round them up, you know."

Delancy clapped the sergeant on the shoulder. "I do know, and I really appreciate it."

"Don't thank us – thank your pal Gillespie."

"Right." Delancy nodded at the corpse of the one he'd recognized. "Hey, can I get a picture with Mr Filibusted?"

The soldiers grinned, despite having been angry with Delancy a few minutes ago. "Yeah, I think we can arrange that." They rolled back a few feet of the curls of barbed wire, jumped down, grabbed the one in the suit, and hauled him up on to the dock, grunting and sweating from the effort of moving dead weight, leaving a thick trail of gore.

Once they had him up there, they arranged the corpse into a sitting position propped up against a box. Then one of them grabbed a fistful of hair and yanked the zombie's bloody face up, and Delancy crouched down next to it, holding his rifle and smiling for the soldier with the smartphone camera. They snapped a few shots, and then Delancy stood. "I need a beer."

One of the soldiers gestured towards the offices. "We've got a whole case on ice for you back here, sir."

They started off towards the far side of the building. "Don't forget to send me that picture," I heard Delancy say.

"Already sent, sir. It's a good one."

Then they were gone.

I waited a few seconds to make sure they were clear, and I returned to the elevator. I made it back unseen. I'm confident that Delancy is completely unaware that he was followed.

(See attached video file, labeled hunting.mp4)

Chapter Thirteen

THE PRESIDENT LOOKED up from the tablet and leaned back in her chair. "Dear God."

Steele and Ty exchanged a look, and then Ty started around the desk. "Did you want to see the video . . .?"

"No. I don't need to see it."

Ty hesitated, stepping back. "He returned to his office about fifteen minutes ago. I think he's in a meeting right now with John Olesson and Gary Hronis."

"I don't care if he's in a meeting with the ghost of Ronald Reagan – get him in here *now*."

Ty blinked once before turning to leave. "I'll have him in five."

Steele watched Ty rush out of the room. "You were right about him. He's good."

"Maybe I should make him Vice President."

Steele couldn't suppress a smile. When the President looked up at her, though, the smile faded. "Steele, I want you here for this meeting. Knowing Delancy, his first concern will probably be to figure out who followed him, and as good as Ty is, I'd rather have him think it was you."

"I agree."

"Now the question is: what do we do with him?"

Steele considered before answering. "I'm almost more concerned with Gillespie. We frankly shouldn't be surprised at behaviour like this from Delancy, but Gillespie is apparently willing to both endanger his best employees *and* put the security of our entire complex at risk just to satisfy Delancy's whims."

The President nodded, picked up a pencil and tapped it in frustration. "True. Unfortunately, he just killed his replacement. Marissa Cheung would have been the only real choice. And how do we discipline him? Take away his company car?"

"I don't know, Madame President. I really don't."

Steele's cell phone chirped. She picked it up, heard Ty's voice. "We're here."

She looked up at the President, who nodded. "Okay, send him in. And Ty, you don't need to wait around."

The office door opened and Delancy entered, crossing the room and dropping his bulk into a groaning metal chair. "What's this about? I was in the middle of some important negotiations with—"

The President cut him off. "Sure you weren't sharing your latest trophy snaps?"

Delancy's mouth hung open for a split second before he remembered to close it. "Trophy snaps?"

As the President stared coolly at Delancy, Steele brought up Ty's video on her own phone and held it out for him to see.

"By God, I know this one – this dipshit tried to filibuster a bill I sponsored once."

"We knew you'd like that one, sir."

Steele asked, "Do I need to keep going?"

"No, I think I got it."

Steele stabbed at the phone screen as the sound of bullets popped out of the tiny speaker. Delancy turned his gaze from the phone to Steele and then to the President. "So, what – are you spying on all of us now, or just me?"

With a chill in her voice, the President answered, "No, just you, Bob. You're the only one who's been disappearing for long stretches of time with a woman who recently turned up infected with HRV and who's now dead."

"Now, that's not my fault."

"Really? So you weren't there when—" The President paused to pull the tablet closer to her and scroll briefly through the report. "—Cheung accidentally stepped to the edge of the loading dock and was scratched on the ankle?"

Delancy's eyes narrowed. "Well, you got the whole goddamn story, didn't you?"

"Yeah, Bob, we did." She pushed the tablet away, rose from her chair and turned furiously on Delancy. "What the hell were you thinking? You put our people in danger – you *killed* the best analyst we had left – just so you could have your own private shooting gallery? Can you imagine what kind of damage this story could do if it got out?"

Delancy didn't stand as he shouted back, "Got out to *who*? In case you hadn't noticed, we don't exactly have to worry much about the press any more. Or foreign intelligence. Or some douchebag kid who thinks he'll be a hero if he gives our secrets away. In fact, about the only thing I can see that we have left to worry about is some zombie king named Moreby, and I hope to Christ he *does* hear about it! Let him know that not all of us are ready to roll over and hand our country to him just yet."

"Is that what you think we're doing, Bob?"

Now he did rise. "All I know is we've been down here for weeks now, and all I see happening is you giving out jobs to used-up losers like Ty Ward. Oh, and don't think I'm so dumb that I don't know it was him who followed me. That's his tablet on your desk, Madame President. Now, if you'll excuse me, I'm going back to my meeting so that some of us with a little fire in our bellies can figure a way out of this mess."

Delancy strode from the office.

Steele rose and started after him. "Do you want me to bring him back?"

"No. Let him go."

Steele closed the door and looked back to see the President sagging into her chair, hand to her chin in her characteristic manner. "He's right."

"How so?"

"We *have* spent too long talking and planning and wasting time, while our enemies have evolved and expanded their hold."

Steele didn't like the direction this conversation might take. She prided herself on caution; it was how she'd built her career. She'd never been an impulsive person; she'd always taken time to analyse every possible manoeuvre, every potential outcome. She'd stopped assassins and broken counterfeiting rings that way. When she'd rescued this President, she'd even predicted how many men and women she'd lose in the attempt, and had been off by only one.

She saw a loss of 100 per cent if they took military action against the zombies now.

The President must have seen Steele's trepidation and guessed rightly at its source. "Don't worry, Steele, we're not going to rush into anything. But we need to push Ames Parker harder."

Steele exhaled in relief. "That we can do."

"Oh, and send Gillespie to see me. I'm going to tell him that if he can't get Landen Jones to tell us everything he knows about Moreby, they'll both be spending twelve hours a day brewing coffee in the cafeteria."

Steele grinned. "You got it, ma'am."

As she left the office, Steele still thought they were on their way to a devastating loss, but at least they wouldn't slowly starve to death buried half-a-mile under the ground and forgotten by history.

If there was any history still to come.

Videos

▶ Benfootball.mp4

▶ BenHalloween.mp4

▶ fallhike.mp4

▶ hunting.mp4

▶ WarrenBen.mp4

5 items, 651.76 GB available

Chapter Thirteen

TY TOOK ANOTHER sip of vodka, refilled his glass and stared again at the computer screen.

hunting.mp4

It would be so easy . . .

The idea had come to him ten minutes ago, as the clock had passed midnight and he'd slipped fully into drunkenness.

Post the video. Make it public.

It would solve the Delancy problem. Steele and the President would be blameless and could focus on other, more important issues.

Parts of the Internet were still operating; there were enough protected and powered nodes that it worked, although it was slower than it had been. Many of the major pre-HRV sites were gone, but others hung on; Ty wondered if they were completely automated, or had hordes of dedicated nerds who'd simply refused to leave their desks for something as minor as the end of the world.

He'd already checked, and learned that the major video-sharing site was still online. He clicked on it again and it came right up. He had an account there because he'd once posted a video of Ben making a touchdown for his school's football team. The account read "UncleMan", and fed to an email account that also didn't include Ty's name. Of course it would take a real hacker only minutes to trace it back to him . . . but he wasn't sure there were any real hackers left.

All he had to do was hit the UPLOAD button.

His gaze drifted down from that temptation to the "Most Popular" section. Because he was drunk, and because it was late at night and he was preoccupied with the thought of possibly betraying his country's Vice President, it took him a few seconds to realize what he was seeing.

Every one of the "Most Popular" videos featured zombies.

Curious, he clicked on the first one, something called "Zombie Sings the Blues". It took several minutes for the video to load and begin playing, and Ty saw a shaky, phonecam image of what looked like the interior of a barn. A zombie was chained to the unpainted wooden wall; it had been a wiry man in his forties, with cropped hair and flannel shirt, but now it was a gaunt spectre with gaping mouth and grasping, claw-like fingers. In the background, rap music played, the bass throbbing.

A young man stepped into the frame. He wore a butcher's apron over his sweats and a welder's mask, the visor already down. "You ready for this?" he asked the camera, grinning.

He lifted a chainsaw up and yanked the starter rope several times until the engine caught to noisy life.

As Ty watched, he felt the vodka's pleasant haze draining away. The young man turned to the squirming zombie and used the chainsaw to sever its left arm. Dark liquid gushed from the stump and the camera tilted down to the arm, still wriggling on the barn's dirt floor, until a boot kicked it away.

The image came back to the man, now covered in the zombie's blood, as he severed the other arm and then went to work on the torso. Clotted blood and tissue flew as the spinning blade bit into the stomach; the chainsaw man stepped back and throttled the chainsaw down so he could be heard whooping as blue and grey intestines spilled out, sliding down the zombie's legs to the floor. The zombie looked down, its mouth twisting in either shock or pain.

The butcher made a motion to the camera – an upheld finger, promising one more magic moment – and then revved the chainsaw again and raised it. This time he sawed the zombie's head from its neck, sending it tumbling. When he was done, he turned off the chainsaw, set it aside, and ripped the welder's mask free and dropped it. He bent down out of frame, and when he came up again he was holding the zombie's head.

He walked it forward, so it took up most of the image. The head was still alive, the mouth moving. The butcher shouted, "Hey, Mikey, turn down that fuckin' noise!" The rap music died and the butcher moved the head even closer to the camera.

Now a faint sound could be heard from the mouth; because there was no larynx or vocal cords attached, what would probably have been wailing came out as an eerie, toneless rush of air, like the sound of wind through distant trees.

"Ain't that a kick?" said the butcher. He put his face next to the zombie's and widened his grin.

Ty hit the video player's PAUSE button. He felt nauseous and knew it wasn't the vodka. He didn't need to see what the young man and his friends finally did to the severed head.

He clicked the BACK arrow, returning to the site's main page, and glanced at the "Most Popular" videos again. He already knew, though, without watching any of them, that they were all like this one.

He did vomit, then. When it was over, he sat on his bunk, weak and shaken, and turned his computer off.

Because he knew if he released the Delancy video into that world, the man would be a hero.

MEMO

Dear Ward:

I'm sorry to report that we've hit a wall with the HRV vaccine research. We've tried every variant:

1) Live, attenuated – we were unable to prepare a strain that did not infect the human host. We even attempted one in which we passaged the virus through 300 cell cultures, but the virus never lost the ability to replicate in human cells.

2) Inactivated – we were, put simply, unable to kill HRV. We tried heat, formaldehyde, some chemical cocktails that should have killed anything ... but HRV wouldn't die.

3) Recombinant vector – this showed the most promise, and I still believe it might be possible to create a vaccine in this fashion. We did manage to isolate the protein in HRV, and when introduced into an attenuated adenovirus, initial results seemed good. Volunteer test subject #89 was vaccinated, and then received a bite from one of the infected. The subject showed no signs of HRV for the first 72 hours ... but then the disease progressed quickly, and the subject had to be terminated.

I probably don't need to add that we've tried various dosages. In the case of live vaccines, the size of the dosage seemed to make little difference, and we're frankly still trying to understand the processes by which HRV replicates so efficiently.

If we had another three years, we could also investigate production of a DNA vaccine. But the fact is ... we don't have three years. I doubt if we have one year.

Ward, we're out of *everything*. Are you still in touch with Landen? We need everything from more volunteers/test subjects to plain old food rations. It's bad enough that we all live at one of NWP's facilities now, but we ARE running out of food and drinking water. And security could use a boost, too. Tell Landen to lobby his friends in DC (if he still has any) to get us what we need. We could at least keep going. Right now we have nothing. This could be the only time I have ever hoped that one of our competitors is ahead of us.

Brewster

Chapter Fifteen

KEVIN HAD BEEN driving for an hour on the 95 heading north when he pulled up to the roadblock.

In the past, he might have approached a line of military vehicles with sweating palms. In LA, he'd once encountered a police checkpoint late on a Saturday night, searching for drunken motorists; fortunately, his last beer had been three hours earlier and the cops had waved him on through. Even sober, it'd been enough to set his heart pounding.

But today he approached with cautious optimism. The trucks lined up across the road were plainly military, as were the young soldiers who stood before them. Even their rifles – which in the past would have intimidated him into turning around and going the other way – gave him a measure of comfort.

He pulled the Hummer to a stop and three soldiers approached. The one on the driver's side made a motion and Kevin rolled down his window. The soldier was younger than Kevin, barely twenty; he had acne-scarred skin, blonde fuzz and mirrored sunglasses he didn't remove.

"Good morning, sir."

"'Morning to you," Kevin said, trying to sound as friendly as possible.

"Can we ask where you're headed?"

"I'm not sure. I came from California to see a friend in Virginia, but . . . that didn't work out. Guess I'm just trying to find a place to stay now."

The young soldier saw something that made him frown, and he walked back three steps, lowering the rifle just enough to let Kevin know he was serious. "Can I ask you to get out of the vehicle, sir?"

Kevin's confidence vanished. He was starting to shake as he undid his seat belt, opened the door and got out of the Hummer. The soldier waved his friends over, and together they all peered at Kevin's face.

The scratches. Of course.

"How'd you get those?" That was one of the others, a wiry man who seemed closer to forty.

"It's okay – I'm not infected."

The blonde kid's jaw tightened. "Answer the question, sir."

"The friend in Virginia gave them to me."

The older man asked, "Was that friend alive or dead?"

Kevin's mouth opened, but he couldn't find an answer.

All three soldiers tensed. "I'm going to have to ask you to come with us," the blonde boy said, motioning away with the rifle barrel.

Kevin looked where he was pointing, and saw that one of the trucks seemed to be filled with people. He glimpsed pale, desperate faces peering out the back; some were obviously very sick, while others were still well enough to regard the armed soldiers below them with fear.

"No, I'm not—"

The older man lowered his gun. "Get to the truck *now*."

Kevin thrust out his hand, and all three men instantly leveled their rifles at him. He didn't care; he hadn't come all this way and *survived* to climb into a truck with sick victims who were obviously bound for a convenient trench and an early meeting with those rifles. "No, no, look at this – this bite, I got it more than three weeks ago from a dead woman, and I haven't developed any symptoms, I'm—"

A rifle barrel in his armpit interrupted. It was the third man, who hadn't spoken so far; now that he did, his voice was thick with both a rural accent and uncompromising iron. "Sure, and I'm the tooth fairy. Now get your ass to that fuckin' truck."

"I swear, I'm immune! Don't you get it? *I'm immune to HRV—*"

The blonde boy placed the barrel of his rifle up against Kevin's head. "Or you could be one of those new smart ones, in which case we'd be perfectly justified in shooting you right here."

"'Smart ones'? What does that mean?"

A push from behind sent Kevin sprawling. He looked back up to see the older one standing over him, leering. "Haven't you heard? We got zombies who can think now, and maybe you're one of those."

Kevin gulped, trying to grasp what he was hearing – *the zombies can think?* "That's fucked up, but I'm—"

The man who'd pushed him cut him off. "You got five seconds to get to your feet and start walking. One . . . two . . . three . . ."

Scrambling to his feet, Kevin started stumbling back. "You guys are making a big mistake—"

He barely noticed a fourth soldier approaching until he heard a feminine voice. "What's going on here?" He looked more carefully at the new arrival and saw a young woman appraising the scene. The other soldiers pulled back slightly. "Just trying to get this infected to join the others, Sarge."

Something about her seemed different – her eyes glinted with intelligence, even humour. He held up his hand for her to see. "Look – I got this *weeks* ago from a woman in Oklahoma. A *dead* woman. And I'm still not infected."

The older man exhaled heavily, moving his rifle barrel towards the truck. "Just shut up about that already and keep walkin'—!"

"Hold on." That was the woman, who took Kevin's hand and studied the shallow bite marks. "These have completely healed over."

"Right. That's what I've been trying to say."

She examined his face, her eyes settling on to the three furrows left there by Bobby. "What about those?"

"Also more than two weeks old. From another infected."

"Any fever? Delirium? Chills, sweats?"

"No."

She locked gazes with him, and Kevin felt a glimmer of hope. The quiet soldier hissed, "Oh, fuck me, LaFortune, you don't actually buy this shit, do you?"

"That's *Sergeant* LaFortune to you, Private. Do I need to write you up again?"

He drew himself up to attention, but kept one lip curled as he threw back, "No, Sergeant, you don't."

LaFortune returned her attention to Kevin's hand. "Those bites on his hand are healed, and he doesn't look sick to me. If he's telling the truth . . ."

Kevin's response was low but urgent. "I am."

She studied him, and finally nodded towards a tent set up by the side of the freeway. "I'll take him to Command, have the doc go over him, and we'll see."

The other three soldiers were plainly irritated, but backed off. "He's all yours, Sarge," said the blonde kid. As they strode away, Kevin heard the tall one laugh and add, "Just don't be surprised when we make *you* march to the truck after this cocksucker turns and bites you."

LaFortune stopped, turned back and glared at them. "Hope you boys all like peeling potatoes, because you just earned yourselves some extra kitchen duty."

Three sets of jaws ground together, but they remained silent.

LaFortune turned back to Kevin and they continued walking. He was shaking now from relief. "Thank you."

"What's your name?"

"Kevin Moon."

"Well, Mister Moon, if you're right, you're the most important man in the world. And if you're not . . ."

She pulled her own holstered pistol and pointed it squarely at Kevin's head, and his relief froze.

Right then, he wished more than anything that he'd stayed in the little farmhouse with the lacy curtains and the shelves of jams and jellies.

My fellow undead citizens –

I send greetings today to those of you who have only recently joined us, via virus, death, rebirth and consumption. More and more of you are coming to consciousness, swelling our ranks with undead vigour, and we will soon be an invincible force.

I must first commend the work of my associate Marianne Willson. She has been instrumental in helping us to realize our great dream of a truly evolved society; she has spread self-awareness and intelligence wherever she has gone. However, we still have far to go, as the human resistance continues to thwart our progress. Thanks to Marianne's valiant efforts, every hour new brothers and sisters rise again to join us.

I also want to address rumors of a working human government, located somewhere near Washington D.C. Let me assure you, my hungry kin, that I am personally hard at work locating and exterminating this paltry, pathetic attempt at coordinating human combat efforts. Our forces remain in control of all important areas of this new nation's Capitol, and we are completely confident in our ability to retain that control. We anticipate crushing this human administration in days, if not hours. Let me assure you that I *will* taste their leader, and I will take this so-called leader into myself. The human end will be painful and bloody.

It is also with tremendous pride that I announce today the formation of a great new civilization. It is time for us all to cast off our old identity, and claim our resurrected heritage. We will henceforth no longer be the United States of America, for that land is a dead thing, buried under the weight of its own failures and destined never to rise again. We instead will embrace who and what we are, and from this day forward let us be known as the first nation of the New Zombie Order.

A great society will unfold here at last, bringing with it something the world has never seen before: a place where all citizens are truly equal, where none are poor or cold or alone. Even now we are beginning work on our human internment and breeding camps, which will ensure that none of us go hungry. I can feel and think through each of you, and we are like one great host; we are truly legion. We will grow and evolve and, in time, we will even reach back out to the stars, finding new worlds to consume and bring into our great fold.

The future belongs to the New Zombie Order and, from this day forward, the New Zombie Order is *us*.

Chapter Sixteen

AARON GILLESPIE LOOKED like shit.

He sat at the head of the table, facing Steele, Ty and the President; his eyes were sunken, his jaw stubbled, clothes wrinkled. He looked like a man who hadn't slept in weeks, and while Steele knew she would never trust him again, a part of her worried for the man.

"Aaron," the President said, "you called this meeting, so suppose you get on with it. What's going on?"

"This . . ." Gillespie had a laptop on the table before him. He turned it around to face them, and they saw a frozen image on a video player: it looked like a woman in a cell made of cement blocks, seated on a bench, while a muscled, bearded man stood over her.

"Yesterday a group down in San Antonio captured Marianne Willson."

Steele thought back for a moment, and then said, "Marianne Willson . . . she was Moreby's cohort, wasn't she?"

Gillespie nodded. "Correct. In his big speech, Moreby claimed she was moving around the country spreading the HRV strain that creates intelligent zombies. Well, this group that got her filmed an interrogation and sent us a copy. I think you'll find this part of it most interesting." Aaron hit a button on the laptop and the video began to play.

Now Steele could clearly see that the woman on the bench was dead; she was middle-aged, but with the gaunt, dried skin and gummy eyes of the living dead. She wore an incongruously pretty dress, although its once-cheerful floral print was now rendered ghastly by extensive blood splatters. Her hands were cuffed before her, and were chained to shackles on her feet.

The man who stood over her asked, "What can you tell me about Moreby?"

"He's our king."

"Is he James Moreby, the President of the New Zombie Order?"

"He is . . . and he is not."

The bearded man gritted his teeth and took a threatening step forward. "Give me straight answers, you dead bitch."

Marianne smiled up calmly. "That *is* a straight answer, but I'll see if I can phrase it in a way you'll understand. Thomas – Moreby, that is – was rather badly damaged when we escaped from The Bunker. Rather than continue on in that slowly decaying form, he summoned his descendent, James Moreby, and placed both his consciousness and his virus strains into the newer, more intact body."

"How did he do that?"

"Our weak flesh may eventually rot and perish, but there's a way for the intellect to continue after physical death. In fact, he's about to bring back his Well of Seven in a somewhat similar fashion—"

"Who's the Well of Seven?"

Marianne seemed to go blank for a second, then she looked up coyly at her interrogator. "He wants me to tell you that it's only a matter of time until he finds out."

"Until he finds out what?"

She turned her pale eyes up to the camera, and the camera operator took that moment to zoom in. Steele felt a chill at the thought that Moreby was somehow addressing her directly through Marianne and the camera lens. "Until he finds out where your President and her lackeys are hiding. And when he does find her, he will cut her skull open and eat her brain with a silver spoon."

"Yeah?" The anger in the interrogator's voice was palpable; when the camera zoomed back out, the man was nearly dancing in his fury. "Well, let me give you a message to send back to your King of Shit—"

He abruptly pulled a pistol and shot Marianne through the head. Dark gore splattered the cement block wall behind them, and the nearly headless body fell forward out of frame. "Let's see you resurrect out of *that*, bitch," the bearded man said, before turning to the camera, holding up his still-smoking pistol, and exclaiming, "Long live the U.S. of A."

The video ended. Gillespie pulled the laptop back, turning it to face him again.

"So," Ty said, slowly, rolling it over in his mind, "the zombies have some kind of . . . mental telepathy or something with Moreby?"

Gillespie said, "I think the British were right when they called it a 'hive mind'. Moreby can share their senses and direct large groups of them. The intelligent ones, I mean."

"And," the President asked, "do we have any idea yet of how many of them there are now?"

Exhaling slowly before answering, Gillespie said, "Enough to form armies."

"Thank you, Aaron," the President said, dismissing him.

Gillespie folded up his laptop and rose; however, he stopped before leaving the room and said, "Oh, about that thing with Delancy—"

The President cut him off. "We'll get to that later, Aaron."

When he still didn't move, Steele repeated, "*Thank you*, Aaron."

Frowning, he left.

Steele turned to Ty, but nodded towards the President. "So, Ty – which one of us is going to try to talk her out of this plan to retake the White House now?"

Ty looked pale and hollow-eyed today, and Steele suspected he'd been drinking the night before. She wondered if she'd need to watch that in the future; even shaking his head slightly seemed an effort. "Not me."

The President surprised Steele by saying, "It's more important than ever now. If we can take both the White House *and* Moreby, we can really cause them some pain."

"I thought they didn't feel pain," Steele said.

"C'mon, Steele – we know now that Moreby's the head. If we cut that head off, they're going to feel *something*."

Ty shifted in his chair, troubled. "Are we prepared to lose Ames Parker in this attack? Because it's a possibility, you know."

The President didn't hesitate to answer. "Yes, it's a possibility. But General Parker is our only real shot at this. There's really no other way."

Steele saw her boss' determination, and she didn't argue the point further.

"I might be right, you know," the President said, and for a second Steele wondered if Moreby was the only mind-reader on the planet.

From: General Ames Parker <a.parker@whitehouse.gov>

To: Colonel Scott Harkins <scottharkins@letterkenny.army.mil>

Sent: MON, Aug 5, 10:13 AM

Subject: Depot Inventory Query

Colonel Harkins, can you provide an inventory of what you've got on hand there at Letterkenny? I'm specifically interested in RCVs and any other armored vehicles. Be prepared for a major requisition to come through later this week; I'll also need all the troops you can spare.

Chapter Seventeen

THEY ENDED UP spending more than three weeks preparing "Operation Oval".

Ty's computer skills proved invaluable. He scrounged half-a-dozen monitors from storage or unused offices (as well as routers and cables), claimed an unused room that was large and provided with plentiful sockets and cable, and created a command centre. They'd have cameras attached to both drones and soldiers, so that the President and her immediate staff would be able to follow the course of the attack as it happened.

They flew drones over Washington, studying the resulting data. There were still thousands of zombies mulling aimlessly around the South Lawn. They'd have to clear that mass to move in ground troops.

"No missiles. No rockets or hand grenades," the President told them at the beginning. "We need to maintain the integrity of the buildings."

"That's going to make it harder," Parker said.

Ty brought up another problem: even if they managed to use aircraft or ground troops to terminate the thousands of infected, what would they do with the bodies? They'd need hundreds of men just for disposal.

"Maybe not . . ." Parker was making a note as he spoke.

The President asked, "What are you thinking, Ames?"

"I may have the best of all possible worlds. Give me a day and I'll come back with a plan."

Parker didn't wait until morning. He called a meeting with the President, Ty and Steele late that night and laid out his plan.

"RCVs." He looked at them expectantly.

Ty thought for a moment, and then said, excitedly, "Right! Route clearance vehicles!"

Parker nodded.

Steele asked, "What are we talking here?"

"RCVs are special armoured vehicles that were created largely for mine clearance and securing roads in overseas conflicts. They're designed to withstand driving directly over mines."

"But," the President said, "we're not talking mines here . . ."

"No. But look at this." Parker turned his tablet screen around to show them a photo of a vehicle that looked like a cross between a bulldozer and a dune buggy. The driver sat up high in a completely enclosed cage, and all sides were heavily plated. Something that looked like a thick version of a bulldozer shovel was attached to the front. "This is the Husky. Again, designed for mine clearance in a combat situation, but—"

Steele got it and looked up at Ames. "—with that front plate, it could clear out zombies, too."

"Right. The Husky's fast and manoeuvrable. It could push through waves of the infected pretty well, back them up against something, and a few rounds would finish them off in nice neat piles."

"Okay," the President asked, "how many of these things do we have, and where are they?"

"Letterkenny Army Depot up in Pennsylvania was producing them and shipping them off to the Mideast, but they've got a dozen on hand. The Depot is still well-guarded and in good shape, and they've also got a few Bradley tanks. They're ready to wade in."

Ty said, "I saw a train of those Huskys over in Iraq. They move pretty fast."

Parker nodded. "As soon as we are ready to go, they can probably get a caravan of the RCVs and Bradleys down here in half a day."

"So," Steele asked, "what's the rest of the plan?"

"Clearing the South Lawn below the White House is Phase One. Once we've accomplished that – and hopefully we can get right up to the Rose Garden and the Oval Office – we position the vehicles to create our perimeter and get some emergency fencing in place. In Phase Two, we use trucks to bring in ground troops who will clear out the buildings, which obviously won't be as congested; I'm thinking a dozen in the liquid Kevlar suits can handle it. Phase Three is a final clean-up crew and units stationed around the West Wing to secure all entry points. Phase Four, we set up video crews and we film a bird with the Presidential seal on its side landing on the South Lawn, and then following Madame President as she steps out and moves into the Oval Office."

"Ames," the President said, fixing him with an intense look, "be realistic: even if we can re-take the West Wing – and I think we can – how long can we hold it?"

The General shrugged. "I wish I knew. A lot of that depends on Moreby, and he's still a big question mark. We just don't know enough about him. I've heard him described as everything from ancient sorcerer to charlatan who was once a janitor. Now Gillespie has told us that Moreby may have some sort of mental control over the infected, especially the intelligent ones. We don't even know if he can be killed in the same way the rest can."

"That's a lot of questions," Steele said.

"Madame President . . ." Parker trailed off, apparently struggling with how to phrase something. "We need answers from New World Pharmaceuticals. If Gillespie can't or won't provide us with the intelligence we need . . ."

"It's time for Landen Jones to provide some real intel." The President turned to Steele and Ty. "Let's see if we can't put a little fear into Landen to loosen him up a bit."

Steele smiled, anticipating an assignment she'd actually enjoy.

They waited until lunch was served and the mess hall was full of senators and representatives and staffers. Jones was there, chatting up several members of the Senate Committee on Health. Steele entered, accompanied by two of the biggest, baddest soldiers Parker had been able to round up.

"Mr Jones," Steele said in a voice loud enough to be heard throughout the room, "I need you to come with me."

Jones had flashed his trademark smile, glancing at his companions as if to say, "Okay, who put her up to this?" When the senators didn't respond, Jones turned to face Steele. "What's this about?"

"I'm here at the request of the President."

Jones looked at her for a moment before nonchalantly turning away. "You've got no authority over me, Steele. If she wants to see me, she can set up an appointment time like everyone else—"

Steele flashed a look to the two soldiers with her, and they took a half-step forward, to where they loomed over Jones. Although he didn't react, Steele was secretly amused to see the senators all inch away from him. "All right, sir – we need to talk about possible conspiracy and obstruction charges."

"Am I being arrested?"

"Not *yet*. But I should warn you: proving uncooperative won't look good if this goes to trial, Mr Jones."

Steele had bluffed. She and the President had cooked up this plan to embarrass Jones in front of his cronies and get him into an interrogation, but they hadn't gone into an extensive Plan B, in case Jones refused to come. "Conspiracy and obstruction charges" had popped into Steele's head out of nowhere, but they proved effective – Jones rose to his feet.

"I really don't have time for this, but if you insist—"

"I'm sure it won't take long." She stepped aside and motioned towards the exit. Parker's soldiers positioned themselves on either side of Jones and walked him out. As Steele followed, she was pleased by the absolute silence she left behind.

They walked Jones to an office she and Ty Ward had set up just for today. They'd cleared all furniture but a simple, battered metal desk and two chairs; the room had been stripped bare of decoration and comfort. They wanted it to look as much like an interrogation room as possible.

Ty was waiting as they entered. The two soldiers deposited Landen in the folding chair behind the desk, and then Steele nodded to them. "We'll be just outside," one of them said as they exited.

The door closed behind them, and Steele leaned up against a wall facing Jones, her arms crossed.

"Well, this is comfy," he said, the way he shifted in the hard metal chair indicating that it clearly was not. "Now, can we finish up here quickly so I can get back to something that matters?"

Steele shot a look at Ty, who smiled slightly. They'd discussed this in advance and Steele had opted for the role of tough interrogator, while Ty played silent partner. He sat in the other folding chair opposite Jones and pretended to take notes on his tablet.

"Landen," Steele said, "we think you know more about Thomas Moreby than what you've told us so far."

"Is that right? Well, I'm flattered that you find me so all-knowing."

Steele uncrossed her arms and walked up to lean on the desk. "Cut the shit, Landen. I don't like you, and don't care who knows it at this point. You can play best friend to all of those senators and representatives, and they might be dumb enough to fall for it, but I'm not. I know your bosses at New World had Moreby until something happened. I want to know exactly what they did with him, what they learned about him, and how they lost him. I'm not prone to hyperbole, so you better believe me when I tell you that any future the United States has might rest on your answers."

Jones at least dropped the near-perpetual smirk, but Steele didn't like the look of hooded anger that replaced it. "So, what, Sandra, is this where you bring in the thugs from the hallway and torture me if you don't like my answers? Maybe a little waterboarding for old times' sake?"

"I don't believe in torture, Landen. Besides, I abide by the Geneva Convention."

"Great. How noble of you. Then my last question is – and forgive me if I'm not clear on the protocol in our current circumstances – do you have the power to arrest me?"

"I do . . . but I'm not going to."

Jones started to rise. "Then we're done here—"

Steele blocked his movement with her own body as she called past him, "Ty, what was the number of that bill again?"

Ty glanced at his tablet. "HR 203."

"Right." She turned to Jones, who had stopped moving halfway out of his chair. "HR 203. Remind me again what that bill is, Landen."

Jones dropped into his chair, and Steele almost wanted to clap her hands in glee as an honest expression – of fear – finally crossed his features. "You know goddamn well what that bill is, Steele. And I shouldn't have to tell you how important it is that it gets passed. New World's close to developing a vaccine. They need all the resources they can get right now."

"They need more than our military forces? The people who are keeping us safe?"

Jones fixed Steele with an intense glare. "You don't want to fuck with this, Steele. I'm better at this than you are."

Lowering herself down until she was just inches from his face, Steele said, with soft power, "Do you really want to test that, Landen? Do you really want me to pull each of those reps aside in a hallway and have a little private chat just like this one with them? I can make them *very* afraid. Hell, I don't even have to get to all of them to make sure that bill fails."

Steele heard breath huff from between Landen's teeth, and she pressed her point. "Or you can do the right thing and tell me everything you know about Moreby right now."

Jones looked from Ty to Steele and then said, "I want your assurance that you'll not only let 203 pass, but you'll even give it a little push."

"The waterboarding's sounding pretty good about now. No assurances, Landen. Just *do the right thing*."

After a moment, he began: "It's really not much more than what you already know . . ."

||| CellNet   5:40 PM   89% ▬▬

◄ Messages   **Sandra Steel**   Contact

Today 5:38 PM

CAN YOU MEET ME TONIGHT?
8:00, YOUR OFFICE?

Text Message   📷   Send

Chapter Eighteen

AMES PARKER LOOKED up from the report and stared, incredulous, at Steele. "They're now taking on the memories of each person they consume? Do we really believe this?"

"The doctors at New World Pharmaceuticals do."

The General exhaled heavily and leaned back in his chair. "Do they know how it's accomplished?"

"I don't think so. Moreby got away before they could fully study the process. But we have footage of an intelligent zombie talking about eating someone's brain, so I'm guessing that's basically how it's done."

"And Moreby's been out there spreading this new strain of HRV that makes zombies who grow more intelligent with every person they eat."

Steele didn't answer. She couldn't.

She'd always been a believer in practicality, in evidence. She wasn't even sure she still believed in God. When she'd been married to Grant, they'd dutifully attended services every Sunday morning at the local Methodist church, and she'd enjoyed the gatherings. But when Grant had been gunned down, Steele had given up any last shreds of belief in a benevolent presence.

Now, though, she'd begun to wonder if there wasn't some omnipotent force after all . . . but just not a benevolent one. Maybe the universe really was ruled by something black and always hungry, something that chose monsters like Thomas Moreby to bequeath part of itself to.

"So, Steele," Parker said, pulling her back to earth, "how'd you get Jones to open up?"

"Well, let's just say I'm probably up shit creek if I ever need medical attention and he's the only doctor around."

Parker smiled, then looked away and tapped a finger on his desk. "Our plan is a good one, Steele. With those CRVs, we've got a real shot at winning, and with a minimal loss of life."

"I know, Ames, but . . . you can't go."

He gaped at her, stunned. "What are you saying?"

"That's why I wanted to see you tonight, before I showed this report—" she gestured at the computer screen where Landen Jones' words glowed, "—to anyone else, even the President. We've had our suspicions for a while now about the intelligent zombies taking on the memories of whoever they eat, and now we've had that confirmed. Do you see where I'm going with this, Ames?"

"I think so, but . . . tell me anyway."

"We're living almost literally right under Moreby's nose. Now he's assembling an intelligent army. There's only one reason they haven't shown up down here yet: *they don't know we're here.* Or they know – maybe have only guessed it – but they don't know how to get down here. If you go up to lead the attack on Moreby and anything goes wrong . . ."

Parker sagged back in his chair. "Oh my God."

"Right – if they get you, Ames, they'll know exactly where we are, who's down here, and how to get us."

Parker looked away, thinking before he said, "But wouldn't that be true of any of our men?"

"Most of the ground troops will be coming with the vehicles from Letterkenny, right? Do any of them know about this complex, other than just that it's somewhere beneath Washington? Do they know who is here?"

"No . . . but even if we don't send any of our troops from down here, they'll need someone to lead them. Colonel Harkins from Letterkenny will be with them and he's a good, capable soldier, but he doesn't know the White House and the grounds like I do."

"Guide him via phone. Ty will have cameras watching everything. You don't need to be there."

Parker clenched a single fist, his jaw working as he looked away. Steele took the moment to press her point. "Ames, *you can't risk all of us.*"

He finally swallowed and uncurled his fingers. "You're right, of course. What about the President?"

"I'll explain it to her. You should work with Ty to make sure you have all the communications you need."

Parker nodded. "Okay. It's just . . ."

"I know," Steele said.

BULLETIN FROM SURGEON GENERAL LANDEN JONES TO ALL FIELD TROOPS

PLEASE BE ADVISED THAT WE ARE RECEIVING REPORTS OF POSSIBLE HRV SURVIVORS. IN ORDER TO FURTHER OUR RESEARCH AND RESPONSE TO THE THREAT POSED BY HRV, WE ARE REQUESTING THAT ANYONE WHO CLAIMS TO HAVE SURVIVED HRV INFECTION (DELIVERED BY BITE, SCRATCH, OR SOME OTHER FORM OF TRANSMISSION) BE DETAINED IMMEDIATELY AND REPORTED TO THIS OFFICE, AT WHICH POINT YOU WILL RECEIVE FURTHER INSTRUCTIONS. REMEMBER, YOU ARE FIGHTING MORE THAN THOSE WHO HAVE ALREADY SUCCUMBED TO HRV; YOU ARE FIGHTING FOR THE VERY FUTURE OF THE UNITED STATES, AND WE CAN ONLY GUARANTEE THAT FUTURE IF WE CAN STAMP OUT HRV AT THE SOURCE. THANK YOU FOR YOUR COOPERATION.

Chapter Nineteen

THE ARMY HAD moved Kevin to a small abandoned office building they'd seized not far from their freeway encampment. He was placed in a windowless storage closet with nothing but a few blankets and a bucket. LaFortune showed up three times a day with food.

Neither of them talked much, but Kevin came to look forward to her visits for more than just meals. He knew she was wary of him, but he tried to smile at her and stay calm, and do his best to indicate that he wasn't sick.

One morning she came early, unlocked the door and motioned him out. "What's up?" Kevin asked, uncertainly.

LaFortune looked tense. "I've notified the Surgeon General's office about you, but they're not convinced you're immune. They want another test." She loosened her pistol in its holster, making clear that she both had no intention of pulling it but would if necessary.

Even though he knew he was better off with LaFortune than any of the other soldiers he'd encountered so far, Kevin's anxiety ramped up. "Where we going?"

"Not far," was all she said.

They exited the building in silence, Kevin walking in front of LaFortune. In the parking lot he saw his old Hummer and felt a small pang as he realized the Army had appropriated it.

"So am I being transferred or something?"

LaFortune didn't – or couldn't – look at him. "Maybe." She gestured at a chain-link fence that enclosed the lot. "Over there."

They reached the fence and she tossed a pair of handcuffs to him. "Put those on one wrist."

He dangled them before his eyes. "You're kidding."

"I'm not." Her hand rested on her gun.

Heart racing, Kevin snapped the cuffs around his left wrist.

She motioned at the fence. "Now close the other cuff around the fence."

Kevin saw no choice. He heard the click as the cuffs locked into place, and wondered if that sound would be one of the last he ever heard. "And you can't tell me what we're doing here . . ."

"Kevin . . ." Now she did look at him, and he saw compassion in her eyes. "I'm really sorry for this. For all of it."

She turned away, her eyes scanning the horizon. Looking for something.

"You're not my executioner, huh?"

She turned back to him. "Oh God, no. I actually think you'll be okay. Which is more than I can say for myself."

"Why?"

"They're transferring me. Apparently they're bringing a shitload of equipment down from Letterkenny to launch an assault on Washington. They say they 'need me'." Her tone was bitter, and Kevin felt a surprising surge of compassion for her.

"You don't seem like career Army."

She smiled. "You mean I'm not like the rest of the assholes?"

Laughing, Kevin said, "Yeah, that's what I mean."

"Well, you're right. I'm not." After a second, she turned to him and said, "Call me Rocky."

"Rocky? Really?"

"It's short for Raquelle, but nobody calls me that except my mother. When she's mad at me. Which used to be pretty much all the time."

"Okay, Rocky. So what *are* you doing in the Army?"

She ran fingers through her short hair before she spoke. "Really, I'm looking for someone. My partner, Jo . . . Jolene. She was the one who actually wanted a career in the Army. Her outfit was stationed in New York when the shit really went down, and they . . ." She broke off.

Kevin remembered: Manhattan had been nuked. "Oh. I'm sorry. I mean, do you know . . .?"

Rocky shook her head and looked down at her feet. "I like to think she got out. I keep emailing her messages, pictures . . . but I haven't heard anything. I know realistically she probably . . ."

In that instant, Kevin wished he'd met this woman under other circumstances, preferably ones that didn't involve her being his guard . . . or something worse. "I'm really sorry."

"Me, too."

"So how did you end up as a sergeant?"

That brought her head up, and she wiped at her eyes. "I joined up to look for Jo, then they quickly found out I was smart and had a college degree."

"In what?"

"History, if you can believe it. I was going to be a teacher – you know, a college professor. I pictured myself opening young minds and arguing the finer points of feudalism with my fellow academics, and writing books that exactly forty-two people read. Instead, I'm an ex-chauffeur and current Army sergeant with pretty much no future."

"At least you've still got a job."

They both laughed then.

A few seconds later, Kevin heard a truck approaching.

"Here they come," Rocky muttered.

"Who?"

A big semi was approaching now, coming from the direction of the road block. Kevin realized it was one of the trucks they'd used to transport the infected in.

Rocky turned to him with sudden urgency. "Kevin, listen: I won't be around any more to protect you. I think you're right and that you're valuable, and I think these other assholes will figure that out after today but . . . you just have to get through this. I'll be right here. Okay?"

"Uh . . . sure . . ."

The truck rumbled into the parking lot, turned, and began to back towards Kevin and Rocky, its reverse warning signal beeping. It finally stopped, the engine died, and two men in Army uniforms leapt down from the cab and joined Rocky.

They held long black rods that it took Kevin a few seconds to identify as cattle prods. And something inside the back of the truck was banging on the closed roll-gate.

One of the two soldiers was the blonde boy who'd first approached Kevin at the blockade. He grinned as he saw the handcuffs. "Well, looks like we're about to put your theory to the test, Mr 'I'm Immune'."

"Knock it off, Forbes!" Rocky nodded at the rear of the truck. "Let's get this over with." She backed away a few steps, drew her pistol and hefted it in both hands.

The two soldiers – the blonde boy and a middle-aged African American who looked too old to be an Army private – stepped up to the gate. The boy yanked a lever back and grabbed the handle. The pounding inside increased, and now Kevin heard desperate moaning.

"One . . . two . . ." The boy's fingers tightened, ". . . three."

The roll-gate rattled up, the two soldiers jumped back, lifting their prods – and the zombie in the truck tumbled out.

It was a twenty-something woman, still dressed in the remains of bloodied hospital scrubs with a teddy bear print. She hit the ground and crumpled, and Kevin hoped she wouldn't get back up . . . but after a few seconds she lifted her large body with difficulty. She was missing much of the meat between her neck and one shoulder, and it made her head wobble to one side. It would have been comical if her eyes hadn't fixed on Kevin, a crimson-tinted froth spilling from her cracked lips.

She staggered forward, and the blonde boy called out to his companion, "Pepper, get behind her." In that instant, she turned on the boy – and he jabbed forward with the prod, which erupted in a crackling buzz as it connected with her chest. She drew back, her moan increasing. The other soldier gave her a touch of his prod, and she turned his way. He zapped her again and she stumbled away from him . . .

Towards Kevin.

He instinctively shrank back as her eyes fixed on him. "Rocky—!"

There was no answer. He didn't dare look away from the dead thing.

She shambled forward, head lolling, and reached out for him.

He pulled back as far as the cuffs would let him. He tried to call out again, but his voice died in his throat.

The zombie grabbed his cuffed arm. She opened her mouth.

Kevin screamed as her head darted downwards and her teeth clamped on his arm.

"Okay, that's it!" Kevin heard Rocky calling. He saw the two soldiers leap forward with the prods, both jabbing the zombie at the same time.

The zombie's jaws opened in shock, and it turned, seeking the ones with the prods.

Rocky stepped in, raised her pistol three feet from the zombie's head and shot it. It hit the ground, truly dead.

Kevin felt pain and looked at his arm, where a ring of bite marks had broken the surface, but the wound didn't look deep or serious.

"Get that thing out of here," Rocky told the two soldiers. They set the prods aside and started to drag the corpse away. Rocky opened a small pack attached to her belt, withdrew a roll of gauze and tape, and began wrapping Kevin's arm as he panted, more from the aftermath of fear than pain.

She talked to him softly as she dressed the wound. "The brass needed to be sure that you're immune to HRV and they didn't completely trust your stories about where your scratches came from. So they ordered this. They'll watch you for a few days now, make sure you don't get sick, then . . . well, they'll probably treat you pretty well from that point on."

Kevin watched her finish with the gauze and said, "You could've told me."

"Maybe. Hell, it wouldn't be the first mistake I've made. Might be one of the last, though."

She unlocked the handcuffs, shoved them back into a pouch, and said, "I'm sorry, but now's when we say goodbye. The tanks are almost at Washington, and I've got to be there."

She started to walk off but Kevin called after her, "Rocky – I hope you find Jo."

"Well, one way or the other, I think we'll be together again soon."

As the two soldiers walked Kevin back to his cell in the office building, he was already missing Rocky.

CRCVG1: We've cleared the area around the South Lawn Fountain and now have all RCVs in place.

PARKER: Tanks?

CTB1: We're lined up behind the RCVs. Encountered some heavy resistance in the Ellipse, but the ground troops coming in with us cleared it out pretty well. The flamethrowers were what really turned it for us, but it stinks like barbecue gone bad down here.

PARKER: Losses?

CTB1: Minimal so far. A few of the ground troops. One RCV got swarmed and we lost both crew and vehicle.

PARKER: Hold position and wait for my command.

CRCV1: Yes, sir.

CTB1: Copy that, sir. We're holding.

Chapter Twenty

STEELE LOOKED OVER the monitors Ty had set up. Next to her, Gillespie, the President and Vice President watched, seated in office chairs. In front, Parker and Ty waited, their fingers tense above controls.

The situation still looked close to impossible.

The vehicles were equipped with cameras, so they'd followed the progress of the modified RCVs and the Bradley tanks through Washington, with ground troops walking behind and at the sides. West of the Potomac, the dead had still been light and clearing them out had been relatively easy. But crossing the Theodore Roosevelt Memorial Bridge had taken an hour, as they'd angled two RCVs to open the way, with the foot soldiers turning flamethrowers on the dead and trying to push the smouldering bodies to the side. They'd finally created enough of a path that the RCVs and tanks were able to roll forward, bumping awkwardly over piles of scorched flesh.

Just beyond the bridge the roads had been packed, but they'd had more room to manoeuvre and they'd moved quickly. The tanks had sent in rockets, squads on the RCVs equipped with assault rifles had kept firing, and the soldiers had picked off stragglers with fire and bullets. The number of truly dead mounted into the many hundreds.

"It's working," Gillespie had noted at one point, as the vehicles had rolled on to the spacious lawns south of the White House.

"It's not over yet," Parker said. Steele knew "over" would mean that Moreby had been terminated and removed from the Oval Office.

There were still tens of thousands of the dead between the human soldiers and the White House.

Parker studied the screens for a moment, and then said, "Launch the second wave."

They'd already used drones once to help open the central area of the lawn known as "the Ellipse", and it had proven to be an effective tactic. Flying in MQ-9 Reapers armed with Hellfire missiles, they'd cleared an astonishing amount of square footage in seconds. The President had initially objected to the use of the Reapers and the Hellfires closer to the White House – she didn't trust the accuracy of the missiles – but Parker had told her it was the best way to achieve victory with minimum human casualties, and she'd relented.

Steele wondered briefly about the drones' operators; they were working from an Air National Guard base in Hancock Field near Syracuse, New York. She imagined young boys who'd probably won video-game competitions before joining the military; to them, these missions were probably not much different from a scenario in which they levelled up after beating the computer.

The Reapers had been hovering overhead, and they couldn't see the actual aircraft – but they saw the missiles hit, and heard the tank and RCV crews whoop and holler.

The Hellfires struck the ground like angry gods, their fury blinding the cameras for a second before they showed hundreds of the infected being blown apart. The OC was too far away to feel the impact, but Steele knew those on the ground were feeling the shockwaves rumble through them.

"That is *damn* pretty," she heard Delancy say.

As the explosions died away, the extent of the devastation was astonishing . . . and astonishingly gruesome. Severed limbs littered the scorched and cratered grass. Corpses, now truly dead, cluttered the grounds, some headless, others merely faceless. Zombies who had lost everything below the waist continued to pull themselves along the ground, still driven by the need to consume.

"Oh, shit, you're not gonna believe this."

Steele thought she recognized the voice coming over the speakers as belonging to one of the RCV drivers.

"Hold on – I gotta pan the camera down . . ."

The view on one of the monitors tilted down, revealing first a complex dashboard; then the picture jittered as the camera was apparently removed from a mount and walked over to a side window. It manoeuvred past bars until it had a clear shot of the tan side of one of the RCVs . . .

. . . and the two zombies who had somehow been fused by heat, skin melted together until the midsection of one had merged with the chest of another. Two of the arms were missing and only one of the four legs was still complete, so the thing's efforts to climb the side of the RCV were constantly hobbled by its own unsteadiness. The faces – a heavyset middle-aged man and a muscular African American in a sports jersey – snapped at each other in frustration.

"Looks like we got us zombie Siamese twins now," the driver said, and chuckled.

"Driver of the RCV, get that camera back inside your vehicle *now*," Parker said, watching the monitor where the camera was plainly held out past the safety of the bars.

"What's that? No, it's cool, they can't get up here. Look at 'em, fer Christ's sakes, fucker can't even stand—"

Steele flinched as a scream echoed around the command centre. On the monitor, the view whip-panned, revealing a split-second image of a desiccated hand reaching in, an open mouth dripping saliva bearing down . . . then the screen went black. The screams, however, continued for several seconds, not drowned out by the babble of other voices crying out in alarm.

"Ty—!" Steele saw Ty was also grimacing from the shocking sounds. It took him a few moments to locate the matching audio channel and mute it.

"We've lost one of the RCVs," said the tank commander.

Beside her, Steele heard a small groan from the President.

"Listen up," Parker answered, "I don't want any more fuck-ups from this point on. No matter what happens, or what you might see, everybody needs to stay focused on the mission – is that understood?"

A chorus of answers sounded over the speakers.

The lawn between the White House and the vehicles was only sparsely occupied now – Steele could even glimpse the Rose Garden just outside the Oval Office. But she knew they'd have to move quickly, before the dead returned (there were always, impossibly, more of them) and overwhelmed the human forces.

Parker was already ahead of her. "Reaper pilots," he said into his headset, "we're done with you now, so you can fly your birds home, but reload them and keep those engines warm. RCVs, move forward and commence clean-up."

The RCVs trundled forward, the thin horizontal plates affixed to their fronts pushing zombies, both moving and inanimate, aside. The President asked, "Do the RCVs always come with bulldozer shovels?"

Parker answered, "Actually, those aren't shovels – they're blast shields. The RCVs are designed first and foremost as mine detectors. But we realized they'd function equally well to clear masses of infected."

On the monitor, cameras mounted in the RCV cabs showed the vehicles lumbering forward and quickly piling up heaps of bodies on the plates. When they reached maximum capacity, they stopped, backed away, turned and moved the bodies to the side, where the foot soldiers helped scrape them off the makeshift shovels into mounds. If any of the bodies moved, a single bullet to the head quickly put a stop to that.

Nearby, Steele heard a small mutter of revulsion, and thought it might have been Gillespie. Of course the intelligence chief liked to keep his hands clean.

Parker let the clean-up continue for a few minutes, and then ordered, "Get the trucks in and the perimeter secured."

Ty tabbed commands on his screen, and several of the monitors switched to views from cameras mounted at the rear of the RCVs. Semi trucks rolled up now from behind the tanks and positioned themselves to form as much of a barricade as possible, crews leapt out, rolled up the truck gates, and began unloading sections of emergency fencing. While snipers picked off approaching zombies, the crews swiftly assembled a solid wall of chain link, stretching between the West and East arms of Executive Avenue. When Parker was satisfied that the South Lawn was locked down and cleared, he gave the order for the ground troops to move into the West Wing.

Steele wished they had DEVGRU – more popularly known as SEAL Team Six – to handle this; or the Army equivalent, Delta Force. She would have settled for a team of expert hired mercs . . . but they had to work with what was left, and what was left was a ragtag team of veterans from different military branches and enthusiastic rookies. The commander, Scott Harkins from Letterkenny, had served with distinction in Afghanistan and was a smart, capable leader with the lined, dour face of hard-won experience.

If Harkins succeeded today, he'd be one of the most famous military men in history. He'd be the commando who took down Thomas Moreby and set the human race back on the path to its rightful future.

One monitor hung on the wall before them had a piece of masking tape with the name HARKINS scribbled on it in black marker, and all eyes now turned to that screen.

The picture bobbed. A hand entered the frame, gesturing and pointing. A dozen armoured and armed soldiers ran up; two carried a portable metal ram. Occasionally a zombie staggered up, but they all went down with ruthless efficiency.

This might work, Steele thought.

The team had cleared a path to the edge of the West Wing now . . . where the Oval Office was. They circled it, fingers tensing on triggers.

Harkins moved forward and gave unheard orders to his troops. They centred on a French door. One of them stepped forward and ran a scanner around the door, then nodded and stepped back. Another soldier reached down and rested a hand on the knob. She took a breath, looked at her companions and tried the knob. It turned. The door opened.

The soldiers poured into the office. Harkins waited.

The audience in the command room waited. Silence.

Finally Harkins moved forward. He stepped up to the opened door, through it and into the Oval Office. The camera panned around the circular interior, past elegant fixtures, paintings of past presidents, chairs and the large desk.

The room was empty. "Nobody home, sir," Harkins reported.

"Copy," Parker answered, "search the building."

Most of the soldiers ran out through the interior door of the office, combing through the West Wing. Two of the men stayed with Harkins, guarding the all-important office.

"Where the hell is Moreby?" That was Gillespie.

"You should know that," Parker answered. "The intelligence part of this was *your* baby."

"General, our intelligence was good. We know Moreby was still in that office yesterday."

Parker stayed quiet. Steele knew he didn't trust Gillespie any more than she did, but right now he had to focus on the military operation, not divert his attention to a squabble about an agency's failure.

After a few minutes, a soldier ran back into the office and said something to Harkins. The camera view bobbed up and down slightly, and Harkins said, "Okay, General Parker: we've now searched and secured the West Wing. We took out a few zombies, but there was no sign of Moreby. We're continuing on to the East Wing now."

"Copy that. Good work, Harkins." Parker pulled off the headset and turned to address the President. "Madame President, we believe the South Lawn, the Oval Office and the West Wing are now secured, and the East Wing should be shortly. But there's no sign of Moreby."

"So what's our next move?"

"Let's see if anything turns up in the East Wing. If there's still no sign of Moreby . . . we'll proceed from there."

"Fine."

It took forty minutes for Harkins' troops to report that they'd searched and cleared out the East Wing. The front entrances had been sealed and barricaded, and the building was now under human control.

The President asked, "General Parker . . . recommendations?"

He considered for a moment, and then rose. "Director Steele, may I see you privately, please?"

Steele blinked in surprise. "Of course."

The President restrained her as she walked by, grabbing Steele's arm even as she addressed Parker. "Hold on here – what's this about? What would you say to Director Steele that you couldn't say in front of anyone else here?"

Parker fixed the President with a look of such silken intensity that Steele felt the other woman's grip on her loosen. "Madame President, I'll have to ask you to trust me, at least for a few more minutes."

The President held the look for a beat, and then released Steele. "Of course, Ames."

Parker led the way out into the corridor. He found a quiet space a few feet away and turned to Steele, speaking softly. "Something's wrong, Steele. We won that battle way too easy."

"Maybe it was just well planned and executed—"

He cut her off. "Maybe, but I don't believe that's why we won, and I don't think you do, either."

"Maybe . . ."

"Think about it: Gillespie's been feeding us reports for days about intelligent zombies, a new strain created by Moreby."

Steele thought back to the battle she'd just witnessed on the monitors. "If that were true . . . they would have been using weapons against us."

Parker nodded. "That's right. But what we saw out there today were nothing but the same old mindless dead things. And where's Moreby?"

"Do you think Gillespie has deliberately been giving us disinformation?"

Parker exhaled and sagged back against the metal wall. "I don't know, Steele. I hope not. If our own intelligence director was working against us, he could probably have fucked us over before this. So no, I don't think it's anything planned. He's as clueless as we are about Moreby's plans."

"So you think it's a trap?"

Parker nodded. "Yes. They know how important it is to us to get the President back into that office. And they know what a blow it would be to the human resistance to show her reanimated corpse stumbling around. It'd be completely over."

"So you think they're just waiting for her to show up?"

"You got it."

Steele let out a long, shaky breath. "So what the fuck do we do? Every moment that we sit here waiting is giving them more of a chance at building up their forces again. Soon all the fences and barricades in the world won't matter . . ."

"Right. And I don't think we're going to convince the President that getting into that office with a camera crew is not a great idea."

"But what if we're wrong? What if we really *did* win the battle today? Can we be so sure we didn't?"

"No, we can't. But we *have* to be sure. If this is all a trap, they're probably waiting for us to fly a 'copter in there, land it on the lawn, and her to step out."

"But we're not going to do that. I mean, we can't, right?"

Parker didn't answer; instead he looked away.

Steele stepped closer, her voice lower, more urgent. "Parker, you *know* there is no way I'm going to let that happen . . ."

"Of course I know that. And that's not what I'm suggesting."

Steele stopped, staring . . . and realized what it was that Parker couldn't say to her, what had made him turn away. "You want me to pretend to be her."

He nodded. "I won't ask you to do it alone, Steele. I'll be on that bird with you. They'd probably be expecting me by her side anyway."

Turning to pace a few feet, Steele mulled it over. "So we fly in, step out – and if we don't trigger an attack, we know it's safe to bring the real thing in."

"And if we *do* trigger something, you and I are probably the best equipped to handle it. We wouldn't go in defenceless."

Steele laughed weakly. "You know, Parker, this means we're probably going to die because of an *office*."

Parker smiled. "Well, it does have a great view."

"Yeah, except right now that view is mountains of dead zombies." Steele turned to Parker, serious again. "She'll try to stop us, you know."

"I know. And that's why I think we shouldn't tell her. I can have that 'copter ready to go in ten minutes."

"Give me fifteen – I'm going to need a blonde wig and a pantsuit that looks like hers."

Parker offered her a warm look. "You got it. Meet you at the elevators in fifteen minutes."

Steele turned, but was stopped when Parker said, "Oh, and Steele . . ."

She looked back to see him drawing a holstered pistol at his side. "I haven't forgotten about our earlier discussion, so . . . the last two bullets will be for us."

Steele walked off, and a strange calm descended on her. She'd never felt it before, and it took her a few seconds to recognize it: she expected to die today, and had already accepted that fact. She'd felt this day coming for sometime, and it arrived with neither fear nor relief.

Suicide was simply another part of her job.

From: Landen Jones <landenjones@nwpharm.com>
To: Dr. Brewster Gilray <bgilray@nwpharm.com>
Sent: THU, Aug 29, 3:16 PM
Subject: Merry Christmas!

know it's still summer, but I think you're about to get the best present ever: we're getting reports of an HRV survivor. Will keep you advised when I track down name and location.

Love,

Landen Claus

Chapter Twenty-One

"WAIT – YOU'RE KIDDING, right?"

Forbes, the blonde soldier, gestured with a rifle. "Do I look like I'm kidding? Now *put it on*."

Any ideas Kevin had had about being taken to a high-tech research facility, or even a low-tech one, had gone out the window when the back of the truck had opened and he'd found himself facing the overgrown front yard of a rambling house in the country. It didn't look as if it had ever been a proper farm – there were no outbuildings or fenced-in corrals, no fields of long-dead crops – but Kevin, city boy that he was, couldn't imagine why else anyone would have built a huge house in the middle of bugfuck nowhere.

Forbes and the fifty-something black man, who Forbes called "Pepper", had led him out of the truck at gunpoint, to a large steel post in the middle of the yard. A length of chain was attached to the bottom of the post, with a set of handcuffs at one end. "Put that around your ankle," Forbes had just said.

"Didn't you guys hear? I'm immune—"

Pepper cut him off. "Maybe you are, and maybe you aren't. We all watched you get bit, so now we wait to see if you turn."

Forbes added, "Oh, he'll turn, all right," with a lopsided grin.

"How many other guys are here?"

Forbes and Pepper looked at each other in perplexity, and then Forbes turned to squint at Kevin. "What the fuck difference does it make?"

"Because if it's just us three, you could easily lock me in a room in that house and still have plenty of space to yourselves."

Forbes ran his finger over the rifle's trigger as he glared at Kevin. "You're not goin' into the house. Now I'm not gonna tell you again – put on the fuckin' cuff!"

Kevin saw there was no point in arguing; he believed that Forbes would be happy to shoot him, and Pepper would probably yawn and stroll away. Reluctantly, he sat on the grass and picked up the open cuff.

It was stained. It'd been used for this before, maybe a lot.

He rolled one sock down and snapped the cuff around his ankle. He had a small build, but even on him the cuff was tight, designed as it was for wrists. He realized the stains were from where it had bit into the flesh of someone who was larger.

"Snap it closed."

"I did!" Kevin gave the chain a yank to prove it. He regretted the action instantly, as he felt the metal bite into his leg.

"Okay. Welcome to your new home, asswipe. You need to take a piss or a shit, you just do it right there in the grass."

"How long will I be here?"

They were already turning away. Pepper called back over one shoulder, "However long it takes." He and Forbes guffawed and headed off to the house.

It wasn't a hot day, but it was clear and sunny, and Kevin was soon covered in sweat. He took off his jacket and laid it aside, intending to use it as a cushion later on; then his T-shirt came off, he folded it into a triangle, and tied it around his head. At least it might keep him from getting heat stroke.

He settled back in the grass to wait.

The sun had just set and Kevin had put his shirt back on when Forbes ambled out of the house. From his unsteady gait, Kevin knew he was drunk. He had an unwrapped candy bar in one hand; he paused a few feet from Kevin.

"We're supposed to feed you an' shit," Forbes said, gesturing with the candy bar, "but you know what? This is chocolate, so you're shit outta luck." He tore off the wrapper and bit the candy bar in half, chewing noisily.

Kevin's stomach rumbled and rolled through a cramp. He hadn't eaten since yesterday, and that meal had been small, just a half-plate of canned hash, not even heated. "Hey, man," Kevin said, trying to sound light and amiable, "you could spare half of that, couldn't you?"

The way Forbes' face twisted up made Kevin think of a mask – a sculpted work of art that perfectly embodied hate. "Sure," he said, before tossing the uneaten half of the bar into the dirt driveway thirty feet away.

For a second Kevin wanted to pound the ground in pure frustration, but he wouldn't give Forbes the pleasure. "You know, if I really am immune and you guys starve me to death, your superiors aren't going to be very happy."

"Well, first off," Forbes said, his words slightly slurred from drink, "you fuckin' *aren't* immune. And second off – we don't give a rat's ass what our superiors think. What're they gonna do – replace us? Nope. Get a clue, you dumb chink."

Ahhh, Kevin thought, *there it is. Of all the soldiers I could've been handed off to . . .*

"I'm not Chinese – I'm Korean-American."

"Oh, excuse me. So you eat that kimchi shit. Yeah, that's a big improvement."

Kevin stood, his hands starting to tremble with anger he couldn't release. Some small part of him told him to sit down, shut up, don't make it worse than it already is . . . but he was hungry, and thirsty, and his ankle was already bruised from the restraint, and unloading on this cretin suddenly seemed like the best idea in the world. "Yeah, I eat kimchi . . . but I didn't drop out of school in the ninth grade to marry my cousin."

Forbes' face flushed instantly, and he staggered forward, trying to throw a punch. But the alcohol made him clumsy, and Kevin ducked easily. He came up again behind Forbes, grabbed his arm, and bit into the man's forearm, tasting blood. Forbes screamed, jerked away and stumbled back, clutching his arm. He screamed for Pepper as Kevin spat Forbes' blood out and grinned at the soldier.

Pepper finally appeared, running clumsily from the house, obviously as drunk as his comrade. "What the fuck—?"

"He bit me! *He fuckin' bit me!*"

Kevin lunged forward, not caring that the cuff was drawing blood now. "Yeah, that's right, asshole, I bit you, and now you're gonna turn and be *just like me*. Soon you'll be craving all the kimchi you can get—"

Pepper drew a pistol and pointed it at Kevin. "You – shut the fuck up."

Kevin's fury ebbed instantly. He drew back, giving the chain slack, as Pepper turned to look at Forbes' arm. "Let me see . . ."

Forbes started to hold his arm out – then grabbed for Pepper's gun. Pepper saw the grab and moved the gun hand up, putting it out of range of the smaller Forbes. "Whoa, whoa, what the hell you doin'—?"

"I'm gonna kill this fuckin' asshole, that's what I'm doing. Don't you get it? He bit me! I'm *dead*!"

Pepper holstered the gun and grabbed Forbes' wounded arm; blood was smeared across the flesh, but not gushing. "Yeah, he got you, man. You better hope he's right and the HRV doesn't take with him. Now, c'mon – let's get back inside and clean that up."

Forbes began to cry as Pepper led him back towards the house. Kevin called after them, "Hey! Aren't you gonna chain him up in the yard, too?"

Pepper didn't turn around but called back over his shoulder, "You're goddamn lucky I didn't just kill you."

They went back into the house. It was full night now, the temperature dropping, and Kevin tugged on his jacket as he sank down into the grass. At least the greenery was soft and he might be able to get some sleep.

If one of his guards didn't realize he was also gay and blow his brains out in the middle of the night.

||| CellNet　　　　　　7:05 PM　　　　　　89% ▬

◄ Messages　　**Sandra Steel**　　Contact

Today 6:56 PM

Ty, plz cut tv feed on lawn cameras in 5. Sorry but youll hav 2 make up excuse. Will tell u when to turn on again.

Text Message　　📷　　Send

Chapter Twenty-Two

STEELE LOOKED DOWN through a window in Marine One at the seething mass below. "How can there be so goddamn many?"

Parker heard her and glanced out his own window before responding. "Whole lot of people in the world. And with the older corpses resurrecting as well, there are now more dead than there were alive."

"I know, but . . . they always seem to group together like that."

"The live ones did it, too, if they got hungry enough."

The pilot called back to them, "One minute."

Steele gave her short blonde wig a tug, and then put on sunglasses. "How do I look?"

"Like a Secret Service agent disguised as the President."

Grimacing, Steele shot back, "You know, I've never said this before to a four-star general, but – fuck you."

Parker looked at Steele seriously. "If we both get out of this . . . I'd like you to meet my wife. You two would have a lot in common."

"I'd like that."

The squat olive-and-white 'copter began its descent, and Steele reached under her blazer, instinctively checking the Glock holstered there. She hoped the bulge wouldn't show, but reminded herself that nobody would be watching. At least nobody alive.

Parker, who had no need for disguise, brought out his own pistol and held it loosely in his hand. "Remember, we just walk to the Oval Office, nice and slow. Colonel Harkins and his troops will be waiting for us."

"Right."

The bird manoeuvred slowly down to the scorched ground, turning while still in the air so that the front hatch faced the Oval Office, perhaps fifty yards away. When the landing was complete, the pilot stepped out of the cockpit, opened the front hatch, and lowered the steps. Steele undid her seatbelt, took a deep breath and rose. She was starting forward when Parker put up a hand to stop her. "Remember, you're the President today. I go first, to make sure it's clear."

"Sorry – old habits."

Parker turned to the pilot. "Keep the engine hot. When I give the all clear, you return to base and await further orders."

"Yes, sir." The pilot returned to the cockpit.

Parker and Steele both scanned the area outside. The earth was pitted and blackened from the recent battle, and there were still a few corpses littering the ground, but most had been cleared away. Behind them, the tanks, RCVs and trucks formed a solid ring; before them stood the White House. Harkins waited just outside the Oval Office with four of his soldiers, all standing at attention now.

It looked safe.

Parker spoke softly, the words picked up by the tiny throat mike that was connected to his earpiece. "Ready?"

Steele pushed her own earpiece in tightly and arranged a lock of hair over it. "Let's do it."

Parker stepped out of the 'copter and turned to wait for her. She moved down the steps, trying to mimic the woman she'd rescued and advised and admired, her careful but self-assured walk. Steele was bigger than the President, but knew that crouching down to appear smaller was wrong; confidence was the key.

She tensed as she reached the ground, and tried to imagine what the President would do. She saw the soldiers back around the tanks staring in her direction, and raised one hand to them. She thought she heard a cheer.

She started to follow Parker across the lawn. They walked slowly, eyes constantly scanning.

There were no signs of danger.

They were halfway across the lawn when Steele stepped up beside Parker and said softly, "Still looks good . . ."

Parker nodded – but his scrutiny didn't let up for a second. "It does, but . . ." He trailed off and stopped walking, his head cocked as if listening.

"What—?" Then Steele heard it, too – a high-pitched whistling, growing louder.

"*Down!*"

Parker threw himself at her and they both went down . . .

As Marine One exploded.

For a second Steele was stunned . . . *what the fuck happened?* Then she felt Parker's weight partly on her, and heard his voice in her ear. "Javelin."

"What?"

Parker rolled aside, giving Steele the room to look up and back. Their ride was gone, nothing but flaming metal chunks. She saw smoke billow up from Parker's back and instinctively reached out. "You're hit . . ."

He waved her off. "Later. Move!"

Steele got to her feet, taking a few seconds to orient herself. She heard more explosions, and saw two of the trucks near the fences going up in blinding balls of light. Soldiers were running and shouting. She heard voices screaming in her earpieces; one of them was Ty, demanding to know what was happening. Two soldiers were on fire, their arms waving frantically. Several were streaming blood from head and chest wounds. The tanks had already opened fire. At first Steele didn't see what they were shooting at.

Then smoke from one of the exploded trucks cleared, and she saw where a large section of the fence had already gone down – and soldiers armed with assault rifles were pouring through. Steele stared at them, unable at first to comprehend what she was seeing. These new attackers moved with trained expertise and obvious cunning; they were ruthless and efficient, and the human ground troops were being decimated.

Who were these attackers – some terrorist group? Humans allied with the dead? As they drew closer, she saw that the advancing soldiers – who all wore Stormtrooper-style combat helmets – were grey-skinned and red-eyed.

Intelligent zombies. Hordes of them. They'd obviously hidden among their slower, thoughtless kin, waiting. What was it Parker had murmured in her ear? *Javelin*. It took her a moment to remember: the Javelin was a standard anti-tank guided missile, fired by a two-man team. They had weapons as well as training, and linked minds that enabled them to act in unison.

The humans didn't stand a chance.

In that instant she felt Parker tug at her. "Go!" He was pulling her towards the Oval Office, where Harkins and his troops were already crouching and offering covering fire. Steele collected her wits, pulled her Glock, and ran with Parker.

Bullets traced the ground beside her. She dodged, expecting to feel the fatal impact any second. Thirty feet away, Harkins was frantically waving her forward . . .

A bullet exploded Harkins' face. He fell back, dead.

Steele stopped and whirled, the Glock already raised. A zombie with a pointed rifle was fifty feet behind her. She sighted and fired. The zombie's helmet caught her shot, and the impact threw the dead man back, but he regained his footing and raised the rifle again.

"Fuck," Steele said.

Unfortunately for the zombie, Steele's first shot had also knocked his *Stahlhelm* helmet askew, and her second shot lodged perfectly the middle of his forehead; he collapsed, a look of surprise frozen on his face.

Parker, beside her, was shouting now to be heard over the gunfire and explosions. "We can't stay. The tanks are our only chance."

Steele nodded and looked back. The Bradleys were firing their big guns at the advancing wave, holding them back . . . but not for long.

Parker pulled her down behind the temporary shield of a smouldering hunk of metal as he spoke into his headset. "Tank commanders, this is General Ames Parker. Prepare to retreat, but not until my signal. We're going to try to reach you first."

Steele heard several voices bark, "Yes, sir!"

Parker looked around. "At least we've got a shot at an escape route."

Steele was about to ask Parker how he suggested they get to the tanks when he rose. "Where are you going?"

He looked towards the Oval Office. "I need to take control of Colonel Harkins' unit, tell them to get the hell out of here with us."

"Right."

"Cover me."

Parker ran.

Steele saw that the zombies all seemed to be preoccupied with the combat surrounding the tanks. She saw one glance at Parker and raise an assault rifle, but she fired first, from behind the safety of the metal wreckage. Her shot knocked the zombie off-balance and gave Parker time to finish running.

But then she saw the zombie lower the rifle and lift a phone instead.

She risked another shot, and it was good – the phone exploded with most of the zombie's hand. It looked down with something like mild irritation, and then began scanning the area for her. Steele ducked behind the wreckage and hoped she hadn't been spotted. She glanced towards the Oval Office – and saw chaos.

Parker and two of Harkins' troops (*the last two?*) were popping off shots from just inside the room; several of the zombie soldiers were advancing on their position, spraying the area with assault rifle fire. From her vantage, she could see Parker clearly through one of the tall windows that circled the Oval Office; he looked up, saw her, and waved towards the tanks. "Start moving, Steele!"

Steele shook her head. "Not without you," she said into her own headpiece.

He gestured angrily. "Dammit—!"

Steele fired at the nearest zombie. Her shot went wide. A second shot caught it in the chest. It staggered slightly, but kept going, inexorable.

One of the soldiers next to Parker took a round in the heart and dropped. It was now just Parker and one other soldier, trying to hold the Oval Office.

Steele surveyed the area. She knew it was unlikely that she could reach the White House alive; there were two zombie soldiers striding forward, both carrying automatic weapons. They'd cut her down in a firestorm. If only she had a grenade, or even a Molotov cocktail . . .

"You know, if you served under me I'd court martial you."

It was Parker's voice. Steele looked across the fifty feet of lawn separating them, and saw him speaking into his headset. He stopped talking and shot at the nearest zombie, who returned fire. The remaining human soldier with him fell dead. Parker reached out as the young soldier collapsed – and a bullet caught him in the arm.

"Parker—!" She leapt to her feet.

"Steele, *go!*"

She didn't. She ducked down again.

All she could do was watch and listen.

Parker tore off his belt, formed it into a loop, and cinched it tight around his left bicep, slowing the flow of blood from the bullet hole just above his elbow. "Steele," he said into the headpiece through gritted teeth, "if I can take out these two coming in, I want you to run." His firing arm was still unharmed, and he lifted the pistol, sighting on the two dead men stepping through the French windows . . .

And so he didn't see the squad that entered the room behind him until it was too late.

From where he crouched by a window, Parker spun and lifted his pistol, aiming at the one in front. The bullet went right through the zombie's throat but missed the brain. Angry, the zombie brought a foot down on Parker's gun hand. Steele nearly yanked her earpiece out as it filled her head with Parker's shrieks while the zombie ground its foot down on to his hand. When the torment finished, Parker stopped screaming, but he breathed raggedly, the gasping after-effects of pain.

The zombies grabbed him by the arms, and he groaned as they dragged him across the Oval Office to a couch. They hauled him up on to it, leaving a thick trail of blood. He lolled there, weak, trying to remain conscious.

"Parker," Steele breathed into the mike.

He didn't answer.

Steele knew Parker was dying. She should run now, while their focus was on him . . . but she couldn't. She had to see this play out. If she couldn't save Parker (she couldn't), at least she could possibly give his death meaning by gaining some useful intelligence.

So she crouched, unseen, behind the wreckage, and observed.

Zombie soldiers moved in and out of the room, relaying information and exchanging positions. In a few minutes, Parker (whose dark skin had greyed as his blood soaked into the expensive upholstery of the couch) was guarded by two dead men in suits, one armed with a rifle, the other holding his hands clasped politely near his holstered pistol.

Steele felt a surge of rage: the two men were Secret Service. One she even recognized, as distant as she was: Michael Barber was a thirty-four-year-old African American who'd once been a champion body builder and who Steele had regarded highly. She remembered him as a crack shot who'd defeated an Army sniper in an impromptu shooting contest; now he gripped a rifle that she knew he'd turn on her without hesitation. Seeing him there, as an agent of the living dead, made her hands shake in unsatisfied rage.

A few seconds later, a new figure entered the office, moving authoritatively. He was dressed in an elegant grey suit, only lightly spattered with blood, and there were others entering behind him. Steele was astonished to realize that she recognized all of them: there was the one-time Governor who'd had fifteen minutes of fame as a vice presidential candidate; there was the elegant Speaker of the House who'd gained a reputation for blocking every piece of legislation initiated by the other party; and the woman with the brunette hair and unblinking stare, wasn't that the Minnesota Representative who'd scoffed at evolution?

It took Steele a few more seconds to recognize the first man, the one whose bearing and position in front of the others marked him as leader. Of course: she'd seen this man's face in photographs and on videos of speeches. He was James Moreby, the would-be president of the New Zombie Order.

"Welcome, General Parker," Moreby said, and Steele heard him over Parker's mike, his voice hinting at a British accent, but one buried beneath an American tongue. "It is an honour to have you."

A feminine giggle sounded somewhere. Steele guessed it belonged to the former Governor.

Moreby also heard the sound and said, "Pardon my ministers, General. They have only recently been incarnated in these bodies, and their thinking, I fear, is somewhat addled by hunger right now."

The giggling woman turned towards Moreby, and Steele thought she saw fury on her features. "Moreby—"

"That is *President* Moreby, my dear, and you will remain quiet until my business with the General is concluded."

The Governor started to respond, then crossed her arms and stayed sullenly silent.

Moreby returned his attention to Parker. "We have been most curious about where your human president is being kept, General. I applaud you for managing to keep that rather large secret . . . until now, that is. Time for a little taste . . ."

Moreby began walking forward, his mouth already opening.

Steele tried to steady her hands as they gripped the pistol. Could she get a shot from here? Moreby wore no helmet; he was vulnerable. One shot . . .

There was still sporadic fighting going on behind her, and one of her former best agents held a rifle in front of her. If she took the shot, she'd be dead, whether she succeeded in killing Moreby or not.

She was still weighing her chances when she saw Parker move. His uninjured arm jerked up and reached for the holstered pistol on the nearest guard's hip. The man tried to wrestle the pistol away, but Parker pulled the trigger and blew most of the agent's hand apart. The big guard, Barber, was trying to swing the rifle around . . .

But Parker had already levelled the stolen pistol on Moreby, who stood six feet away.

At first Steele didn't understand what Parker was waiting for. "*Take the shot*," she involuntarily said.

Parker heard it. "Trying, but . . ."

Then she realized: he was weakened by blood loss and shock, and his hand was shaking so badly that even at close range he couldn't guarantee a hit.

Moreby smiled down at Parker with almost parental concern. "Ames, Ames . . . just give it up. I am betting that your vision is fading, that your hands are shaking . . . do you even still have the strength to pull the trigger?"

"Yes," he said, his voice little more than a whisper.

Before they could stop him, he turned the gun around, put the barrel in his mouth and squeezed. An explosion sounded in Steele's ear.

She gasped and sagged, her own strength failing. Her gun hand fell to the grass, all thoughts of action gone. Everything . . . gone.

After a few seconds she became aware of voices in her earpiece, and she looked up. In the Oval Office, Moreby was reaching down to the ruined remains of Ames Parker. He peeled something away from the General's head, and at first Steele had the notion that it was tissue from the inside of Parker's skull . . . then Moreby ran his fingers along it, wiping it clean, and when Steele heard a tiny thump in her ear, she knew what it was.

Moreby licked his fingers clean of Parker's blood, and tentatively placed the earpiece in his own ear and the mike near his throat. He walked to the nearest window and looked out at the tanks. When he spoke, Steele realized he wasn't addressing her directly, but she thought he might as well be.

"*We will be coming for you next.*"

She pulled the earpiece out, flung the headset aside, hefted her gun and took off.

She circled wide around the sheltering wreckage, trying to move from one large piece to another. She was making progress, closing in on the nearest tank. At thirty yards, she saw its hatch open and a soldier popped up, waving her on.

There was no more wreckage between her and the tank. She'd have to try for it.

She inhaled – and ran.

She heard gunshots, but didn't know how many were pointed in her direction. She saw a trio of zombies in front of the tank explode into pieces of tattered flesh as a grenade landed at their feet. When another stepped into view from around the rear of the vehicle, she fired into its chest, only to knock it back and give her time.

The rear hatch started to lower. She waited, her palms sweating on the Glock's handle.

The zombie she'd hit in the chest began to rise. She raised the Glock – but didn't need to fire, when the hatch suddenly fell open, pinning the zombie beneath. Soldiers inside waved her in. "Come on! Quick!"

Steele jumped up – and tripped when her ankle was grabbed by the zombie beneath the hatch, who had reached over the edge with its free arm. Steele struggled briefly, lowered the Glock and fired at the elbow. The arm was severed, her bullet ricocheted off the metal and away from the tank, and she reached down and pried the still-grasping hand from her ankle, tossing it out as the hatch began to rise. She ducked as she saw more attackers trying to pump bullets into the tank before the hatch sealed, but they were too late; their last few shots pinged off the metal outside.

Steele was helped to a padded metal bench by two soldiers, a young woman with short hair and a wide jaw, and an older man with a prematurely lined face. The vehicle suddenly jounced as it began to roll forward, and the man grabbed Steele before she was thrown from the bench. "Hang on – it's liable to be a bumpy ride."

She nodded and forced herself to wind down; adrenaline was still racing through her, making her heart slam and her fingers jitter. "Pretty rough, huh," said the young woman.

"Yeah."

"Were you hurt? Y'know . . ."

"Bitten?" Steele asked.

The woman nodded.

"No," Steele answered.

The two soldiers eyed her strangely – the man with mild curiosity, the woman with uncertainty – and Steele remembered that she still had on the blonde wig. She reached up and removed it, setting it in her lap.

After a moment, the female soldier asked, "You're not really her, are you?"

"No, I'm not." Steele looked down at the wig and for a moment was struck by the power of image. She'd seen an almost worshipful look on the soldier's face when she'd first set foot in the tank, but that had changed to uncertainty and finally disappointment. And she understood how vitally important the woman she worked for was, how her likeness on a stranger could inspire courage and hope.

Steele turned her gaze from the cast-off wig in her lap to the female soldier, and she stuck a hand out. "Sandra Steele, Director, United States Secret Service."

Her eyes widening, the twenty-something soldier accepted the offered hand. "It's an honour, ma'am. Sergeant Raquelle LaFortune, but my friends call me Rocky. And this redneck is PFC Willson Danning."

Danning shook her hand as well. Rocky said, "You're the first female Director, aren't you?"

Steele nodded. "They had to bring me in when the boys couldn't keep their pants zipped. Oh, sorry, Danning – no offence meant."

"None taken—" Danning broke off as something rocked the tank with a deafening roar. "Another fuckin' rocket," he noted. He waited a second to make sure the tank was still moving forward, and added, laconically, "They didn't quite get us."

"Danning's a master of understatement," Rocky said.

Steele tried to smile, but couldn't. She was thinking of the man she'd left behind, Ames Parker. She suffered the first flash of guilt at having abandoned him, and the second for having watched him die.

She knew she'd feel that guilt for the rest of her life . . . which she didn't expect to be long.

From: Dr. Brewster Gilray <bgilray@nwpharm.com>
To: W. Leonard Paryder <big_daddy@deadbolt.com>
Sent: THU, Aug 29, 5:27 PM
Subject: URGENT – Patient Omega

Landen has finally relayed information on Patient Omega, including name and location. Subject is Kevin Moon, of Korean descent, 23 years old, height 5' 10", weight 170. GPS coordinates for his present location will be relayed separately. Please pick up subject and clean location per the usual; then return subject to HQ.

Ward, this is the missing link. Put your best team on it and make sure we don't blow this one.

Chapter Twenty-Three

KEVIN WAS DYING.

At least that was what he thought, as the sun dawned on his fourth day without food or water. The hunger left his insides in knots, but the thirst had taken away his ability to think of anything else. Water was all he could imagine, all he could dream about, what his world had constricted to.

Water.

Yesterday Pepper had ambled out into the yard, a big litre bottle of water in his hands. He'd stood just beyond Kevin's reach, gulping half the bottle at once; he'd then poured most of the rest over his head. When he finished, droplets running down his shaven, dark brown pate, there'd been two inches left in the bottle.

"You want it?"

Even slightly unfocused from hunger and thirst, Kevin heard the edge in the man's voice. "C'mon, man, yeah – of course I'm thirsty."

"Tell me you want me to give you water."

Under any other circumstance, Kevin would've told him to fuck off, or laughed and turned his back . . . but thirst was controlling his tongue, his eyes riveted to those two inches of water. "Okay. I want you to give me water."

"You want my water?"

"Just . . . any water."

"Okay."

With that, Pepper had tossed the bottle behind him, unzipped his pants, and pissed on Kevin.

Kevin had jerked back, already gagging at the acrid smell and the hot liquid on his sunburned skin, but the chain pulled him up short, digging anew into the ragged flesh of his ankle. Pepper was laughing while he continued to spray the ground with urine. Finally he finished, shook himself and zipped up again. "You wanted it, you got it, dipshit."

Using his shirt to wipe his head clean, Kevin snarled, "What are your superiors gonna say when you hand me over dead, asswipe?"

Pepper squatted down to get closer to Kevin, feigning a friendly chat. "Well, see, in the first place – we all know you're gonna start to turn any time now; and even if you're not – we don't take kindly to having our brothers bitten by either the dead or the living. You're gonna pay for that, and nobody's gonna know the difference when you turn. See, I'm just gonna make your death as unpleasant as possible." Pepper winked, rose and walked away.

Later in the day he and Forbes had eaten lunch (microwaved burritos) in front of Kevin, they'd set up bottles behind him and fired away with their rifles, intentionally coming close to him, and they'd blared country music at ear-splitting volumes. After the sun had gone down, they'd started drinking again, and Forbes at one point had staggered out of the house with a freshly dead rat that he'd tossed to Kevin, shrieking with laughter before he'd wandered back inside.

The worst part had been that Kevin had seriously considered eating the rat. Instead, he'd finally removed the temptation by picking it up and tossing it out of his reach.

At least they'd drunk enough to pass out, and he knew they'd both be suffering from hangovers. Of course even with throbbing heads, they'd still spent a warm night in comfortable beds, while he'd huddled under his jacket for warmth, shivering as the night temperatures dropped to a few degrees above freezing. He was bare-chested under the jacket since his T-shirt had served as everything from pillow to towel, and he'd tossed it aside after wiping off Pepper's urine with it.

Now, on this third morning, he was thankful for the sunrise and the increasing warmth, but weak and wary of what the day would bring.

He guessed it was about noon when Pepper staggered out, blinking in the sun, downing another bottle of water. Pepper stopped, looked down at him. "Well, you don't look so good today, you little freak."

"I'm not turning, if that's what you're thinking. I'm hungry and thirsty and just spent the night freezing out here, thanks to your hospitality."

Pepper actually frowned and stepped closer, eyeing Kevin carefully. "You don't look like somebody with HRV . . ."

"I don't have HRV! For fuck's sake, what does it take to get through to you? *I'm immune.* Get it?"

Doubt flickered across the soldier's dark face. He jiggled his half-full bottle uncertainly, and for an instant Kevin thought he might offer it to him, realize he'd made a terrible error . . . but instead he poured it on to the ground before rising and dropping the empty bottle. "Yeah, well, whatever. Forbes ain't lookin' so good. That place where you bit him is all purple, and he's got a fever."

"You probably just didn't disinfect the wound well enough. Does it look like HRV?"

Again, uncertainty clouded Pepper's expression, but was swiftly replaced by anger. "Just shut the fuck up. I got somethin' special in mind for you tonight, *boy*. Somethin' that's gonna make Forbes feel better, and you feel a whole lot worse. I'm tellin' you now just so you'll have somethin' to look forward to all day long. You just lay there and think about the shitstorm that's comin' your way."

Pepper turned and walked off. And as much as Kevin hated it, his body did exactly what Pepper wanted – anxiety ramped up his cramping another notch, and he shook, not from cold this time but from stark, undeniable fear.

Just before sunset, Kevin heard the door to the house bang open. He turned to see both Pepper and Forbes walking towards him, purposefully.

Pepper held a long butcher's knife in one hand and a length of white nylon rope in the other. Forbes had a roll of duct tape.

Kevin's heart started to hammer.

They stopped just beyond Kevin's reach, glanced at each other, and then looked down at him with hard eyes. Forbes had dirty gauze wrapped around his bite wound, and he looked pale, but he obviously wasn't suffering from HRV.

He began rubbing his crotch.

"You ready for playtime?" Pepper asked.

Kevin crawled back as far as the chain would allow. He pulled at it, knowing it wouldn't give but driven by instinct to seek any escape. They both walked forward now, and Pepper gestured with the knife as he spoke. "Flat on your stomach, hands behind your back."

"No." Kevin sat and stared up with what he hoped was defiance.

Pepper drew back a boot. Kevin had just enough time to see the steel in the toe before it impacted with his head.

Pain exploded, vision darkened. He didn't completely lose consciousness, but he couldn't seem to make anything work. He felt himself hit the ground, and then his arms were being pulled up behind his back and tied, duct tape was wound several times around his head, sealing his mouth shut. They didn't tape his nose, though. They wanted him to live through this.

The next thing was the sound of an engine approaching.

He heard Pepper and Forbes question each other. The engine noise grew louder and then tyres crunched on gravel. Someone new had arrived.

Kevin turned his head, and his sight cleared; he saw car lights, a heavy vehicle like his former Humvee, the doors opening. Four men got out. It was dark and he couldn't make them out clearly from his vantage on the ground, but he saw they wore some sort of uniforms and were armed.

"That him?" He didn't recognize the voice.

"Oh, what the fuck . . ." Another newcomer.

Forbes laughed nervously. "Hey, c'mon, we're just fucking around, we didn't mean anything—"

One of the new men pulled a pistol and shot Forbes right in the head, a perfect, clean kill.

Pepper cried out and tried to lunge with the knife and the man shot him, another direct head hit.

"Jesus," one of the men said.

They walked over to Kevin, two knelt down. "Are you conscious?"

Kevin nodded, scraping one cheek on the ground. He tried to grunt.

Someone pulled the duct tape away, while someone else undid the knots tied around his wrists. Freed, they helped him sit up. He tried to talk and had to choke first, then rasped out, "Water."

One of them ran to their vehicle and returned with a bottle. They tilted it to his lips, and Kevin started to gulp, but felt his stomach contract around the liquid and threaten to repel it. He gasped and sputtered, waited, but the water stayed down.

"You're Kevin Moon, right? The one who's immune?"

Kevin nodded.

"Can you hold out your right arm for me?"

He did, although his arm was trembling. One of the men took it, gently, and held up a mag flashlight until he located the place where the zombie had been allowed to bite him. The teeth marks were still obvious, although they'd scabbed over and bruised. "Yeah, that's him. There's the control mark."

"Good. Can you stand?"

"I . . . I don't know."

They helped him to his feet, and saw the chain that still held him captive. "Oh for fuck's sake . . . do you know where this key is?"

Kevin tilted a chin towards the bodies of Pepper and Forbes. "Probably on one of them."

Upright now, with the last light of the sunset and the Humvee's headlights outlining them, Kevin made out his saviours: the four men wore black jumpsuits with gun belts, and they all possessed a lived-in toughness he hadn't seen in any of the other soldiers so far. He was thankful they'd rescued him, but also fearful of their obvious strength and the mystery of who they worked for. Two of them searched the bodies of Pepper and Forbes while the other two held Kevin upright.

"How long you been out here?" That was the oldest man; he was built like a linebacker, must have been in his forties, had a thick sand-coloured moustache and piercing blue eyes. Somehow Kevin knew he was in command here.

"Three days. No food or water."

"Oh Jesus Christ."

The two searchers returned with keyrings, and went through them until one key fit the handcuff around his ankle and it sprang open. As that man pulled the cuff away, he examined Kevin's leg by his maglight. "That ankle's infected. He's going to need treatment for that."

"Right." The commander gave Kevin a slight, reassuring smile. "Relax. You're in good hands now."

Kevin shook his ankle, making sure it still worked after three days of being shackled, and he would have fallen had the commander not caught him.

"Whoa, take it easy. We're going to get you to the medical help you need. We've got some food with us you can have now, but you'll have to eat it slowly or it'll come right back up. Do you understand?"

Kevin tried to nod, but the movement made his head spin. "Where are we going?"

"It's a medical facility. We've got about a four-hour drive. Think you can handle it?"

"Can I have a little more water?"

One of the men handed him the bottle. He took it, swigged from it, but didn't swallow all of it. He kept a little in his mouth, swishing it around, working it into a slight froth as he limped over to where the two dead men were sprawled in the grass – and he spat on Pepper's face. He poured the last of the water on to the corpse, and let the empty plastic bottle bounce off the dead man's chest.

Kevin asked for a few moments to clean up. They helped him into the house, where he used two precious bottles of water to sponge himself off. He found some old clothes in a bedroom closet that he put on. Flannel and denim weren't exactly his style and the clothing was two sizes too large, but anything was better than smelling like Pepper's piss.

It was full night by the time they climbed into the Hummer. Kevin glanced back one last time at the two corpses they'd be leaving behind.

"Let's get the fuck out of this shithole."

The Commander clapped him on the shoulder, and they headed out.

[Text message sent from Ty Ward to Sandra Steele]

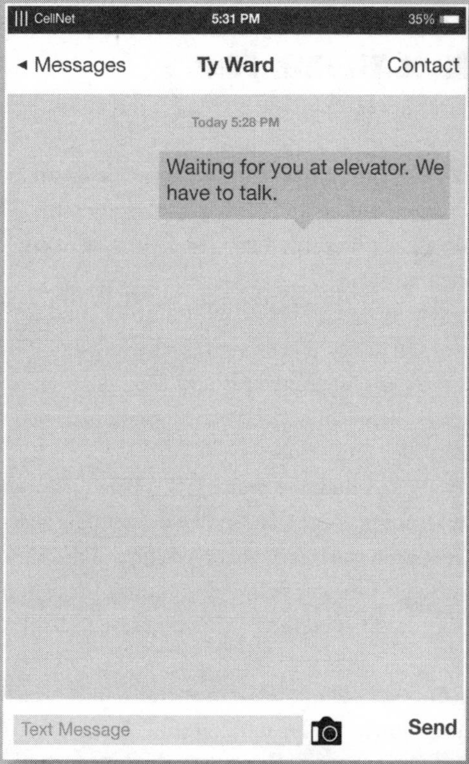

Chapter Twenty-Four

TWO OF THE tanks and three of the RCVs made it back to Bolling. The other had been taken out by anti-tank rockets before they'd left the South Lawn. Steele knew she'd gotten lucky, and she also knew the odds were against it happening again.

The intelligent zombies had been concentrated around the White House, and had thinned out as the remaining vehicles rolled out of the area. The undead ranks were sparse afterwards and they made good time getting home through the encroaching darkness. Steele was relieved to see the base was still well patrolled and secure.

As the tanks parked and the rear hatch opened, she bid farewell to LaFortune and Danning; she'd come to like the young female soldier a great deal and had been prepared to offer her a position in the bunker, but Rocky was searching for someone and wanted to continue the fight on the ground. They wished each other good luck. "Guard her well," Rocky added. Steele nodded.

Steele went through security clearance and found herself alone in the elevator heading down to the underground complex. For a moment, unaccompanied and unseen, she let herself slump; she was exhausted, drained by defeat, burdened by guilt she couldn't imagine bearing for the rest of her life. She wanted to retreat, to hide, especially from herself.

Instead she stood straight again as the elevator stopped and the doors opened.

Ty stood just outside. "She knows," he said.

"Oh, Christ. How?"

"She had one of the tank drivers on a private line."

They walked together through another security check, punching in codes, and continued on towards the heart of the OC.

Steele asked, "Does she know I'm back?"

"No. The guy she was talking to got blown up with his tank. She doesn't know what happened to you, but . . . I think you need to see her right away."

Steele stopped. She wasn't sure she could do this. Her feet wouldn't move; her lungs barely worked. She forced herself to breathe again, and Ty waited, patient, as she collected herself. Finally she looked up and asked, "Where is she?"

"Still in the Command Center. It's pretty loud in there right now."

Steele nodded and pushed past Ty. She walked for another minute before arriving outside the Command room, and she spent those sixty seconds trying to go blank. She was even partially successful.

Ty had been right: she heard raised voices through the closed door.

She opened it and paused.

Delancy was just shouting, "—equal response that will—" But he broke off as he saw her.

The President turned, took one look at Steele, and said, with quiet forcefulness, "Everybody but Steele out *now*."

Gillespie and Jones rose. Delancy didn't. "Madame President, I—"

"*Now*, Bob. We'll continue this later."

This time he didn't argue. He rose and left the room. As he walked past Steele, he muttered, "Good luck."

The door closed behind him. Steele stood, rigid, staring straight ahead.

"You know that if the situation were any different I'd fire you right now."

"Yes, ma'am."

"Is Parker dead?"

Steele nodded. When she spoke, she could only manage a whisper. "Yes."

"Did he compromise our position?"

"No." She cleared her throat and said, "He shot himself first."

The President looked away for a second, struggling with her own emotions. After a few seconds, she turned back to Steele. "Why? If you and Parker had come to me, the three of us together might have found a different way, a real solution. Or I might have ended up agreeing with you and letting you do what you did. But you didn't respect me enough to give me that choice."

"I . . ." Steele had no answer.

"Let me explain something: it's not about me being the only one to make decisions, or to have the power. It's about the fact that I need all of you who are left operating on top form, and you can't do that if you're thinking about your failures or drowning in guilt. If people are going to die as a result of a decision, then *I* need to be the one to carry that load."

Steele felt the weight of the other woman's eyes on her, and the judgement felt like a sentence. She waited, hoping the President would follow through and relieve her of this terrible duty.

Instead, the President asked, "Did you at least learn anything useful?"

Steele nodded. "Moreby's got intelligent zombies, all right. And not just a few – we're talking an army's worth, all combat ready. Some of them seem to be equipped with special bulletproof helmets, so we should assume they have their own research and development teams and manufacturers. And Moreby's got some kind of cabinet with him—"

"The Well of Seven."

Steele broke off, looking at the President, curious. "Sorry . . .?"

"Were there seven of them? These people with Moreby?"

She tried to replay the Oval Office scene in her head, mentally counting. "I think so. Yes."

"The 19th-century Moreby had a group of followers who he practised all his rituals with and called 'The Well of Seven'. Apparently he's reincarnated them somehow and plans to make them his puppet government."

Remembering the former Governor and the others, Steele said, "Wait until you see who they are. It's like a police line-up of people who probably wanted to kill you even before they turned."

"The big difference is now they want to eat my brain."

The President and Steele exchanged a smile, and Steele began to relax slightly. Maybe, she thought, there really is still a place for me here. Maybe the work will help me to forget . . . to stop thinking about Ames Parker.

She heard a scraping sound and saw the President sliding a tablet across the desk to her. "Another reason you should have consulted with me before you rode off into the sunset today: we've got a situation developing that we need to discuss."

"Situation?"

The President gestured at the tablet. "Aaron decrypted some New World Pharmaceuticals communications that indicate they've found an HRV survivor."

Steele had to force her mind back to business; it spun up slowly, like a cold engine on a winter day. The tablet showed an email about a young man named Kevin Moon, and gave coordinates for a location. "Did we get a team out to this location already?"

The President retrieved the tablet. "A little while ago. They found two dead guards. Moon was gone. One of the dead men was found with a bite mark on his arm, and both had been shot in the head. So, maybe Moon really wasn't immune after all, came back, attacked his guards and took off. But if that's the case . . . who shot the guards? And why wasn't Moon found dead with them?"

"We think New World Pharmaceuticals has him now?"

"Landen Jones is missing. He left while we were all preoccupied with the attack. Security topside reports that he took a car and left the base, claimed it was 'official business'. It doesn't take much to put that together with the encrypted email and our missing survivor."

Steele looked at the President, saw the puffy bags under her eyes, knew she was sleeping only a few hours every night, and yet she felt both admiration and envy at the fact that the woman still functioned better than everyone else. "Well," Steele said, hoping she didn't sound as unsure of herself as she felt, "even if that is what happened . . . is that necessarily a bad thing? I mean, New World still has the best research resources and the capability to mass-produce any cure or vaccine they come up with, right? Even if some other team found a cure first, we'd still have to farm out production to NWP, wouldn't we?"

The President's slight smile boosted Steele's confidence. "That's exactly right . . . which is why I think they're up to something else. They certainly were with Moreby."

"Right. So . . . what do we do? Try to get this Kevin Moon back? Do we even know where they might have taken him?"

"I've got something else in mind. Congress just passed a bill to funnel resources to NWP. I'm going to let that stand . . . but we're going to make damn sure those resources never actually reach them. That's where I'll need your help."

Steele rose. "Whatever I can do. Now if you'll excuse me, I think I need to go wash some blood off."

The President didn't say anything until Steele was halfway out the door, then she added, "Oh, and Steele – I'm sorry, but you just can't work the pantsuit like I can."

THE WHITE HOUSE
WASHINGTON

BULLETIN FROM THE OFFICE
OF THE PRESIDENT OF THE UNITED STATES

Contact: Ty Ward, Chief of Staff

It is with great sadness that we announce the death of General Ames Parker, Joint Commander of the United States combined military forces. General Parker, 61, died during combat against the forces of James Moreby's New Zombie Order.

General Parker was

Chapter Twenty-Five

TY STARED AT the bulletin again, mentally writhing over the inadequacy of the words, unable to even complete the last sentence. He knew he should just finish the goddamn thing with Parker's Wikipedia bio, vet it with the President, and then send it out . . . but it just didn't feel right.

Of course *none* of this felt right. Parker dead. The human forces defeated. Ty in charge of reassembling the military forces.

And then there was the phone call to be made.

He pushed the tablet screen with the barely begun press release aside and picked up Parker's phone. Push "1" – it was all he had to do. Well, that, and tell Parker's family that their centre was gone.

He'd tried out different ways of telling them in his head: *I'm so sorry, but . . . I'm afraid I've got some very bad news . . . This is going to be hard . . . It is with great sadness . . .*

"Fuck it," Ty muttered to himself. *Get it over with. Just do it. Say it. Don't overthink this.*

He pressed the "1" and raised the phone to his ear.

The number went through, and the call rang on the other end. And rang. And rang.

Ty was on the verge of hanging up when the call was answered. On the other end, a frantic female voice came on. "Ames—?"

"Hello. Is this Mrs Parker?"

In the background he heard young voices shouting and muffled poundings. "Yes. Who is this? Where's Ames? I need to speak to him right now – we're locked in the basement and they're in the house upstairs, the soldiers are gone or dead, it's just me and the kids—"

Ty's throat tightened and he shut his eyes. "Mrs Parker, my name is Ty Ward. I'm acting as Chief of Staff in the President's office, and I'm so sorry to have to tell you that . . . Ames is dead."

"No!" There was a choked sob. "No, no, no . . ." Another cry farther away from the phone came over the line.

What was he supposed to do or say next? Ty wondered what training policemen and real military leaders had for these situations. "Mrs Parker, you should know that he died a hero, on the battlefield—"

"But that doesn't help *me*. I knew something was wrong when he didn't return the calls – I've left a dozen over the last few hours. If he'd gotten them, he would have done something, something to help us . . ."

"Did you say the soldiers who'd been protecting you are gone?"

There was a brief blurt of static, and then Ty heard her say, "—all gone. I think some of them have already . . . come back."

After a second, Ty said, "Mrs Parker, stay where you are and I'm going to try to get help."

"Okay. Please, tell whoever comes to hurry – the way they're pounding on the basement door, it can't last long . . ."

The poundings in the background were louder, and one of the youthful voices screamed.

Ty said, "Goodbye, Mrs Parker," and severed the connection. He clutched helplessly at the phone. The truth was there was *nothing* he could do. Even if he could find a squad willing to leave the safety of whatever the nearest base was and make their way through treacherous country, they wouldn't reach Parker's house in time. They'd probably end up losing their own lives in the attempt, and right now they didn't have enough lives on the human side to spare.

He had to let them die, even while a part of him itched with the (irrational) thought that Parker would have done something to save them . . . even when he hadn't been able to save himself.

Trying not to imagine Ames Parker's wife and children backing away into the corner of a dusty basement as the hungry dead shambled down the creaking stairs towards them, Ty pulled the tablet computer and the keyboard over, erased what he'd already done, and retyped:

It is with deep sadness that we report the death of General Ames Parker, who died earlier today in combat during a human offensive against the forces of James Moreby's New Zombie Order. Effective immediately, the acting Joint Commander of the United States Armed Forces will be Ty Ward. A decorated veteran of the Iraq War, Ward is dedicated to restoring the human forces of the United States, and will begin preparing new strategies and offensives with all major commanders.

Leaning back, Ty read over what he'd just typed, and thought Ames Parker would have approved.

||| CellNet   3:16 PM   50%

◄ Messages   **B. Gilray**   Contact

Today 3:10 pM

Patient Omega acquired safely. Testing proceeding. Awaiting your arrival.

Text Message   Send

Chapter Twenty-Six

KEVIN WOKE SLOWLY, allowing himself to drift up from sleep, a feather caught in a gentle draft. The crisp, cool sheets were delicious against his skin, his stomach was happily rumbling in anticipation of breakfast, and even the chemical scents of hospital disinfectants were welcome after days of smelling sweat and urine and blood.

He still hurt in places – mainly his right ankle, where the metal shackle had rubbed a red circle and led to an infection – and he was weak. He thought he might try getting out of bed and walking a little . . . but later.

When he'd been brought in last night, he'd barely been conscious enough to know what was happening. He was exhausted and feverish. He remembered isolated images: a security gate; a large complex of some kind; armed guards patrolling; a stretcher rolled up to the van; white-coated doctors and nurses asking him questions and tending to him.

They'd all treated him with compassion he could barely recognize.

Now, with dawn spilling in through a nearby window, he had a chance to look around. He was in a hospital room, but an elegant one with high-tech medical equipment Kevin had never seen before, spotless floors and fixtures, a flatscreen television facing the single bed, and two luxurious leather armchairs.

This was obviously no ordinary hospital.

Kevin was hooked up to an IV, and he thought he recognized a heart monitor, but there were wires taking readings from him that he couldn't guess at. He needed to urinate, and glanced under the sheet just to make sure he didn't have a catheter; instead, he saw he wore simple cotton pyjamas. He was thankful to realize he'd been thoroughly cleaned, although he had no memory of that happening.

He found a call button tucked into the guard rail on the bed's right side, and he pressed the button. Within seconds, the door opened and a man in a white lab coat entered. He smiled at Kevin and said, "Well, good morning, Mr Moon. I'm Dr Singh. How are you feeling?"

What Kevin felt at that exact moment was incredulity: Dr Singh was one of the handsomest men he'd ever seen. With gleaming black hair tousled in a boyish cut, skin the colour of cherry wood and perfectly white teeth, Kevin was tempted to ask if he was a real doctor or an actor playing one.

"Mr Moon . . .?"

"Oh, sorry. Still a little out of it, I guess, but much better today. *Much* better."

"Good."

Dr Singh bent forward to examine readings on the equipment, and Kevin saw that there was a patch sewn on to his lab coat – the logo for New World Pharmaceuticals Group. "Is that where I am – some facility or something for New World Pharmaceuticals?"

"Exactly right. This is our US headquarters just outside Baltimore. We have a large and very secure complex here, so you're quite safe. Now, what can I help you with?"

It took Kevin a few seconds to remember that he'd pressed the call button. Singh helped him out of bed and the few steps to the bathroom, while rolling the IV stand. When he'd finished, Kevin was startled to realize how much just that small action had fatigued him, and he was grateful for the solace of the bed. Once he was settled, Singh said, "Whenever you're ready, Mr Moon, I'm going to need to ask you a few questions."

"I'm ready now."

Singh pulled up a chair, and for the next ten minutes they went over Kevin's entire medical history, beginning with childhood vaccinations and winding up with three days of exposure, dehydration and starvation. Singh tapped some notes into a keyboard attached to a metal extension over the bed, and when he finished he eyed Kevin with fresh appreciation. "It's a wonder you've survived everything that's happened to you, Mr Moon."

"Could you call me Kevin? Mr Moon sounds like my Dad."

Singh smiled, and Kevin was dazzled again. "Of course, Kevin."

"So . . . what's going to happen to me here?"

A flicker of trepidation crossed Singh's face, but was replaced almost instantly by warmth and reassurance. "You're going to be very well looked after here, let me assure you. I'll be frank with you, Kevin: you're the first human survivor of HRV, or at least the first one who we know of. At this point, that makes you a pretty important guy and we'll take good care of you. I'll be overseeing your medical care, so we'll be getting to know each other pretty well."

"Okay. And how long will I be here?"

"I think you'll be ready for regular quarters by tomorrow. After that . . . well, it'll be pretty comfortable here, especially compared to what's going on outside."

Kevin nodded, and realized he wouldn't mind staying anywhere that was near Singh.

The doctor rose and reached into a pocket for a syringe. "Now, if you don't mind, Kevin, I'm going to need to draw some blood . . . for tests. I'm afraid you may be feeling like a pincushion in another few days."

"Hey, doc, I'll take pincushion over punching bag any day."

Singh took Kevin's right hand, turned it over to expose the wrist, and found a vein. His fingers were sure and warm, and lingered slightly as he removed the needle and pocketed the vial of blood. He taped a band-aid over the pinprick, told Kevin he'd be back in the afternoon and left.

Kevin closed his eyes, letting comfortable drowsiness settle in, luxuriating in the possibility that everything might actually be fine at last.

CENTRAL INTELLIGENCE AGENCY

AARON GILLESPIE, DIRECTOR
CONFIDENTIAL

Two days ago, as you may recall from the bulletin I sent at that time, the self-proclaimed NZO government under the control of James Moreby restored power to most of the eastern seaboard, including Washington and, specifically, the White House. As of yesterday, we were able to access all intelligence-gathering devices in the structure with the exception of those in the Oval Office, the Rose Garden, and the South Lawn, all of which were destroyed or damaged in the recent combat operations.

This morning, September 21, at 6:41 am, Moreby convened a meeting of what our earlier intelligence indicates to be his "Well of Seven". They met in the Roosevelt Room, and we were able to obtain a complete and clear audio recording of the meeting, which has been transcribed herein.

The choice of time and date – at dawn, on the day of one of the eight Pagan Sabbats known as "Mabon", the time of the Autumn equinox – is consistent with reports from the early 1800s of Thomas Moreby's meetings with his acolytes ("The Well of Seven"). As hesitant as I am to suggest some sort of occult method of reincarnation, we believe that "James Moreby" is in fact Thomas Moreby, and the ministers who took part in this morning's cabinet meeting represent some of the original Well of Seven; that is to say, their consciousness has somehow been transplanted into contemporary bodies. As you'll note from the transcription, their manner of speech and level of familiarity with modern technology and American society would indicate that they do indeed possess an early 19th-century British sensibility.

The members of The Well of Seven have evidently always been intended to serve as Moreby's ministers in a crude, largely dictatorial government. We can only guess that the earlier version of Moreby promised them this form of extended life in return for their services at his side.

In addition to Moreby, we have identified five male voices ("Jonathan", "Charles", "General Arnold", "Sir William", and "Lovett" – there is some confusion on the gender of this latter, as you'll see – and two female voices ("Cecilia" and "Dr. Fremont"). You'll also note that each discusses his or her role in Moreby's government.

TRANSCRIPTION:

Moreby: I hereby call this first meeting of the provisional NZO government to order, President James Moreby, presiding—

Cecilia [interrupting]: Are we not to call you "Thomas", then?

Moreby: Dear Lady Cecilia, I must request that you not interrupt me, especially in my capacity as President – it would appear entirely disrespectful were any outside of this group to witness it.

Cecilia: But I—

Moreby: In private, I care not how you address me, but in public situations you will refer to me henceforth as *President* Moreby. Is that quite clear, my dear?

Cecilia: Yes, Thomas.

Moreby: And please, Cecilia, in the future, I think we'd all appreciate it if you could attend our meetings in a less gruesome state. Being covered in blood is not acceptable for a minister of my government.

Cecilia: Oh. My apologies. I shall address my hygiene more carefully in the future.

Moreby: Very good. Now, I trust you all understand the importance of—

Lovett [interrupting]: Before we go any further, Mr. Moreby, I must protest the body you have assigned to me.

Moreby: Why? It is really quite handsome, I believe.

Lovett: But that is just it – the "handsome" part. It is *male*, your Lordship.

Moreby: Yes, I am aware of that, Mrs. Lovett.

Lovett: How can you call me "Mrs." when I've got this . . . well, you know, this bit in my trousers? It's just not fittin' for a lady, it ain't.

Moreby: I do apologize for the confusion. But at the time of the incarnation ritual, this body was the best one present. It's almost entirely undamaged and still quite presentable. I thought its strength might be useful to us should you decide to gift us with one of your delicious pies.

Lovett [laughs, then]: Oh, it might at that, guv'nor.

Moreby: That's *President* now – why must I continue to remind you all of that? And my dear lady, you must understand that the incarnation ritual is dependent on place, availability of suitable subjects, *and* time. The next date when I can successfully perform a ritual as difficult as an incarnation is more than a month distant, I am afraid, so I suggest you reconcile yourself to your new form for now. And I should not have to remind you why you are perhaps most suited to this gathering regardless of gender – you are the only one amongst my lieutenants who subsisted on human flesh even before the change.

Lovett: Fine, fine. I'll muddle through, I will.

Moreby: Excellent. Does anyone else have a complaint?

Sir William: Mine is not famed.

Moreby: What was that, Sir William?

Sir William: My body was no one. Lord Charles and Lady Cecilia both have famous bodies. Dr. Fremont, who was not even counted amongst our original Well of Seven, has a famous body. Mine belonged to little more than a carriage driver.

Moreby: They call them "cars" now, Sir William. And I would also point out that yours is the youngest of all those assembled here.

Cecilia: Also the most becoming.

Moreby: Cecilia, please, contain yourself. But she is right, Sir William. And you know that Dr. Fremont is here to replace the unfortunate Dr. Hawkins, whose consciousness was lost in transit. Now, may we proceed with business?

Dr. Fremont: I must protest as well. You've placed me in the body of a woman who was a laughingstock. And with good reason – using this brain is like trying to use a butter knife to perform cardiac surgery.

Moreby: Dr. Fremont . . . Clare, I can see to it that you have *no* body, if that is your preference.

[No response]

Moreby: Very well. I presume you have all had time by now to study your relative positions and the information you have been provided with. While I understand that we will all be spending many hours, if not indeed years, understanding the 21st century in which we now find ourselves, it is vitally important that we begin reconstruction of this country into the shape that I have outlined in your reports. Firstly, I would like to ask General Arnold, as our Minister of War, to report on the military situation.

Arnold: Thank you, *President* Moreby.

[A small feminine snort is heard here, presumably from Cecilia. Arnold clears his throat and continues.]

Arnold: Our armies continue to grow in number and are in control of an estimated 82% of the former United States now. In the west, Major General Harland Dawson has proven especially effective in quashing human resistance, and we should have most of Southern California under control within two or three weeks. We owe our successes in part to advanced military equipment research, which has provided our troops with bulletproof helmets based on a Germanic style designed, so I am informed, to induce primary dread in the minds of our enemies; and also to Operation Darwin, which selects the human prisoners that our military commanders will consume on the basis of military knowledge and experience.

Moreby: Well done, Minister. And on a personal note . . . I trust you are enjoying crushing the same Americans who have blackened your good name for so long, Benedict?

Arnold: I am, sir.

Moreby: Excellent. Next, I call upon our Minister of Administration – Lord Charles?

Charles: Yes?

Moreby: Your report?

Charles: I do not have a report. I do not even know what my job is supposed to be – what on earth is a "Minister of Administration"? It sounds like some sort of sodding amanuensis.

Moreby: Charles, we discussed this. Your job is second only to mine; you oversee all of the essential functions of the government – the sub-ministers, the governors, the mayors, the local ministers. They all report to *you*. And I even secured a powerful body for you – he was only two steps removed from the presidency. You have learned from his memories, have you not?

Charles: I have tried, but by God, Moreby, this man had no interest in real government. He lived only to create discord.

Moreby: Charles, did you not hear General Arnold? We have taken most of the former U.S.; soon we will hold it in its entirety, and we will need to govern it. It is *your* job to see to it that we begin to establish political order out there . . . if you are not up to the task then please inform me thusly *now*.

Charles: No, President Moreby, I shall apply myself and prepare a report for you by the morrow.

Moreby: See that you do. Dr. Fremont, what progress on securing our food supply?

Lovett: I'm starving, by God I am. I could do with a pie right now.

Moreby: I understand that dear lady, but—

Cecilia: I am, too. Why can we not have a human brought in here? We are the rulers of this world now – we should be feasting.

Moreby: You arrive at this important gathering looking like some overstuffed harlot from an abattoir, and now you demand *more*?

Cecilia: *You* are the one who conferred upon me a body with significant appetites, dear sir.

[There is the sound of a chair being pushed back.]

Moreby: Sir William, why are you rising?

Sir William: We are all hungry, Moreby. I have not eaten in days. Surely you cannot expect us to function in this state.

Moreby: Surely not.

[Other chairs are pushed back.]

Moreby: Oh, very well. This meeting is adjourned.

Charles: Oh, do not sound so dour, Thomas. I would say that we accomplished as much as the last government's typical meeting did.

Chapter Twenty-Seven

THE PRESIDENT STARED at Delancy in disbelief. "Say again?"

"We need to hit back *hard*. Now."

The rest of the group gathered around the conference room – Steele, the President, Ty and Gillespie – all gaped at Delancy in unison.

"Mr Vice President," Steele said, no longer caring if she offended the man or not, "in case you weren't paying attention . . . less than a month ago we got our ass handed to us by our enemies. We don't have the manpower right now to kick back *soft*."

Delancy leaned forward, urgently. "But see, that's the great thing about ass-whuppings: you learn from them. We know now what it is we really face."

"Yes," the President said, "we face intelligent, heavily armed opponents with a 300-year-old leader who is apparently an immortal black magician. Just exactly how did you propose we strike back against that?"

"A special team – strictly covert. Just like we did with Bin Laden: they go in under cover of night, they find Moreby and take him out, then they extract themselves. We even have an advantage SEAL Team Six didn't have: We know exactly where our target is. No guesswork."

The President appeared to consider before turning to Gillespie. "Aaron: analysis?"

Gillespie laughed. "You're kidding right? I mean, you do know it's ridiculous, don't you? We don't have any highly trained men left. We don't have the equipment. We can't get through thousands of their troops, and we're not even sure if a bullet will take out Moreby."

Delancy swung his hands wildly. "So are we supposed to just sit down here and wait for them to find us? Maybe hand all of us a cyanide capsule so we don't have to be eaten when they burst in?"

"Bob," the President said as if speaking to a very young child, "we've been working on other things."

"Like *what*?"

The President nodded at Ty, who glanced at his tablet. "We've got a CDC research team looking into medical alternatives to combat—"

"Aw, bullshit," Delancy blurted, "we all know that's a dead end. NWP would've found something by now if there was anything to find. You better have something more than that."

Silence. Delancy stared from one to the other. Only the President held his gaze, but she remained mute.

After a few seconds, Delancy rose. "Well, if you'll excuse me, I figure I might as well go finish off my will and then see how far up my ass I can stick my thumbs while I wait for some zombie to sink its teeth into my scalp." He strode out, not bothering to close the door behind him.

Ty got up and pulled it shut, and returned to his chair. The President cleared her throat lightly, said, "Aaron, I know your agency has a long relationship with the Vice President, but I have to tell you: he's on the verge of becoming a liability."

"I agree," Gillespie said.

"I want to know where he goes and what he does when he gets there, twenty-four hours a day. If you need assistance in tracking him, you have my authorization to pull help from other agencies and positions. Take Steele and Ty, if necessary; but make tracking Delancy a priority."

Steele asked, "Why? What is it that you think he might do?"

The President exhaled a long, heavy breath. "I'm not even worried about him stirring up the other hawks in Congress. At this point, I wouldn't put it past him to try to take command of what's left of our military."

"A coup?" Ty asked.

"Maybe. Anyway, let's not give him the chance."

Steele muttered, "Agreed."

The President turned her attention back to Gillespie. "What about this Kevin Moon? Any idea yet where he disappeared to?"

Gillespie shook his head. "We've been unable to ascertain where NWP might be holding him, or even if they've really got him. At this point their security is better than ours. They've got hired mercenaries and a network we can't get a toe into."

"Keep working on it."

"Right."

The meeting ended shortly thereafter. In the hallway outside, the President pulled Steele aside and spoke to her in hushed tones. "Steele, stay on Gillespie about Delancy. My gut tells me Bob's going to try something stupid, and I want one of us to be there when he does."

"Will do."

The President walked away, her shoulders sagging in fatigue, and Steele found herself thinking, *And my gut tells me we are seriously fucked no matter what Delancy does.*

MEMO

Dear Ward,

My God, I think I may have an answer. Start polishing up my Nobel Prize. After today, there may even be enough of us left to still form Nobel Prize committees.

We've been thinking about HRV all wrong, Ward. In fact, the name itself – Human Reanimation *Virus* – is a misnomer. It's not a virus any more than 3D printing is really printing; it's a convenient media term that made television news reports easier for the masses to digest.

We should not be thinking of this situation as a viral epidemic, but as a mass envenomation.

After all, the sickness occurs when a zombie *bites* a healthy human being (and yes, I know it can be spread in other ways, but let's not split hairs for the moment). In that respect, it's not much different from a rattlesnake bite. And how do we treat rattlesnake bites? Not with a vaccine, but with an *antiserum*.

And how do we create an antiserum? By finding an individual who has survived the bite, and using their blood in a passive antibody transfusion.

We have such an individual in our possession. Ward, I propose we skip the usual protocols – while there are still enough human beings left to save – and test this immediately on a real human.

I can't believe I hadn't seen this before. Zombies as rattlesnakes. Cure as antiserum, not vaccine. I know this will present certain difficulties – quickly inoculating someone in a combat zone who has been bitten, for instance – but it's our best hope at the moment.

Brewster

Chapter Twenty-Eight

KEVIN LOOKED UP from his morning coffee when a knock sounded on the door. He rose to answer it and was delighted to find his friend Garud – Dr Singh – at the door.

"Good morning," Garud said, offering up that smile that always melted an edge off Kevin.

"Hey, Garud. Come on in."

Kevin stepped back, and Garud entered the former office that now served as Kevin's studio apartment. It was a large room and had obviously once housed an important figure at NWP . . . a figure probably now long dead or living dead. Given free rein to do as he pleased with the space, Kevin had moved out a bank of filing cabinets and a huge heavy bookcase, had moved in a hospital bed and had kept the desk. Digging through an old storage garage, he'd found some warmer paints and had painted the sterile white walls, and he'd rescued some Dorothea Lange photos from another abandoned office. On the desk, he'd framed printouts of a few favourite photos from his Facebook account: him with Scotty at a Hollywood premiere. A friend's wedding. Walking on the beach with Bobby.

"Wow. Nice job." Singh took it all in, nodding slowly.

"Thanks. It's finally starting to feel slightly less like some dead guy's office."

Singh smiled wryly. "I know. I wish we had something better, but at least we're safe in here. And yours looks like a real living space. Mine still looks like my office."

"You should let me fix it up for you." Kevin immediately regretted the statement; he'd thrown in a small coy look, and hoped he hadn't offended Singh, who felt like his only real friend.

Instead Singh smiled more broadly. "I'd like that. If you wouldn't mind."

"Well, I'll try to fit it into my busy schedule."

Kevin motioned at the armchair he'd stuffed with cushions and set up near the room's sunniest window. "I was just having some coffee. I've got two mugs . . ."

"No, I've already had too much caffeine today."

A silence fell then, as Kevin wondered what this was about. Was Singh here for NWP or himself? "So . . .?"

"Oh. Well, first I just wanted to check on how you were feeling."

Kevin lifted up a pants leg and displayed his ankle, which had only a few small scabs and a faint ring-shaped bruise. "Almost back to normal. Thanks to you."

"Good. Well . . . I was wondering if you might like to join me for something I have to do today."

"Sure. What?"

"I . . ." Singh broke off.

Kevin realized he was anxious. "Garud, what is it?"

"Just . . . come with me."

They left Kevin's office/apartment, walking down a wide hallway in one of the NWP facility buildings. This one had a few other "tenants" who had also taken shelter here, but it was quiet and seemingly empty now.

As soon as they stepped outside into the cool, clear morning, walking between big two-storey brick buildings that housed labs and offices, Singh seemed to relax slightly and said, "We've had some . . . let's say, internal politics going on here this week."

"At a big pharmaceutical company? I'd think you'd be used to that by now."

Singh shrugged, bemused. "You'd think so, but . . . I'm still fairly new here. I had just started with NWP right before the zombie epidemic hit, so I didn't know exactly how the game was played at that point."

Kevin squinted at his friend. "And just how *is* the game played?"

"They hire really smart, young and very naive researchers like me, and then when we actually find something that works, somebody higher up takes the credit."

"Ahhh . . . well, I think a lot of companies work that way."

They now left the main part of the complex behind, and headed for an older concrete building – a big squat, ugly square.

"Here's the thing, Kevin: using your blood, I think I created a cure for HRV, or at least a dominant strain of it."

Kevin stopped dead in his tracks, frozen in astonishment. It took Singh a few seconds to realize Kevin was no longer at his side; he stopped and looked back.

All Kevin could say was, "What?"

Singh answered, "I've been saying for months that we were all mistaken in approaching this thing as a virus. Just because it spreads quickly doesn't really mean it's a viral infection – it's actually more like what happens when you get bitten by a venomous animal. Have you ever seen what the bite of a brown recluse spider does? It causes severe necrosis – dead tissue."

"Like zombies."

"Yes," Singh said, nodding. "And if we were looking at something more akin to venom than virus, then we needed an agent from which to produce antiserum. That agent is *you*."

"Because I'm immune."

"Essentially. And I have indeed now produced what I believe is an effective antiserum, thanks to you. But there are others here at NWP who want to take over the project. It may be petty on my part, but . . . I believe I deserve the credit."

The look on Singh's face – pride, desperation, anger – made Kevin want to take his friend's hands in his, to let him know he wasn't alone . . . but he still didn't know Singh well enough yet. He thought Singh might be gay, but he hadn't simply asked. Instead, he said, "It's not petty. Garud, if you've got – what, a cure for HRV? – you deserve everything."

Singh locked on to Kevin's eyes for a moment, with gratitude, but after a few seconds he looked away. "There's just one thing: it hasn't been tested yet. We don't have time to do this right, and I'm afraid if I wait any longer that they'll just take the whole thing away from me. That's why I asked you to come with me today: I want to test it. Now. On myself. And frankly . . . you're the only one here I can trust."

Warmth exploded throughout Kevin, and he actually stammered. "I . . . I'm really . . . you know whatever you need, just tell me how I can help."

Without another word, Singh turned and walked to the concrete block building.

As he stepped through the glass doors into the sterile interior, Kevin realized what this place reminded him of – a veterinary clinic. The air was cool and he heard the hum of air-conditioning units, but there was a slight sour smell barely masked by cleaning agents: the smell of death. There were living dead here.

They paused before a locked metal door, and Singh turned to address Kevin. "I promise you, you'll be in no danger today. We will be in the proximity of infected subjects, but they have been restrained."

"I don't understand, Garud, what . . .?"

Singh swiped a card key through an electronic lock. There was a buzz, and he pulled the door open.

The stench that hit Kevin was stronger here. He was facing a hallway lined with heavy doors. Each door had a small window inset.

He heard zombies moaning behind several of the doors.

Garud reached into a pocket of his white lab coat and removed a capped hypodermic needle, which he extended to Kevin, who took it gingerly. "This is the antiserum. I'd like you to hang on to it."

"Why? You're the doctor."

"Today," Singh said, removing the lab coat to reveal that he wore a short-sleeved polo shirt beneath, "I'm also the test subject."

Kevin abruptly put it all together. He put the syringe down carefully on the desk where Garud had folded his lab coat. "Oh no. No, no, no. Don't do this. Surely there's somebody else—"

"Even if there was, I couldn't ask them to do it." Singh moved to the closest door and looked in through the small window.

Kevin moved up next to him and saw a zombie on the other side. The cell was small, plain, not even a built-in bunk or toilet. The zombie was missing both arms (Kevin realized, with a disgust that brought an actual physical wave of nausea with it, that the thing's arms hadn't been chewed off, but looked to have been neatly sawn away), and a metal collar around its neck was attached to a chain that connected it to a wall. It had once been a middle-aged man who still wore the traces of a dark suit, and Kevin wondered what position he'd once held at NWP.

As it saw them, the zombie snarled and lunged, but it could only jerk forward a few inches as the chain pulled taut. Pink froth flew from its lips, and its red-rimmed eyes burned with the most primitive and overwhelming hunger imaginable.

Singh slid his security card through a slot next to the door. The door popped open.

"Garud, I'm not a doctor, I don't even know how to administer a shot."

"You don't have to – I'll do that. I need you here to restrain me after the shot."

Kevin's jaw dropped. "What? Why?"

"In case . . . it doesn't work."

There was no more room for argument. Kevin watched in mute horror as Garud stepped into the room with the zombie, whose moans ramped up to near-screams now, its armless body twisting in vain. He stepped closer – one step, two, three – until he was within two feet of the thing's gnashing jaws. Then, taking a deep breath, Singh raised his left arm and extended it to the zombie.

Its teeth snapped. Singh flinched and jumped back, clenching his fists in frustration. "Fuck!"

"Garud, there's got to be another way to do this . . ."

Kevin's words seemed to galvanize Garud, who lifted his head, tightened his fist, and offered his bare forearm.

The zombie's mouth clamped shut around the meaty part of the arm. Singh gasped as teeth penetrated his skin. He tried to pull away, but the zombie hung on.

Before Kevin could stop himself, he leapt into the room and drove a fist straight into the zombie's temple. The monster was stunned, and its jaws involuntarily popped open in shock. Kevin jerked his dazed friend back and propelled him from the room.

The toothmarks in Singh's arm were deep and gushing blood, but at least no flesh or tissue had been torn away.

Panting in pain, Singh managed, "Under the desk . . . medical kit."

Kevin sat Singh down in an ancient rolling desk chair, and found a large first-aid case under the desk. Sweat was popping out on Singh's face and he was pale, but he was able to work with Kevin on cleaning and dressing his arm. Once they had bandages in place and the bleeding seemed to be slowing, Singh nodded at the syringe. "Now," was all he said.

Kevin handed him the hypo. Singh removed the cap and cleared the needle of bubbles, squirting a small amount of liquid into the air. His hand was shaking, and Kevin put both of his around Singh's, guiding the needle-point to Singh's left bicep. Together, they managed to complete the injection, and then Singh dropped the empty hypo and fell back into the chair. "Thank you, Kevin. I'm not sure I could have done that without you."

Kneeling down before his friend, looking up into his stricken face, Kevin asked, "Now what?"

"Now I want you to lock me in one of these cells and wait."

Kevin was about to respond when the sound of the security door buzzing open interrupted him. He looked up to see three men enter: a security guard, a doctor in a white lab coat and a perfectly groomed man in a business suit. "Thank you for your service, Mr Moon," the latter said, "we'll take it from here."

Singh groaned, and Kevin wasn't sure if it was from the pain of the bite or the arrival of the three men. As he watched, the doctor checked the dressings on the wound and examined Singh while the guard, a tattooed bull of a man, stood over them.

"Who are you?" Kevin directed the question to the suited man, who looked vaguely familiar.

"I work with New World Pharmaceuticals. My name is Landen Jones. Now, perhaps you'd care to join me for coffee and we can chat about a few things . . .?"

Jones slid his card key through the slot beside the security door and then gestured Kevin out. Kevin was reluctant to leave Singh, but the beefy security guard eyed him in a way that left him no possibility of staying.

Kevin left his friend, wondering which one of them was moving into greater danger.

CENTRAL INTELLIGENCE AGENCY

CONFIDENTIAL REPORT ON V.P. BOB DELANCY

Prepared by Aaron Gillespie, Director, C.I.A.

The activities of Bob Delancy continue to present a growing concern. Delancy has been using a satellite phone to make a number of calls recently. Although we are unable to trace these calls, we do know from other sources that at least one of the calls was to Colonel Douglas Schrader, commander of the Tobyhanna Army Depot. We can find no previous history of Delancy and Schrader, so it seems unlikely that this was a casual personal call. We believe it is possible that Delancy is acquainting himself with commanders of a number of military bases, camps, and depots, and we are of the opinion that surveillance of Delancy should not only continue, but be made a top priority.

Chapter Twenty-Nine

STEELE, TY AND the President all looked up from Ty's stock inventory report when the office door burst open and Delancy stood there, his already florid features redder than usual. "We need to talk," he said looking pointedly at the President.

Steele rose, slowly; Delancy radiated aggression, and she wanted to make herself as imposing as possible in return. The President, however, sighed and gestured at a chair. "Have a seat, Bob."

Glancing at Steele and Ty before returning his gaze to the President, Delancy said, "Alone."

"Whatever you have to say can be said in front of everyone here."

Delancy huffed briefly, then said, "You vetoed S. 110."

The President peered at Delancy with barely disguised contempt. "You mean the immigration bill? Of course I vetoed it. It was a joke."

"My party didn't think it was a joke."

"Bob, in case you and your party haven't noticed, we don't have a problem right now with immigration. Or with borders that need to be protected. In fact, I'm not even sure we still have borders. That bill wanted to allocate resources we don't have to something that may not exist and which is certainly not a problem. If your party wants to pass legislation, might I suggest they look at the shit we're in up to our necks right now?"

Delancy blinked once, in surprise, before saying, "Maybe we're planning for the future. Maybe we don't believe we won't recover from this. Maybe we believe in the United States of America."

Steele couldn't restrain a laugh. "You've got to be kidding me."

Delancy shot her a quick, hooded look, but the President intervened, gesturing to the tablet computer screen on her desk. "See this? This is what we were working on when you came in. It's an inventory of our food stocks. Down here in the bunker system, we're in pretty good shape – with rationing, we can hold out for two years. But we've got fighters topside who are starving, so we're trying to figure out how much of our supplies we can spare. Are you willing to risk giving up a few meals so our Armed Forces can keep eating? Because we are. That's the reality, not these nonsense bills about immigration and tax reform and drug enforcement."

The Vice President stared for a few seconds, as if weighing what he'd just heard. Finally, he said, "You know, that's funny, because I've been talking to a few of our field commanders and I'm not hearing anything about a problem with food. In fact, the men and women I've spoken to all have more food than action."

"What does that mean?"

Delancy ignored the question and turned to Ty. "Mr Ward, you follow the chatter around here. Have you heard rumours of impeachment proceedings?"

Ty shrugged. "Rumours, yes, but—"

The President cut him off, her own temper flaring now. "Impeachment? On what grounds?"

Delancy, seeing that he'd managed to anger her, smiled slightly. "Does it matter?"

"It does if you want to call it 'impeachment' and not a 'coup'. It matters if you want to maintain the illusion that this is a democracy and not a mob."

"Well, here's a news flash, Madame President," Delancy said, rising, "however many of the American people are left out there, don't think of this as either a democracy or a mob. I'd say the best comparison might be a really boring movie, maybe one of those French things where you have to read subtitles and you realize after a while that all that reading isn't making this movie any better. Our people want – no, *need* – action. If you don't have the balls to give it to them, somebody else will."

Delancy left, doing his best to slam the door on the way out.

There was silence for a moment following his departure, and the President said, "I need to know exactly who he's been talking to on that phone. I don't care what it takes – we have to know who he's calling and what's being said. If any of our military leaders plan on joining him in a takeover, I don't want to find out when they've got us up against a wall with guns to our heads."

A few short weeks ago, Steele would have thought the President was overreacting; but today she said, "I agree."

Ty made notes on his tablet and asked, "Do we know which side Gillespie would fall on?"

Steele shrugged. "I don't think he's ever quite forgiven Delancy for what happened with Marissa Cheung. We already know he's been watching Delancy pretty closely anyway. I think he's okay."

The President said, "Can you check into that, Steele? I'm not quite as confident as you are."

Nodding, Steele said, "Okay. I'll pay Aaron a visit later today."

"Good. And if we have to pull people from some other project to keep tabs on Delancy, do it."

Ty stabbed a finger at his tablet and said, "Yes, ma'am. Are we done here?"

"I think so."

Steele and Ty started to leave, but the President stopped them at the door. "Oh, and I'm sure you both know this, but: I'm not worried about us if Delancy manages to take over. I'm worried about the fact that a government further fractured and weakened by that sort of infighting will stand even less chance to make real progress than we do."

Ty answered, "Oh, we get that. We know you're the best shot."

Steele remained silent. As she turned to go, she couldn't shake a feeling of impending doom.

We can face the walking dead and apocalypse, but if we start turning on each other, it's all over.

STAY STRONG
HELP IS COMING!

You are receiving these food rations from your United States Government because we want you to know that we are STILL HERE, working for YOU.

In addition to food and water, in coming weeks we will supply you with weapons, ammunition, clothing, fuel, medicines, batteries, and tablet computers. You will receive instructions on how to connect to our network, so we can communicate directly with you over safe (encrypted), clear channels.

Most importantly, we want to assure you that we have research teams of the best doctors in the world finding ways to halt the spread of HRV. We believe we may soon have a vaccine. Rest assured that you will receive distribution of any new drugs as soon as they are available.

In the meantime – fight on! We know many of you are exhausted and see no end to the conflict, but do NOT give up hope. We WILL beat HRV. We WILL re-establish the United States of America. Be brave, be resolute, and together we will WIN.

Chapter Thirty

FOR EIGHT DAYS, Kevin was not allowed to see Singh.

On the first day after the bite and the injection, Kevin had ventured over to the squat concrete block building and had tried the outer door, but it was locked. He sought out Landen Jones, who seemed to be in charge throughout the NWP complex. Jones agreed to see him in his office.

"What can I do for you, Mr Moon?"

"I want to see Dr Singh."

"I'm afraid that's impossible."

"Why?"

Jones' smile and poise never flickered, and Kevin was seized with an irrational urge to slap the man until his expression changed. "Dr Singh is under quarantine right now. You were there when he was bitten, so surely you understand the need to keep him secured until we know if the antiserum worked or not."

"Secured, yes . . . but why does that mean I can't see him?"

"If he survives, you'll be allowed to see him."

"When will that be?"

Jones laughed. "Really, Mr Moon, what's with the urgency? It's not as if you still have any medical condition he needs to oversee."

Fresh anger flared in Kevin. "He's my friend, okay? Got any of those yourself?"

Jones peered at Kevin, scrutinizing him. "Are you sure he's just a friend?"

"What does that mean?"

"That means, Mr Moon," Jones said, waving a hand at his desktop computer, "that I've read all of your files. I know that you're a Korean from

Los Angeles, that your mother's name is Jung-ah but her American friends call her June, that you got poor grades in chemistry and math but did well in history, that your favourite drink is a blended margarita, and that you're gay."

Kevin sat stunned for a moment before asking, "How did . . . how did you know all that?"

"The average citizen would probably be surprised if they found out what their government really knows about them."

"So you got my government file?"

Jones spread his arms wide. "Mr Moon, really – I *am* the Surgeon General."

Kevin remembered then where he'd seen Jones: in the early days of the outbreak, there'd been a few photos of him posing with Ames Parker, who was then in charge. He'd heard gossip that Parker had died during a failed attempt to take back the White House, and he was sorry – he'd always thought the General seemed like a decent man. Jones, on the other hand . . . Kevin had always found his square-jawed grin and styled hair too perfect to be likeable. Now he knew he'd been right.

"Okay," Kevin said, rising and turning to go.

"Mr Moon—"

Kevin turned back, and Jones continued. "I'm truly sorry, but we simply can't allow you in to see Dr Singh at this time."

"Sure. Whatever."

Kevin left.

That night he waited until late, when work at the facility had ceased, and he strolled down a hallway lined with offices that were no longer in use. The first few he went into were empty; the third one he tried still had the previous tenant's belongings in place, including a white lab coat with an ID card clipped to it. Kevin grabbed the card and left, heading for the building where Singh was being held.

The card admitted him through the outer door, and he made his way quickly past the first block of cells, down the central hallway to the second security door. He slid the pass card through the slot, the door buzzed, he pushed it open – and faced the muscular, tattooed security guard who'd come in with Jones. The man held a nightstick in one hand and said nothing, just stared at Kevin, making his warning clear without words.

"C'mon, I just want to see Singh," Kevin said, knowing it would do nothing.

"You can use your stolen card to find your way out."

Kevin tried to peer past him. He even shouted, "Singh—!"

The door closed in his face. For a second he imagined sliding the card through the security slot again, reminding the guard that his blood was valuable and trying to push past the man . . . but he doubted that the guard would hold his blood in high esteem. He'd be more likely to thoughtlessly spill it.

Instead he turned and stalked out. He went back to his office-cum-apartment and stashed the stolen card in the desk. He'd try again tomorrow, during the day. Maybe a different guard might be easier to reason with. Or fight.

None of the guards let him in. In fact, by the third day the stolen card key no longer worked on the outer door.

Kevin paid another visit to Landen Jones. He caught up with him in the main hospital area, as Jones was walking and talking to a doctor. "Jones –!"

Jones stopped, and without glancing back said to his companion, "Will you excuse me a moment?" He walked back to Kevin, smiling as always. "Yes, Mr Moon?"

"At least tell me how Singh's doing. You can do that much, can't you?"

"You know, after reading Dr Singh's file, I'm still not sure if he's straight or gay. The Indians can be somewhat mysterious that way, don't you think?"

"Stop fucking around and be a human being for once in your pompous life."

Jones almost blinked, the tiniest of cracks revealed in his exterior. His smile fell, and he leaned forward and whispered, "It's too soon to tell. Now, if you come near me again, I'll have you locked into your room."

With that, Jones strode off.

The next morning, Kevin's door was locked. He hadn't even realized it was possible to lock it from the outside. At least they weren't consigning him to one of those featureless cells in the concrete building.

The windows didn't open, and he considered busting one out to escape, but the idea of possibly cutting himself on glass just so he could flee into the waiting jaws of zombies – who might not infect him but could still devour him – didn't appeal. So instead he waited.

In the evening they brought him dinner. There was a knock on the door, followed by the sound of locks being drawn back. The door opened to reveal a frightened-looking young nurse. Kevin remembered her name from when he'd been a patient; she'd been kind to him. "Hi, Rebekah."

The burly, tattooed guard – who's name Kevin had been told was Joker – was behind her.

She passed Kevin a tray that held several covered dishes and two bottles of water. She didn't speak, or look at him. He took the tray from her. "Thank you."

"I . . ." Whatever she'd been about to say trailed off as she remembered the man standing behind her, glowering. Instead she turned and strode off. The door was closed and locked again.

This went on for three days. Kevin was brought breakfast, lunch and dinner. It was always Rebekah and Joker. Neither of them spoke. By the second day, Kevin didn't, either; he simply took his tray of food in silence. In the evenings, Rebekah collected all the empty dishes and trays.

On the fourth day, Rebekah arrived without Joker.

"Where's the gorilla?" Kevin asked, looking behind her.

"He got called off to handle something else." Rebekah, anxious, set down the tray and turned to go.

"*Hey*—!" Kevin called after her. She hesitated in the doorway, and Kevin said, "I'm not going to try to escape. There's nowhere to go, anyway."

She relaxed and turned to look back at him. "That's good."

"Do you have to rush right off? Could we just . . . you know, talk for a few minutes? It gets kind of boring in here alone."

Rebekah offered a half-smile. "Sure. I guess I could spare some time."

They ended up talking for an hour. Rebekah told Kevin about how she'd been fresh out of nursing school when NWP had hired her to work in their experimental facility two years ago, and how the pay had been great but she had seen terrible things she couldn't talk about, and how she still held on to her Catholic beliefs and missed her parents and sisters and her old church. She'd listened with interest to Kevin's account of his trip from Los Angeles, she was sorry to hear of the fate of Bobby, and she was horrified by Kevin's brief description of the treatment he'd received from the two soldiers. "Monsters," she said.

"Well, I probably owe my life to you," Kevin said.

"Thanks, but it was really Dr Singh. He's amazing."

"Rebekah," Kevin asked, nervously, "do you know if he's okay?"

She shrugged. "I've heard he is, but I haven't seen him in nearly two weeks. I hope so."

When she left, Kevin thanked her for being his friend. She smiled and nodded.

The next day, a knock was followed by the appearance of not Rebekah, but Landen Jones and Joker. "Good morning, Mr Moon," Jones said, with false amiability. "I trust your short . . . shall we call it an enforced vacation . . . has been satisfactory?"

"Sure. Next time I want cable TV, too, though."

"Don't we all. God, I used to love HBO. Well, on to the matter at hand today: Would you like to see Dr Singh now?"

Kevin was jolted by both hope and dread. "Is he alive?"

"Oh yes, he is. All the tests indicate that the antiserum worked. Shall we?" Jones gestured out of the office. Behind him, Joker flexed his arms, causing the ink marks (barbed wire, a death's head in a rose) to ripple.

Left with little choice, Kevin shrugged and exited the office.

They walked down the hall to the end of his building and stepped outside. The early October weather had turned cold, colder than Kevin had expected (or was used to, being a Californian), and he shivered and clutched at himself. Then, to his surprise, they turned left and entered the building that housed the facility's hospital rooms.

"This way," Jones said, obviously relishing Kevin's confusion.

They passed the room where Kevin had recovered and stopped at one a few doors down.

It was locked.

Jones slid his key through a reader, and the door buzzed open. Jones entered first, followed by Kevin and Joker.

Kevin took one step into the room – and froze, staring in disbelief.

Singh was on the room's only bed, and although he was covered by a thin sheet Kevin could see that his hands and feet were strapped to the bed's rails. There were wires attached to his chest, and multiple intravenous needles fed in and out of his arms. One tube was bright red, and draining into a pouch.

They were collecting Singh's blood, a lot of it, judging by the greyish tone of his normally richly hued brown skin; and they were collecting the blood against his will.

Singh was drowsy, but he did hear the visitors enter, and he smiled. "Kevin . . ."

Kevin started forward, but Joker interposed himself, and Kevin turned furiously on Jones. "What the hell is this?"

"Well, Mr Moon, here's the deal: the antiserum created from your blood successfully fought off the HRV infection Dr Singh sustained after receiving the bite. We have now determined that Dr Singh's blood can be used to create antiserum, just as yours can."

"But why is he strapped down? You're killing him—"

"No, no, we aren't, of course not. He's of no use dead. Neither are you."

Before Kevin could react, Joker grabbed his arms from behind. He started to cry out, to struggle, then he felt something cool pressed against his neck. The last thing he saw was Singh's face, looking stricken and desperate.

CENTRAL INTELLIGENCE AGENCY

CONFIDENTIAL REPORT ON V.P. BOB DELANCY
Prepared by Aaron Gillespie, Director, C.I.A.

Pursuant to my earlier report on the activities of Bob Delancy, I believe it is possible that our Vice President is attempting to parlez with the enemy, i.e. New Zombie Order President James "Thomas" Moreby.

Although I have been unable to trace calls made by Delancy on a satellite phone, I do have two pieces of evidence which support this:

On Tuesday evening, at approximately 11:00 pm, Delancy took the satellite phone to an unused office, which he obviously believed to be clean. Fortunately for us, we have installed microphones in all unused offices now, and we were able to obtain a clear recording of Delancy's side of this conversation, which ran as follows:

DELANCY: Yes, it's Delancy. You know that proposition we discussed earlier? I'd like to act on it, so I need to know where we start . . . I understand, but I . . . that's going to be difficult for me, and I . . . no, of course it's not that I don't trust you – we're going to be partners in this enterprise, after all – but I do have concerns about some of the others around you, and I don't think I'm asking too much to have my safety guaranteed . . . well, let's both think about it, then, and I'll contact you again tomorrow.

The following day, Wednesday at 2:30 pm, we recorded a call that Moreby picked up in the Roosevelt Room in the White House, which we still have undiscovered transmitters in. The following is a record of Moreby's side of that conversation.

MOREBY: President Moreby . . . yes, hello, Bob . . . oh, that is good news, and I certainly think it is the correct decision for both our sides. So when should we expect you? . . . Are you sure you cannot make it sooner? . . . No, I quite understand . . . Thank you . . . yes, I look forward to seeing you, then.

In light of these two conversations, I think we must consider that Delancy is attempting to create an alliance with Moreby, to further his own ambitions.

I'd also like to suggest that we seriously consider the possibility that Delancy is possessed. While I know this might sound preposterous at first, please consider that we now accept the existence of zombies (creatures returned from the dead to consume human flesh), black magic (since we believe that Moreby created the virus which has spread the occult infestation), and reincarnation (Moreby's "Well of Seven"). Given that, we should also consider the existence of other supernatural entities as well, which could include ghosts, vampires, or demonic forces.

Delancy was always a friend of this office and a solid American in the past, but his recent behavior suggests a turnabout so severe that it might be attributable to the intercession of unearthly powers. If this is the case, perhaps we can exorcize Delancy and restore him to his former self. I will begin investigating this immediately.

Chapter Thirty-One

STEELE TOOK A deep breath, and pressed the buzzer set into the wall below the hand-written sign that read CIA DIRECTOR AARON GILLESPIE. After a few seconds, the intercom sounded.

"Yes?" asked Gillespie's voice.

"Aaron, it's Steele. Can you buzz me in?"

"How do I know you're really Steele?"

Steele made a fist and let her head droop. After reading Gillespie's last report, the President had immediately ordered Steele to pay a visit on Gillespie and assess his mental state. Steele had never completely liked or trusted the man, but she would never have believed him to be the type who would develop mental illness . . . until now.

"We exchanged emails an hour ago. You agreed to see me. You do remember that, don't you?"

"Jesus, Steele, of course I remember." The door buzzed open and Steele entered.

When she'd last been in the large open room with multiple workstations that Gillespie had claimed for the CIA, it'd been an orderly space with bulletin boards on the walls displaying printouts and photos, and Gillespie's glassed-in office at the other end a hive of electronic activity with numerous monitors and computers.

Now, however, it was anything but orderly. The walls were covered in layers of printouts and copies of pages from old files; they were taped over each other without apparent reason, and when Steele flipped a few pages up, she realized they were at least six sheets deep in places. Parts of the prints were circled or highlighted; a few had large exclamation marks in the margins.

Every story on view was either about Thomas Moreby and the HRV epidemic, or paranormal events from the past. As Steele walked slowly along the walls, taking it all in, she saw reports and articles on hauntings, lake monsters, Mothman, telekinesis, clairvoyance, chupacabras, vampires, Bigfoot, strange sounds heard around the world, the "Slender Man", shapeshifters, UFOs and a race of serpent people living beneath the streets of downtown LA. In some cases large black arrows had been drawn between articles, linking a supposed ghost sighting in Japan to a mysterious death in a small town in Alberta, Canada; articles on time travel were allied with an old cemetery in London, England; cattle mutilations in Wyoming were connected to crop circles in rural France.

And on one wall, cases of possession surrounded printouts on Bob Delancy.

"So, do you get it, Steele?"

Steele almost jumped – she'd been so intent on the lunatic collage surrounding her that she'd forgotten about its maker. "No, I don't. Explain it for me."

"It starts here . . ." Gillespie jogged to a far corner of the room, lifted pages and gestured at an article that looked like a copy of a newspaper page. "This is when crews in London excavating an old church came upon Moreby instead. They released him, and – and—" Gillespie broke off, frowning. After a few seconds, he spun to the right, made his way along the wall, and stopped at a stack, sorting through the taped pages. "Or maybe it really starts here, in 1803, when we have accounts of Moreby and The Well of Seven performing a ritual to call forth the demon Anarchon—" Again, Gillespie stopped abruptly, but this time his eyes went wide in revelation. "Holy shit – of course! Anarchon could be who's possessing Delancy . . . Jesus, it was so obvious, how did I miss it before?" Gillespie began tearing down pages, running them to the area on Delancy and taping them there.

"Aaron . . ." Steele barely knew where to start. "When did you start working on all . . . *this*?" She waved a hand around the room.

"Maybe two weeks ago. I think I've made excellent progress, don't you?"

"How long has it been since you've slept?"

Gillespie turned to her with a shaky grin. "Sleep? We don't have time for that any more, Steele. None of us do."

Curious, Steele walked past him. Gillespie was so intent on drawing marks around parts of the newly rearranged Delancy wall that he ignored her as she entered his office.

There was a half-full vial of pills on the desk. Steele raised it to read the label: "Dexedrine."

She put the container down and glanced into the trash can by the side of the desk; it was nearly full of empty vials. She didn't need to pick them up to know: their intelligence chief had been doing massive amounts of amphetamines for at least two weeks, probably more, and was suffering psychosis as a result.

Steele left the office and returned to Gillespie, who finished drawing symbols with a Sharpie and stepped back to examine his work. "This all makes sense: Moreby enacts a ritual to allow Anarchon to possess Delancy, thereby gaining entrance to our facility, and . . . oh my God, what if our attempt to retake Washington was nothing but a giant sacrifice to Anarchon? Dear God, Steele, what if we were set up all along?"

"Aaron, where did you get all the Dexedrine?"

"Our medical stocks down here are quite good, you know. There's still plenty left."

"Do you think you should be taking this much of it?"

Gillespie turned his red eyes on her, and the force of his fear and paranoia was almost a physical sensation, like a rat sinking teeth into an exposed ankle. "Steele, we should *all* be taking this much of it. Every one of us who are left, who are still human. We can only beat them if we *think* our way out, and we can only keep thinking if we stop sleeping. *They* don't sleep, you know, and it's a luxury we can no longer afford. And before you tell me I've taken too much Dex and I'm not thinking straight, let me ask you: Is anyone else down here coming up with anything better?"

Steele held his gaze for a few seconds, and asked, "Just answer me one thing, Aaron: were those transcriptions of Moreby's and Delancy's phone conversations accurate?"

"I swear they were. Think whatever else you will, but I will never falsify evidence like that."

Steele nodded. "That's all I need to know for now, Aaron. Thank you for your time."

She turned and left. When she reached the hallway and heard the door close behind her, she exhaled and realized she'd been holding her breath until she'd escaped the madman's room

18:58

[A jeep is seen approaching the gate. It pulls to a stop before the guard booth, and a uniformed soldier steps out. A single man is seen in the jeep; he hands an ID to the guard, who eyes it and almost does a double-take.]

GUARD: Good evening, Mr. Vice President.
DELANCY: 'Evening, soldier.
GUARD: What can I do for you, sir?
DELANCY: You can open the gate. I've got urgent business to attend to.

[The guard peers into the jeep, then returns his attention to Delancy.]

GUARD: Sir, you don't have anyone with you, not even Secret Service . . .
DELANCY [laughs harshly, then]: Don't get me started on the Secret Service. And it's all right, soldier I'm meeting extremely secure forces just a short distance from here.

[The guard glances out past the gate; strong spotlights are trained on the area just outside and reveal that the exterior perimeter is clear, as is the road leading away from the field.]

GUARD: Are you sure, sir? We keep the immediate area clear, but you won't go very far before there'll be swarms of them . . .
DELANCY: Soldier, don't make me bring the word "insubordination" into this. Open the goddamn gate now.
GUARD [salutes]: Yes, sir!

[The guard hits a button, and the heavy chain-link fence topped with barbed wire that serves as Bolling's main gate begins to roll back; the soldier steps out of the booth and stands ready with a rifle to take out any of the infected who might appear. Delancy waits until the opening is barely wide enough for his jeep, then guns the engine and roars out into the night. The soldier reverses the gate controls, stands his ground until it is again secure, then returns to the guard booth where he writes the encounter down in a log, then picks up a phone.]

Chapter Thirty-Two

THE PRESIDENT PUSHED the tablet away in disgust. "Jesus Christ . . . this happened last night! Why are we just now hearing about this?"

Ty and Steele exchanged a look, and then Steele said, "It's my fault, ma'am. Colonel Marcus from Bolling did contact us promptly last night, but unfortunately . . . his message went to Aaron Gillespie. I've now corrected the mistake, and all incoming communications for the CIA or Gillespie will go through me."

"Has Gillespie officially been relieved yet?"

"Not officially, no. There's no real point in doing that until we can find a replacement, is there?"

The President looked from Steele to Ty. "Get to work on that. If we have to fly someone across the country, Ty, I want somebody here overseeing intelligence in a week. It's too much to ask us to take it on – we're already stretched so thin we're making mistakes. We can't afford too many more."

"On it." Ty began tapping out notes on his computer.

Rising and pacing, the President said, "So, Delancy . . . we think he met with Moreby last night, is that correct?"

Steele answered, "Yes. I think we can assume that part of Gillespie's report was accurate."

"Is Bolling on security alert now?"

"Yes. The drones are flying surveillance, but they're all ready with Hellfires in case Delancy shows up at the head of Moreby's army. The Bolling perimeter is in good shape."

The President paced a few more steps. "Opinion, Steele: would Delancy really try to sell us out to Moreby?"

Steele thought it over . . . for about one second. "Truthfully, ma'am . . . absolutely I believe he would. If Delancy thought he could gain power by allying himself with a housefly, he'd do it."

"I agree. I guess we wait, then."

So they waited.

From: Landen Jones <landenjones@nwpharm.com>
To: NWP Board of Directors <BCC>
Sent: MON, Nov 04, 8:01 PM
Subject: The solution to Human Reanimation Virus

Gentlemen and Ladies: I am very pleased to inform you that my team has finally been successful in engineering an antiserum that combats HRV. We realized a short time ago that our search for a vaccine would ultimately prove fruitless, and so I directed my people to consider other alternatives. Working from the notion that a zombie bite might be treated in the same fashion that a snake bite is, we created an antiserum that counteracts HRV completely, and we are ready to begin producing the antiserum. Due to limited resources, production will necessarily be slow at first, but we expect it to increase quickly.

I'd like to suggest now how we might best serve our species while maximizing NWP's position, and I'm going to make a rather radical proposal: given the country's current wartime situation, with two governments (the United States of America and the so-called New Zombie Order) both claiming control and resources either split between the two or simply gone altogether, I believe it's time for NWP to rethink its profit-making strategies. Put quite frankly, we now live in a world where the once-almighty dollar is essentially worthless. I believe the new system may rely not on the gold standard, but on the power standard.

What I am suggesting is this: our HRV antiserum will shortly be the most powerful bargaining chip in the world. I suggest we offer it to neither the U.S. government nor Moreby's nation, but distribute the drug ourselves in exchange for signed loyalty agreements. In other words: We will create our own country. Our citizens will be protected from HRV, and they in turn will protect us and our interests. As we solidify and expand, we will continue to arm and feed our people, further ensuring that they feel comfortable as citizens of New World Pharmaceuticals. We will create history's first true corpocracy, and we will spread our influence and product around the globe.

If any of you are hesitant to consider this bold plan, I'm currently working on a more complete proposal that will include realistic timelines, production estimates, and potential profits.

Ladies and gentlemen, you will no longer be merely Directors of a corporation; under my plan, you will be Rulers of a world.

Chapter Thirty-Three

KEVIN HAD SPENT nearly four weeks strapped to the bed.

Granted, they allowed him – under Joker's baleful eye – to get up twice a day and walk the length of a corridor. Rebekah took expert care of him; he was fed and bathed and his bed pan was changed promptly; and he was allowed to choose the movies he could watch on the room's flat-screen television. But as long as Joker was present, he and Rebekah almost never spoke . . . and Joker was *always* present.

Kevin also spent two hours a day watching his blood drain away.

They pumped him full of supplements, but he felt his energy and strength diminishing with his blood. Each day it was a little harder to get out of the bed and walk, even a short distance. They kept assuring him they wouldn't drain him, that soon he'd be freed, and he'd be a wealthy, protected citizen under the upstart government of New World Pharmaceuticals; but Kevin also guessed they'd gleefully bleed his life away for whatever their version of a buck would be, and feel no shame or guilt whatsoever.

He also knew he wasn't alone. Sometime during the first week, he'd heard a scream of agony from a room near his.

The scream had belonged to Singh.

Later on, he'd broken the silence and asked Rebekah what had made Singh scream like that. "Oh," she told him, not meeting his eyes, "he's really okay. It was just . . . well, one of the other nurses missed the vein."

In the background, Joker stood by, mute, watching, listening.

Then there was the day Rebekah had arrived with a new patch sewn on the breast of her white nurse's uniform. The patch had the letters NWP framed by the Earth seen from space, with the motto A NEW WORLD FOR ALL scrawled across the bottom.

"What's that?" Kevin had asked.

The young nurse glanced at the patch and said, "I'm not sure, but we all have to wear them now, even the doctors."

Rebekah might not have been sure, but Kevin was when he took his afternoon walk, and saw the new flag placed behind the nurse's station. It was a larger version of the patch, and left no doubt in his mind: New World Pharmaceuticals was trying to take over the country – or maybe the entire planet. What he didn't know was whether they'd already succeeded or not.

Then one day, as Kevin got out of bed in the morning, the world darkened and spun around him, and only the sure hands of Rebekah kept him from collapsing. She lowered the bed rail and got him seated on the edge of the bed.

"I'm getting so weak," Kevin said, waiting for his vision to clear.

"Maybe we should get you up three times a day."

The world around Kevin sharpened and he saw Joker standing six feet away. "Rebekah . . . they're going to kill me, you know."

Rebekah shot one nervous glance at Joker and said, too loudly, "No one's going to kill you, Mr Moon. You're in good hands here. The *best* hands."

But something in her look told Kevin she knew it wasn't true.

Three nights later, Kevin was re-watching *Avatar* – a movie he didn't especially like, but had seen fewer times than the other movies that were available via NWP's own streaming media – when the door buzzed open and Rebekah entered pushing an empty wheelchair.

Joker was noticeably not with her.

Kevin muted the sound and sat up straighter, eyeing her curiously.

"So you had a little accident in the bed, Mr Moon? Well, let's get you cleaned up."

"I didn't—" Kevin started to say, but her fierce look cut him off.

She took the remote and unmuted the sound, then turned up the volume. Kevin let her pull him forward, and she whispered, "Play along. You're leaving tonight." Her eyes shot briefly towards a corner of the room, and Kevin realized that what he'd always taken to be a smoke alarm was probably a camera.

No wonder she'd never spoken freely here.

"Yeah, I'm really sorry. I just kind of lost control . . ."

"Here, let's get you into the wheelchair until I can get this cleaned up." Kevin took a seat in the chair, and Rebekah positioned herself between him and the camera. She deftly unplugged his various tubes and sensors, and leaned forward again to whisper, "There's a bag with your clothes under the chair." She pretended to strap his wrists to the chair arms, but she left the straps so loose he could easily pull free. She stepped away and said loudly, "I'm going to have to push you out of the room while I strip the bed. Don't try to get up, Mr Moon – you're strapped to the chair for your own safety."

"I'll be good, I promise."

Kevin's heart began to hammer as she rolled the chair towards the door – was she really doing this? She pulled the door open and moved him out into the corridor, which was empty this time of night. Leaning forward to set the brakes on the chair, she said with soft urgency, "There's a supply truck that makes a delivery from Washington on Saturday nights; they should be arriving any minute. I can hide you in the back of the truck while they wheel in the drop-offs, then it'll be up to you to figure out what to do on the other end. Can you walk?"

He nodded.

"Okay. I'm going back into the room. Where you're at right now is out of any camera range, so change your clothes. There's also a white doctor's coat in there – put that on. Then when I come out again, I'll walk you out to the truck."

She turned to go back into the room, but Kevin pulled his hands from the straps and grabbed her wrist, causing her to turn back. "Rebekah – I'm not leaving without Singh."

Rebekah's gaze darted away, guilty. "You have to, Kevin. He can't even walk."

"Then I'll carry him. But I won't let him stay here to die."

For a second he thought she'd argue, but she finally said, "Okay, just get dressed. I'll be right back." She went back into Kevin's room, the door shutting behind her.

Kevin reached under the wheelchair, found the bag, stood up, and had to throw a hand out to brace himself against the wall as he nearly blacked

231

out. When he was steady again, he yanked on the clothes and the lab coat just as Rebekah re-emerged, carrying an armful of bed sheets which she threw aside. She slid her card through the slot for Singh's room, and nodded at the wheelchair. "Bring that, he'll need it. And act like a doctor."

She led the way into the room. For the second time, Kevin found himself staring at Singh in disbelief.

The doctor looked like death. He was emaciated and colourless, sleeping or comatose, his breathing shallow. "My God," Kevin murmured.

Rebekah stepped up to the bed, saying loudly, "Good evening, Dr Singh. Dr Jacobson is here to see you."

Singh gave no sign that he'd heard.

"We have to move you for a few minutes, Dr Singh. Dr Jacobson's going to assist me. Okay?"

Still no response.

Rebekah plucked the needles from Singh and motioned to the chair Kevin still gripped. "Doctor, can you bring that over here and help me get him into it?"

Kevin nodded, and wheeled the chair over. His throat constricted as he got even closer to Singh, and he had to work not to groan. Rebekah got Singh's light body sitting up, and they managed to wrestle him into the wheelchair. He was barely conscious.

"Doctor, can you take him outside?"

Kevin started to push, but Singh whispered, "Wait." Kevin did, and Singh raised one hand – the effort costing him – and reached under the mattress. He dug for a few seconds, and withdrew a USB stick which he handed to Kevin. "Go," he croaked.

Kevin wheeled the chair out the door and into the hallway. After a few seconds, Rebekah joined him with a blanket that she tucked around Singh's limp body.

"Is he going to make it?"

Adjusting the blanket, Rebekah said, "I really don't know. But we have to go *now*."

She walked swiftly down the hallway and Kevin struggled to keep up, pushing Singh in the chair. At the end of the corridor Rebekah indicated they wait as she looked outside. Kevin risked a glance past her and saw a man wheeling a laden trolley away from a large delivery truck. A guard with an assault rifle lounged against the side of the vehicle, smoking a cigarette.

"Wait here until I call you," Rebekah said. She stepped through the doorway and approached the guard.

Standing as far back in the shadows as possible, Kevin watched as Rebekah walked to the guard, said something, and pointed off to the right. The guard looked in that direction, dropped his cigarette, stubbed it out with a booted foot and walked off. Rebekah waited a few seconds, checked for the man with the trolley and finally waved to Kevin.

He pushed Singh before him, moving as rapidly as he could, until they reached the back of the truck. Two boards served as a ramp up to the truck bed, and Kevin prayed he had the strength to get Singh up there. He glanced in and saw racks of linens, cases of medicines, and stacks of plastic crates. It would be easy enough to hide in there, but the chair wouldn't fit – he really would have to carry Singh.

"Hurry," Rebekah said.

Kevin knelt beneath Singh, grabbed him around the waist, and managed to lift him in a fireman's carry over one shoulder. Even as slender as Singh was, the weight nearly buckled Kevin's knees. He didn't know how he'd get him up the boards.

He made it halfway up and could go no further, but it was enough – leaning forward as gently as possible, he deposited Singh on the edge of the truck bed, then gently laid him back. Rebekah ran the wheelchair back to the facility, and Kevin got behind Singh to drag him. Somehow that seemed harder, and he was only halfway to the back when Rebekah reappeared and whispered, "They're coming!"

"Okay," Kevin said, before adding, "and thank you."

Rebekah didn't respond. Instead she stepped around the side of the truck. Kevin heard the sounds of the trolley wheel's trundling over asphalt, and Rebekah in conversation with the guard, their words dulled by the metal side of the truck.

Redoubling his efforts, Kevin hauled Singh all the way to the back – then dropped to his knees and crouched behind boxes as the man with the trolley came into view. If the man looked carefully, or had a flashlight, he'd see Singh's legs plainly visible at the end of the truck . . .

Instead, the man pushed the two planks up on to the bed, lifted the trolley and set it next to the boards, closed the rear doors and sealed them. The interior of the truck was completely dark, and Kevin clutched on to Singh as if the void might suck him away.

Kevin didn't allow himself to breathe yet. He waited until the truck's engine rumbled to life and it rolled forward. After a few turns, it stopped, and he overheard a brief conversation with NWP's perimeter guards. At last the truck started moving again.

Kevin exhaled in relief. They'd made it – they'd escaped New World Pharmaceuticals. "Singh, we did it – we're free."

Kevin felt something hard in a pocket of the lab coat, and reached down; there was a stethoscope and a small Maglite there. Whether Rebekah had planned the maglite or not, Kevin was grateful to find it. He twisted the end and the small bluish beam shot out. He aimed it down at Singh, who still seemed to be only semi-conscious.

"Singh . . ." Kevin tried shaking him slightly, but the doctor's head just rolled to one side. Kevin began to panic. He aimed the light beam into Singh's face, holding it close to his eyes. "Singh . . .!"

Singh groaned, and Kevin cried out. "Singh, we're out of NWP."

His eyes bleary and half-focused, Singh looked up at Kevin. "The drive . . . has my research . . ."

The truck bounced over a large object, and Singh gasped as his back hit the hard metal floor. Kevin bent down, concerned. "Are you all right?"

"No . . ."

Peeling off his bogus white coat, Kevin wadded it up and shoved it under Singh's back to try to provide some cushioning; the doctor's head rested on his knee. "Is that better?"

"That's . . ." Singh had to swallow before he could go on; talking, even just a few simple words, was obviously difficult. ". . . not . . . the problem. I'm dying."

"No . . ."

"They . . . took too much." Singh's hand fluttered up like an injured bird, and Kevin took it in his own.

"Just hang in there, Garud. This truck's headed for Washington. We can get help there—"

A faint trace of a smile crossed Singh's face. "I won't . . . but you must . . ."

"Garud—"

Singh's fingers tightened around Kevin's. "I'm sorry . . ."

His eyes closed, his grip loosened.

"No, Garud – don't do this . . ."

Kevin squeezed Singh's hand harder, but there was no response. In the noisy, dim, bouncing truck, it was impossible to tell if his friend was dead, but Kevin knew it didn't matter; even if he had merely lapsed into unconsciousness, Singh wouldn't make it to Washington.

Kevin turned off the Maglite, lowered his head and sobbed.

STEELE: Steele.

MARCUS: Director Steele, this is Colonel Marcus up in Bolling.

STEELE: Yes, Colonel. What can I do for you?

MARCUS: Your boy Delancy is outside our front gate asking for admittance. How would you like us to proceed?

STEELE: Is he alone?

MARCUS: Confirmed. Both ground and air surveillance are negative on other targets.

STEELE: Okay. Follow standard protocol for dealing with extremely dangerous subjects. Assume he's armed, carrying explosives, the works. Oh, and also assume he's HRV-positive. Then bring him inside and get him in your best cell, round-the-clock guards. I'll be there in an hour.

MARCUS: You got it, Director. We'll make sure Delancy's not carrying so much as a toothpick.

Chapter Thirty-Four

BY THE TIME Steele arrived at Bolling's brig, Delancy had been X-rayed, frisked, stripped and examined. He'd been provided with a simple dark jumpsuit, and when Steele looked at the monitor hooked up to the cell's camera, he was seated calmly on the room's bunk.

"So, speak to me," she said, addressing Bolling's commander, Colonel Paul Marcus.

"He was unarmed and alone. He cooperated fully with our instructions. Just one thing, though . . ." Marcus looked at Steele, enjoying drawing out the suspense.

"And that is . . .?"

"He's dead. We found a chunk missing from his side, and the doc confirmed that he shows all the signs of reanimation after HRV infection. Well, I should say *almost* all the signs – the one he doesn't show is a complete lack of higher brain function. He's completely aware and lucid; in fact, we had no idea he was dead until we found the bite wound."

On the monitor, Delancy looked straight up into the camera and smiled, and Steele had the eerie notion that he could somehow see her. "Did he have his security card?"

"Yeah. We confiscated that safe and sound." Marcus hesitated, and then asked, "Steele, what the hell is this? Are they all smart now?"

Steele weighed her words carefully. "We're still trying to figure it out ourselves."

"So what do we do with him?"

Steele pulled away from the monitor and drew her Glock. "He's a zombie, Marcus."

237

Marcus nodded. "Okay, then, Steele – he's all yours."

He led her down the short hallway to Delancy's cell, where he unlocked the door and motioned her inside. "I'll wait just out here."

Steele nodded, and the door locked behind her. She held the Glock steady with both hands and stared down at Delancy. The Vice President rose; his eyes were filmy, skin paler than usual, but otherwise there was little sign of his transformation. He possessed the same swagger, the same thin veneer of amiability hiding a core of cunning and greed, and the reasons he made Steele's skin crawl hadn't changed, although they'd perhaps been amplified slightly. "Put that down, Steele," he said, gesturing at the gun, "you won't need it."

"You're not just a zombie, Bob – you're a zombie *and* a traitor. I could shoot you right here and be perfectly justified twice over."

"A traitor to what exactly? Not the United States of America, surely . . . because that great state hasn't existed for quite some time."

"Bullshit. Moreby hasn't won yet."

"Moreby?" Delancy barked a harsh laugh, and when he grinned Steele nearly winced at the sight of his death-blackened gums. "Moreby's not what killed this nation. It's that bloodless excuse for a President you serve."

Steele gaped in disbelief, and then said, "You're dead *and* insane."

"Oh, please – don't confuse me with your little CIA dog Gillespie. I assure you, I'm far from some paranoid junkie hyped on uppers and running around spouting conspiracy theories. Or maybe the problem is *you*, Steele. Maybe you just can't face the fact that you backed a loser."

"So, let me guess: you figured you'd make a little deal with Moreby to hand her over so you could take her place?"

Delancy nodded. "See? I always knew you were the smartest one in the bunch."

"Smarter than you at least, Bob, if you actually believe for a second that Moreby will honour that deal."

Steele experienced a deep satisfaction when she saw Delancy's expression flicker briefly. "Why wouldn't he?"

"Jesus, you're an idiot. Have you read his files? This is a man who was willing to sacrifice his own wife. He'll use you just to get the real power out of the way, then toss you aside like a piece of peeled-off dead skin. Christ, he's already eaten part of you."

Delancy's fingers involuntarily reached for his wound. "That was a necessary sacrifice . . ."

"Like his wife?"

Delancy peered at Steele as he said, "Let me ask you something: if he wasn't interested in working with me, why didn't he just eat my brain, get what I know and go from there? Why turn me and let me come back?"

"Well, our intelligence – and yes, we *do* still have some, regardless of what you think of Aaron Gillespie – suggests that Moreby is somehow in contact with those he personally turns. I think he's using you as a sort of walking camera. Maybe he thought we'd take you back to the President, and he'd learn everything about us that way."

His expression suddenly guarded, Delancy said, "You don't know everything, Steele."

"What? Tell me what I don't know, and maybe you'll live a little longer."

Delancy laughed so hard the wound in his torso started oozing, creating a large darker spot on the side of his jumpsuit. "You can't kill me, Steele. I'm not one of those mindless monsters shambling around outside, scrabbling over scraps of flesh. Can you imagine how it would look to the rest of my party if they found out you'd murdered me in cold blood?"

"The rest of your party? My God, Delancy, is that all you're thinking about?"

He took a step forward and Steele found herself reacting instinctively to tighten her grip on the gun. The motion caused Delancy to stop walking, but he spoke urgently. "My party is going to come out ahead this time, because we've been prepared for this, we've been thinking about it for a long time. The end of the world, I mean. We'll work with Moreby to save whatever we can of humanity and then we'll help him forge a new nation, a new *world*, where our foresight and our strength will be respected."

Steele had heard enough. She reached back to rap on the door, never taking her eyes off Delancy or lowering her gun. As she heard the door buzz open, she stepped backward carefully.

Just before the door closed behind her, Delancy called out, "Just remember, Steele: it's *your* end coming, too. Will you be ready?"

REPORT FROM COL. JOHN SIROCO, ACTING COMMANDER, FORT IRWIN MILITARY TRAINING CENTER

TO: WASHINGTON COMMAND

DATE: 5 November

Relying on data collected from both civilian and military forces fighting the insurgents in the Southern California area, I am attempting to assemble here a comprehensive picture of the current situation in the area.

Throughout September and October, the New Zombie Order Army Southwest (NZOASW) under the command of Major General Harland Dawson swept north from San Diego, moving largely via the inland route around the 5 freeway. They have established a base camp at what used to be USMC Camp Pendleton, situated 46 miles north of San Diego. The NZOASW stormtroopers are highly organized and well equipped.

The sizeable civilian resistance movement in that area is providing heavy opposition, but they desperately need resupplying now that the NZOASW has successfully cut their supply lines via air, land and sea. Not only are they in need of food, but they also require automatic weapons and ammunition if they are to stand any chance of halting the zombie advance.

We are also receiving so far unconfirmed reports that the NZOASW has started setting up Human Internment Camps across Southern California where those freedom fighters they capture are being incarcerated for god knows what fate.

We believe Harland Dawson was part of Operation Darwin, an NZOASW project that groomed military leaders by feeding them only the brains of the finest and most devoted human fighters, allowing the zombies to gain their memories and experience.

However, the situation changed on or about 30 October. At that time, Dawson (probably acting against orders) recklessly led a small squad against human resistance fighters in south Los Angeles County. We believe Dawson may have been driven by hunger to eat a couple of the resistance leaders, and that the knowledge he acquired at that point caused him to forsake his NZOASW command. On 2 November, Dawson fled, in search of the human children of the husband and wife he'd consumed; he was last seen stealing a vehicle in Hollywood. His whereabouts are currently unknown.

Since Dawson's disappearance, the NZOASW has been unable to proceed any further; their forces seem to be in disarray, in fact.

We recommend monitoring the situation closely. Here in Fort Irwin, we are located approximately 150 miles from Los Angeles. While we are secure and see few insurgents (none intelligent so far), it also makes obtaining information from the metropolitan areas more difficult.

Respectfully submitted by
Colonel John Siroco

Chapter Thirty-Five

KEVIN WASN'T SURE how long he'd been unconscious in the lightless back of the truck when the first explosion hit. It wasn't direct, but it was close enough to rock the truck from side to side, jostling Kevin awake. The brakes squealed, and he collided with a metal rack as the truck slammed to a halt. Outside he heard gunshots, screams and more explosions.

He had no idea if bullets could penetrate the metal sides of the truck or not, but he instinctively crouched down, his hands over his head. Another explosion – this one uncomfortably close – struck nearby, and the sound nearly deafened him.

When the ringing passed he listened, trying to piece together what he was hearing. He thought he heard the driver and the guard shouting from the cab, and the rapid-fire blasts that followed he guessed might be the guard's rifle. He heard poundings, as if hands were slapping the outside panels; a few seconds later, a high-pitched scream might have been the driver. There was another, more distant burst of gunfire, and then it was quiet for a few seconds.

He waited in the dark, anxious, not sure what to dread more – never being found, or being found by whoever had just won the battle outside.

A few moments later the handle on the rear opening was lifted, and as the doors were thrown open Kevin did his best to withdraw behind a stack of crates.

The truck bounced slightly as someone climbed up on to the bed, and a single pair of footsteps walked slowly towards him; otherwise, it was quiet outside. Kevin trembled, from weakness and fear, as the unknown visitor stepped nearer . . . nearer . . .

The click of a gun was followed by a question: "You, at the front – are you still alive?"

"I'm alive, I'm human," Kevin said, his voice as tremulous as his hands, "please don't shoot."

"Come out where I can see you."

Crawling slowly, Kevin edged around the crates. A single man stood silhouetted against the early morning daylight pouring into the truck through the open doors.

"Are there two of you?"

Kevin stood slowly and nodded down at Singh. "Yes, but . . . my friend didn't make it."

"Come on out where I can see you."

The man backed away towards the rear lip of the vehicle, keeping a rifle trained on Kevin, who walked forwards slowly, his hands up. As he drew nearer the light, it blinded him, a stabbing pain, and he flinched.

"How long have you been in here?"

"I'm not even sure."

"Are you hurt? Or . . .?"

His eyes adjusting slowly, Kevin tried to see the man, but could still make out only a silhouette. As he realized what the man was asking, he laughed, a small, mirthless sound.

"What's so funny?"

"You're asking if I've been bitten, right? No, I haven't, but it wouldn't make any difference if I had, because I'm immune."

There was an instance of silence before the man said, "Bullshit. Nobody's immune."

"Yeah, well . . . I am. I was being held by New World Pharmaceuticals so they could use my blood to create antiserum." Kevin reached into a pocket and withdrew Singh's USB stick. "This has my friend's notes on making the antiserum. New World stole his research, then bled him dry and I was next. I'd probably be dead by now if I hadn't escaped."

"Do you have any weapons?"

"No."

The rifle lowered, and the man turned to walk out of the truck. "You're too trusting – if I was a bad guy, I would've just known that you were unarmed and valuable. Now, let's get out of here."

Kevin walked forwards, still squinting against the sunlight, moving carefully. He reached the edge, sat down and lowered himself to the ground, his knees nearly giving way. The man with the gun was walking towards his own vehicle, a big dented and battered 4 x 4 pickup. Kevin followed, unsteadily. He stumbled on something, and his stomach lurched when he looked down and saw a corpse in the road. He stepped around it, realizing as he did that it was the corpse of a corpse – a truly dead zombie, its brains sprayed across the asphalt, its blood lacking any hint of crimson. He looked to the sides, and saw at least five other prone figures; from the grey messes surrounding them, he guessed them all to be zombies.

"You took all these out?"

"Yep. Unfortunately I was too late to save the two men in the cab."

Kevin looked up as the man turned to face him . . .

And he staggered back, gasping, as he saw it wasn't a man at all, but a glassy-eyed, bluish-skinned zombie, fresh blood staining his chin. His breath quickening, Kevin looked to the right, wondering how far he could run before his legs gave way and the monster was on him . . .

"Hey, whoa there – sorry, I should've warned you. Yeah, I'm dead, but I'm not one of them."

The voice seemed sincere, the zombie made no threatening moves, and Kevin hesitated, eyeing him uncertainly.

The dead man gestured back towards the truck. "Look, if you don't trust me, maybe you'll trust my friend."

Following his wave, Kevin saw another figure in the front of the truck. It looked like a small person, or . . . a child. Incredulous, Kevin stumbled forward until he could clearly see a little boy, no more than twelve, and with the brown skin and glossy black hair of a Latino. Even though he eyed Kevin uncertainly, he glowed with health and was clearly human and living.

"That's Maxi – short for Maximiliano," said the zombie. "We came all the way from Los Angeles."

"Los Angeles?" Kevin turned to look at the zombie. "That's where I came from, too."

"And where are you headed now?"

"I don't know," Kevin confessed. "Anywhere away from New World Pharmaceuticals, I guess."

"Well, if you'd like to come with us, Mister . . .?"

"Moon. Kevin Moon."

"Mister Moon, we're headed for Washington. I'm sure the human government would be most grateful to have the world's only immune man and a thumb drive full of instructions on making a cure."

Kevin eyed the zombie, curious about his bearing, his air of authority. "And you are . . .?"

"Harland Dawson. I was a general in the zombie army. In fact . . . I led the troops who took Los Angeles."

The thought that Los Angeles – his hometown – was now under control of these marauders left Kevin chilled. He realized he had no idea how long it had been since he'd left the city, how long he'd been tossed from one captivity to another, and that the world had changed while he'd hidden, been beaten and tormented, examined and drained.

Los Angeles belonged to the zombies now.

Dawson stood by the truck, not moving, waiting calmly, his glassy eyes fixed on Kevin.

"So why exactly should I trust you?" asked Kevin.

"Because I abandoned my command and went AWOL. I work for the human resistance now. Maxi's parents were leaders, and I'm . . . carrying on their legacy."

Kevin's gaze moved past Dawson and his pickup to the surrounding landscape, an area of open fields and distant structures, and dotted with the dead . . . all moving in this direction. He wouldn't make it far on foot, and even if the delivery truck was still operable, he didn't know how to drive it. There didn't seem to be much choice.

"I'd suggest you decide quickly, Mr Moon," Dawson said. He raised the rifle, sighted along it, and picked off the nearest zombie.

"Okay." Kevin forced his legs to walk to the truck. "I guess if you were gonna eat me, you could've done it already."

"I'm not going to eat you. I already ate the two men who were in the front of the truck."

Kevin was about to climb into the truck, but now he stopped and stared, seeing again the fresh blood staining Dawson's chin. Dawson reached the side of the truck and added, "I didn't kill them – they were dying by the time I reached them."

"Let's go," said a small voice. Kevin looked down and saw the little boy, Maxi, glancing around anxiously as zombies staggered towards them. That voice – so young, so human – spurred him, and he crawled into the rear seat. Dawson got in, stashed the rifle in a gun rack, locked the doors and started up the engine. As he drove forward, moving around the delivery truck, carelessly rolling over corpses, Kevin thought about Singh's body and issued a mental farewell and apology.

His reverie was interrupted when Maxi turned around and thrust a hand over the seat back. "Hi, I'm Maxi."

Kevin took the offered hand and tried to smile. "I'm Kevin. I'm from Los Angeles, too."

"Cool." Maxi held a candy bar out to Kevin. "You hungry? We lucked out and got a couple of crates of these."

"Yeah. Thanks." Kevin took the candy bar and wolfed it down. When he looked up, he saw Dawson's eyes on him in the rearview mirror, and even behind the covering of death there was compassion.

Kevin thought, *Goddamnit, Singh . . . we almost made it*; then he sank back into the truck's seat and tried not to sob.

FROM: NZO PRESIDENT JAMES MOREBY

To all living citizens of the former United States of America:

I applaud you all. You have fought a courageous, valiant war; you have survived against difficult odds.

But the war is over. You must realize by now that your old world is dead. Or perhaps I should say that the dead have taken that world.

Your United States is gone. Despite rumors to the contrary, the human Government is no more. If you have received supplies or communications recently, know that those lines have been severed and you are now abandoned.

But you are not forgotten. My Government would welcome you. Surrender now and I guarantee your safety. You will not be harmed. You will not be consumed.

I'm pleased to inform you that NZO scientists have succeeded in creating synthetic human meat. We are now in the initial stages of mass production of this foodstuff, and we will soon begin distributing it to all of NZO's citizens in need. You will be protected as we transition to this new nourishment.

NZO is dedicated to achieving – for the first time in the history of Earth's intelligent species – world peace. Humans and zombies will live side by side, securely and happily. Together we will wipe out poverty, crime and misery; even death will be a thing of the past. We will rebuild a shining new future from the ruins of the old.

Join us now. Lay down your arms. And welcome the future.

**Yours in Brotherhood,
President James Moreby**

Chapter Thirty-Six

STEELE FINISHED READING the report and couldn't resist hitting the DELETE button on the tablet. She missed the days of paper printouts – she would have enjoyed wadding this particular report up and hurling the crumpled remains against the nearest wall.

The President looked up from her own copy and addressed Ty. "There's not a chance that they've really created a synthetic meat, is there?"

Ty shrugged. "It's remotely possible, I suppose, but even if they have . . . you'll note that little missive contains no mention of the millions of *unintelligent* zombies staggering around out there. Unless Moreby is prepared to begin shooting his own kind, there's no way they can guarantee human safety."

"It's absolute bullshit." Steele couldn't restrain herself, and the President and Ty both turned to look at her. "This is the same kind of disinformation Moreby's been distributing for a while. This is about as valid as that ridiculous thing he sent out which was supposed to be from you, the little speech that made you look about as sane as a schizophrenic serial killer off her meds."

"Oh, I don't know," the President noted, "I enjoyed the part about the First Spouse dying in the Lincoln Bedroom with a young intern."

Steele knew that in reality the President's late husband had died in the first battle for Washington, and that he'd been found with a gun in his hand on the National Mall near the Vietnam Veterans Memorial, not in *flagrante delicto* with another woman. The fact that the President could claim to find that fictitious slur amusing left Steele admiring her anew.

"I agree," Ty said. "And I'll add: I think this disinformation campaign on Moreby's part is actually a good sign. We are winning in many areas – we know, for example, that human forces have retaken both Albuquerque and Denver – and I think Moreby's getting a little desperate."

Ty's phone sounded. He glanced at the caller ID, and said, "It's Marcus from Bolling. Excuse me for a minute . . ."

He rose and stepped out of the President's office. Steele looked at her boss, who returned her gaze with determination. "We've still got a shot, Steele."

"I believe you, but . . . I can't help but wonder what happens even if we win. We've all lost so much; our families, our friends, our homes, our security. How do we go back?"

"We don't go back. We go forward."

"I know, but . . ." For a second it all threatened to overwhelm Steele. She struggled to keep from screaming, sobbing, laughing, throwing herself on the floor and letting everything just drain away. Giving up.

The President's voice had softened when she spoke again. "It won't be easy. We may win the war and fail in the reconstruction. I know that. But if we fail, we at least tried. It's all we can do."

Steele nodded. "It's just . . . I'm so tired."

"We all are."

The office door re-opened and Ty Ward stood framed in the entrance, his expression one of astonishment. He seemed speechless.

The President asked, "Ty . . .?"

"That was Marcus up at Bolling. Major General Harland Dawson just surrendered to him. And he's got Kevin Moon with him."

"Is Dawson talking?"

Ty nodded to the President. "He says he wants to help us."

Steele and the President could only look at each other, wondering. Thinking.

And daring to hope.

Interrogation conducted by Sandra Steele,
assisted by Ty Ward

The interrogation took place in a conference room within
Bolling Air Field. Steele and Ward were already present
as Dawson was led into the room by two armed guards.

STEELE: Good afternoon, General Dawson. I'm Sandra
Steele, serving as Director of Secret Services and Aide
to the President, and this is Chief of Staff and Acting
Joint Commander Ty Ward.

DAWSON [nodding]: Ms. Steele, Mr. Ward.

STEELE [to the guards]: Thank you, we'll take it from
here.

GUARD #1: Are you sure, ma'am? He's a zombie . . .

STEELE [sets her pistol on the conference table]: I'm
sure it will be fine, soldier.

GUARD #1: Yes, ma'am.

[The two guards exit]

STEELE: Have a seat, General. [He does] Are you
comfortable? Can we get you anything? Oh, sorry, strike
that.

DAWSON: I don't need anything.

STEELE: Okay, then let's get started. General Dawson, I
should inform you that not only is this interrogation
being recorded, but the President is listening live as
we proceed.

DAWSON: I'm honored. Thank you, Madame President. I look
forward to offering you my complete cooperation.

STEELE: Let's talk about that, then. Until recently, you
were a general in the NZOA.

DAWSON: Correct. Specifically, I commanded the New Zombie
Order Army Southwest.

STEELE: And I believe your last act as their commander

was to lead the NZOA against the human resistance in Southern California.

DAWSON: Correct. We had taken San Diego and Orange County, and were pushing into Los Angeles.

STEELE: When you abandoned your command.

DAWSON [hesitates, then]: Yes.

STEELE: Why did you do that, General?

DAWSON: Are you familiar with Operation Darwin, Director Steele?

STEELE: That's the NZO project in which military commanders are fed specially selected humans to acquire additional military knowledge, yes?

DAWSON: That's correct. I was a primary participant in Operation Darwin. However, during the incursions into Los Angeles, my superiors were delayed in providing me with sufficient subjects. I . . . was starving. I disobeyed orders and engaged in the consumption of a subject who was not approved by Operation Darwin.

WARD: Yes, we've got that here. You consumed Hector Robles, a leader in the Southern California resistance forces.

DAWSON: Yes.

[After several seconds of silence]

STEELE: What happened then?

DAWSON: I . . . changed. I disobeyed orders, sought out Robles' wife, and consumed her as well. I now possess the sum knowledge of both their lives. I experienced their commitment and passion, and I saw that we -- those led by Moreby, I mean -- will ultimately fail. We can only increase our numbers by destroying lives, and we can only create by building on what others have done. We are a people destined to slowly decay and fade out.

WARD: General, do you know if there's any truth to Moreby's claim that NZO scientists have developed synthetic human meat?

DAWSON [laughs]: I know they *haven't*. Look, the only reason his tech guys were able to come up with better helmets for zombie troops was that it was a process one of them had designed *before* he died. I guarantee that none of them are capable of creating anything as new as fake human flesh. It's a lie.

STEELE: Let's go back to what happened after you consumed Hector and Alejandra Robles . . .

DAWSON: The Robles had two children, Maribel and Maximiliano. I made it my mission to find them and protect them.

STEELE: That's Maximiliano you arrived with?

DAWSON: Yes. Maribel was already gone when I reached them.

STEELE: Why were you coming to Washington?

DAWSON: Because I have both inside knowledge about Moreby's operations, and considerable skill as a military expert, something I think you've needed since you lost Ames Parker. No offense, Mr. Ward.

WARD: None taken.

STEELE: General Dawson, you'll understand if I tell you that we will need considerable proof of your intention to aid us, and even then we will proceed with extreme caution.

DAWSON: Of course, Director. I expect no less.

STEELE: Is there anything you can tell us right now, sir?

DAWSON: I was turned as the result of a direct bite from Moreby, just as your Vice President Delancy was . . .

WARD [interrupting]: How do you know about Delancy? We haven't gone public with that.

DAWSON: Those of us who were infected by Moreby himself are reborn with a sort of direct mental connection to Moreby.

STEELE: Are you telling me you share Moreby's mind in some way?

DAWSON: Yes, although . . . it's hard to explain. We're like . . . I think you might call it a hive mind. Those of us turned by Moreby or turned by Moreby's original victims -- the intelligent zombies, in other words -- have both our own thoughts and general, overwhelming directives. If Moreby wants us to perform some task for him, we all work together to do it.

STEELE: Although you can also apparently deny the instructions.

DAWSON: Yes, but . . . most don't. It's always easier to go with the rest of the tribe, isn't it?

STEELE: If you know about Delancy, what else do you know?

DAWSON: We know where human forces are mobilizing. We know how well armed they are and what their numbers are. We know your Government is in tatters and hidden in a complex beneath Washington. And we know of the occult nature of that complex.

STEELE: "Occult nature"?

DAWSON: Yes. You do know of Benjamin Henry Latrobe, one of the original architects, don't you?

[A few seconds of silence]

DAWSON: My apologies. Even Moreby thought you'd discovered that already.

STEELE: Discovered what exactly?

DAWSON: That the complex housing you was always intended to serve as Moreby's American center. Latrobe was Moreby's acolyte, and designed much of the underground system working from detailed plans they created together when Latrobe studied with Moreby in London. Later, Latrobe adjusted the plans on-site, to accommodate certain geological features of Washington. Unfortunately for Moreby, when Latrobe disappeared soon after construction was completed, he took the final plans with him.

STEELE: So Moreby knows about the underground facility, but not exact details like how to get into it?

DAWSON: Correct. He knows the ground-level entrances are located somewhere on this base, but he knows neither their exact locations nor how to access them.

STEELE: Why hasn't he attacked Bolling, then?

DAWSON: Oh, he will, Director. He just plans on attacking it in a way that leaves those entrances undamaged and open to him.

Chapter Thirty-Seven

"MR MOON, I'M so pleased to meet you. And you must be Maximiliano."
The President took Maxi's hand as the boy looked away shyly.

"Everybody just calls me Maxi."

"Well, Maxi, I know you've had a long trip, and I'm glad you could join us."

"Where's Mr Dawson?"

An uncomfortable silence passed among the adults – Steele, Ty, Kevin,
the President. Finally Kevin said, "He's okay, Maxi. They can't bring him
down here because he's . . ."

The boy filled in the gap. "Dead. But he's an okay dead. He knows all
about my Mom and Dad."

Steele found herself responding to the boy on a primal level; she wanted
to keep him safe and comfortable. She knew Moon felt the same way –
he'd refused to leave Maxi's side since they'd arrived. Whether it was some
latent parental instinct, or something even deeper – guarding the future of
the species? – she didn't know. Perhaps she just liked Maxi because he was
street-smart and tough without being cruel.

The President smiled down at him. "He did a good thing in saving you,
and we're going to take very good care of you. You'll be safe down here."

Maxi shrugged and glanced around. "I guess, but . . . don't you miss
the sun?"

The others were rendered as dazed by that simple question as Steele was.
She realized abruptly that she *did* miss the sun, and the sky and trees and
clouds and grass underfoot. From the silence of the others, she knew they
felt the same way.

"Yes, we do," said Ty. "But we know it's only temporary. We'll get it all back someday. And soon."

Maxi looked unconvinced.

The President motioned at Ty. "Ty, could you take Maxi out for a few minutes so we can talk to Mr Moon?"

"Sure—" Ty started to leave, but stopped when he realized Maxi wasn't following. He was standing rigidly by Kevin's side.

"I'm staying with Kevin," Maxi announced.

Kevin clamped a friendly hand on the boy's shoulder. "Dude, it's okay – I'll just be a minute. I'll bet they've got some radical candy bars down here."

Ty grinned. "I've even got ice cream."

Kevin gave Maxi a gentle push and the boy acquiesced, although his expression made it clear that he wasn't especially interested in candy or ice cream. "It's probably that fake ice cream that comes in a little silver pouch."

Ty grinned. "Guilty as charged. It's still pretty good, though . . ."

"This won't take long, I promise," Kevin said, as Ty led the boy out.

The door closed behind them and Steele said, "He's really bonded with you."

Turning back to her, Kevin smiled warmly. "He's a great kid. We've both been through a lot, so there's that in common."

The President returned to her desk chair and, as she seated herself, said, "Kevin – if I may . . .?"

"Of course."

Steele indicated a chair and Kevin sat. He was still shaky from what he'd been through – he'd filled them in briefly on his ordeal at New World Pharmaceuticals – but he was recovering and Steele sensed he was a genuinely decent man.

"Kevin," the President said, "we know a little of what you've endured, and so we hate to ask this, but we have to . . ."

"You need my blood," Kevin guessed.

"Yes. Our own doctors assure us that just a sample will do. There's a medic up at Bolling who can take it. The doctors have already been through the files you provided and believe it will be enough to recreate NWP's success in generating an antiserum. I want to assure you first, though, that you will be treated with kindness and respect here. You'll be free to come and go, to do what you like, although we will ask that if you choose not to stay here that you understand and respect the delicacy of our position . . ."

"I'm happy to stay here and do whatever I can to help. Which probably isn't much – I was just a waiter before."

"I'm sure Steele can find a job for you."

Steele smiled. "Of course, Kevin. I'll talk to you about it more later."

"Good." Kevin hesitated, before adding, "Oh, one thing: I'd like to take care of Maxi. I mean, as an official guardian or whatever."

For a second, Steele felt a pang of regret; she'd been ready to make the offer herself. But there was no denying the boy's connection to Moon, and a male authority figure would probably be better for him.

"Of course," the President said. "That's very kind of you."

Kevin started to rise, but remembered: "Oh, and I don't know how good your intelligence on NWP is, but . . ."

Steele stepped in. "What've you got?"

"There was this guy there – Landen Jones – who I think is planning to use the antiserum as a pretty big bargaining chip with you. I didn't get all the details, but . . . well, he may not know I'm here, so maybe you can use that."

The President answered first. "Yes, Kevin, maybe we can. Thank you."

Kevin left. As the door closed behind him, the President released a long sigh. "So the question now is who's the bigger enemy: cannibalistic zombies or a multinational drug company?"

Steele couldn't answer.

REPORT FROM COL. PAUL F. MARCUS,
BOLLING AIR FIELD

Re: Incident involving R. Delancy and H. Dawson

As you know, earlier today I passed on a request from detainee
Harland Dawson to visit detainee Bob Delancy. The request
was approved by Ty Ward, provided the meeting was secure
and under observation.

At 14:30, Dawson was accompanied by guards to Delancy's
cell. Delancy's cell is equipped with functioning security
cameras; and, since both detainees are already infected with
HRV and dead, they were believed to present no threat to each
other. The guards placed Dawson in Delancy's cell and locked
the door.

The following is a transcript of what occurred between the two
detainees:

DELANCY: Well, if it isn't the traitor himself. To what do I owe
the honor, General?

DAWSON: It's no honor, Delancy. And you're in no position to
judge someone else as a traitor.

At that point Dawson moved towards Delancy, who backed
away. Dawson abruptly punched Delancy in the temple, then
grabbed his head and pounded it against the wall. By the time
the guards were able to unlock the door and re-enter the cell,
Dawson had broken Delancy's skull against the wall and
damaged the brain, which as you know terminates the living
dead.

As the guards entered, Dawson finished, turned to them calmly, and held up his hands, which by then were considerably stained with Delancy's remains.

DAWSON: I'm done here. Gentlemen, as you're still among the living I'd advise you to proceed with caution in escorting me and cleaning this up.

He was then returned to his own cell. A medic was called, who determined that Delancy was truly dead.

Although Dawson's visit to Delancy was approved by Ty Ward, I accept full responsibility for this incident.

Submitted by:
Col. P. F. Marcus, Bolling Air Field

Chapter Thirty-Eight

WASHINGTON WAS IMPLODING and Ty Ward was in the black hole centre of it.

He'd spent the morning trying to keep angry Congressmen away from the President. Word of Delancy's (second) death had spread fast, and every member of his party seemed to think the killing had been an act of partisanship. They demanded to know why Dawson had done it, how he'd been given access to Delancy, when his trial would begin and who would preside over it. The other party, meanwhile, stayed quiet but, behind closed doors, they snickered and celebrated and toasted Dawson.

Ty himself had interviewed Dawson after the . . . what, murder? Execution? Termination? Dawson had stated that not only had Delancy committed an act of high treason, but he knew that Moreby had been planning to use Delancy to infiltrate the human government. Dawson claimed his action had saved them all. Ty believed him.

That didn't help when trying to fend off three-dozen angry politicians. He knew the President needed time to prepare her response to what Dawson had done, that it was his job to give her that space, but he had little patience for these senators and representatives who, only a day ago, had been worried about banning gay marriage in order to "keep America fruitful and multiplying".

He'd been trying to calm down a senator from Florida when a young woman he knew as an aide to a representative from California had run up and told him she'd seen blood pouring from under the door that led into the CIA offices. Even though blood was seldom a good sign, Ty was secretly relieved to be pulled away from the shrieking middle-aged Floridian. He followed the woman through corridors and around corners until they reached the office with a hand-written sign that read CIA DIRECTOR AARON GILLESPIE.

There was a large amount of blood pooling out from beneath the door.

Ty told the woman to leave, which she did, quickly. He knew he should wait for help – preferably armed help – but if someone was still alive, bleeding to death while he stood by outside . . .

He tried the door, which was unlocked. Heart hammering, he looked in, moving cautiously.

There was a body on the floor just inside.

Ty knelt, trying to keep one eye on the surroundings – but when he saw the knife still clutched in one of the dead man's hands and verified that the blood streams were pouring from slit wrists, he put aside caution. The corpse lay face down, and even though he knew, he put two fingers beneath the chin and tilted the head up enough to verify the identity: It was Gillespie. Dead. Suicide.

Rising, Ty stepped around the blood and body, making sure there was no one else present, no signs of struggle, nothing out of the ordinary.

That was when he saw the gruesome message written across the walls, three red words scrawled in blood atop layers of taped-up printouts and articles:

WE CANT WIN

"Jesus," he muttered to himself.

He found a tape dispenser on Gillespie's desk, a blank sheet of paper, and a Sharpie pen. He used the pen to write DO NOT ENTER on the paper, then left the room, stringing tape across the opening and attaching his handmade sign. He'd worry later about cleaning up. Maybe he'd tell the shrieking Florida senator to do it.

In the meantime, he'd have to tell the President that whatever little intelligence Gillespie had recently been supplying would now be gone.

From: Dr Willson Armitage <w.armitage@cdc.gov>

To: Sandra Steele <s.steele@whitehouse.gov>

Sent: THU, Nov 14, 4:27 PM

Subject: HRV antiserum

Please advise President that attempts at creating HRV antiserum from files of G. Singh and blood of subject Moon completely successful. Expect to be able to produce large quantities shortly. Complete report to follow.

W. A.

Chapter Thirty-Nine

"YOU'RE NOT GOING to believe this, but . . . Landen Jones is requesting a video conference."

Steele looked up from a report on human casualties incurred in the previous week to where Ty stood in the doorway of her office. "With the President?"

Ty nodded. "She wants you present."

Without another word, Steele rose and headed to the President's office with Ty. "Do we have any idea what this is about?"

He shook his head. "No, but . . . wild guess here: it ain't good."

As they reached the President's office and entered, she looked up wordlessly, only nodding. Ty opened a program on the President's computer and Jones' face appeared on the screen, looking as immaculate and falsely amiable as ever. "We're ready, Mr Jones." Ty stepped back. Steele joined him at the edge of the President's desk, where they could be seen.

"Good morning, Madame President," Jones started, and Steele remembered again how much she loathed this man.

"Why are you calling, Landen?" The President's voice was firm, with just a hint of anger.

"Well," Jones said, his expression never changing, "I see the gloves are off. Good – it should make this move a little more quickly. Here's the deal: New World Pharmaceuticals has successfully created an antiserum that counteracts HRV. We've already begun mass production, and have shipped several thousand vials already. We are prepared to work with your people on distribution of the antiserum, which I think we all agree could turn the tide of this war. However, we have several non-negotiable requirements."

"I'm sure you do. And what are they?"

If possible, Jones' smile grew broader. "Effective immediately, the United States of America will become a subsidiary of New World Pharmaceuticals."

The President burst into laughter. When she stopped, she stared at Jones on the screen. "Are you telling me that NWP is now a *country*, Landen?"

"No. Countries are a thing of the past. The United States operated more like a corporation every year, didn't it? Well, NWP is just taking that to the obvious next level and saying it's time for the real corporations to take over. It's simple, really: the world is dying and we have the cure. We *should* be the ones in charge. And you should be happy to work with us towards that goal."

Jones looked down for a second, punched a few keys, and then returned his gaze to the camera. "I've just sent a comprehensive proposal package. You'll see that you would all be treated as top-level executives with excellent compensation, including profit participation. Of course we recognize that we have a long road ahead of us, but together we can rebuild."

An icon appeared on the screen, and the President said, "Your attachment has come through."

"Excellent. Oh, and let me just add: any attempt to retaliate against NWP with any police or military action will result in the immediate destruction of all materials related to the antiserum. You would be damning the world, should you make that unwise decision."

The President's next words jolted Steele like an electrical bolt. "We'll need some time to go over this, of course."

"Of course. But we need to move quickly, so we are calling for an answer in three days. Any failure to respond in that time will be interpreted as an act of aggression, and our numbers are growing."

"We'll get back to you." The President closed the call and logged off the computer for good measure. Once the screen had shut down, she turned to Ty and Steele, speaking with urgency. "Ty, get as big a force assembled as you can immediately and hit New World's main facility outside Baltimore. If we can get Landen Jones alive, so much the better. They obviously don't know yet that we have Kevin Moon and our own antiserum, and I want them shut down before they find out."

Ty grinned, a wolfish look on his lean face. "You got it, Madame President. We've got a couple of boys in that area just itching to fight something other than zombies." Ty strode out.

The President smiled bitterly. "I'm not sure whether to call this secession or a hostile takeover."

Steele said, "How about just extraordinary assholery?"

The President agreed.

||| CellNet   10:32 AM   35% ■■

◄ Messages   **Ty Ward**   Contact

Today 9:56 AM

ETA one hour bird. Have your men ready as soon as I arrive. Ward

Text Message   📷   Send

Chapter Forty

TY'S INSIDES FELT like a Gordian knot.

As he sat in the back of the truck with the rest of the troops, heading towards NWP's headquarters, he was surprised by his own reactions. The rush of adrenaline – related for a change to real action, not emotional situations – was even refreshing. And the part he'd dreaded (image of a dead boy with a gun) hadn't surfaced. The dread he felt was only what any soldier experienced going into a potential combat situation. He joked with some of the other soldiers, easing tension; he laughed when one of them called it "a drug bust". He shared a bottle of water, and teased the one man who lit a cigarette.

Still, he was relieved when the "battle" turned out to be brief. There were a few brief exchanges of gunfire, but New World's hired security forces gave up easily when faced off against eighty heavily armed soldiers. Only one – a tattooed brute whose name was apparently Joker – had tried to keep firing and he'd been taken down before he'd hit anyone.

An explosion startled them, but it came from the other side of the facility. Ty realized that Landen was living up to his threat – he had apparently just destroyed the labs where the antiserum was produced and stored.

Jones surrendered shortly thereafter, telling them they'd made a mistake but there was another lab somewhere else producing the antiserum, and he was still willing to negotiate. When Ty stepped forward, Jones openly smirked. "Ah, I see it's the office boy. You might want to get your boss on the phone pronto, Ward."

Ty motioned two of the soldiers forward, who frisked and cuffed Jones. "Landen Jones," Ty said, relishing this moment, "you're under arrest on charges of sedition and treason. Oh, and by the way – you're also an idiot, because we've got Kevin Moon and our own antiserum."

The way Jones' face fell was a memory Ty would cherish for the rest of his days.

||| CellNet   12:48 AM   30%

◄ Messages   **Ty Ward**   Contact

Today 12:46 AM

NWP shutdown accomplished. Landen Jones in custody. Returning to Washington now. Gillespies was wrong. We CAN win.

Text Message   📷   Send

Chapter Forty-One

STEELE WAS BEGINNING to think that they really might come out of this.

They had an antiserum for HRV. They had the opposition of NWP locked down – Ty had returned to Washington with Landen Jones, who was in detention. Delancy's attempted treason had failed. US troops and independent resistance fighters all over the country were starting to win, even against the intelligent zombies.

All that really was left was Moreby.

Steele decided to interrogate Dawson further. The President had managed to calm down much of the uproar over Delancy's death by issuing a statement regarding "a complete investigation and pursuant trial", but Steele knew that had just been spin control. If Dawson could help them defeat Moreby, the President would release him regardless of who screamed.

She met Dawson in his cell. She'd had a hog brought to him earlier in the day; the zombies could survive eating animals, although Dawson said it was unpleasant. Still, Steele preferred knowing that he might be less likely to view her as a next meal.

Marcus admitted her into the cell, locking the door behind her, but she felt no need to draw her Glock. She'd already decided she trusted Dawson.

"Director Steele," he said, greeting her simply.

"General Dawson."

"Thanks to you and the President for protecting me after the incident with Delancy."

"How did you know we've been protecting you?"

Dawson's grey lips formed a wan smile. "It doesn't take psychic connections to figure out that must have caused a hell of an uproar."

"You're right." Steele leaned against a wall. "We truthfully don't quite know what to do with you, General."

"Well, to start with, you can stop calling me 'General'. Harland will do just fine."

"Okay." Steele paced a few steps, and turned to face him. "We need to know how to get to Moreby and how to kill him, Harland."

"I have to tell you the truth, Director: I'm not sure he can be killed."

It was what Steele had dreaded, but still refused to believe completely. "You can't just destroy the brain like you can with all the rest?"

"Well, let me put it this way: sure, you can destroy Moreby's brain, and sure, that might stop him . . . for a few days, or even a few weeks maybe. But remember that Moreby's not just a zombie – he's also some kind of sorcerer or whatever you call it, who seems to have mastered a form of reincarnation. We know that he somehow placed his consciousness into this current body, and that he did something similar for the group he calls The Well of Seven. If we destroy his current body's brain, what's to stop him from simply manifesting into another individual?"

Steele stopped, not seeing the barren cell, not seeing Dawson or herself, only seeing a future that grew ever bleaker. "So . . . do we just give up?"

"No, I think there might be another way. Do we have much on Moreby's history?"

Thinking back over what she'd read, Steele half-remembered police reports and British intelligence reports about Moreby being buried in some crypt. "Some, yes. As I recall, the speculation was that crews excavating an old church for a festival or something broke into a crypt and accidentally released him."

"Yes. A crypt . . ."

Steele looked at Dawson with sudden realization. "He may have been in that crypt for centuries."

"He was. In 1803, a ritual went badly and a mob threw Moreby into that crypt. He was sealed there until that construction crew accidentally freed him. So what happened during those two hundred years?"

Steele thought back – she'd seen newspaper clippings reporting rumours of sounds, hauntings, unexplained visions . . . but they'd been little more than the usual urban legends. "Nothing happened."

"That's right. So, even if he can't be killed, we know that he can be rendered powerless by imprisonment."

"But surely we can't just lock him into a prison cell and believe that's going to work."

Dawson shook his head. "It won't. No, it has to be a particular kind of chamber, one with occult powers . . ."

"Didn't you say the original architect of our underground system followed certain occult practices?"

"Benjamin Henry Latrobe – yes." Dawson thought for a few seconds before asking, "Do you know if you have any of the original plans for the complex?"

"I've never seen any, but we have a storage room that houses old records. I assumed it was mainly old food inventories, that kind of thing . . ."

Dawson stepped up closer to Steele, and an unpleasant odour of dead flesh made her stomach turn over once. "Find those plans, Steele. There may be something there you can use."

Steele nodded. "We'll start looking. If there is . . . then we'd just need to figure out how to lure Moreby down there."

"Well, that part may be easier than you think."

That thought sent a small chill down Steele's spine.

DIRECTOR STEELE: IN REGARDS TO YOUR QUERY RE: THE CRYPT BENEATH ALL HALLOWS CHURCH, LONDON, WHEREIN WE BELIEVE THOMAS MOREBY WAS INTERRED BEFORE THE OUTBREAK OF HRV, WE CAN TELL YOU THAT HE DESIGNED THE CHURCH AND CRYPT HIMSELF IN THE STYLE OF ARCHITECT NICHOLAS HAWKSMOOR.

HAWKSMOOR WAS WIDELY ADMIRED IN THE EARLY 18TH CENTURY, PRINCIPALLY FOR HIS LONDON CHURCHES, ALTHOUGH THERE HAVE SINCE BEEN SUGGESTIONS THAT HAWKSMOOR HIMSELF DABBLED IN MAGIC AND SATANISM, AND THAT HIS CHURCHES TAKEN TOGETHER FORM AN OCCULT PENTAGRAM THAT SPANS THE PARAMETERS OF THE OLD CITY.

MOREBY WAS A GREAT ADMIRER OF HAWKSMOOR'S WORK, AND EVEN STUDIED UNDER HAWKSMOOR FOR SOME TIME. HOWEVER, AS TO WHETHER THE CRYPT BENEATH ALL HALLOWS HUES TO ANY SPECIFIC OCCULT THEORY OR PRACTICE, I'M AFRAID WE CANNOT CONFIRM.

WE WISH YOU THE BEST OF LUCK IN WHATEVER PLANS YOU MAY HAVE FOR SECURING MOREBY. AS YOU KNOW, BRITAIN IS IN A SHAMBLES AND HUMANITY THROUGHOUT EUROPE IS CONFINED TO POCKETS. RUSSIA IS BASICALLY GONE, AS IS MUCH OF THE SOUTHERN HEMISPHERE, AND NOBODY HAS HEARD ANYTHING OUT OF CHINA SINCE THE INITIAL OUTBREAK. AT THE RISK OF SOUNDING VERY CLICHÉD, IT'S PROBABLY QUITE TRUTHFUL TO SAY THAT THE FATE OF THE WORLD RESTS ON YOU AT THIS POINT.

Chapter Forty-Two

STEELE AND TY had been rummaging for two hours, with no success.

The storage room for the OC's documents was located at one far end of the facility; beyond its concrete walls was nothing but raw stone and soil. It was a medium-sized space stocked with a dozen file cabinets – old metal monstrosities that rattled as their dented drawers were yanked open – and stacks of white cardboard boxes. Ty had taken the file cabinets while Steele sat on the floor going through the contents of the boxes. They'd seen thousands of invoices and packing slips for supplies, work orders for construction, signed confidentiality agreements, and modern maps, but nothing pertaining to Latrobe's original design or construction.

They were running out of drawers and crates.

Ty pulled open a final drawer, saw one hanging file inside full of useless receipts, and exclaimed, "Damn. There's just nothing here." Angry, he slammed the drawer home hard enough to shake the entire cabinet.

Something rattled behind it.

Ty walked around to the edge of the row of filing cabinets and tried to look behind. He grabbed the end cabinet and, huffing with the exertion, managed to move it away from the wall slightly.

There was a large frame back there.

He tried to reach it, but could only wedge his arm into the space up to the wrist.

"What is it?" Steele asked, looking up from the floor.

"There's something back here, but I can't reach it." He struggled again with the cabinet, but couldn't get it to move any further.

"Maybe I can," Steele said, rising and joining him.

"Be my guest."

Steele's arm was thinner than Ty's, and she was able to reach hold of the large framed piece. She got a good grip on an edge and slid it out from behind the cabinets.

It was a framed blueprint. Large (about four feet by three feet), and obviously old, in an ornamental wooden frame, protected behind glass.

"Holy shit, Steele, I think this is it." Ty propped the piece up against the cabinets, used his sleeve to wipe dust from it, and knelt to study it.

It showed a layout similar to the modern maps of the complex, but with rooms named differently. The ink had faded to brown, and in one corner was the legend WASHINGTON DC UNDERGROUND / BENJAMIN HENRY LATROBE, ARCHITECT, in archaic script.

Ty reached up to the top of one of the cabinets, where he'd set a modern map of the underground complex. "Okay, let's see what we've got." He unfolded the modern map and held it beside the framed plans.

Steele joined him to compare the two. The layout matched almost exactly on the two documents, although some rooms had been divided up or repurposed on the modern map.

"There." Ty jabbed a finger at the plans, and brought the matching part of the map up close. Squinting, Steele saw that there was indeed a large chamber indicated on the plans that did not appear on the map. "There's an extra room on the original plans that's not on the later map."

"Meaning . . .?"

Ty turned to her excitedly. "Meaning this room was walled off and removed from the map."

"How do we know it was actually built?"

"Well, we don't . . . but Latrobe's original plans are otherwise exactly the same as the map. Let's see, this room – if it existed – would be . . ." Ty drew a finger along both the plans and the map, then sat back and looked up, " . . . right on the other side of this wall."

Steele followed Ty's gaze, seeing nothing but bare concrete wall, not even painted or panelled. "Are you sure?"

"Yeah . . ." Ty went over the plans again, and pushed them closer to Steele to show her. "See, we're at the far western end of the OC. On the new layout, this is the last room . . . but on the old ones, there's one more room beyond this, and it's larger. The opening would have been right behind the file cabinets."

"Where you found the plans," Steele added.

"Right." Ty leapt to his feet and ran a hand along the smooth concrete surface. "This concrete's probably eight inches thick. We'll need somebody with experience and the right equipment to get through it."

Rising to join Ty, Steele found herself reluctant to touch the wall. "Ty . . . even if you're right, and there's a room behind this one . . . what are you hoping to find there? I mean, is it something we *want* to break into?"

Ty turned to her, surprised. "Somebody didn't want us to find this room; maybe that somebody was even Moreby. This could be the answer we need."

"Or it could be something even worse than Moreby."

"Steele . . . do we really have a choice at this point?"

Steele wanted to say, *Yes – we can walk away, hide those prints, say we found nothing* . . . but she knew Ty was right.

Whatever was behind the wall might save them . . . or complete their damnation.

||| CellNet   8:57 AM   63%

◄ Messages   **P. F. Marcus**   Contact

Today 8:50 AM

We've got a private up here who says his brother was a contractor and he once helped use a cut-off saw on a concrete wall. That and a couple of sledgehammers should get you through.

Text Message   Send

Chapter Forty-Three

BY THE TIME Private Larsen was done with the cut-off saw, both he and Ty were covered with tiny cuts from flying concrete chips.

Fortunately they'd both worn safety goggles and heavy gloves. Ty had opted to keep the operation small, partly because they were working in a confined space already, and partly to keep anyone else out of jeopardy. He had two other soldiers working to haul away the concrete as he hammered chunks down, but he'd asked everyone else to stay clear of this section until they were done.

As soon as they'd created the first large hole, they saw old-fashioned bricks and mortar behind. They removed more concrete, and it soon became clear that the bricks had been used to cover a doorway; the wall on either side was made of massive blocks of stone, and the bricks were set within a granite archway. The ornamentation at the top of the arch consisted of an ornate flying skull.

Most dreadful, however, was the skull and crossbones crudely painted on the bricks. The paint was centuries old and had faded, but it was still a plain warning that death awaited behind the wall.

Ty got the last of the concrete they'd broken through removed, thanked Private Larsen for his work, and told him he could return to Bolling. Larsen, a young man with thinning red hair, seemed relieved to go.

Left alone before the brickwork, Ty studied it and considered his options. Whatever the room held was likely long crumbled to dust. The old plans he'd found were dated 1803, the same year that Benjamin Henry Latrobe had disappeared; had Latrobe placed anything in this room, it would be more than 200 years old.

Ty placed his hands on the brickwork; it was still solid, and cold to the touch, with a musty smell. Curious, he put one ear up against the construction. He listened for a few seconds, hearing only . . .

Something thudded on the wall from the other side.

Ty leapt back, startled. Hands were on him from behind and he gasped. He spun – and saw Steele there.

"Whoa, it's just me. You okay?"

Panting, Ty looked from Steele to the wall. "Yeah, I . . . thought I heard something is all."

Steele looked at the bricks and the primitive white icon painted thereon. "Jesus. I can see why you'd be spooked."

"Yeah. Pretty weird, huh?"

Looking from the bricks to Ty, Steele said, "You were right again, Ty."

He shrugged. "Right about the room, but . . . I have no idea what we'll find in there. Whatever it is, somebody went to great pains to make sure it wasn't found."

"Or that something wasn't getting out."

"What could—" Ty broke off as a muffled thud sounded from beyond the brick wall. He knew he'd likely turned as pale as Steele just had.

"Ty . . ."

"I know. I heard it, too. Something is in there."

"What I was going to say was . . . do you remember the reports from the British, the ones about how when Moreby was freed from the crypt beneath the church, they think he released fleas that may have started the spread of HRV?"

Ty's jaw dropped. How had he missed that?

A crypt . . . He looked again at the macabre flying skull that sat at the apex of the arch, and he knew. This was a crypt, too. And something was in there that was probably long dead, but still alive.

"You can't open it, Ty. You might be condemning everyone down here if you do."

"We *have* to open it, Steele." When she started to protest, he cut her off. "We can do it carefully."

"No."

"Listen to me: we'll clear everyone out of this section, then we'll send in one man and seal everything behind him."

Steele shook her head. "You can't do it, Ty. It's suicide—"

Ty grinned. "It's not suicide for someone who's already dead. It won't be me going in – it'll be Dawson."

"Dawson . . ." Steele glanced at the brickwork one last time and made her decision. "You get everything you need – whatever it'll take to seal this area off. While you do that, I'll go talk to Dawson."

"Good."

Steele was nearly out the door when Ty called after her, "It'll work, Steele. You know it will."

She wished she could believe that.

A NEW WORLD FOR ALL

For immediate release:

Yesterday, Dr. Landen Jones, former Director of Research and Development for New World Pharmaceuticals, was arrested by Federal troops and escorted to Washington, D.C.. Dr. Jones is being held on a number of charges, including treason against the United States of America.

The Board of Directors of New World Pharmaceuticals is hereby going on record as stating that it had no prior knowledge of Dr. Jones's activities and had not authorized his actions. NWP fully acknowledges the vitally important role that Dr. Jones played in the recent development of an antiserum to counteract Human Reanimation Virus (HRV), and we applaud his leadership and ingenuity on that project. However, Dr. Jones then withheld distribution of this crucial drug to the United States Government, and made numerous demands, acting entirely on his own.

Again, we repeat: Dr. Landen Jones at no time acted on behalf of or with the approval of NWP. We suspect that, due to the stress of recent events, Dr. Jones may be suffering some sort of breakdown or psychotic snap; although such psychological illness obviously doesn't excuse his alleged crimes, we do nonetheless hope that he can receive the help he clearly needs and find some sort of peace.

NWP obviously remains dedicated to serving the people and the Government of the United States of America; we are committed to working hand-in-hand with the Government to control the spread of HRV and improve the lives of all humankind. Saving lives and improving health, longevity and happiness have always been NWP's core mission, and recent events have not changed that.

To further demonstrate our commitment, NWP will be offering the first 10,000 doses of our antiserum to the United States Government free of charge.

Chapter Forty-Four

"LOOKS LIKE THEY'RE throwing you under the bus, Landen," the President said as she slid a printout of the NWP press release across her desk.

Jones, seated on the other side with Steele positioned behind him, picked up the release, scanned it, and put it back down. "Can't say that I blame them. I would've done the same thing."

"Whatever happened to honour among thieves?"

"I'd say it went down about the same time that the myth of the United States as a force to be reckoned with did."

Steepling her fingers beneath her chin, the President said, "We're still a force, Landen. Do you understand the severity of what you've attempted to do, or of the punishment you face? Treason can carry a death sentence."

Steele couldn't see Jones' face, but she could imagine that his trademark slight smile hadn't shifted an inch. "And what will killing me gain you?" he said. "I can still be useful to you."

"Yes," the President answered, "you can: you can show the rest of the world that we are still the United States of America and we stand proud against those who seek to bring us down. Get him the hell out of here, Steele."

Steele put a hand under Jones' arm and tugged him to his feet. "With pleasure, ma'am."

As she led Jones back to his cell, he said, "I thought you were smarter than the rest of them, Sandra. You should know that the US doesn't have what it takes to survive."

"We've got more than you know," she said, hoping it would put a chink of doubt in Jones' delusion.

It worked. "What've you got?"

"Landen," Steele said, as they reached the OC's two-cell jail, "it gives me tremendous pleasure to tell you to go fuck yourself."

She thrust him into the cell, locked the door behind him, and walked away. She had more important things to worry about right now – like getting Harland Dawson to be the "more" they needed right now.

||| CellNet	5:32 PM	90%
◂ Messages	**Sandra Steel**	Contact

Today 5:32 PM

Dawson agrees. will bring him down to O.C. blindfolded to minimize information leaking to Moreby. Get your shit together and let's do this.

Text Message · Send

Chapter Forty-Five

"OKAY, HE'S IN and I'm sealing the doors now."

Steele and the President, seated in their Command Center, looked from Ty's monitor, where he was closing a door and using duct tape to seal all the edges, to Dawson's, which showed him walking towards the storage room. Steele leaned forward and turned up the volume as Dawson began to speak.

"Am I coming through?" he asked.

"Loud and clear, Dawson," Steele answered.

Dawson turned two more corners and reached the storage room. He entered, closed the door behind him, and repeated Ty's door-sealing routine with a roll of tape that had been left in the room for that purpose. When he finished, he looked up at the room's only vent, already sealed over with a metal square. "Vent seal in place."

The President nodded. "Go for it," Steele said into her Bluetooth.

Dawson picked up a sledgehammer and began pounding on the bricks.

As he worked, Ty Ward entered the Command room, taking a seat beside Steele. "Anybody bring the popcorn?"

Steele couldn't manage a smile; she'd been unable to shake the feeling that today's events would lead to disaster. She had no rational basis for that feeling, and she tried to tell herself that it was likelier to yield answers . . . but the most primitive part of her – the part that still believed in ghosts and feared spiders and fled at the thought of death – shrieked in protest.

On the monitor, Dawson was laying waste to the bricks. The construction was two centuries old, and it only took him minutes to clear most of it away. He set the sledgehammer aside and looked into the hole he'd created. "We've got a wooden door behind here. It's barred from this side, so it should be easy to open – just give me a minute or so . . ."

He kicked aside the bricks he'd scattered, moving them into a neat pile out of the way. Once he had a clear path, he picked up the main item he'd been provided with: a flamethrower. He'd received a crash course on how to use it before they'd brought him down, blindfolded and with ear muffs, to the OC. He donned the backpack holding the cylinder tanks, released the ignition valve, pulled the ignition trigger and a small jet of blue flame burst from the nozzle. "I'm hot. Here we go."

Dawson stepped forward and pulled up the heavy metal bar that was laid across the door. He set the bar aside and Steele held her breath as he grasped the iron handle set near one edge.

"Hinges are rusty," Dawson said, effort audible in his voice as he pulled.

Steele wondered, *Is Moreby somehow tuning in on all of this? Have we already given him some information he needs to defeat us?* Unfortunately, there'd been no way to ask Dawson to complete this task without removing the blindfold and ear muffs. It was one big overall risk package.

Beside her, the President flinched as the Command Center filled with the nerve-wracking sound of the hinges squealing. The door opened outward, one inch, two . . .

Fingers appeared from the other side, grasping the door, fingers that were nightmares of tattered flesh and bone. An inhuman cry sounded over the speakers, and Steele's heart leaped into her throat.

"What the fuck was that?" Ty whispered beside her.

Even Dawson had jumped back, startled. He stood two feet away from the door now, watching.

The door was abruptly shoved all the way back. Something stood there, lit only by the dim glow of the fire from the tip of the flamethrower. "Wait . . ." Dawson said, and the view from his camera jostled as he evidently reached down for something. A Maglite appeared, was turned on and revealed the thing in the doorway.

It had once been human, but was now little more than a living scarecrow – a creature of ragged shreds and stained bones. The head was a skull with a few wisps of colourless hair and strips of skin, putty-like eyes sunken within the sockets. The remains of a frock coat, shirt, waistcoat and trousers hung from it, and it rattled, bone on bone, as it moved. Its jaws were moving, but no words came forth, just a whistling moan, somehow old and distant.

"Dear God," Dawson muttered.

Beside Steele, the President tensed; Ty was halfway out of his chair.

The spectre took a step forward, and Dawson backed away; even the dead man was unnerved. He lifted the flamethrower, and the sight of the small blue flame caused the skeletal thing to stop. It looked from the fire to Dawson, and Steele shivered as she realized that there was still some intelligence trapped within that ghastly frame.

"Who are you?" Dawson asked.

The thing looked at him for several seconds, as if trying to work out the solution to a difficult problem. Its jaws moved and Dawson reluctantly moved closer, trying to hear. It spoke again, and a sepulchral whisper sounded in the Command Center: "*Latrobe* . . ."

Ty rose excitedly. "Fuck me – it's Benjamin Latrobe."

The President asked, "The architect?"

"Yes. I'm sure it's him."

On the monitor there was sudden movement. Latrobe had apparently rushed forward, colliding with Dawson, who stumbled back. The image spun and shook as they heard crashes and blows on the speakers.

Ty called out, "Dawson, what's happening?"

The image continued to shudder. Latrobe reappeared, falling back, and Dawson seemed to right himself. "He attacked me. The poor mad bastard tried to eat me . . ."

Latrobe was chewing something, but he turned aside and spat it out, moaning, eyeing the camera with pain and confusion.

"Are you all right?" Steele asked.

Dawson answered, "He got a chunk of my shoulder, but I can live without it. Afraid I didn't agree with him, though."

Latrobe turned his back to Dawson and shambled back into the hidden room, making scratchy, choked sounds that actually made Steele pity that terrible, mad thing.

Dawson followed, warily; although Latrobe seemed to present no threat, the area beyond the storage room was lightless, unknown. The flashlight beam picked out a featureless round chamber, high-ceilinged but windowless, with the doorway the only entrance. The walls were rough stone, the only decoration some sort of rock table set up on one side of the space.

"What the hell is that?" Dawson muttered.

Ty said, "It looks almost like . . . some sort of . . . altar."

Latrobe avoided the stone table and moved to the other side of the chamber, where a few pages of parchment rested against the curved wall. He gestured at the pages, indicating that Dawson should take them.

"What are those?" Ty asked.

The monitor image bobbed down as Dawson picked up the pages and held them before the camera in one hand, training the Maglite on them with the other. The pages were torn and brown, covered with cramped handwriting in black ink. "They look like . . . some sort of journal or something."

Behind the pages, Latrobe sagged against the stone wall, a decrepit, sick thing. He looked on dully as Dawson scanned the sheets.

"What do they say?" Steele asked.

"It looks like . . ."

Dawson's camera image went black.

Leaning forward in alarm, Ty called out, "Dawson? What happened? Are you there?"

Dawson's sure voice boomed over the speakers. "I'm here, but I need you to come down here, Ty. I'm suspending all other communications." His voice was replaced by dead air.

Although she already knew the answer, Steele called into her mike, "Harland?"

Nothing.

The President turned away from the screens to look at Ty and Steele. "You two know Dawson better than I do: any speculation on what just happened?"

"Are you asking," Ty responded, "if this might be a trap?"

"Frankly, yes."

Ty shook his head. "Dawson's a hundred and ten per cent committed to us. He wouldn't turn on us."

Steele said, "It doesn't matter either way, because you can't go."

"Steele, I have to."

"We don't know what's in there, Ty. You could be walking into a nest of Moreby's fleas, or some other infectious agent."

"We've got an antiserum—"

The President cut him off. "Steele's right. Even if you can survive HRV, there might be something else in there that's lethal to humans. And frankly, you're too valuable to risk."

"Well, I appreciate that, Madame President, but I know Dawson, and he wouldn't have told me to come down there if he thought there was any risk to me. Maybe he's worried that our lines are being tapped, or—" Ty broke off in sudden realization, and saw that Steele knew, too. "Moreby."

The President sat up, alarmed. "Moreby? Do we have any reason to think he's got a direct line to our coms?"

"No," Steele said, "but he has some mental link to the intelligent zombies. Maybe Dawson's found something big down there, and he's . . . I don't know, trying to block Moreby or something."

Ty said, "I have to go. I can use a hazmat suit – that'll protect me from any infectious agents. You can set up a quarantine team right outside the sealed area, have them waiting for me when I come out. And I'll go in armed, just in case. But I *have* to go in. This could be the answer we need."

After a few seconds, the President said, "I don't like it, but . . . all right."

Ty rose, shouting back over his shoulder as he left, "Fifteen minutes, and I'll be ready."

The door closed behind him, and the two women looked at each other. "I don't know about you," the President said, "but I could use a drink about now."

Steele agreed.

MOREBY: Damnation . . .

CECILIA: What is it?

MOREBY: General Dawson seems to be dead. And just when he was making himself useful again . . .

CECILIA: How was he useful? I thought he betrayed us.

MOREBY: [sighs, then]: Cecilia, my dear, do not make me regret giving you this position more than I already do.

Chapter Forty-Six

TY PULLED AWAY the last strip of duct tape, took a deep breath and said, "I'm going in."

He opened the heavy steel door that separated this section of the complex and stepped through, the bulky hazmat suit and the pistol holstered from a utility belt making it difficult to move. He closed the door behind him, and used the roll of duct tape to seal it again from the inside. When he was satisfied that the seal was air-tight, he said, "We're secure again."

Steele's voice came over his earpiece. "We're with you."

He began walking towards the storage room. The hallways seemed normal enough – the glow of fluorescent lights was steady, no sound audible through the suit, no movement but him – but Ty's heart was thrumming with suspense. What had Dawson found? Was he still alive? Would Ty himself make it out again?

Reaching the storage room, he tried to open the door and found it wouldn't budge. He yanked harder and it moved slightly; he remembered that Dawson had also secured the inside of this room and he was pulling against tape. He pulled with all his strength and the door tore away from its seal. Moving cautiously, he looked into the room.

There was no sign of either Dawson or Latrobe. There was one stack of boxes that had been knocked over, papers scattered about, and there was a fist-sized glob of meat on the floor that made Ty swallow back a wave of nausea.

"Ty . . .?"

"I'm at the storage room, Steele. Nothing yet. Stay tuned . . ."

Stepping into the room, Ty closed the door and sealed it up with tape; then he set the tape roll down and hefted the pistol. He walked to the hole in the wall, stopped when he reached Dawson's pile of bricks and the sledgehammer, and stared at the wooden door he'd seen on the monitor only half-an-hour earlier.

The door was closed. Dawson had to be on the other side of it.

Ty stepped up to the door and called out, "General Dawson . . .?"

"Is that you, Ty?"

It was Dawson's voice. Ty felt a small surge of relief . . . but reminded himself to proceed with caution.

"Yes, sir."

"Come in, Ty, but close the door behind you. *Quickly.*"

Ty pulled the heavy wooden door open, the hinges grating. He caught a glow from within and saw it emanated from a normal flashlight, not some ethereal device or creature. Dawson held the Maglite, aimed at his own face; it painted his already gaunt features with deeper, menacing shadows.

"The door," he said, motioning.

Steele's voice sounded in his headset. "Ty, is that—?" He pulled the door closed, struggling slightly with its weight. Steele's voice cut out. "Steele?" There was no answer.

"They won't receive anything so long as you're in here and that door is shut," Dawson said.

Ty looked around the room, but could see little by the dim flashlight beam. He stepped up to a wall and reached out to the stone surface, which he realized curved around him.

"Where's Latrobe?"

Dawson aimed the flashlight beam towards a far corner of the chamber. "There."

Ty followed the light and saw a pile of blackened, broken bones covered with ash and a few last shreds of clothing. He stepped back, repulsed. "What . . .?"

"He's been trapped in here for over 200 years. There was almost nothing human left, just hunger. He attacked me but realized too late he couldn't eat me. I used the flamethrower. He was suffering, and that way anything he might have carried died with him."

"God," muttered Ty.

Dawson moved the beam of light from Latrobe's remains to the walls of the room. "This place was designed to be unassailable, on both natural and supernatural levels. Sound can pass through the door, but nothing else – not our communication devices, and not Moreby's clairvoyance. In other words, I'm free of the hive mind in here."

"So that's why I had to come to you?"

Dawson gestured with some pages, and Ty recognized the ancient parchment sheets he'd seen on the video. "Well, these are why I couldn't leave here."

Ty stepped closer, trying to peer at the pages. "What are they?"

"Basically, Latrobe's suicide note." Dawson held a sheet up before the light and read: "'I, Benjamin Henry Latrobe, am yet of sound mind, but my body is now anything but sound. I have been infected by a terrible ailment which, I believe, has killed my body and placed abominable appetites within it . . .'"

"HRV," Ty said.

"Yes. He talks about being bitten by 'one of Moreby's damned fleas', and when he realized what he was, and that Moreby had meant him to infect the entire New World, he immediately withdrew from public life and had himself sealed in this chamber, which he made sure was erased from all future plans." Dawson lowered the papers and looked at the small mound of Latrobe's bones. "My God . . . he condemned himself to be locked in here, in the dark, alone, for centuries, unable to feed or even communicate. Of course he went insane – anyone would."

"So why are *we* here, General?"

Dawson gestured around the chamber. "I think Latrobe knew this room was impervious to exterior discovery; he wanted to put himself away where he'd never be found . . . by Moreby, specifically."

Something started to tickle at the edge of Ty's thoughts, but he couldn't quite grasp it. "Then . . ."

Dawson grinned, and with his dead face, in the half-light of the narrow beam, it wasn't a comforting sight. "Think about it, Ty: if we could get Moreby in here . . ."

Ty did understand now, " . . . he'd be trapped. Truly trapped – he couldn't reach out, move on, any of it."

"Right. And I'm betting it would also sever his connection to the intelligent ones. No more hive mind. Hell, it might even remove their intelligence altogether."

"But . . ." Ty looked anxiously up at Dawson. "Wouldn't that mean that . . . you . . .?"

"Not if I'm in here with him."

In the brief time he'd known Dawson, Ty had come to like him a great deal; like Ames Parker, he took his duty seriously and displayed compassion along with courage. But this was too much – damning himself wasn't listed on the job description. "You can't do it. We're talking about sealing him in here forever, Dawson. My God, you saw what it did to Latrobe."

"I did, and I'm prepared to accept that fate. I don't want to find out later on that Moreby found a way out of here when nobody was looking . . . so, I'll stay and look." Dawson turned away for a moment, then said, softly, "Besides, if this works and you win . . . it'll be your world, not mine."

Ty pushed down his emotions (fury at the unfairness, despair at the chance of ever winning) and focused on the situation. "Okay, fine. That just leaves the biggest question, then: how do we get him down here?"

Dawson stepped closer to Ty. "That's why you had to come down here: I know how to do it, and if I leave here Moreby will know, too."

"How?"

Dawson told him.

Steele: Mr. Moon, we of course invite you to stay with us—

Moon: Me and Maxi, right?

Steele: Of course. But we'll need to find a job for you.

Moon: Great. I want to work.

Steele: Is there anything in particular you'd be interested in doing?

Moon: Well . . . I don't know much about politics, and I'd be a pretty crappy soldier, but I'm organized and I've got a good memory, and . . .

Steele: Weren't you majoring in Business in College?

Moon: Yeah, but I dropped out in my second year – couldn't keep up with tuition any more. I was going to work for a while to save up enough to go back . . . my goal's always been to open my own restaurant.

Steele: Do you have any accounting experience?

Moon: A little. My boss had me doing some of the books at my last restaurant job.

Steele: Good enough. I'm thinking we can find you something in either an aide position or maybe the GAO . . . once we get an economy up and running again.

Moon: Wow . . . um, that would be amazing. Ms. Steele . . . this might sound like bullshit, but – well, I really want to help. I want to see us come back, and if I can help make that happen . . . well . . .

Steele: That doesn't sound like bullshit at all, Mr. Moon – I think most of us here feel that way. Welcome to the team.

Chapter Forty-Seven

PEPPER AND FORBES had come back.

They lumbered towards Kevin, and he turned to run, but he couldn't – he was still chained to the post in the yard, but the chain was so heavy now he couldn't even move his feet. He remembered something – they'd been shot. He'd seen them, they'd both taken bullets to the head, so how could they be moving . . .?

They came closer, and he saw the blossom-shaped wounds each carried in their foreheads. He wanted to scream, to tell them they couldn't possibly be alive, because even the intelligent ones were dead when the brain was damaged, and these two had never been intelligent, but here they were reaching out for him, so close, and he couldn't move or scream or—

His eyes snapped open. He was panting, his heart was drumming a frantic rhythm, his breath fast and shallow. For a second, Kevin was disoriented – he saw metal walls, soft lights, a blanket bunched around his body . . .

It came to him: he was in the OC, deep beneath Washington, in the room he shared with Maxi. It'd been a dream; Pepper and Forbes were long dead, and he was safe.

When his heart slowed to a reasonable pace, Kevin thought of Maxi and hoped he hadn't woken the boy. He looked over to Maxi's bunk, on the other side of the room . . .

It was empty.

"Maxi?"

There was no answer.

"Damn it," Kevin muttered to himself, mainly because the panic had flared again, this time for real. There was no reason to panic; Maxi had probably just gone for a walk, maybe looking for a snack.

But Kevin knew there'd be no sleep until he'd reassured himself about Maxi's safety, so he swung out of his own bunk, pulled on jeans and a jacket, ran his fingers through his hair, and stepped over to the main door of the room.

He opened it, and blinked at the light – the hallways remained lit at all times, and the glare was painful as Kevin came from their room, where the only illumination was provided by a lamp they left turned low at all times. Kevin heard a voice from his right, and turned to see Maxi a few feet away, sitting with his back against one wall of the corridor, talking on a cell phone.

"Maxi?" Kevin said.

The boy looked up, and guilt flashed across his dark features. "Hey, I gotta go," he said into the phone, speaking in a quiet rush, "I'll talk to you later." He ended the call and lowered the phone.

"Who was that?"

"Nobody. Sorry, did I wake you?"

"No, a nightmare did that. So you know somebody named 'Nobody'?"

Maxi rose and walked past Kevin to return to their room, obviously feigning a yawn. "Didn't realize how late it was. I'm goin' to bed . . ."

Kevin followed him, closing the door behind them. Maxi tried to ignore him as he took off his shoes and jeans, but Kevin turned on the overhead light, letting Maxi know that sleep wasn't going to be happening right away.

He's a little kid, Kevin reminded himself. *This is where I have to be the adult.*

Kevin sat on the end of Maxi's bed, trying to sound gentle yet firm. "Maxi, I need to know who you were talking to."

Turning away from Kevin, Maxi said, "You don't trust me."

"No, I . . ." Kevin trailed off, realizing it was true – he didn't trust Maxi on this. But he had to. He was still learning the ins and outs of dealing with a twelve year old, and was slowly realizing that Maxi was no regular twelve year old. When Kevin had been twelve, he'd liked comic books and performing magic tricks; Maxi, however, had seen people die and be eaten, he'd lost his parents and he'd travelled across a post-apocalyptic America with a dead man. If Kevin treated him like a child, he'd lose him.

"I'm sorry, Maxi, I didn't mean to . . . look, I trust you. I was just concerned, that's all. If you don't want to tell me, it's cool."

Kevin rose from the boy's bunk, turned off the overhead light, and was halfway across the room when he heard Maxi whisper, "Maribel."

Kevin froze, then turned around. "Maribel? You mean your sister? But I thought she was . . ."

. . . dead.

"Oh my God . . . she turned, didn't she?"

Maxi nodded. "She told me to hide when they came. I did. She tried to run, but they got her. Three of them. I was in a closet, and I heard her scream, and they didn't just kill her and eat her . . . they *played* with her first. They made fun of her, they shouted mean shit at her, and they made her cry, and when they finally got bored and ate her I saw parts of it, through a crack in the door. And then they left, and she got up. She came over to the closet to get me, but instead she told me to run." Maxi's eyes filled up and tears spilled over, washing down his cheeks. "I knew she was hungry, but she told me to run. I did, and that was when I found Mr Dawson. He was just outside, and if he'd come just half-an-hour earlier . . . I told him my sister was dead, and we left."

Kevin reached out and put a comforting hand on Maxi's shoulder. "I'm so sorry, Maxi. God, I'm sorry."

Wiping at his eyes and sniffling, Maxi said, "She still had her cell phone when I called her. We couldn't talk much because the phone wouldn't work in most places across the country, but it works here, with the Wi-Fi."

"Have you talked to her a lot?"

Maxi nodded. "Since we got here, yeah. She says LA's a mess – the zombies took over for a while, but the humans are fighting back now and doing pretty good. She's afraid to go out, afraid she'll get shot."

"Maxi . . . how much have you told her? About where we are, I mean?"

The boy's eyes went wide and he blinked away tears as he looked up at Kevin. "N-nothing. Why? . . . Hey, she wouldn't—"

"I know she wouldn't do anything deliberately, but there are rumours that the zombies – the intelligent ones – can all kind of talk to each other, you know, mentally."

"I swear I haven't said anything."

Kevin looked at the boy closely, and decided he believed him. "Okay," he said, smiling, and then added, "but it's probably a good idea if you don't tell anyone else down here you've been talking to her."

"I won't. I promise."

"You rule."

That got a weak smile from the boy. Kevin gave him a final pat and stood. "Think you can sleep now?"

The boy nodded.

"Okay. Good night."

"Good night, Kevin."

Kevin walked across the room and sat down on his own bed. He knew sleep wouldn't come soon, not because of nightmares, but because of the waking thought he couldn't shake:

Please, God, don't let us be trapped down here because of something a twelve-year-old kid did out of love.

I, Benjamin Henry Latrobe, am yet of sound mind, but my body is now anything but sound. I have been infected by a terrible ailment which I believe has killed my body and placed abominable appetites within it.

I believe this to be the work of Thomas Moreby, the British architect to whom I so foolishly apprenticed myself. Moreby, as I discovered during our work together, was less interested in the beauty of structures than in their potential occult powers. I allowed myself to be guided by him, and now I fear what I have given my art to. This new

Capitol – this "New Rome" – could someday be a source of great evil and, should that ever come to pass, then I will be partly to blame.

My last correspondence with Moreby suggested that he has embarked on a great and sinister plot, and that I am his link to America. The letter included one of Moreby's damned fleas, a plague-carrier which infected me with this terrible ailment created by Moreby. Now I suffer from the hungers of the damned; I yearn to taste the flesh of my fellow man. Dare I even call another man "fellow" now? Am I beyond humankind, some sort of new species?

I suspect that I am now Moreby's flea, that if I should give-in to these terrible desires, I would spread this hellish infection. Moreby likely meant me to infect the New World in preparation for his arrival.

This I will not allow to happen.

I know not if I can die at this point, so I am left with only one alternative: After swiftly putting my affairs in order, I shall seal myself away in a place where I can cause no harm or risk discovery. There is a room that Moreby bade me construct and which my brother Masons conducted certain rituals within to ensure its security. This chamber is located in the underground structure beneath Washington, and at the extreme end of it. It will be easy enough to seal it away. I will place myself within it shortly, and bid my trusted construction foreman to bar and then wall-in the only doorway. I will further request that he seal the two entrances to this entire subterranean system. My final building will, as it must, become my tomb.

I will spend my internment praying for forgiveness and for sweet death. If these words are ever found, beware he who reads them; should I still live, you will be in mortal — and possibly immortal — danger. If you possess the knowledge to destroy me, please act upon that knowledge. If not, then flee this place and seal it away again.

And if you who enter should bear the name Moreby, may God damn you to even worse Hells than that to which you have damned me, sir.

Benjamin Henry Latrobe

Chapter Forty-Eight

JONES LOOKED UP as Steele and a medic entered his brig cell. Steele enjoyed the way his expression changed to trepidation when the medic held up the syringe.

"What is this? Surely you're not resorting to truth serum."

Steele smirked. "Surely not. No, Landen, this is even worse, at least for you: we've got an HRV vaccine, and everyone gets a dose – even a worthless piece of shit like you."

"Well, Steele, nice to see your true colours coming out at last."

"Just shut up and roll up your sleeve."

The medic shot Steele a look that she hoped Landen hadn't noticed; she knew the man was a dedicated healer and didn't like being part of this deception, but their country's future rested on the lie.

Jones took his time unbuttoning his cuff and rolling up the sleeve. The medic swabbed his arm and said, "Make a fist, please." Landen did, the medic found a vein, and the shot was quickly delivered.

"Ow," said Jones with exaggerated boredom, looking at Steele.

She was just following the medic out when Jones said, "Oh, by the way, Steele – be sure to congratulate the President on the creation of the vaccine. I'm not quite sure how your research team was able to figure that out when ours wasn't . . . looks like you won all the way around."

"Sometimes the good guys do," Steele said, just before stepping out and locking the door.

She sent the medic back up to Bolling, and then met Ty down the hallway. "Did he buy it?" Ty asked.

"I didn't leave him much choice," Steele said. "So, what's next?"

They started walking towards the Command Center. "The message has gone out to Moreby," Ty said. "If he has any IT experts on hand they might figure out it didn't come from New World Pharmaceuticals and we'd be fucked then, but that's a chance we'll have to take. If we don't get an answer in the next twenty-four hours, we probably won't hear from him at all and the plan will be off."

Steele took a deep breath and answered. "We wait, then."

"We wait," Ty agreed.

Dear Landen: I am certainly most interested in hearing what my old friends at NWP have to offer, and I would appreciate the opportunity to discuss this further. Is tomorrow at 1:00 p.m. here in the Oval Office acceptable? You of course have my personal assurance that you will be unharmed, provided you come unarmed and alone.

Chapter Forty-Nine

IT WAS 12:15 pm the next day when Steele opened the door to Jones' cell. As she left the door open, he eyed her curiously.

"C'mon, Landen, let's go," she said, jerking her head towards the outside hallway.

Jones didn't rise from his seated position on his bunk. "You'll pardon me, Director Steele, if I indulge myself enough to ask . . . let's go where, exactly?"

Steele did her best to look irked. "You're free to go."

That got him to sit a little straighter. "Am I, now? How did that happen?"

"Your NWP masters made some kind of deal for you. I can't tell you the details. They just want you back for some reason, it seems."

Jones' brow furrowed, and for a moment Steele wondered what would happen if he simply refused to leave the cell. Finally, though, he rose. "It's almost enough to make one believe in miracles. A moment, please."

Steele stepped out slightly as Jones straightened his clothes and hair. As he left the cell, she handed him his jacket. "Your phone's in the pocket."

Jones put the jacket on, then withdrew the phone and hit the power button. When the screen glowed, he said, "How nice of your intelligence experts not to drain the battery when they went through it."

"We don't have intelligence experts any more – Aaron Gillespie committed suicide a couple of weeks ago."

For a split second, Jones seemed to display a genuine emotion. "I'm sorry to hear that. I always liked him."

"Let's just get this over with." Steele turned and led the way towards the elevators.

As they rounded a corner that led away from the brig, Ty joined them, exchanging a look with Steele. Jones didn't notice – he was too intent on meeting his freedom. "Mr Ward, come to hug me goodbye?"

"More like to make sure you don't scrawl obscenities on the elevator walls."

The rest of the ride up was completed in silence. The doors opened, and Steele and Ty accompanied Jones through the nondescript office building that disguised the entrance to the OC and out to where a reinforced jeep awaited, the keys in the ignition.

"This is mine?" Jones asked.

Steele said, "Sorry it's not your colour – blood red. It was all we could spare."

"As long as it gets me away from here, it'll do."

Jones climbed in behind the steering wheel, and Steele leaned through the open passenger-side window. "Follow this road to the front gate – they're expecting you. From there you're on your own."

Jones started up the engine, and said, "Wish I could say it's been a pleasure." He rolled up the window.

Steele moved back to join Ty a short distance away. They spoke together softly, Steele facing away from the jeep. "What's he doing?"

Ty glanced behind her and smiled, then spoke softly. "He's looking down. Pretty sure he's going through his phone. Wait – he's frowning. Yeah, he just got it."

Steele knew what the "it" was: the message they'd sent Jones that purported to be from NWP's Board, directing him to meet with Moreby at 1:00 pm to offer the zombie government an exclusive licence to NWP's antiserum.

Steele heard the jeep's engine rev up and the tyres squealed as Jones peeled out. Ty watched the jeep head off and said, "I'm pretty sure he just realized he has about fifteen minutes to get to the White House and make that meeting."

A few seconds later, Steele's phone rang. She answered it, said only, "Got it," terminated the call and turned to Ty. "He's through the gate."

Ty nodded, pulled out his own phone and punched a number. "Ready Alpha Team."

Steele returned to the office building and ducked into the first cubicle, where a computer waited for her. She brought up the data from the GPS tracker hidden in Jones' jeep, and followed his progress through the streets of Washington. When he turned on to State Place and pulled up to the White House gates, Steele ran back out to where Ty waited, now surrounded by a dozen men in protective armour and bearing assault rifles.

"He's there," she said.

Ty finished pulling on his own armour, made sure his headset was in place, and shouted at his team, "We're live! Let's go." He indicated a Black Hawk that waited a few hundred yards away, and the soldiers jogged towards it. Just as he was about to follow, Steele grabbed his arm and he turned back.

"You sure you want to do this yourself?" she asked. "They're good men. They can handle this on their own."

"Probably, but . . . I think I *need* to do this. Ames wanted me to take over for him, and he would have led this personally, you know?"

She did. She nodded and said, "Good luck."

"I'll see you soon."

Ty turned and ran across the field. As soon as he was aboard the Black Hawk, it lifted off. Steele watched it go, gaining altitude and then turning to head towards the White House.

Even while she was sure she'd never see Ty alive again, she hoped she was wrong.

Moreby: Ahh, the guest of honor has arrived. Welcome, Mr. Jones! We have saved you a seat at the head of the table. These ladies and gentlemen are my principal ministers.

Jones: Hello, everyone. Thank you for having me here today.

Cecilia: Are we having him, Thomas?

Moreby: Cecilia—!

Cecilia: Oh, it was just a little joke. Calm yourself.

Moreby: Now, Mr. Jones . . .

Jones: Landen, please. I'm sorry, I don't mean to stare, but - I well, President Moreby, your ministers are familiar faces; in fact, I hadn't even realized that a few of them were . . .

Moreby: Dead, I think you mean.

Jones: Well . . . yes.

Cecilia: Something else you may not have realized, Landen: my body's previous owner found you quite attractive. In fact, she seems to have even harbored some rather erotic fantasies about you—

Moreby: Enough, Minister! I apologize on behalf of my cabinet, Landen.

Lovett: I'd like to see him on my butcher's block, I would . . .

Moreby: *Cease*!

⟦A few seconds of silence, then⟧

Moreby: Now, we are very interested to hear
more about this offer which your
Government is prepared to make.

Jones: Well, Mr. President, New World is
technically not a government . . .
yet . . .

Moreby: New World? I know more about New
World Pharmaceuticals than you can
possibly imagine . . . *Landen*. I am
talking about the Federal Government.

Jones: I'm sorry, sir - I'm not following.

Moreby: The message that I received
indicated that you would be
representing the United States of
America here today.

Jones: ⟦stammering slightly⟧: No, sir - I'm
here from New World Pharmaceuticals.

Moreby: Interesting. We seem to have had
some sort of . . . breakdown in
communications.

Jones: ⟦very nervous⟧: Look, I'm sure this
is just a simple misunderstanding.
I can still be of use . . .

Moreby: Oh, I *know* you can.

Jones: Why is he getting up? What's he
doing?

Moreby: Lord Charles, sit down.

Charles: But Thomas, he looks so delicious.

Moreby: I should have given you the body of a pig. Now, please give me the courtesy of saving this one for myself.

Jones: Now, hold on there, Mr. President – you don't have to come so close, sir, I—

〖Jones screams, and there are ripping and chewing sounds.〗

Moreby: You were quite right, my dear – he *is* delicious! Here, have a taste . . .

〖Jones's screams are muffled, and fade to a series of gulping whimpers. More chewing sounds are heard, indicating multiple acts of consumption going on. Suddenly a retching noise is heard.〗

Arnold: President Moreby . . .?

〖Moreby gasps, but forms no coherent words. Now there are other choking and vomiting sounds.〗

Cecilia: What is happening . . .!

〖There's the sound of a body falling. It's soon followed by several more. Two voices are still moaning and gasping, and then those are silenced as well, followed by the final two thuds.〗

Chapter Fifty

AS THE BLACK Hawk prepared to set down on the South Lawn, Ty addressed his team again. "Remember, quick in and out – we only want Moreby."

They nodded. They were good soldiers; all seemed prepared, confident, cool. Ty wished he felt that way.

Breaking into New World Pharmaceuticals had been easier because he hadn't been the real commander – he'd been a tag-along figurehead. Now, however . . . he couldn't help but think over and over that he wasn't Ames Parker – or Steele, for that matter. He'd done reasonably well as the President's Chief of Staff, but this was *real* combat.

He glanced out the side of the bird as it descended, and noticed that what Steele had told him minutes before – "I think it worked; we're getting reports from all over the country that the zombies seem to be suddenly in disarray, confused" – was happening here as well. Dead soldiers with guns, who'd stood at alert attention until Moreby's attempt to eat Landen Jones, now moved erratically, without direction. One young male was trying to eat the laser sight atop his assault rifle.

Dawson had guessed right: consuming a human injected with the HRV antiserum had in essence poisoned Moreby; although they had no visual confirmation, they believed that he'd fallen into some sort of unconsciousness, since his connection with the zombies had apparently been severed. Now they could only hope that he would not recover before they could get him out of the White House and to the underground chamber where Dawson waited.

The Black Hawk touched down, and Ty was (guiltily) relieved to see that he didn't even have to shout commands – his forward units were already on the ground, laying down fire. Fortunately the zombies were spread out, and although they had started to converge on the 'copter, they were still moving slowly. Soon their remains littered the lawn and the Rose Garden.

Next, they focused on clearing a path to the West Wing. Ty's team aimed first at any zombie in a uniform or carrying a weapon, but no gunfire was returned. Ty had chosen his men and women well, and they worked with practised efficiency.

Steele had indicated that they'd likely find Moreby in the Roosevelt Room, only a few feet from the Oval Office. It should be a simple operation to enter through the Office, cross a corridor and pick up Moreby from the Roosevelt Room.

Ty knew things were rarely simple, though.

With half his troops now forming an armed line leading to the Oval Office, Ty and the rest of his unit ran forward. The door was unlocked, and his forward leaders ran in first, rifles ready. They shot three of the dead in the Office, and shouted, "Clear!"

Ty entered, crossed to the President's desk and unplugged a laptop sitting there, which he handed to another of his men who stored it in a backpack. Working quickly, Ty checked around the desk, yanked open drawers and circled the room, but found nothing else that might contain useful information.

Remembering the plans he'd studied, he walked to the door that should face on to the corridor and the Roosevelt Room just beyond, and risked a glance out. There were several zombies in the corridor; the door on the far side was closed.

Ty nodded to his troops, who stepped into the corridor and took down the approaching dead with a single shot each. They moved up to the closed door of the Roosevelt Room, two on either side, and looked to Ty. He nodded again.

One of them tentatively tried the knob, which turned. He abruptly threw the door back and raised his rifle, tensing.

No sound came from the Roosevelt, but from his vantage point in the Oval Office Ty saw bodies on the floor.

As his troops moved into the room, Ty followed. There were figures sprawled everywhere, in chairs, on the floor, slumped across the table. Blood was splattered on faces and clothing; in several cases, where the fallen faced up, Ty was startled to realize he recognized some of them from news coverage of the past, when they'd been Congressmen and Governors who'd made news by arguing or accusing or preening.

A choked moan sounded from one corner, and rifles were raised in immediate response. "Sir," one of the soldiers said, gesturing Ty over. Ty joined him, and it took him a moment to identify who he was looking down at.

Landen Jones was still alive, even though he'd been partially eaten. Half his scalp, with his styled hair still attached, now hung on one side of his head, revealing a crimson-splotched white skull. One cheek was a gaping hole, his jacket had been ripped off and his left arm ended a few inches below the elbow, a bone protruding from the torn, red-soaked flesh. His crisp white shirt had turned almost entirely red, and one of his Italian loafers was missing.

One eye had filled with blood, but he could still see well enough with the other one to recognize Ty. "You set me up," he rasped out.

"You know, Landen," Ty said, for the first time not trying to disguise the contempt in his voice, "I prefer to think that I finally gave you a chance to serve your country."

A rush of blood burbled up over Jones' bottom lip, he convulsed and died. Ty raised his own rifle until the barrel was a few inches above Jones' ruined forehead and he squeezed the trigger. Landen Jones wouldn't be coming back.

"Sir," a man called from a few feet away, "target identified."

Ty stepped over another prone figure and looked down. The man in the grey suit, with the blood-spattered face of a one-time janitor, was unquestionably Moreby. He was moving weakly, spasmodically, and Ty knew he might recover at any time. "That's him. Let's move quickly."

Ty stood back and let two others step forward. One had a white hockey mask that he secured around Moreby's head, removing his ability to bite. "You're kidding me," said another soldier who lifted Moreby forward and secured his wrists behind him.

"No," said the man who'd put on the mask, "got the idea from that movie, the one with the serial killer—"

"Let's stay focused," Ty said. Something felt wrong here. He couldn't put his finger on it, but a dread of terrible failure was building in Ty, something . . .

His right leg flared in pain. He gasped and instinctively jerked back, looking down.

A woman who had once represented Minnesota in the House of Representatives and who had become well known for her fundamentalist beliefs had pushed up the leg of Ty's protective suit and sunk her teeth into the soft flesh of his calf just above his boot. "Goddamnit," Ty cried out, as the zombie refused to relinquish her hold on him. He was lowering his rifle when one of his soldiers stepped forward, pulled her own pistol and shot the former Congresswoman in the head. "I always hated that dumb bitch," the soldier said, before bending to look at Ty's leg.

"I'm okay. We've got antiserum in the bird – let's just get back there before the rest of them wake up and get hungry."

A black sack was thrown over Moreby's head and a large soldier – who'd been brought along for his ability to lift – knelt, hefted the zombie President over one shoulder, rose and started out.

They made the trip back to the Black Hawk safely. Once everyone was on board, the 'copter lifted off, returning to Bolling.

An Asian soldier named Chu was acting as their medic. He squatted in the middle of the bird, pulled back Ty's blood-soaked pants leg and examined the wound. "It's deep, but I don't think anything major has been severed. Can you still move the foot?"

"Yes," Ty answered.

"Good. You should be okay." The medic swabbed out the wound, applied a field dressing, gave Ty some painkillers, and then raised a hypodermic needle and a vial of antiserum. "You'll be out of it for a few days," the medic said as he gave Ty the injection, "but you should be just fine afterwards."

"Good job. Thanks."

Ty settled back against the side of the Black Hawk. The pills were already working, the pain in his leg subsiding, but he still felt the first anticipatory tingle of illness. They'd told him to expect a day or so of reduced symptoms. This was stronger than what he'd expected, though, and he wondered what it must be like to die of HRV if this was how a lesser version felt. The fever was already spreading, his limbs weakening, his concentration fading . . .

"You okay, Commander?" The medic was eyeing him with some concern.

"You're sure you gave me the right dosage on the antiserum?"

The medic held up the syringe and examined it, even though it was now empty. "Yes. Why?"

"I feel . . . strange . . . maybe once the antiserum works its way through . . ." Ty's voice trailed off as he passed out.

FIELD REPORT FROM 76TH INFANTRY BRIGADE COMBAT TEAM

HEADQUARTERED AT FORT BENJAMIN HARRISON,
LAWRENCE, INDIANA
COL. JACK WHITTAKER, COMMANDING

DATE: 11/24/13

As has been previously reported, the 76th BCT has been successful in holding our ground (including armory), despite constant threat of both intelligent and non-intelligent dead insurgents. The intelligent are members of the NZOAMW, and they are armed and knowledgeable about our strategies and defenses. They were victorious once in breaking our perimeter, but were repelled by a combination of explosive arms and close combat.

Since that time, the NZOAMW has continually mounted attacks. Although we have taken casualties (49 wounded, 12 dead, 5 transformed and MIA), we still have 212 troops stationed here, and ammo and supplies are good. We continue to take in civilians, although their numbers grow less with time.

Today at approximately 13:40 hours, we encountered a phenomenon we hadn't hitherto witnessed: intelligent members of the NZOAMW, who had set up a machine-gun nest a few dozen yards from our southwest perimeter, abruptly ceased the attack. Initial assumptions were that they'd run out of ammo or experienced technical problems, but they failed to respond to our counter-attack, and the three members of NZOAMW manning the post were terminated with ease. A sweep of the area revealed eight other NZOAMW soldiers, all of whom seemed equally unaware and unfocused; only one tried to brandish a rifle as our squad approached, and he moved so slowly that he hadn't finished raising the weapon before he was shot.

Since then, scouts have reported that the NZOAMW soldiers seem to be regaining awareness, but many are running from our troops and fleeing their posts.

We cannot account for this behavior, but it has – temporarily, at least – turned the tide here at Fort Benjamin Harrison, and for the first time since the rise of the NZOAMW we can safely state that we have won a battle against them.

Respectfully Submitted,
Col. Jack Whittaker

Chapter Fifty-One

STEELE RAN A finger down her tablet screen, glancing at the emails. "They're coming in from all over: reports of Moreby's troops flopping over like their batteries just ran out. Even when they sort of wake up, they seem disorganized. It's a major victory for human forces everywhere."

The President nodded and smiled. "We're owed one, I think . . ."

Steele's phone sounded. She glanced at the screen, murmured, "Marcus," and then answered.

The news was only partly good: Moreby was on his way down, but Ty had been injured. "How severe is it?" Steele asked.

"He was apparently bitten by one of Moreby's ministers. They administered antiserum promptly, so he should be okay, but he passed out on the flight home."

"Christ. Okay, I'll meet your group at the elevators." Steele told the President what had happened, put the phone in a pocket and rose. "They're bringing in Moreby now. With Ty out of order, I'll need to take him to Dawson."

The President started to rise. "Good. I'll—"

Steele raised a hand and her voice both. "You'll do nothing but stay in this office until you hear from me. We still need to consider Moreby extremely dangerous, and I won't let you go anywhere near him."

The President opened her mouth to argue, but instead dropped back into her chair. "Sorry, you're right, of course. It's just that . . ."

Softening, Steele said, "I know – you wanted to see him, especially as he's locked away. I understand that, but . . . this is one historic scenario you'll have to only hear about second-hand."

With that, Steele left.

She stopped at Supply long enough to secure a hazmat suit, which she donned immediately. She issued orders to clear all the hallways between the elevators and the room where Dawson waited; all doors were to be locked, no one was to venture out again until she gave the all clear.

Steele was ready in the protective suit when the elevator arrived and the doors opened. Two men in suits like hers wheeled a gurney with Moreby strapped to it . . . or at least she had to assume it was Moreby, because a black sack still covered his head.

The men saluted, and Steele waved them forward, leading the way to the secret room. Walking this close to Moreby, even if he was strapped to a gurney and accompanied by two armed soldiers, made her anxious and she didn't resist the urge to occasionally look back. He didn't seem to be moving, but she knew he wasn't dead.

They reached the storage room and Steele turned to the two soldiers; there was no point in exposing them to either further potential danger or the knowledge of the secret room. "Dismissed. I'll take it from here."

They didn't argue, but instead turned soundlessly and left.

Steele struggled slightly manoeuvring the gurney into the cramped storage room. When she had it in, wedged between piles of bricks and filing cabinets, she closed the outer door and walked to the heavy wooden door behind which Dawson waited. She hauled it open and called his name.

He emerged from the darkness of the room, his filmy eyes going immediately to the figure on the gurney. After a few seconds, he looked into Steele's suit, his brow furrowing when he saw her behind the transparent faceplate. "Steele? Where's Ty?"

"He was injured capturing Moreby."

"Was he infected?"

"Yes, but he received a dose of antiserum. He should be all right."

Dawson nodded. He looked down at the prone figure of Moreby again, his hand inching towards the black hood, but he hesitated. "I wish you didn't have to be here, but . . . someone will need to lock us in again."

"I understand." After a second, Steele added, "Harland, are you sure you need to do this? We can just put him in there and seal it behind him . . ."

"I'm sure. But, I need to ask a favour . . ." Dawson nodded at the belt around the hazmat suit, one from which Steele's holstered pistol was slung. "I need your sidearm."

Steele blinked in surprise, and realized she was reluctant to give the Glock up; she'd used it for a decade now, and recently it had saved her life on more than one occasion. "Of course, but . . ."

"I'm going to try to kill Moreby."

Something moved on the gurney. Steele's gaze jerked down, and she saw that Moreby's fingers were twitching; as she watched, they began to flex. Dawson moved quickly, unbuckling the straps that held Moreby to the gurney. "We may not have much time. We need to get him in there *now*."

Steele nodded, and worked on the straps around Moreby's legs. When the restraints were undone, Dawson hefted him under the arms and dragged him off the gurney; Moreby's legs hit the floor with a thump and scraped along the painted concrete as Dawson, lurching backwards, dragged him into the secret room. By the time Dawson laid Moreby out in the centre of the chamber, he was beginning to moan softly. Dawson looked up at Steele, who hesitated in the doorway.

"The Glock," he said.

Steele removed the weapon from its holster and passed it to Dawson. "The magazine's full."

Dawson accepted the Glock and weighed it in his hand, satisfied. "As soon as you seal that door, I'm going to put this to his head and pull the trigger."

"But, if it works . . . you'll be . . ."

"No, I won't. Because if it works, the second shot will be for me. And if it doesn't work, I'll be here to guard him."

Moreby began to rustle under the cowl. Dawson jerked back and pointed the gun at Moreby's head. "Get out, Steele – *now*!"

Steele stepped back and closed the door, sliding the heavy bar into place. She paused there, listening. She thought she heard the sound of the gun firing, but she couldn't be sure.

She stayed a few more minutes before turning to go. At the entrance to the storage area, she turned off the lights, closed the door and tested the lock.

It was done for now.

MESSAGE FROM THE PRESIDENT
OF THE UNITED STATES OF AMERICA

My fellow Americans,

Today, America is renewed. We've come through the darkest storm clouds and we can, at last, see a future of light and promise.

I'm pleased to inform you that our great enemy, the zombie President James Moreby, is no more. Approximately eighteen hours ago, Moreby was taken by a special team under the leadership of Ty Ward, and has been placed in a maximum security facility. Without Moreby's direction, his forces are in disarray, and within the last day our forces have successfully retaken many key locations, including San Francisco, Chicago, and Providence. Here in Washington, we are in the process of securing the White House once again, and we hope to have the American Government reinstalled in that most significant of landmarks within days.

The tide has turned. We have new drugs that are helping us to survive HRV, and we have already begun distribution of these drugs on a mass scale.

I know most of you hearing or reading this have suffered

immense losses; we all have. I myself have lost my husband, my daughter, and many others who were dear to me. But I've survived, as you have, and now I'm very proud to be able to lead this great nation into a new era of hope, as we come together and rebuild.

It's not over yet; I know that. We have almost unimaginable hurdles in front of us. We have cities to reconstruct, roads to clear, mouths to feed, and hearts to heal. We don't know yet the full extent of HRV infection around the world. As much as we could mutually benefit with help from our neighbours, we may have to move ahead alone, at least at first.

So I must ask more of you. I know you're all exhausted, hungry, heartsick. But if we can all endure just a few more days, life will begin again. Don't let down your guards yet – our foe is still plentiful, strong, and intent on defeating us. But without their leader – who we now believe was also the creator of HRV itself – they cannot win.

The end is near . . . and the end is victory.

Good night, and God bless the United States of America.

H.

Chapter Fifty-Two

AS STEELE HELPED the President pack up the office, she was surprised to realize she might actually miss this concrete-and-steel, sunless tomb that had been their home for far too long.

She knew there was still a chance they'd be returning to it; the situation around the country was still far from stable. When their troops had returned to the White House yesterday, two of Moreby's ministers couldn't be accounted for. But the zombie army was in a shambles; the human fighters had moved quickly to take advantage of the living dead's disorientation, and they'd absolutely secured the White House. By the end of today, they'd have a real President – a human President – back in the Oval Office.

There was, however, one other reason Steele would be glad to leave the OC: there were fresh rumours about sounds coming from the end of the complex around the storage room. Even though they'd concreted up the hidden entrance and sealed off the entire block of rooms and corridors, people working in surrounding offices or trying to sleep in their quarters said they heard the distant echoes of inhuman shrieks. Little Maxi, playing in a corridor that was some distance from the storage room, came back terrified, saying he'd heard not one but *two* voices screaming.

Steele loaded more files into a box and tried to push those thoughts away. Moreby was done; and even if he wasn't, there was no way he could have been heard through the walls surrounding the secret room. No, it was coincidence, or another urban legend . . .

"Oh my God. Steele, look at this." The President pushed her tablet towards Steele, who set down the latest handful of Manila folders and picked it up.

On the screen was a press release from New World Pharmaceuticals. They were pleased to announce that they'd just concluded negotiations with the Chinese, and would shortly be relocating their personnel and operations to Beijing.

"Wow," Steele said, as she finished reading the email, "talk about sore losers."

"How are you at other languages? Think we need to start learning Chinese?"

Steele smiled. "If they still had an army to worry about, they would've taken us over already."

"True." The President reclaimed the tablet, glanced through the rest of her messages, and leaned back in her desk chair with a long, exhausted sigh. "There's still so much to do. Just getting food to people is going to be hard for a while, and medical care . . ."

"Well," said Steele, "look on the bright side: maybe you can finally put through your proposal for universal healthcare."

The President burst into laughter, and Steele was glad; she hadn't seen the woman laugh in weeks, and that had worried her.

They were still chuckling when the office door opened and Ty Ward entered.

Steele blinked in surprise. She hadn't seen Ty since yesterday, when she'd checked on him in his quarters. He'd been in bed, looking pasty and feeble, but had assured her he was feeling better. Now he was upright and walking . . .

But he was walking stiffly, and his face had regained none of its old colour. His eyes were rheumy, and when he finally spoke his voice sounded hollow. "Steele, we need to talk."

"Sit down, Ty." She motioned to a chair, but he hesitated, his eyes moving from her to the President and away.

He was afraid.

The President saw it, too. "What is it, Ty?"

He ignored the President to focus on Steele. "Do you have a gun?"

Steele had replaced her beloved Glock with a Smith & Wesson M&P9. It held the same number of rounds and was a similar weapon, but she was still getting used to the feel of it and had set it down in a corner of the office, in its holster. Now her eyes glanced towards it, darted back to Ty and . . .

She knew. "Oh, God, Ty. Oh God, no . . ."

"I died."

Steele saw the yearning in his face, the way his mouth hung open slightly when he wasn't speaking, and she walked quickly over to where her gun rested. Out of the corner of her eye she saw the President rise slowly, backing away . . . although there was nowhere to go. If Ty should spring quickly . . .

Sliding the M&P9 free of its holster, she levelled it on Ty. He looked at her with boundless despair. "I think I know why: the virus is different with the intelligent ones. A whole other strain."

The President gasped. "Oh my God. If that's true . . ."

"The antiserum is useless now," Ty said.

"*No.*" Steele blurted the word out without meaning to – her mind rebelled at the possibility that they'd made a crucial mistake and had actually failed when they thought they'd succeeded. "No, the antiserum still works on the old strain. We just have to contain the other version . . ."

She broke off as they all realized what that meant. Shooting Ty made the most sense.

"That's why you have to kill me, Steele."

"No, Ty, you're still *you*. You've still got your reason—"

"You want to know what I've got, Steele? *Hunger.*" Ty's dead eyes blazed now, and he took a half-step towards Steele. "There's only one thing I want right now, and that's to do whatever it takes to make that hunger stop. I want to eat you, Steele. I want to tear parts of you off with my teeth, swallow them, feel your blood in my mouth, running down my throat . . ."

"Don't come any closer, Ty." Steele pushed her thumb against the M&P's safety.

The President said, softly, "He's right, Steele. You have to do it. Or I will."

Steele thought back to when she and the President had first met, when the President had taken a rifle that Steele couldn't use and finished a task that should have been Steele's. She'd been grateful then . . . but she couldn't allow that to happen twice, not if she wanted to finish the rest of her own life with any grain of self-respect.

"Do it," Ty said. "Before I can't . . . before I can't . . . stop it . . ." A thread of saliva slid down Ty's chin.

Steele fired.

THE WHITE HOUSE
WASHINGTON

Bulletin from <u>WhiteHouse.gov</u>

Effective immediately, Sandra Steele, formerly Director of the Secret Service and Special Advisor to the President, has been named to serve as Vice President, replacing Bob Delancy, who succumbed to HRV earlier this year.

Vice President Steele is taking office just as the President and her administration return to occupancy in the White House, after regaining control from the New Zombie Order leader James Moreby. Moreby is currently being held captive in an unspecified location.

"I'm honored to accept this position and look forward to moving America into a revitalized future," said Vice President Steele. "The President and I have worked together for some time, and we believe we can not only re-establish this nation's greatness, but set it moving on some exciting new paths. We'll be focusing first on making sure our citizens are safe, fed, housed, and receiving proper medical care; then we'll turn our attention to the economy, our international relations, and our environment."

(Biography of Steele attached)

Chapter Fifty-Three

KEVIN WAS STARTING to worry that he'd never fit in on Capitol Hill.

Since Steele's promotion, he'd seen little of her and the President. His job put him in contact throughout the day with senators, representatives, lobbyists, aides, secretaries, under-secretaries, and a variety of other political animals . . . and he'd realized quite soon that he liked almost none of these people. Perhaps it was because he'd trekked across an America ripped open and consumed by death; maybe he'd seen the face of a brutality they wouldn't even admit existed.

Whatever the reason, he found himself disgusted by the amount of deception and self-aggrandizement he was surrounded by. He wanted to stand in the middle of the Senate floor and scream, "Don't you idiots get it? *That world is gone.*" Because they tried to pretend things were the same; in their little sealed enclave, the old battles were still being fought while the greater war went almost unacknowledged.

He would have already left if it hadn't been for Maxi. He knew the boy didn't much like it here, either, but there were people helping to care for him, and they were safer here than they would have been anywhere else. Kevin had come to rely on Maxi in ways that surprised him; returning home at the end of another frustrating day to find Maxi waiting for him, with a game or a DVD, kept him going.

It was 4:00 pm, and Kevin was just returning from another pointless meeting with several representatives who wondered why his department – the Government Accounting Office – wasn't doing more about the deficit. Until the perimeter could be expanded to include more of Washington, most of the politicians worked now from the Eisenhower Executive Office Building. Kevin was negotiating one of its long, marble-tiled hallways when he heard his name called. He turned to see a man just exiting one of the offices and waving him back. It took a minute for him to remember: Senator Davis Tilich was the big, red-faced Texan who chaired the Senate Committee on Health, Education, Labor and Pensions.

"Mr Moon," Tilich said as Kevin approached, "I've been familiarizing myself with your files. Do I understand correctly that you possess a natural immunity to HRV?"

Kevin answered, "Yes, sir."

"And it was your blood that was used to create the antiserum?"

"Initially, yes."

The Senator's eyes crinkled slightly beneath his white brows, his mottled red flesh turned into a mask of disapproval. "One thing that wasn't clear in your files: Mr Moon, are you a homosexual?"

Everything in Kevin turned to ice, ice that was impossibly superheated. "Yes," was all he managed.

Senator Tilich said, "I thought there was a reason the antiserum didn't work. Good day to you, Mr Moon." He turned and strode off.

Several seconds passed before the red cleared from Kevin's vision, before he could force his legs to walk in a direction that didn't involve following Tilich and driving a fist into his florid jowls. Before he knew it, Kevin was back in his office, where Maxi waited. As Kevin entered, Maxi was on his phone, but when he saw Kevin he said, "I'll call you back," and hung up.

"Are you okay?"

Kevin saw the look on the boy's face, and it quenched the flames that had nearly engulfed him. "Yeah, I'm sorry, just . . . a rough day." He threw himself on to the office couch, loosening his tie. After a few seconds, Maxi sat beside him. "Maybe . . . we shouldn't stay here."

Frowning, Kevin looked at Maxi. "What?"

"I was just talking to Maribel, and . . . everything's different out there. She's different. She says she no longer feels like something is directing her, making her do stuff she doesn't want to do. She still gets . . . you know . . . *hungry*, but she says she can control it." After a few seconds, Maxi looked away and added, "I want to go see her."

Kevin sat up straighter and said, "You know it's still not safe out there, no matter what Maribel says. Right now we're winning, but—"

Maxi cut him off. "We're not winning. Not really. There are too many of them. They're already coming for this place again. I can hear them outside the fences."

Everyone could hear them. And yet most of those living here ignored the moans and the scrabblings, the gunshots that took one down so four more could take their place. They all heard the sounds and pushed them away into a corner, behind their petty concerns and useless meetings.

"You're right," Kevin said. "It's already dead here."

Kevin could get a car. He probably wouldn't be able to put together many supplies, so they'd have to forage along the way. It would be dangerous, but they'd be moving, and they'd be together, and they'd have a goal.

"Pack whatever you need," Kevin said.

Maxi grinned, and rushed off. Kevin felt a weight slide from him. He briefly considered calling Steele – to thank her, to say goodbye and good luck – but decided not to. He didn't want to risk anyone stopping them.

A few minutes later, Kevin and Maxi walked out of the Eisenhower building, each carrying a few precious items. It was already late in the day, but they wouldn't stay here one more night. Not in this land of the trapped, home of the failed.

Life was waiting.

May 1st, 1802
London

My Dear Benjamin,

If you are reading this missive, it means that you
are now in possession of that single most important
piece of our plans for the New Rome. Although I
trust you completely, I would still request the
favour of a response, letting me know that it crossed
the Atlantic ocean and arrived unmolested.

Now, to the piece: We have spoken of it before,
but I think you deserve to know the full history
and importance of this unique and remarkable
relic. It is not merely a slab of rock, but sandstone
hewn from the highest mountain and shaped by the
hand of the great Leonardo himself. Note the

geometric figures, smooth indentations and lidded chambers carved into its surface. Why, you may be asking, would I entrust an item of such obvious value and antiquity to you, an architect on the other side of the world, for use in a city that as yet is little more than a foetid swamp?

Because, Benjamin, I have seen not only the past, but also the future. My vision is, granted, limited and far from all-encompassing, but through certain herbs and other occult means at my disposal, Anarchon has gifted me with enough prescience to see that your Washington will become the greatest seat of power the world has ever known, surpassing even the first Rome. Washington will be the nexus from which a magnificent empire springs, and what you and L'Enfant and Ellicott and Hoban have built is nothing less than the foundation for this future wonder.

Given Washington's standing in centuries to come, it is of course of primary importance to my plans. I will one day arrive in Washington; it will be my last step to achieving my own destiny and thus the world's.

You have built a special chamber in your underground system, which we have dubbed "the Altar Room", to contain the sandstone slab. I have provided specifications for how the stone is to be placed in that room. Please follow my instructions precisely — the power of the stone will be bleached should it not be situated with proper rituals and measurements. The design of the Altar Room is such that it contains all energies and powers, of both natural and supernatural means, and so the stone will be safe within.

Once I am entrenched in Washington, an exact date — of great significance — will arrive, and on that date I will adjourn to the Altar Room. There and then, I will offer Anarchon a sacrifice; this sacrifice will be no mere pure girl-child, but a man of experience and importance. If all is found pleasing to the Great Lord, I will ascend. I am not at liberty to describe my ascension to you, but rest assured that it will be the single most important event in human — or inhuman — history. The date is currently more than two centuries in the future, but I am patient and can wait.

I congratulate you on being an integral part of this accomplishment, and I know you sense the majesty of our shared future. And rest assured, dear Benjamin Henry, that it will happen. The road to ascension will appear treacherous and complicated, but it is all part of the plan.

Yours,

Thomas Moreby, Esq. quo

Acknowledgements

Many thanks to Duncan Proudfoot (as always), Nicola Chalton and Pascal Thivillon (without whom . . .), Max Burnell, Joe Roberts, Michael Marshall Smith, Pat Cadigan, Peter Crowther, Christopher Fowler and John Llewellyn Probert. Special thanks, of course, to Lisa Morton for ensuring that this novel will never be favourably reviewed on Fox News Channel. Dedicated with grateful thanks to the memory of Nick Robinson. —SJ

My thanks go to Stephen Jones, who I now officially owe twenty years' worth of gratitude to. —LM

Lisa Morton is a screenwriter, author of non-fiction books, award-winning prose writer, and Halloween expert whose work was described by the American Library Association's *Readers Advisory Guide to Horror* as "consistently dark, unsettling, and frightening". Her most recent books include the novels *Netherworld: Book One of the Chronicles of Diana Furnaval* and *Malediction*, and the Bram Stoker Award-winning *Trick or Treat: A History of Halloween*. She lives in North Hollywood, California, and can be found online at lisamorton.com.

Stephen Jones is the winner of three World Fantasy Awards, four Horror Writers Association Bram Stoker Awards, three International Horror Guild Awards and multiple British Fantasy Awards, as well as being a multiple recipient of the British Fantasy Award and a Hugo Award nominee. A former television producer/director and genre movie publicist and consultant (the first three *Hellraiser* movies, *Nightbreed*, *Split Second*, etc.), he has written and edited more than 125 books, including the *Fearie Tales: Stories of the Grimm and Gruesome*, *A Book of Horrors*, *Curious Warnings: The Great Ghost Stories of M.R. James*, *Psycho-Mania!*, *The Mammoth Book of Best New Horror* and *Zombie Apocalypse!* series. You can visit his website at stephenjoneseditor.com.